CROWN PRINCE, PREGNANT BRIDE!
BY
RAYE MORGAN

AND

VALENTINE BRIDE
BY
CHRISTINE RIMMER

MILLS &
BOON

Dear Reader,

For the island nation of Ambria, the time of reckoning is fast approaching. The storm is gathering. Retribution for what was done to the DeAngelis royal family when their country was torn from them is at hand — and Pellea Marallis, promised to the usurper's heir, knows it very well.

Monte DeAngelis, the Crown Prince, has come back to claim what is his. For most of his life he's known exactly what that is. Only now does he see that his need has grown. Though he never thought he would let a woman blur the intensity of his determination, Pellea is doing just that. In the grand scheme of things he is afraid he may just ache for her more strongly than he craves revenge.

The more he tries to deny it, and the more Pellea tries to hold him off, the deeper his desire goes — and once he realises she is carrying his child he knows there is no turning back. They make their way through the castle corridors, exploring secret rooms, tricking guards, attending a masked ball and stealing a prized artifact. But when Monte escapes along an ancient passageway Pellea refuses to go with him. She's torn between her love for Monte and her devotion to her dying father. Will she be caught up in the coming war and pay the ultimate price for her divided loyalties?

Well, you know the drill — you'll have to read the book to find out!

Hope you enjoy it — all the best,

Raye Morgan

CROWN PRINCE, PREGNANT BRIDE!

BY
RAYE MORGAN

First published in Great Britain 2011
Harlequin Mills & Boon Limited,
Eton House, 18-24 Paradise Road, Richmond, Surrey TW9 1SR

CROWN PRINCE, PREGNANT BRIDE! © Helen Conrad 2011

ISBN: 978 0 263 88860 7

23-0211

Harlequin Mills & Boon policy is to use papers that are natural, renewable and recyclable products and made from wood grown in sustainable forests. The logging and manufacturing processes conform to the legal environmental regulations of the country of origin.

Printed and bound in Spain
by Litografia Rosés S.A., Barcelona

Raye Morgan has been a nursery school teacher, a travel agent, a clerk and a business editor, but her best job ever has been writing romances — and fostering romance in her own family at the same time. Current score: two boys married, two more to go. Raye has published over seventy romances, and claims to have many more waiting in the wings. She lives in Southern California with her husband and whichever son happens to be staying at home at the moment.

This book is dedicated to Baby Kate

CHAPTER ONE

THOUGH MONTE COULDN'T see her, Pellea Marallis passed so close to the Crown Prince's hiding place, he easily caught a hint of her intoxicating perfume. That gave him an unexpected jolt. It brought back a panoply of memories, like flipping through the pages of a book—a vision of sunlight shining through a gauzy white dress, silhouetting a slim, beautifully rounded female form, a flashing picture of drops of water cascading like a thousand diamonds onto creamy silken skin, a sense of cool satin sheets and caresses that set his flesh on fire.

He bit down hard on his lower lip to stop the wave of sensuality that threatened to wash over him. He wasn't here to renew the romance. He was here to kidnap her. And he wasn't about to let that beguiling man-woman thing get in the way this time.

She passed close again and he could hear the rustle of her long skirt as it brushed against the wall he was leaning on. She was pacing back and forth in her courtyard, a garden retreat built right into this side of the castle, giving her a small lush forest where she spent most of her time. The surrounding rooms—a huge closet filled with clothes and a small sitting room, a neighboring compact office stacked to the ceiling with books, a sumptuously decorated bedroom—each opened onto the courtyard with French doors, making her living space a mixture of indoors and outdoors in an enchanting maze of exciting colors and provocative scents.

She was living like a princess.

Did he resent it all? Of course. How could he not?

But this was not the side of the castle where his family had lived before the overthrow of their royal rule. That area had been burned the night his parents were murdered by the Granvillis, the thugs who still ruled Ambria, this small island country that had once been home to his family. He understood that part of the castle was only now being renovated, twenty-five years later.

And that he resented.

But Pellea had nothing to do with the way his family had been robbed of their birthright. He had no intention of holding her accountable. Her father was another matter. His long-time status as the Grand Counselor to the Granvillis was what gave Pellea the right to live in this luxury—and his treachery twenty-five years ago was considered a subject of dusty history.

Not to Monte. But that was a matter for another time.

He hadn't seen her yet. He'd slipped into the dressing room as soon as he'd emerged from the secret passageway. And now he was just biding his time before he revealed his presence.

He was taking this slowly, because no matter what

he'd told himself, she affected him in ways no other woman ever had. In fact, she'd been known to send his restraint reeling, and he knew he had to take this at a cautious pace if he didn't want things to spin out of control again.

He heard her voice and his head rose. Listening hard, he tried to figure out if she had someone with her. No. She was talking on her mobile, and when she turned in his direction, he could just make out what she was saying.

"Seed pearls of course. And little pink rosebuds. I think that ought to do it."

He wasn't really listening to the words. Just the sound of her had him mesmerized. He'd never noticed before how appealing her voice was, just as an instrument. He hadn't heard it for some time, and it caught the ear the way a lilting acoustic guitar solo might, each note crisp, crystal clear and sweet in a way that touched the soul.

As she talked, he listened to the sound and smiled. He wanted to see her and the need was growing in him.

But to do that, he would have to move to a riskier position so that he could see out through the open French doors. Though he'd slipped easily into her huge dressing room, he needed to move to a niche beside a tall wardrobe where he could see everything without being seen himself. Carefully, he made his move.

And there she was. His heart was thudding so hard, he could barely breathe.

The thing about Pellea, and part of the reason she so completely captivated him, was that she seemed to embody a sense of royal command even though there wasn't a royal bone in her body. She was classically beautiful, like a Greek statue, only slimmer, like an angel in a Renaissance painting, only earthier, like a dancer drawn by Toulouse-Lautrec, only more graceful, like a thirties-era film star, only more mysteriously luminescent. She was all a woman could be and still be of this earth.

Barely.

To a casual glance, she looked like a normal woman. Her face was exceptionally pretty, but there were others with dark eyes as almond-shaped, with long, lustrous lashes that seemed to sweep the air. Her hair floated about her face like a misty cloud of spun gold and her form was trim and nicely rounded. Her lips were red and full and inviting. Perfection.

But there were others who had much the same advantages. Others had caught his eye through the years, but not many had filled his mind and touched off the sense of longing that she had.

There was something more to Pellea, something in the dignity with which she held herself, an inner fire that burned behind a certain sadness in her eyes, an inner drive, a sense of purpose, that set her apart. She could be playful as a kitten one minute, then smoldering with a provocative allure, and just as suddenly, aflame with righteous anger.

From the moment he'd first seen her, he'd known she was special. And for a few days two months ago, she'd been his.

"Didn't I give you my sketches?" she was saying into the phone. "I tend to lean a little more toward traditional. Not too modern. No off-the-shoulder stuff. Not for this."

He frowned, wondering what on earth she was talking about. Designing a ball gown maybe? He could see her on the dance floor, drawing all eyes. Would he ever get the chance to dance with her? Not in a ballroom, but maybe here, in her courtyard. Why not?

It was a beautiful setting. When he'd been here before, it had been winter and everything had been lifeless and stark. But spring was here now, and the space was a riot of color.

A fountain spilled water in the center of the area, making music that was a pleasant, tinkling background. Tiled pathways meandered through the area, weaving in among rosebushes and tropical plants, palms and a small bamboo forest.

Yes, they would have to turn on some music and dance. He could almost feel her in his arms. He stole another glance at her, at the way she held her long, graceful neck, at the way her free hand fluttered like a bird as she made her point, at the way her dressing gown gaped open, revealing the lacy shift she wore underneath.

"Diamonds?" she was saying into the phone. "Oh, no. No diamonds. Just the one, of course. That's customary. I'm not really a shower-me-with-diamonds sort of girl, you know what I mean?"

He reached out and just barely touched the fluttering hem of her flowing sleeve as she passed. She turned quickly, as though she'd sensed something, but he'd pulled back just in time and she didn't see him. He smiled, pleased with himself. He would let her know he was here when he was good and ready.

"As I remember it, the veil is more of an ivory shade. There are seed pearls scattered all over the crown area, and then down along the edges on both sides. I think that will be enough."

Veil? Monte frowned. Finally, a picture swam into stark relief and he realized what she must be talking about. It sounded like a wedding. She was planning her wedding ensemble.

She was getting married.

He stared at her, appalled. What business did she have getting married? Had she forgotten all about him so quickly? Anger curled through him like smoke and he only barely held back the impulse to stride out and confront her.

She couldn't get married. He wouldn't allow it.

And yet, he realized with a twinge of conscience, it wasn't as though he was planning to marry her himself. Of course not. He had bigger fish to fry. He had an invasion to orchestrate and manage. Besides, there was no way he would ever marry the daughter of the biggest betrayer still alive of his family—the DeAngelis Royalty.

And yet, to think she was planning to marry someone else so soon after their time together burned like a scorpion's sting.

What the hell!

A muted gong sounded, making him jerk in surprise. That was new. There had been a brass knocker a few weeks ago. What else had she changed since he'd been here before?

Getting married—hah! It was a good thing he'd shown up to kidnap her just in time.

Pellea had just rung off with her clothing designer, and she raised her head at the sound of her new entry gong. She sighed, shoulders drooping. The last thing she wanted was company, and she was afraid she knew who this was anyway. Her husband-to-be. Oh, joy.

"Enter," she called out.

There was a heavy metal clang as the gate was pulled open and then the sound of boots on the tile. A tall man entered, his neatly trimmed hair too short to identify the color, but cut close to his perfectly formed head. His shoulders were wide, his body neatly proportioned and very fit-looking. His long face would have been handsome if he could have trained himself to get rid of the perpetual sneer he wore like a mark of superiority at all times.

Leonardo Granvilli was the oldest son of Georges Granvilli, leader of the rebellion that had taken over this island nation twenty-five years before, the man who now ruled as *The General*, a term that somewhat softened the edges of his relatively despotic regime.

"My darling," Leonardo said coolly in a deep, sonorous voice. "You're radiant as the dawn on this beautiful day."

"Oh, spare me, Leonardo," she said dismissively. Her tone held casual disregard but wasn't in any way meant to offend. "No need for empty words of praise. We've known each other since we were children. I think by now we've taken the measure, each of the other. I don't need a daily snow job."

Leonardo made a guttural sound in his throat and threw a hand up to cover his forehead in annoyance. "Pellea, why can't you be like other women and just accept the phony flattery for what it is? It's nothing but form, darling. A way to get through the awkward moments. A little sugar to help the medicine go down."

Pellea laughed shortly, but cut it off almost before it had begun. Pretending to be obedient, she went into mock royal mode for him.

"Pray tell me, kind sir, what brings my noble knight to my private chambers on such a day as this?"

He actually smiled. "That's more like it."

She curtsied low and long and his smile widened.

"Bravo. This marriage may just work out after all."

Her glare shot daggers his way, as though to say, *In your dreams*, but he ignored that.

"I came with news. We may have to postpone our wedding."

"What?" Involuntarily, her hands went to her belly—and the moment she realized what she'd done, she snatched them away again. "Why?"

"That old fool, the last duke of the DeAngelis clan, has finally died. This means a certain level of upheaval is probable in the expatriate Ambrian community. They will have to buzz about and try to find a new patriarch, it seems. We need to be alert and ready to move on any sort of threat that might occur to our regime."

"Do you expect anything specific?"

He shook his head. "Not really. Just the usual gnashing of teeth and bellowing of threats. We can easily handle it."

She frowned, shaking her head. "Then why postpone? Why not move the date up instead?"

He reached out and tousled her hair. "Ah, my little buttercup. So eager to be wed."

She pushed his hand away, then turned toward the fountain in the middle of the courtyard and shrugged elaborately. "'If it were done when 'tis done, then 'twere well it were done quickly,'" she muttered darkly.

"What's that my sweet?" he said, following into the sunshine.

"Nothing." She turned back to face him. "I will, of course, comply with your wishes. But for my own purposes, a quick wedding would be best."

He nodded, though his eyes were hooded. "I understand. Your father's condition and all that." He shrugged. "I'll talk to my father and we'll hit upon a date, I'm sure." His gaze flickered over her and he smiled. "To think that after all this time, and all the effort you've always gone to in putting me off, I'm finally going to end up with the woman of my dreams." He almost seemed to tear up a bit. "It restores one's faith, doesn't it?"

"Absolutely." She couldn't help but smile back at him, though she was shaking her head at the same time. "Oh,

Leonardo, I sometimes think it would be better if you found someone to love."

He looked shocked. "What are you talking about? You know very well you've always been my choice."

"I said *love*," she retorted. "Not *desire to possess*."

He shrugged. "To each his own."

Pellea sighed but she was still smiling.

Monte watched this exchange while cold anger spread through him like a spell, turning him from a normal man into something akin to a raging monster. And yet, he didn't move a muscle. He stood frozen, as though cast in stone. Only his mind and his emotions were alive.

And his hatred. He hated Leonardo, hated Leonardo's father, hated his entire family.

Bit by bit, the anger was banked and set aside to smolder. He was experienced enough to know white-hot emotional ire led to mistakes every time. He wouldn't make any mistakes. He needed to keep his head clear and his emotions in check.

All of them, good and bad.

One step at a time, he made himself relax. His body control was exceptional and he used it now. He wanted to keep cool so that he would catch the exact right time to strike. It wouldn't be now. That would be foolish. But it would be soon.

He hadn't been prepared for something like this. The time he and Pellea had spent together just a few weeks before had been magical. He'd been hungry to see her again, aching to touch her, eager to catch her lips with his and feel that soaring sense of wonder again. He had promised himself there would be no lovemaking to distract him this time—but he'd been kidding himself. The moment he saw her he knew he had to have her in his arms again.

That was all. Nothing serious, nothing permanent. A part of him had known she would have to marry someone—eventually. But still, to think that she would marry this…this…

Words failed him.

"I'd like you to come down to the library. We need to look at the plans for the route to the retreat in the gilded carriage after we are joined as one," Leonardo was saying.

"No honeymoon," she said emphatically, raising both hands as though to emphasize her words. "I told you that from the beginning."

He looked startled, but before he could protest, she went on.

"As long as my father is ill, I won't leave Ambria."

He sighed, making a face but seemingly reconciled to her decision. "People will think it strange," he noted.

"Let them."

She knew that disappointed him but it couldn't be helped. Right now her father was everything to her. He had been her rock all her life, the only human being in this world she could fully trust and believe in and she wasn't about to abandon him now.

Still, she needed this marriage. Leonardo understood

why and was willing to accept the terms she'd agreed to this on. Everything was ready, the wheels had begun to turn, the path was set. As long as nothing got in the way, she should be married within the next week. Until then, she could only hope that nothing would happen to upset the apple cart.

"I'll come with you," she said. "Just give me a minute to do a quick change into something more suitable."

She turned and stepped into her dressing room, pulling the door closed behind her. Moving quickly, she opened her gown and began unbuttoning her lacy dress from the neck down. And then she caught sight of his boots. Her fingers froze on the buttons as she stared at the boots. Her head snapped up and her dark eyes met Monte's brilliant blue gaze. Every sinew constructing her body went numb.

She was much more than shocked. She was horrified. As the implications of this visit came into focus, she had to clasp her free hand over her mouth to keep from letting out a shriek. For just a moment, she went into a tailspin and could barely keep her balance.

Eyes wide, she stared at him. A thousand thoughts ricocheted through her, bouncing like ping-pong balls against her emotions. Anger, remorse, resentment, joy—even love—they were all there and all aimed straight into those gorgeous blue eyes, rapid-fire. If looks could kill, he would be lying on the floor, shot through the heart.

A part of her was tempted to turn on her heel, summon Leonardo and be done with it. Because she knew as sure as she knew her own name that this would all end badly.

Monte couldn't be a part of her life. There was no way she could even admit to anyone here in the castle that she knew him. All she had to do was have Leonardo call the guard, and it would be over. They would dispose of him. She would never see him again—never have to think about him again, never again have to cry into her pillow until it was a soggy sponge.

But she knew that was all just bravado. She would never, ever do anything to hurt him if she could help it.

He gave her a crooked grin as though to say, "Didn't you know I'd be back?"

No, she didn't know. She hadn't known. And she still didn't want to believe it. She didn't say a word.

Quickly, she turned and looked out into the courtyard. Leonardo was waiting patiently, humming a little tune as he looked at the fountain. Biting her lower lip, she turned and managed to stagger out of the dressing room towards him, stumbling a bit and panting for breath.

"What is it?" he said in alarm, stepping forward to catch her by the shoulders. He'd obviously noted that she was uncharacteristically disheveled. "Are you all right?"

"No." She flickered a glance his way, thinking fast, then took a deep breath and shook her head. "No. Migraine."

"Oh, no." He looked puzzled, but concerned.

She pulled away from his grip on her shoulders, regaining her equilibrium with effort.

"I...I'm sorry, but I don't think I can come with you right now. I can hardly even think straight."

"But you were fine thirty seconds ago," he noted, completely at sea.

"Migraines come on fast," she told him, putting a hand to the side of her head and wincing. "But a good lie-down will fix me up. How about...after tea?" She looked at him earnestly. "I'll meet you then. Say, five o'clock?"

Leonardo frowned, but he nodded. "All right. I've got a tennis match at three, so that will work out fine." He looked at her with real concern, but just a touch of wariness.

"I hope this won't affect your ability to go to the ball tonight."

"Oh, no, of course not."

"Everyone is expecting our announcement to be made there. And you will be wearing the tiara, won't you?"

She waved him away. "Leonardo, don't worry. I'll be wearing the tiara and all will be as planned. I should be fine by tonight."

"Good." He still seemed wary. "But you should see Dr. Dracken. I'll send him up."

"No!" She shook her head. "I just need to rest. Give me a few hours. I'll be good as new."

He studied her for a moment, then shrugged. "As you wish." He bent over her hand like a true suitor. "Until we meet again, my beloved betrothed."

She nodded, almost pushing him toward the gate. "Likewise, I'm sure," she said out of the corner of her mouth.

"Pip pip." And he was off.

She waited until she heard the outer gate clang, then turned like a fury and marched back into the dressing room. She ripped open the door and glared at Monte with a look in her eyes that should have frozen the blood in his veins.

"How dare you? How dare you do this?"

Her vehemence was actually throwing him off his game a bit. He had expected a little more joy at seeing him again. He was enjoying the sight of her. Why couldn't she feel the same?

She really was a feast for the senses. Her eyes were bright—even if that seemed to be anger for the moment—and her cheeks were smudged pink.

"How dare you do this to me again?" she demanded.

"This isn't like before," he protested. "This is totally different."

"Really? Here you are, sneaking into my country, just like before. Here you are, hiding in my chambers again. Just like before."

His smile was meant to be beguiling. "But this time, when I leave, you're going with me."

She stared at him, hating him and loving him at the same time. Going with him! What a dream that was. She could no more go with him than she could swim the channel. If only…

For just a split second, she allowed herself to give in to her emotions. If only things were different. How she would love to throw herself into his arms and hold him tight, to feel his hard face against hers, to sense his heart pound as his interest quickened…

But she couldn't do that. She couldn't even think about it. She'd spent too many nights dreaming of him, dreaming of his tender touch. She had to forget all that. Too many lives depended on her. She couldn't let him see the slightest crack in her armor.

And most of all, she couldn't let him know about the baby.

"How did you get in here?" she demanded coldly. "Oh, wait. Don't even try to tell me. You'll just lie."

The provocative expression in his eyes changed to ice in an instant.

"Pellea, I'm not a liar," he said in a low, urgent tone. "I'll tell you or I won't, but what I say will be the truth as I know it every time. Count on it."

Their gazes locked in mutual indignation. Pellea was truly angry with him for showing up like this, for complicating her life and endangering them both, and yet she knew she was using that anger as a shield. If he touched her, she would surely melt. Just looking at him did enough damage to her determined stance.

Why did he have to be so beautiful? With his dark hair and shocking blue eyes, he had film-star looks, but that wasn't all. He was tall, muscular, strong in a way that would make any woman swoon. He looked tough, capable of holding his own in a fight, and yet there was nothing cocky about him. He had a quiet confidence that made any form of showing off unnecessary. You just knew by looking at him that he was ready for any challenge—physical or intellectual.

But how about emotional? Despite all his strength, there was a certain sensitivity deep in his blue eyes. The sort of hint of vulnerability only a woman might notice. Or was that just hopeful dreaming on her part?

"Never mind all that," she said firmly. "We've got to get you out of here."

His anger drifted away like morning fog and his eyes were smiling again. "After I've gone to so much trouble to get in?"

Oh, please don't smile at me! she begged silently. This was difficult enough without this charm offensive clouding her mind. She glared back.

"You are going. This very moment would be a good time to do it."

His gaze caressed her cheek. "How can I leave now that I've found you again?"

She gritted her teeth. "You're not going to mesmerize me like you did last time. You're not staying here at all." She pointed toward the gate. "I want you to go."

He raised one dark eyebrow and made no move toward the door. "You going to call the guard?"

Her eyes blazed at him. "If I have to."

He looked pained. "Actually, I'd rather you didn't."

"Then you'd better go, hadn't you?"

He sighed and managed to look as though he regretted all this. "I can't leave yet. Not without what I came for."

She threw up her hands. "That has nothing to do with me."

His smile was back. "That's where you're wrong. You see, it's you that I came for. How do you feel about a good old-fashioned kidnapping?"

CHAPTER TWO

PELLEA BLINKED QUICKLY, but that was the only sign
she allowed to show his words had shocked her—rocked
her, actually, to the point where she almost needed to
reach out and hold on to something to keep from falling over.

Monte had come to kidnap her? Was he joking? Or
was he crazy?

"Really?" With effort, she managed to fill her look
with mock disdain. "How do you propose to get me past
all the guards and barriers? How do you think you'll
manage that without someone noticing? Especially when
I'll be fighting you every step of the way and creating
a scene and doing everything else I can think of to ruin
your silly kidnapping scheme?"

"I've got a plan." He favored her with a knowing
grin.

"Oh, I see." Eyes wide, she turned with a shrug, as
though asking the world to judge him. "He's got a plan.
Say no more."

He followed her. "You scoff, Pellea. But you'll soon
see things my way."

She whirled to face him and her gaze sharpened as she remembered his last visit. "How do you get in here, anyway? You've never explained that." She shook her head, considering him from another angle. "There are guards everywhere. How do you get past them?"

His grin widened. "Secrets of the trade, my dear."

"And just what is your trade these days?" she asked archly. "Second-story man?"

"No, Pellea." His grin faded. Now they were talking about serious things. "Actually, I still consider myself the royal heir to the Ambrian throne."

She rolled her eyes. "Good luck with that one."

He turned and met her gaze with an intensity that burned. "I'm the Crown Prince of Ambria. Hadn't you heard? I thought you understood that."

She stared back at him. "That's over," she said softly, searching his eyes. "Long over."

He shook his head slowly, his blue eyes burning with a surreal light. "No. It's real and it's now. And very soon, the world will know it."

Fear gripped her heart. What he was suggesting was war. People she loved would be hurt. And yet…

Reaching out, she touched him, forgetting her vow not to. She flattened her palm against his chest and felt his heartbeat, felt the heat and the flesh of him.

"Oh, please, Monte," she whispered, her eyes filled with the sadness of a long future of suffering. "Please, don't…"

He took her hand and brought it to his lips, kissing the center of her palm without losing his hold on her gaze for a moment. "I won't let anything hurt you," he promised, though he knew he might as well whistle into the wind. Once his operation went into action, all bets would be off. "You know that."

She shook her head, rejecting what he'd said. "No, Monte, I don't know that. You plan to come in here and rip our lives apart. Once you start a revolution, you start a fire in the people and you can't control where that fire will burn. There will be pain and agony on all sides. There always is."

His shrug was elaborate on purpose. "There was pain and agony that night twenty-five years ago when my mother and my father were killed by the Granvillis. When I and my brothers and sisters were spirited off into the night and told to forget we were royal. In one fire-ravaged night, we lost our home, our kingdom, our destiny and our parents." His head went back and he winced as though the pain was still fresh. "What do you want me to do? Forgive those who did that to me and mine?"

A look of pure determination froze his face into the mask of a warrior. "I'll never do that. They need to pay."

She winced. Fear gripped her heart. She knew what this meant. Her own beloved father was counted among Monte's enemies. But she also knew that he was strong and determined, and he meant what he threatened. Wasn't there any way she could stop this from happening?

The entry gong sounded, making them both jump.

"Yes?" she called out, hiding her alarm.

"Excuse me, Miss Marallis," a voice called in. "It's Sergeant Fromer. I just wanted to check what time you wanted us to bring the tiara by."

"The guard," she whispered, looking at Monte sharply. "I should ask him in right now."

He held her gaze. "But you won't," he said softly.

She stared at him for a long moment. She wanted with all her heart to prove him wrong. She should do it. It would be so easy, wouldn't it?

"Miss?" the guard called in again.

"Uh, sorry, Sergeant Fromer." She looked at Monte again and knew she wouldn't do it. She shook her head, ashamed of herself. "About seven would be best," she called to him. "The hairdresser should be here by then."

"Will do. Thank you, miss."

And he was gone, carrying with him all hope for sanity. She stared at the area of the gate.

There it was—another chance to do the right thing and rid herself of this menace to her peace of mind forever. Why couldn't she follow through? She turned and looked at Monte, her heart sinking. Was she doomed? Not if she stayed strong. This couldn't be like it was before. She'd been vulnerable the last time. She'd just had the horrible fight with her father that she had been dreading for years, and when Monte had jumped into her life, she was in the mood to do dangerous things.

The first time she'd seen him, he'd appeared seemingly out of nowhere and found her sobbing beside her fountain. She'd just come back to her chambers from that fight and she'd been sick at heart, hating that she'd hurt the man she loved most in the world—her father. And so afraid that she would have to do what he wanted her to do anyway.

Her father's health had begun to fade at that point, but he wasn't bedridden yet, as he was now. He'd summoned her to his room and told her in no uncertain terms that he expected her to marry Leonardo. And she'd told him in similar fashion that she would have to be dragged kicking and screaming to the altar. No other way would work. He'd called her an ungrateful child and had brought up the fact that she was looking to be an old maid soon if she didn't get herself a husband. She'd called him an overbearing parent and threatened to marry the gardener.

That certainly got a response, but it was mainly negative and she regretted having said such a thing now. But he'd been passionate, almost obsessive about the need for her to marry Leonardo.

"Marry the man. You've known him all your life. You get along fine. He wants you, and as his wife, you'll have so much power…"

"Power!" she'd responded with disdain. "All you care about is power."

His face had gone white. "Power is important," he told her in a clipped, hard voice. "As much as you may try to pretend otherwise, it rules our lives." And then, haltingly, he'd told her the story of what had happened to her mother—the real story this time, not the one she'd grown up believing.

"Victor Halma wanted her," he said, naming the man who had been the Granvillis' top enforcer when Pellea was a very small child.

"Wha-what do you mean?" she'd stammered. There was a sick feeling in the pit of her stomach and she was afraid she understood only too well.

"He was always searching her out in the halls, showing up unexpectedly whenever she thought she was safe. He wouldn't leave her alone. She was in a panic."

She closed her eyes and murmured, "My poor mother."

"There was still a lot of hostility toward me because I had worked with the DeAngelis royal family before the revolution," he went on. "I wasn't trusted then as I am now. I tried to fight him, but it was soon apparent I had no one on my side." He drew in a deep breath. "I was sent on a business trip to Paris. He made his move while I was gone."

"Father..."

"You see, I had no power." His face, already pale, took on a haggard look. "I couldn't refuse to go. And once I was gone, he forced her to go to his quarters."

Pellea gasped, shivering as though an icy blast had swept into the room.

"She tried to run away, but he had the guard drag her into his chamber and lock her in. And there, while she was waiting, she found a knife and killed herself before he could..." His voice trailed off.

Pellea's hands clutched her throat. "You always told me she died during an influenza epidemic," she choked out. She was overwhelmed with this news, and yet, deep down, she'd always known there was something she wasn't being told.

He nodded. "That was what I told you. That was what I told everyone. And there was an epidemic at the time. But she didn't die of influenza. She died of shame."

Pellea swayed. The room seemed to dip and swerve around her. "And the man?" she asked hoarsely.

"He had an unfortunate accident soon after," her father said dryly, making it clear he wasn't about to go into details. "But you understand me, don't you? You see the position we were in? That's what happens when you don't have power."

"Or when you work for horrible people," she shot back passionately.

Shaking his head, he almost smiled. "The strange thing was, the Granvillis started to trust me after that. I moved up in the ranks. I gained power." He looked at his daughter sternly. "Today, nothing like that could happen to me. And what I want for you is that same sort of immunity from harm."

She understood what he wanted for her. She ached with love for him, ached for what he'd gone through, ached for what her own mother had endured. Her heart broke for them all.

But she still hadn't been able to contemplate marrying Leonardo. Not then.

To some degree, she could relate to his obsession to get and hold power. Still, it was his obsession, not hers and she had no interest in making the sort of down payment on a sense of control that marrying Leonardo would entail.

But this had been the condition she'd been in when she'd first looked up and found Monte standing in her courtyard. She knew she'd never seen him before, and that was unusual. This was a small country and most in the castle had been there for years. You tended to know everyone you ran into, at least by sight. She'd jumped up and looked toward the gate, as though to run.

But he'd smiled. Something in that smile captivated her every time, and it had all begun that afternoon.

"Hi," he'd said. "I'm running from some castle guards. Mind if I hide in here?"

Even as he spoke, she heard the guards at the gate. And just that quickly, she became a renegade.

"Hurry, hide in there," she'd said, pointing to her bedroom. "Behind the bookcase." She'd turned toward the gate. "I'll deal with the guards."

And so began her life as an accomplice to a criminal—and so also her infatuation with the most wrong man she could have fallen in love with.

Monte didn't really appreciate the effort all this had cost her. He'd taken it for granted that she would send the guard away. She'd done the same thing the last time he was here—and that had been more dangerous for them both—because they'd already seen him in the halls at that point. The whole castle was turned upside down for the next two days as they hunted for him. And the entire time, she'd had him hidden in her bedroom.

No one knew he was here now except Pellea—so far.

"Was that the DeAngelis tiara you were talking about just now?" he asked her. "I thought I heard Leonardo bring it up."

She glared at him. "How long have you been here spying on me? What else did you hear?"

He raised an eyebrow. "What else didn't you want me to hear?"

She threw her hands up.

"Don't worry," he said. "The wedding-dress-design discussion and your talk with Leonardo were about it."

They both turned to look at the beautiful gown hanging against a tall, mahogany wardrobe. "Is this the gown you're wearing to the ball tonight?"

"Yes."

It was stunning. Black velvet swirled against deep green satin. It hung before him looking as though it was already filled with a warm, womanly body. Reaching out, he spanned the waist of it with his hands and imagined dancing with her.

"The DeAngelis tiara will look spectacular with this," he told her.

"Do you remember what it looks like?" she asked in surprise.

"Not in great detail. But I've seen pictures." He gave her a sideways look of irony. "My mother's tiara."

She shivered, pulling her arms in close about her. "It hasn't been your mother's tiara for a long, long time," she said, wishing she didn't sound so defensive.

He nodded slowly. "My mother's and that of every

other queen of Ambria going back at least three centuries," he added softly, almost to himself.

She shivered again. "I'm sure you're right."

His smile was humorless. "To the victor go the spoils."

"I didn't make the rules." Inside, she groaned. Still defensive. But she did feel the guilt of the past. How could she not?

"And yet, it will take more than twenty-five years to erase the memories that are centuries old. Memories of what my family accomplished here."

She bit her lip, then looked at him, looked at the sense of tragedy in his beautiful blue eyes, and felt the tug on her heart.

"I'm sorry," she said quickly, reaching for him and putting a hand on his upper arm. "I'm sorry that I have to wear your mother's tiara. They've asked me to do it and I said yes."

He covered her hand with his own and turned toward her. She recognized the light in his eyes and knew he wanted to kiss her. Her pulse raced, but she couldn't let it happen. Quickly, she pulled away.

He sighed, shaking his head in regret, but his mind was still on something else.

"Where is it?" he asked, looking around the wardrobe. "Where do you keep it?"

"The tiara?" She searched his eyes. What was he thinking? "It's in its case in the museum room, where it always is. Didn't you hear Sergeant Fromer? The guards will bring it to me just before I leave for the ball. And they will accompany me to the ballroom. The tiara is under guard at all times."

He nodded, eyeing her speculatively. "And so shall you be, once you put it on."

"I imagine so."

He nodded again, looking thoughtful. "I was just reading an article about it the other day," he said, half musing. "Diamonds, rubies, emeralds, all huge and of superior quality. Not to mention the wonderful craftsmanship of the tiara itself. It's estimated to be worth more than some small countries are."

Suddenly she drew her breath in. She hadn't known him long, but she was pretty sure she knew a certain side of him all too well.

"Oh, no you don't!" she cried, all outrage.

He looked at her in surprise. "What?"

She glared at him. "You're thinking about grabbing it, aren't you?"

"The tiara?" He stared at her for a moment and then he threw his head back and laughed. That was actually a fabulous idea. He liked the way she thought.

"Pellea," he said, taking her by the shoulders and dropping a kiss on her forehead. "You are perfection itself. You can't marry Leonardo."

She shivered. She couldn't help it. His touch was like agony and ecstasy, all rolled into one. But she kept her head about her.

"Who shall I marry then?" she responded quickly. "Are you ready to give me an offer?"

He stared at her, not responding. How could he say

anything? He couldn't make her an offer. He couldn't marry her. And anyway, he might be dead by the end of the summer.

Besides, there was another factor. If he was going to be ruler of Ambria, could he marry the daughter of his family's biggest betrayer? Not likely.

"I think kidnapping will work out better," he told her, and he wasn't joking.

She'd known he would say that, or something similar. She knew he was attracted to her. That, he couldn't hide. But she was a realist and she also knew he hated her father and the current regime with which she was allied. How could it be any other way? He could talk about taking her with him all he wanted, she knew there was no future for her there.

"I'll fight you all the way," she said flatly.

He smiled down into her fierce eyes. "There's always the best option, of course."

"And what is that?"

"That you come with me willingly."

She snorted. "Right. Before or after I marry Leonardo?"

He looked pained. "I can't believe you're serious."

She raised her chin and glared at him. "I am marrying Leonardo in four days. I hope."

He brushed the stray hairs back off her cheek and his fingers lingered, caressing her silken skin. "But why?" he asked softly.

"Because I want to," she responded stoutly. "I've promised I will do it and I mean to keep that promise."

Resolutely, she turned away from him and began searching through a clothes rack, looking for the clothes she meant to change into.

He came up behind her. "Is it because of your father?"

She whirled and stared at him. "Leave my father out of this."

"Ah-hah. So it is your father."

She turned back to searching through the hangers. He watched her for a moment, thinking that he'd never known a woman whose movements were so fluid. Every move she made was almost a part of a dance. And watching her turned him on in ways that were bound to cripple his ability to think clearly. He shook his head. He couldn't let that happen, not if he wanted to succeed here.

"Leonardo," he scoffed. "Please. Why Leonardo?"

Unconsciously, she cupped her hand over her belly. There was a tiny baby growing inside. He must never know that. He was the last person she could tell—ever. "It's my father's fondest wish."

"Because he might become ruler of Ambria?"

"Yes." How could she deny it? "And because he asked."

That set him back a moment. "What if I asked?" he ventured.

She turned to him, but his eyes showed nothing that could give her any hope. "Ah, but you won't, will you?"

He looked away. "Probably not."

"There's your answer."

"Where is Georges?" he asked, naming the Granvilli who had killed his parents. "What does he say about all this?"

She hesitated, choosing her words carefully. "The General seems to be unwell right now. I'm not sure what the specific problem is, but he's resting in the seaside villa at Grapevine Bay. Leonardo has been taking over more and more of the responsibilities of power himself." She raised her head and looked him squarely in the eye. "And the work seems to suit him."

"Does it? I hope he's enjoying himself. He won't have much longer to do that, as I intend to take that job away from him shortly."

She threw up her hands, not sure if he meant it or if this was just typical male bombast. "What exactly do you mean to do?" she asked, trying to pin him down.

He looked at her and smiled, coming closer, touching her hair with one hand.

"Nothing that you need to worry about."

But his thoughts were not nearly as sanguine as he pretended. She really had no conception of how deep his anger lay and how his hatred had eaten away at him for most of his life. Ever since that night when the castle had burned and his parents were murdered by the Granvilli clan. Payment was due. Retribution was pending.

"Is your father really very ill?" he asked quietly.

"Yes." She found the shirt she wanted and pulled it down.

"And you want to make him happy before he…"

He swallowed his next words even before she snapped her head around and ordered curtly, "Don't say it!"

He bit his tongue. That was a stupid thing to have thought, even if he never actually got the words out. He didn't mind annoying her about things he didn't think she should care so much about, but to annoy her about her father was just plain counterproductive.

"Well, he would like to see you become the future first lady of the land, wouldn't he?" he amended lamely.

He tried to think of what he knew about her father. Marallis had been considered an up-and-coming advisor in his own father's regime. From what he'd been able to glean, the king had recognized his superior abilities and planned to place him in a top job. And then the rebellion had swept over them, and it turned out Vaneck Marallis had signed on with the other side. Was it any wonder he should feel betrayed by the man? He was the enemy. He very likely gave the rebels the inside information they needed to win the day. There was no little corner of his heart that had any intention of working on forgiveness for the man.

"Okay, it's getting late," she said impatiently. "I have to go check on my father."

"Because he's ill?"

"Because he's very ill." She knew she needed to elaborate, but when she tried to speak, her throat choked and she had to pause, waiting for her voice to clear again. "I always go in to see him for a few minutes at this time in the afternoon." She looked at him. "When I get back, we'll have to decide what I'm going to do with you."

"Will we?" His grin was ample evidence of his opinion on the matter, but she turned away and didn't bother to challenge him.

Going to her clothes rack, she pulled out a trim, cream-colored linen suit with slacks and a crisp jacket and slipped behind a privacy screen to change into them. He watched as she emerged, looking quietly efficient and good at whatever job she might be attempting. And ravishingly beautiful at the same time. He'd never known another woman who impressed him as much as this one did. Once again he had a pressing urge to find a way to take her with him.

It wouldn't be impossible. She thought he would have to get her past the guards, but she was wrong. He had his own way into the castle and he could easily get her out. But only if she was at least halfway cooperative. It was up to him to convince her to be.

"I don't have time to decide what to do with you right now," she told him, her gaze hooded as she met his eyes. "I have to go check on my father, and it's getting late. You stay here and hold down the fort. I'll be back in about half an hour."

"I may be here," he offered casually. "Or not."

She hesitated. She didn't like that answer. "Tell me now, are you going to stay here and wait, or are you going to go looking for Leonardo and get killed?" she demanded of him.

He laughed shortly. "I think I can handle myself around your so-called fiancé," he said dismissively.

Her gaze sharpened and she looked seriously into his

eyes. "Watch out for Leonardo. He'll kill you without batting an eye."

"Are you serious? That prancing prig?"

She shook her head. "Don't be fooled by his veneer of urbanity. He's hard as nails. When I suggested you might be killed, I meant it."

He searched her eyes for evidence that she really cared. It was there, much as she tried to hide it. He smiled.

"I'm not too keen on the 'killed' part. But as for the rest…"

She glanced at her watch. Time was fleeting. "I'm running out of time," she told him. "Go out and wait in the courtyard. I just have one last thing to check."

"What's that?" he asked.

She looked pained. "None of your business. I do have my privacy to maintain. Now go out and wait."

He walked out into the lush courtyard and heard the door click shut behind him. Turning, he could see her through the glass door, walking back into her closet again. Probably changed her mind on what to wear, he thought to himself. And he had a twinge of regret. He didn't have all that much time here and he hated to think of missing a moment with her.

Did that mean he'd given up on the kidnapping? No. Not at all. Still, there was more to this trip than just seeing Pellea.

He scanned the courtyard and breathed in the atmosphere. The castle of his ancestors was all around him.

For a few minutes, he thought about his place in history. Would he be able to restore the monarchy? Would he bring his family back to their rightful place, where they should have been all along?

Of course he would. He didn't allow doubts. His family belonged here and he would see that it happened. He'd already found two of his brothers, part of the group of "Lost Royals" who had escaped when the castle was burned and had hidden from the wrath of the Granvillis ever since. There were two more brothers and two sisters he hadn't found yet. But he hoped to. He hoped to bring them all back here to Ambria by the end of the summer.

He turned and looked through the French doors into her bedroom and saw the huge, soft bed where he'd spent most of the two and a half days when he'd been here before. Memories flooded back. He remembered her and her luscious body and he groaned softly, feeling the surge of desire again.

Pellea was special. He couldn't remember another woman who had ever stuck in his mind the way she did. She'd embedded herself into his heart, his soul, his imagination, and he didn't even want to be free of her. And that was a revelation.

If he survived this summer…

No, he couldn't promise anything, not even to himself. After all, her father was the man who had betrayed his family. He couldn't let himself forget that.

But where was she? She'd been gone a long time. He turned back and looked at the closed doors to her dressing room, then moved to them and called softly, "Pellea."

There was no response.

"Pellea?"

Still nothing. He didn't want to make his call any louder. You never knew who might be at the gate or near enough to it to hear his voice. He tried the knob instead, pushing the door open a bit and calling again, "Pellea?"

There was no answer. It was quite apparent she wasn't there.

CHAPTER THREE

ALARM BELLS RANG IN Monte's head and adrenaline flooded his system. Where had she gone? How had she escaped without him seeing her? What was she doing? Had he overestimated his ability to charm, compared to Leonardo's ability to hand out a power position? Was she a traitor, just like her father?

All that flashed through his mind, sending him reeling. But that only lasted seconds before he'd dismissed it out of hand. She wouldn't do that. There had to be a reason.

The last he'd seen of her she was heading into her large, walk-in closet at the far side of the dressing room. He was there in two strides, and that is when he saw, behind a clothing bar loaded with fluffy gowns, the glimmer of something electronic just beyond a door that had been left slightly ajar.

A secret room behind the clothing storage. Who knew? He certainly hadn't known anything about it when he'd been here before.

Reaching in through the gowns, he pushed the door fully open. And there was Pellea, sitting before a large computer screen that was displaying a number of windows, all showing places in the castle itself. She had a whole command center in here.

"Why you little vixen," he said, astounded. "What do you have here? You've tapped into a gold mine."

She looked up at him, startled, and then resigned.

"I knew I should have closed that door all the way," she muttered to herself.

But he was still captured by the computer screen. "This is the castle security system, isn't it?"

She sighed. "Yes. You caught me."

He shook his head, staring at the screen. "How did you do that?" he asked in wonder.

She shrugged. "My father had this secret room installed years ago. Whenever he wanted to take a look at what was going on, he came to me for a visit. I didn't use it myself at first. I didn't see any need for it. But lately, I've found it quite handy."

"And you can keep things running properly on your own?"

"I've got a certain amount of IT talent. I've read a few books."

He looked at her and smiled. "My admiration grows."

She colored a bit and looked away.

"So you can see what's going on at all the major interior intersections, and a few of the outside venues as well. How convenient." His mind was racing with possibilities.

She pushed away from the desk and sighed again. "Monte, I shouldn't have let you see this."

"You didn't let me. I did it all on my own." He shook his head, still impressed. "Are you going to tell me why?"

She sighed again. "There are times when one might want to do things without being observed. Here in the castle, someone is always watching." She shrugged. "I like a little anonymity in my life. This way I can get a pretty good idea of who is doing what and I can bide my time."

"I see."

She rose and turned toward the door. "And now I really am late." She looked back. He followed her out reluctantly and she closed the door carefully. It seemed to disappear into the background of paneling and molding strips that surrounded it.

"See you later," she said, leading him away from the area. "And stay out of that room."

He frowned as she started off. He didn't want her to leave, and he also didn't want to miss out on anything he didn't have to. On impulse, he called after her, "I want to go with you."

She whirled and stared at him. "What?"

"I'd like to see your father."

She came back towards him, shocked and looking for a way to refuse. "But you can't. He's bedridden. He's in no condition…"

"I won't show myself to him. I won't hurt him." He shook his head and frowned. "But, Pellea, he's one of the few remaining ties to my parents left alive. He's from their generation. He knew them, worked with them. He was close to them at one time." He shrugged, looking oddly vulnerable in his emotional reactions. "I just want to see him, hear his voice. I promise I won't do anything to jeopardize his health—or even his emotional well-being in any way."

She studied him and wondered what she really knew about him. The way he felt about her father had been clear almost from the first. He was wrong about her father. She'd spent a lot of time agonizing over that, wondering how she could make him understand that her father was just a part of his time and place, that he had only done what he had to do, that he was really a man of great compassion and honesty. Maybe this would be a chance to do just that.

"You won't confront him about anything?"

"No. I swear." He half smiled. "I swear on my parents' memories. Do you trust me?"

She groaned. "God help me, I do." She searched his eyes. "All right. But you'll have to be careful. If you're caught, I'll claim you forced me to take you with me."

He smiled at her sideways, knowing she was lying. If he were caught, she would do her best to free him. She talked a good game, but deep down, she had a lot of integrity. And she was at least half in love with him. That gave him a twinge. More the fool was she.

"I only go when no one else is there," she was telling him. "I know when the nurse goes on her break and how long she takes."

He nodded. He'd always known she was quick and

sure at everything she did. He would have expected as much from her.

"Keep your eyes downcast," she lectured as they prepared to head into the hallway. "I try to go at a quiet time of day, but there might be someone in the halls. Don't make eye contact with anyone or you'll surely blow your cover. You can't help but look regal, can you? Take smaller steps. Try to slump your shoulders a little. A little more." She made a face. "Here." She whacked one shoulder to make it droop, and then the other, a tiny smile on her lips. "That's better," she said with satisfaction.

He was suspicious. She hadn't held back much. "You enjoyed that, didn't you?"

"Giving you a whack?" She allowed herself a tight smile. "Certainly not. I don't believe in corporal punishment."

"Liar." He was laughing at her. "Are you going to try to convince me that it hurt you more than it hurt me?"

She didn't bother to respond. Giving him a look, she stepped out into the hallway, wondering if she was crazy to do this. But she was being honest when she said she trusted him to come along and see her father with her. Was she letting her heart rule her head? Probably. But she'd made her decision and she would stick to it.

Still, that didn't mean she was sanguine about it all. Why had he come back? Why now, just when she had everything set the way it had to be?

And why was her heart beating like a caged bird inside her chest? It didn't matter that she loved him. She couldn't ever be with him again. She had a baby to think about. And no time to indulge in emotions. Taking Monte with her was a risk, but she didn't really have a lot of choice—unless she wanted to turn him in to the guard.

She thought about doing exactly that for a few seconds, a smile playing on her lips. That would take them back full circle, wouldn't it? But it wasn't going to happen.

Don't worry, sweet baby, she said silently to her child. *I won't let anything hurt your father.* She said a tiny prayer and added, *I hope.*

Monte wasn't often haunted by self-doubt. In fact, his opinions and decisions were usually rock-solid. Once made, no wavering. But watching Pellea with her father gave him a sense that the earth might not be quite as firm under his feet as he'd assumed.

In the first place, he wasn't really sure why she'd let him come with her. She knew how the need for retribution burned in him and yet she'd let him come here where he would have a full view of the man, his enemy, lying there, helpless. Didn't she know how dangerous that was?

It would be easy to harm the old man. He was still handsome in an aged, fragile way, like a relic of past power. His face was drawn and lined, his color pale, his thin hair silver. Blue veins stood out in his slender hands. He was so vulnerable, so completely defenseless. Someone who moved on pure gut reaction would have done him in by now. Luckily, that wasn't Monte's style.

He would never do such a thing, but she didn't really know that. She'd taken a risk. But for what?

He watched as the object of his long, deep hatred struggled to talk to the daughter he obviously loved more than life itself, and he found his emotions tangling a bit. Could he really feel pity for a man who had helped ruin his family?

No. That couldn't happen.

Still, an element confused the issue. And to be this close to someone who had lived with and worked with his parents gave him a special sense of his own history. He couldn't deny that.

And there was something else, a certain primal longing that he couldn't control. He'd had it ever since that day twenty-five years ago when he'd been rushed out of the burning castle, and he had forever lost his parents. He'd grown up with all the privileges of his class: the schools, the high life, the international relationships. But he would have thrown it all out if that could have bought him a real, loving family—the kind you saw in movies, the kind you dreamed about in the middle of the night. Instead, he had this empty ache in his heart.

And that made watching Pellea and her father all the more effective. From his position in the entryway, he could see her bending lovingly over her father and dropping a kiss on his forehead. She talked softly to him, wiping his forehead with a cool, damp cloth, straightening his covers, plumping his pillow. The love she had for the man radiated from her every move. And he felt very similarly. She was obviously a brilliant bit of sun in his rather dark life.

"How are you feeling?" she asked.

"Much better now that you're here, my dear."

"I'm only here for a moment. I must get back. The masked ball is tonight."

"Ah, yes." He took hold of her hand. "So tonight you and Leonardo will announce your engagement?"

"Yes. Leonardo is prepared."

"What a relief to have this coming so quickly. To be able to see you protected before I go…"

"Don't talk about going."

"We all have to do it, my dear. My time has come."

Pellea made a dove-like noise and bent down to kiss his cheek. "No. You just need to get out more. See some people." Rising a bit, she had a thought. "I know. I'll have the nurse bring you to the ball so that you can see for yourself…."

"Hush, Pellea," he said, shaking his head. "I'm not going anywhere. I'm comfortable here and I'm too weak to leave this bed."

Reluctantly, she nodded. She'd known he would say that, but she'd hoped he might change his mind and try to take a step back into the world. A deep, abiding sadness settled into her soul as she faced the fact that he wasn't even tempted to try. He was preparing for the end, and nothing she said or did would change that. Tears threatened and she forced them back. She would have to save her grieving for another time.

Right now, she had another goal in mind. She was

hoping to prove something to Monte, and she was gambling that her father would respond in the tone and tenor that she'd heard from him so often before. If he went in a different direction, there was no telling what might happen. Glancing back at where Monte stood in the shadows, she made her decision. She was going to risk it—her leap of faith.

"Father, do you ever think of the past? About how we got here and why we are the way we are?"

He coughed and nodded. "I think of very little else these days."

"Do you think about the night the castle burned?"

"That was before you were born."

"Yes. But I feel as though that night molded my life in many ways."

He grasped her hand as though to make her stop it. "But why? It had nothing to do with you."

"But it was such a terrible way to start a new regime, the regime I've lived under all my life."

"Ugly things always happen in war." He turned his face away as though he didn't want to talk about it. "These things can't be helped."

She could feel Monte's anger beginning to simmer even though she didn't look at him. She hesitated. If her father wasn't going to express his remorse, she might only be doing damage by making him talk. Could Monte control his emotions? Was it worth it to push this further?

She had to try. She leaned forward.

"But, Father, you always say so many mistakes were made."

"Mistakes are human. That is just the way it is."

Monte made a sound that was very close to a growl. She shook her head, still unwilling to look his way, but ready to give up. What she'd hoped for just wasn't going to happen.

"All right, Father," she began, straightening and preparing to get Monte out of here before he did something ugly.

But suddenly her father was speaking again. "The burning of the castle was a terrible thing," he was saying, though he was speaking so softly she wondered if Monte could hear him. "And the assassination of the king and queen was even worse."

Relief bloomed in her chest. "What happened?" she prompted him. "How did it get so out of control?"

"You can go into a war with all sorts of lofty ambitions, but once the fuse is lit, the fire can be uncontrollable. It wasn't supposed to happen that way. Many of us were sick at heart for years afterwards. I still think of it with pain and deep, deep regret."

This was more like it. She only hoped Monte could hear it and that he was taking it as a sincere recollection, not a rationalization. She laced her fingers with her father's long, trembling ones.

"Tell me again, why did you sign on with the rebels?"

"I was very callow and I felt the DeAngelis family had grown arrogant with too much power. They were rejecting all forms of modernization. Something was needed to shake the country up. We were impatient. We thought something had to be done."

"And now?"

"Now I think that we should have moved more slowly, attempted dialogue instead of attack."

"So you regret how things developed?"

"I regret it deeply."

She glanced back at Monte. His face looked like a storm cloud. Wasn't he getting it? Didn't he see how her father had suffered as well? Maybe not. Maybe she was tilting at windmills. She turned back to her father and asked a question for herself.

"Then why do you want me to marry Leonardo and just perpetuate this regime?"

Her father coughed again and held a handkerchief to his lips. "He'll be better than his father. He has some good ideas. And your influence on him will work wonders." He managed a weak smile for his beloved daughter. "Once you are married to Leonardo, it will be much more difficult for anyone to hurt you."

She smiled down at him and blotted his forehead with the damp cloth. He wouldn't be so sure of that if he knew that at this very moment, danger lurked around her on all sides. Better he should never know that she was carrying Monte's child.

"I must go, Father. I've got to prepare for the ball."

"Yes. Go, my darling. Have a wonderful time."

"I'll be back in the morning to tell you all about it," she promised as she rose from his side.

She hurried toward the door, jerking her head at Monte to follow. She didn't like the look on his face. It seemed his hatred for her father was too strong for him to see what a dear and wonderful man he really was. Well, so be it. She'd done her best to show him the truth. You could lead a horse to water and all that.

But they were late. She had a path laid out and a routine, and now she knew she was venturing out into the unknown. At her usual time, she never met anyone in the halls. Now—who knew?

"We have to hurry," she said once they were outside the room. She quickly looked up and down the empty hallway. "I've got to meet Leonardo in just a short time." She started off. "Quickly. We don't want to meet anyone if we can help it."

The words were barely out of her mouth when she heard loud footsteps coming from around the bend in the walkway. Only boots could make such a racket. It had to be the guards. It sounded like two of them.

"Quick," she said, reaching for the closest door. "In here."

Though she knew the castle well, she wasn't sure what door she'd reached for. There was a library along this corridor, and a few bedrooms of lower-ranking relatives of the Granvillis. Any one of them could have yielded disaster. But for once, she was in luck. The door she'd chosen opened to reveal a very small broom closet.

Monte looked in and didn't see room for them both. He turned back to tell her, but she wasn't listening.

"In," she whispered urgently, and gave him a shove,

then came pushing in behind him, closing the door as quietly as she could. But was it quietly enough? Pressed close together, they each held their breath, listening as the boots came closer. And closer. And then stopped, right outside the door.

Pellea looked up at Monte, her eyes huge and anxious. He looked down at her and smiled. It was dark in the closet, but enough light came in around the door to let him make out her features. She was so beautiful and so close against him. He wanted to kiss her. But more important things had cropped up. So he reached around her and took hold of the knob from the inside.

There was a muttering conversation they couldn't make out, and then one of the guards tried the knob. Monte clamped down on his lower lip, holding the knob with all his might.

"It's locked," one of the guards said. "We'll have to find the concierge and get a key."

The other guard swore, but they began to drift off, walking slowly this time and chattering among themselves.

Monte relaxed and let go of the knob, letting out a long sigh of relief. When he looked down, she was smiling up at him, and this time he kissed her.

He'd been thinking about this kiss for so long, and now, finally, here it was. Her lips were smooth as silk, warm and inviting, and for just a moment, she opened enough to let his tongue flicker into the heat she held deeper. Then she tried to pull away, but he took her head in his hands and kissed her longer, deeper, and he felt her begin to melt in his arms.

Her body was molded to his and he could feel her heart begin to pound again, just as it had when they'd almost been caught. The excitement lit a flame in him and he pulled her closer, kissed her harder, wanted her all to himself, body and soul.

It was as though he'd forgotten where they were, what was happening around them. But Pellea hadn't.

"Monte," she finally managed to gasp, pushing him as hard as she could. "We have to go while we have the chance!"

He knew she was right and he let her pull away, but reluctantly. Still, he'd found out what he needed to know. The magic still lived between them and they could turn it on effortlessly. And, he hoped, a bit later, they would.

But now she opened the door tentatively and looked out. There was no one in the hall. She slipped out and he followed and they hurried to her gate, alert for any hint of anyone else coming their way. But they were lucky. She used a remote to open the gate as they approached. In seconds, they were safely inside.

The moment the gate closed, Monte turned and tried to take her into his arms again, but she backed away, trying hard to glare at him.

"Just stop it," she told him.

But he was shaking his head. "You can't marry Leonardo. Not when you can kiss me like that."

She stared at him for a moment. How could she have let this happen? He knew, he could tell that she was so in love with him, she could hardly contain it. She could protest all she wanted, he wasn't going to believe her. If she wasn't very careful, he would realize the precious secret that she was keeping from him, and if that happened, they would both be in terrible trouble.

Feeling overwhelmed, she groaned, her head in her hands. "Why are you torturing me like this?

He put a finger under her chin and forced her head up to meet his gaze. "Maybe a little torture will make you see the light."

"There's no light," she said sadly, her eyes huge with tragedy. "There's only darkness."

He'd been about to try to kiss her again, but something in her tone stopped him and he hesitated. Just a few weeks before, their relationship had been light and exciting, a romp despite the dangers they faced. They had made love, but they had also laughed a lot, and teased and played and generally enjoyed each other. Something had changed since then. Was it doubt? Wariness? Or fear?

He wasn't sure, but it bothered him and it held him off long enough for her to pivot out of his control.

"Gotta go," she said as she started for the gate, prepared to dash off again.

He took a step after her. "You're not planning to tell Leonardo I'm here, are you?" he said. His tone was teasing, as though he was confident she had no such plans.

She turned and looked at him, tempted to do or say something that would shake that annoying surety he had.

But she resisted that temptation. Instead, she told the truth.

"I'm hoping you won't be here any longer by the time I get back."

He appeared surprised. "Where would I go?"

She shook her head. It was obviously no use to try, but she had to make her case quickly and clearly. "Please, Monte," she said earnestly. "Go back the way you came in. Just do this for me. It will make my life a whole lot easier."

"Pellea, this is not your problem. I'll handle it."

She half laughed at his confidence. "What do you mean, not my problem? That's exactly what you are. My problem."

"Relax," he advised. "I'm just going to work on my objective."

"Which is?"

"I told you. I'm here to kidnap you and take you back to the continent with me."

"Oh, get off it. You can't kidnap me. I'm guarded day and night."

"Really? Well, where were your wonderful guards when I found my way into your chambers?"

She didn't have an answer for that one so she changed the subject. "What's the point? Why would you kidnap me?"

He shrugged. "To show them I can."

She threw up her hands. "Oh, brother."

"I want to show the Granvillis that I've been here and taken something precious to them."

Her eyes widened. "You think I'm precious?"

His smile was almost too personal. "I know you are. You're their most beautiful, desirable woman."

That gave her pause. Was she supposed to feel flattered by that? Well, she sort of did, but she wouldn't admit it.

"Gee, thanks. You make me feel like a prize horse." She shook her head. "So to you, this is just part of some war game?"

The laughter left his gaze. "Oh, no. This is no game. This is deadly serious."

There was something chilling in the way he said that. She shivered and tried to pretend she hadn't.

"So you grab me. You throw me over your shoulder and carry me back to your cave. You go 'nah nah nah' to the powers that be in Ambria." She shrugged. "What does that gain you?"

He watched her steadily, making her wonder what he saw. "The purpose is not just to thumb my nose at the Granvillis. The purpose is to cast them into disarray, to make them feel vulnerable and stupid. To throw them off their game. Let them spend their time obsessing on how I could have possibly gotten into the castle, how I could have possibly taken you out without someone seeing. Let them worry. It will make them weaker."

"You're crazy," she said for lack of anything else to say. And he was crazy if he thought the Granvillis would tumble into ruin because of a kidnapping or two.

"I'd like to see them tightening their defenses all around," he went on, "and begin scurrying about, looking for the chinks in their armor. There are people here who watch what they do and report to us. This will give us a better idea of where the weak spots are."

She nodded. She understood the theory behind all this. But it didn't make her any happier with it.

"So when you get right down to it, it doesn't have to be me," she noted. "You could take back something else of importance. The tiara, for instance."

Something moved behind his eyes, but he only smiled. "I'd rather take you."

"Well, you're not going to. So why not just get out of my hair and go back where you came from?"

He shook his head slowly, his blue eyes dark with shadows. "Sorry, Pellea. I've got things I must do here."

She sighed. She knew exactly what he would be doing while she was gone. He would be in her secret room, checking out what was going on all over the castle. Making his plans. Ruining her life. A wave of despair flooded through her. What had she done? Why hadn't she been more careful?

"Arrgghh!" she said, making a small wail of agony.

But right now she couldn't think about that. She had to go meet Leonardo or he would show up here.

"You stay out of my closet room," she told him with a warning look, knowing he wouldn't listen to a word she said. "Okay?" She glared at him, not bothering to wait for an answer. "I'll be back quicker than you think."

He laughed, watching her go, enjoying the way her

hips swayed in time with her gorgeous hair. And then she was gone and he headed straight for the closet.

To the casual eye, there was nothing of note to suggest a door to another room. The wall seemed solid enough. He tried to remember what she'd done to close it, but he hadn't been paying attention at the time. There had to be something—a special knock or a latch or a pressure point. He banged and pushed and tried to slide things, but nothing gave way.

"If this needs a magic password, I'm out of luck," he muttered to himself as he made his various attempts.

He kicked a little side panel, more in frustration than hope, and the door began to creak open. "It's always the ones you don't suspect," he said, laughing.

The small room inside was unprepossessing, having space only for a computer and a small table. And there on the screen was access to views of practically every public area, all over the castle. A secret room with centralized power no one else knew about. Ingenious.

Still, someone had built it. Someone had wired it. Someone had to know electronics were constantly running in here. The use of electricity alone would tip off the suspicious. So someone in the workings of the place was on her side.

But what was "her side" exactly? That was something he still had to find out.

The sound of Pellea's entry gong made him jerk. He lifted his head and listened. A woman's voice seemed to be calling out, and then, a moment later, singing. She'd obviously come into the courtyard.

Moving silently, he made his way out of the secret room, closing the door firmly. He moved carefully into the dressing area, planning to use the high wardrobe as a shield as he had done earlier, in order to see who it was without being seen. As he came out of the closet and made his way to slip behind the tall piece of furniture, a pretty, pleasantly rounded young woman stepped into the room, catching sight of him just before he found his hiding place.

She gasped. Their gazes met. Her mouth opened. He reached out to stop her, but he was too late.

She screamed at the top of her lungs.

CHAPTER FOUR

MONTE MOVED LIKE LIGHTNING but it felt like slow motion to him. In no time his hand was over the intruder's mouth and he was pulling her roughly into the room and kicking the French door closed with such a snap, he was afraid for a moment that the glass would crack.

Pulling her tightly against his chest, he snarled in her ear, "Shut the hell up and do it now."

She pulled her breath into her lungs in hysterical gasps, and he yanked her more tightly.

"Now!" he demanded.

She closed her eyes and tried very hard. He could feel the effort she put into it, and he began to relax. They waited, counting off the seconds, to see if anyone had heard the scream and was coming to the rescue. Nothing seemed to stir. At last, he decided the time for alarm was over and he began to release her slowly, ready to reassert control if she tried to scream again.

"Okay," he whispered close to her ear. "I'm going to let go now. If you make a sound, I'll have to knock you flat."

She nodded, accepting his terms. But she didn't seem

to have any intention of a repeat. As he freed her, she turned, her gaze sweeping over him in wonder.

"Wait," she said, eyes like saucers. "I've seen you before. You were here a couple of months ago."

By now, he'd recognized her as well. She was Pellea's favorite maid. He hadn't interacted with her when he'd been here before, but he'd seen her when she'd dropped by to deal with some things Pellea needed done. Pellea had trusted her to keep his presence a secret then. He only hoped that trust was warranted—and could hold for now.

But signs were good. He liked the sparkle in her eyes. He gave her a lopsided smile. "I'm back."

"So I see." She cocked her head to the side, looking him over, then narrowing her gaze. "And is my mistress happy that you're here?"

He shrugged. "Hard to tell. But she didn't throw anything at me."

Her smile was open-hearted. "That's a good sign."

He drew in a deep breath, feeling better about the situation. "What's your name?" he asked.

"Pellea calls me Kimmee."

"Then I shall do the same." He didn't offer his own name and wondered if she knew who he was. He doubted it. Pellea wouldn't be that reckless, would she?

"I've been here for a couple of hours now," he told her. "Pellea has seen me. We've been chatting, going over old times."

Kimmee grinned. "Delightful."

He smiled back, but added a warning look. "I'm

sure you don't talk about your mistress's assignations to others."

"Of course not," she said brightly. "I only wish she had a few."

He blinked. "What do you mean?"

She shrugged, giving him a sly look. "You're the only one I know of."

He laughed. She had said the one thing that would warm his heart and she probably knew it, but it made him happy anyway.

"You're not trying to tell me your mistress has no suitors, are you?" he teased skeptically.

"Oh, no, of course not. But she generally scorns them all."

He looked at her levelly. "Even Leonardo?" he asked.

She hesitated, obviously reluctant to give her candid opinion on that score. He let her off the hook with a shrug.

"Never mind. I know she's promised to him at this point." He cocked an eyebrow. "I just don't accept it."

She nodded. "Good," she whispered softly, then shook her head as though wishing she hadn't spoken. Turning away, she reached for the ball gown hanging in front of the wardrobe. "I just came by to check that the gown was properly hung and wrinkle-free," she said, smoothing the skirt a bit. "Isn't it gorgeous?"

"Yes, it is."

"I can't wait to see her dancing in this," Kimmee added.

"Neither can I," he murmured, and at the same time, an idea came to him. He frowned, wondering if he should trust thoughts spurred on by his overwhelming desire for all things Pellea. It was a crazy idea, but the more he mulled it over, the more he realized it could serve more than one purpose and fit into much of what he hoped to accomplish. So why not give it a try?

He studied the pretty maid for a moment, trying to evaluate just how much he dared depend on her. Her eyes sparkled in a way that made him wonder how a fun-loving girl like this would keep such a secret. He knew he had better be prepared to deal with the fallout, should there be any. After all, he didn't have much choice. Either he would tie her up and gag her and throw her into a closet, or he would appeal to her better nature.

"Tell me, Kimmee, do you love your mistress?"

"Oh, yes." Kimmee smiled. "She's my best friend. We've been mates since we were five years old."

He nodded, frowning thoughtfully. "Then you'll keep a secret," he said. "A secret that could get me killed if you reveal it."

Her eyes widened and she went very still. "Of course."

His own gaze was hard and assessing as he pinned her with it. "You swear on your honor?"

She shook her head, looking completely earnest. "I swear on my honor. I swear on my life. I swear on my…"

He held a hand up. "I get the idea, Kimmee. You really mean it. So I'm going to trust you."

She waited, wide-eyed.

He looked into her face, his own deadly serious.

"I want to go to the ball."

"Oh, sir!" She threw her hands up to her mouth. "Oh, my goodness! Where? How?"

"That's where you come in. Find me a costume and a nice, secure mask." He cocked an eyebrow and smiled at her. "Can you do that?"

"Impossible," she cried. "Simply impossible." But a smile was beginning to tease the corners of her mouth. "Well, maybe." She thought a moment longer, then smiled impishly. "It would be fun, wouldn't it?"

He grinned at her.

"Will you want a sword?" she asked, her enthusiasm growing by leaps and bounds.

He grimaced. "I think not. It might be too tempting to use it on Leonardo."

"I know what you mean," she said, nodding wisely.

He got a real kick out of her. She was so ready to join in on his plans and at the same time, she seemed to be thoroughly loyal to the mistress she considered her best friend. It was a helpful combination to work with.

He lifted his head, looking at the ball gown and thinking of how it would look with his favorite woman filling it out in all the right places. "All I want to do is go to the ball and dance with Pellea."

"How romantic," Kimmee said, sighing. Then her gaze sharpened as she realized what he might be describing. "You mean...?"

"Yes." He nodded. "Secretly. I want to surprise Pellea."

Kimmee gave a bubbling laugh, obviously delighted with the concept. "I think Leonardo will be even more surprised."

He shook his head and gave her a warning look. "That is something I'll have to guard against."

She sighed. "I understand. But it would be fun to see his face."

He frowned, wondering if he was letting her get a little too much into this.

"See what you can do," he said. "But don't forget. If Leonardo finds out…" He drew his finger across his throat like a knife and made a cutting sound. "I'll be dead and Pellea will be in big trouble."

She shook her head, eyes wide and sincere. "You can count on me, sir. And as for the costume…" She put her hand over her heart. "I'll do my best."

Pellea returned a half hour later, bristling with determination.

"I've brought you something to eat," she said, handing him a neatly wrapped, grilled chicken leg and a small loaf of artisan bread. He was sitting at a small table near her fountain, looking for all the world like a Parisian playboy at a sidewalk café. "And I've brought you news."

"News, huh? Let me guess." He put his hand to his forehead as though taking transmissions from space.

"Leonardo has decided to join the national ballet and forget all about this crazy marriage stuff. Am I right?"

She glared at him. "I'm warning you, don't take the man lightly."

"Oh, I don't. Believe me." He began to unwrap the chicken leg. He hadn't eaten for hours and he was more than ready to partake of what she'd brought him. "So what is the news?"

"Leonardo talked to his father and we've decided to move the wedding up." Her chin rose defiantly. "We're getting married in two days."

He put down the chicken leg, hunger forgotten, and stared at her with eyes that had turned icy silver. "What's the rush?" he asked with deceptive calm.

The look in his gaze made her nervous. He seemed utterly peaceful, and yet there was a sense in the air that a keg of dynamite was about to blow.

She turned away, pacing, thinking about how nice and simple life had been before she'd found him lurking in her garden that day. Her path had been relatively clear at the time. True, she had been fighting her father over his wish that she marry Leonardo. But that was relatively easy to deal with compared to what she had now.

The irony was that her father would get his wish, and she'd done it to herself. She would marry Leonardo. She would be the first lady of the land and just about impervious to attack. Just as her father so obsessively craved, she would be as safe as she could possibly be.

But even that wasn't perfect safety. There were a thousand chinks in her armor and the path ahead was perilous. Everything she did, every decision she made, could have unforeseen repercussions. She had set a course and now the winds would take her to her destination. Was it the best destination for her or was it a mirage? Was she right or was she wrong? If only she knew.

Looking out into the courtyard, Pellea shivered with a premonition of what might be to come.

Monte watched her from under lowered brows, munching on a bite of chicken. Much as she was trying to hide it, he could see that she was in a special sort of agony and he couldn't for the life of him understand why. What was her hurry to marry Leonardo? What made her so anxious to cement those ties?

Motivations were often difficult to untangle and understand. What were hers? Did it really mean everything to her to have her father satisfied that she was safe, and to do it before it was too late? Evidence did suggest that he was fading fast. Was that what moved her? He couldn't think what else it could be. But was that really enough to make her rush to Leonardo's arms? Or was there something going on that he didn't know about?

"I suppose the powers that be are in favor of this wedding?" he mentioned casually.

She nodded. "Believe me, everything around here is planned to the nth degree. Public-relations values hold sway over everything."

"I've noticed. That's what makes me wonder. What's the deal with this wedding coming on so suddenly? I

would think the regime would try to milk all the public-
ity they could possibly get out of a long engagement."

"Interesting theory," she said softly, pretending to be
busy folding clothes away.

"Why?" he asked bluntly. "Why so soon?"

"You'd have to ask Leonardo about that," she said
evasively.

"Maybe I will. If I get the chance." He looked at her
sharply, trying to read her mind. "I can't help but think
he has a plan in mind. There has to be a reason."

"Sometimes people just want to do things quickly,"
she said, getting annoyed with his persistence.

"Um-hmm." He didn't buy that for a minute. The
more he let the idea of such a marriage—the ultimate
marriage of convenience—linger in his mind, the more
he hated it. Pellea couldn't be with Leonardo. Everything
in him rebelled at the thought.

Pellea belonged to him.

That was nonsense, of course. How could she be his
when he wouldn't do what needed to be done to take that
responsibility in hand himself? After all, he'd refused
to step up and do the things a man did when making a
woman his own. As his old tutor might say, he craved
the honey but refused to tend to the bees.

Still in some deep, gut-level part of him, she was his
and had been since the moment he'd first laid eyes on
her. He'd put his stamp on her, his brand, his seal. He'd
held her and loved her, body and soul, and he wanted her
available for more of the same. She was his, damn it!

But what was he prepared to do about it?

That was the question.

He watched her, taking in the grace and loveliness of her form and movement, the full, luscious temptation of her exciting body, the beauty of her perfect face, and the question burned inside him. What was he prepared to do? It was working into a drumbeat in his head and in his heart. What? Just exactly what?

"You don't love him."

The words came out loud and clear and yet he was surprised when he said them. He hadn't planned to say anything of the sort. Still, once it was out, he was glad he'd said it. The truth was out now, like a flag, a banner, a warning that couldn't be ignored any longer. And why not? Truth was supposed to set you free.

And she didn't love Leonardo. It was obvious in the way she talked to him and talked about him. She was using him and he was using her. They had practically said as much in front of him—though neither had known it at the time. Why not leave it out there in the open where it could be dealt with?

"You don't love him," he said again, even more firmly this time.

She whirled to face him, her arms folded, her eyes flashing. "How do you know?" she challenged, her chin high.

A slow smile began to curl his lips. As long as they were speaking truth, why not add a bit more?

"I know, Pellea. I know very well. Because…" He paused, not really for dramatic effect, although that was what he ended up with. He paused because for just a second, he wondered if he really dared say this.

"Because you love me," he said at last.

The shock of his words seemed to crackle in the air.

She gasped. "Oh! Of all the…" Her cheeks turned bright red and she choked and had to cough for a moment. "I never told you that!"

He sat back and surveyed her levelly. "You didn't have to tell me with words. Your body told me all I would ever need to know." His gaze skimmed over her creamy skin. "Every time I touch you your body resonates like a fine instrument. You were born to play to my tune."

She stood staring at him, shaking her head as though she couldn't believe anyone would have the gall to say such things. "Of all the egos in the world…"

"Mine's the best?" he prompted, then shrugged with a lopsided grin. "Of course."

She held her breath and counted to ten, not really sure if she was trying to hold back anger or a smile. He did appear ridiculously adorable sitting there looking pleased with himself. She let her breath back out and tried for logic and reason. It would obviously be best to leave flights of fancy and leaps of faith behind.

"I don't love you," she lied with all her heart. Tears suddenly threatened, but she wouldn't allow them. Not now. "I can't love you. Don't you see that? Don't ever say that to me again."

Something in her voice reached in and made a grab for his heartstrings. Had he actually hurt her with his careless words? That was the last thing he would ever want to do.

"Pellea." He rose and reached for her.

She tried to turn away but he wouldn't let her. His arms came around her, holding her close against his chest, and he stroked her hair.

"Pellea, darling…"

She lifted her face, her lips trembling. He looked down and melted. No woman had ever been softer in his arms. Instantly, his mouth was on hers, touching, testing, probing, lighting her pulse on fire. She kissed him in return for as long as she dared, then pulled back, though she was still in the circle of his embrace. She tried to frown.

"You taste like chicken," she said, blinking up at him.

He smiled, and a warm sense of his affection for her was plain to see. "You taste like heaven," he countered.

She closed her eyes and shook her head. "Oh, please, Monte. Let me go."

He did so reluctantly, and she drew back slowly, looking toward him with large, sad eyes and thinking, *If only…*

He watched her, feeling strangely helpless, though he wasn't really sure why. With a sigh, she turned and went back to pacing.

"We have to get you out of here," she fretted while he sat down again and leaned back in his chair. "If I can get you out of the castle, do you have a way to get back to the continent?"

He waved away the very concept. "I'm not going anywhere," he said confidently. "And when I do go, I'll take care of myself. I've got resources. No need to worry about me."

She stopped, shaking her head as she looked at him. How could she not worry about him? That was pretty much all she was thinking about right now. She needed him to leave before he found out about the baby. And even more important, she wanted him to go because she wanted him to stay alive. But there was no point in bringing that up. He would only laugh at the danger. Still, she had to try to get him to see reason.

"There is more news," she told him, leaning against the opposite chair. "Rumors are flying."

He paused, the chicken leg halfway to his mouth. He put it down again and gazed at her. "What kind of rumors?"

She turned and sank into the chair she'd been leaning on. "There's talk of a force preparing for an Ambrian invasion."

He raised one sleek eyebrow and looked amused. "By whom?"

"Ex-Ambrians, naturally. Trying to take the country back."

His sharp, all-knowing gaze seemed to see right into her soul as he leaned closer across the table. "And you believe that?"

"Are you kidding?" She threw her hands up. "I can see it with my own eyes. What else are you doing here?"

He gave her another view of his slow, sexy smile. "I came to kidnap you, not to start a revolution. I thought I'd made that perfectly clear."

She leaned forward, searching his eyes. "So it's true. You are planning to take over this country."

He shrugged, all careless confidence. "Someday, sure." His smile was especially knowing and provocative. "Not this weekend though. I've got other plans."

He had other plans. Well, wasn't that just dandy? He had plans and she had issues of life and death to contend with. She wanted to strangle him. Or at least make him wince a little. She rose, towering over him and pointing toward her gateway.

"You've got to go. Now!"

He looked surprised at her vehemence, and then as though his feelings were hurt, he said, "I'm eating."

"You can take the food with you."

He frowned. "But I'm almost done." He took another bite. "This is actually pretty good chicken."

She stared at him, at her wit's end, then sank slowly back into the chair, her head in her hands. What could she do? She couldn't scream for help. That could get him killed. She couldn't pick him up and carry him to the doorway. That would get *her* killed. Or at least badly injured. She was stuck here in her chambers, stuck with the man she loved, the father of her child, the man whose kisses sent her into orbit every time, and everything depended on getting rid of him somehow. What on earth was she going to do?

"I hate you," she said, though it was more of a moan than a sentence.

"Good," he responded. "I like a woman with passion."

She rolled her eyes. Why couldn't he ever be serious? It was maddening. "My hatred would be more effective if I had a dagger instead," she commented dryly.

He waved a finger at her. "No threats. There's nothing quite so deadly to a good relationship. Don't go down that road."

She pouted, feeling grumpy and as though she wasn't being taken seriously. "Who said we had a good relationship?"

He looked surprised. "Don't we?" Reaching out, he took her hand. "It's certainly the best I've ever had," he said softly, his eyes glowing with the sort of affection that made her breath catch in her throat.

She curled her fingers around his. She couldn't help it. She did love him so.

She wasn't sure why. He had done little so far other than make her life more difficult. He hadn't promised her anything but kisses and lovemaking. Was that enough to give your heart for?

Hardly. Pellea was a student of history and she knew very well that people living on love tended to starve pretty quickly. What began with excitement and promises usually ended in bleak prospects and recriminations.

The gong sounded, making her jump. She pulled away

her hand and looked at him. He shrugged as though he regretted the interruption.

"I'll take my food into the library," he offered. "Just don't forget and bring your guest in there."

"I won't," she said back softly, watching him go and then hurrying to the entryway.

It was Magda, her hairdresser, making plans for their session. The older woman was dressed like a gypsy with scarves and belts everywhere. She was a bit of a character, but she had a definite talent with hair.

"I'll be back in half an hour," she warned. "You be ready. I'm going to need extra time to weave your hair around the tiara. It's not what I usually do, you know."

"Yes, I know, Magda," Pellea said, smiling. "And I appreciate that you are willing to give it a try. I'm sure we'll work something out together."

Magda grumbled a bit, but she seemed to be looking forward to the challenge. "Half an hour," she warned again as she started off toward the supply room to prepare for the session.

Pellea had just begun to close the gate when Kimmee came breezing around the corner.

"Hi," she called, rushing forward. "Don't close me out."

Pellea gave her a welcoming smile but didn't encourage her to come into the courtyard. "I'm in a bit of a hurry tonight," she warned her. "I've got the hairdresser coming and..."

"I just need to give your gown a last-minute check

for wrinkles," Kimmee said cheerfully, ignoring Pellea's obvious hint and coming right on in.

"Where is he?" she whispered, eyes sparkling, as she squeezed past.

"Who?" Pellea responded, startled.

Kimmee grinned. "I saw him when I was here earlier. You were out, but he was here." She winked. "I said hello." She looked around, merrily furtive. "We spoke."

"Oh."

Pellea swallowed hard with regret. This was not good. This was exactly what she'd hoped to avoid. Kimmee had kept the secret before, but would she again?

"He is so gorgeous," Kimmee whispered happily. "I'm so glad for you. You needed someone gorgeous in your life."

Pellea shook her head, worried and not sure how to deal with this. "But, Kimmee, it's not like that. You know I'm going to marry Leonardo and…"

"All the more reason you need a gorgeous man. No one said it had to be a forever man." Her smile was impish. "Just take some happiness where you can. You deserve it."

She looked at her maid in despair. It was all very well for her to be giving shallow comfort for activities that were clearly not in good taste. But here she was, hoisted on her own petard, as it were—taking advice that could ruin her life. But what was she going to do—beg a servant not to gossip? Might as well ask a bird not to fly.

Of course, Kimmee was more than a mere servant.

In many ways, she had always been her best friend. That might make a difference. It had in the past. But not being sure was nerve-wracking. After all, this was pretty much a life-or-death situation.

She closed her eyes and said a little prayer. "Kimmee," she began nervously.

"Don't worry, Pel," Kimmee said softly. She reached out and touched her mistress's arm, her eyes warm with an abiding affection. She'd used the name she'd called Pellea when they were young playmates. "I'm just happy that…" She shrugged, but they both knew what she was talking about. "I'd never, ever tell anyone else. It's just you and me."

Tears filled Pellea's eyes. "Thank you," she whispered.

Kimmee kissed Pellea's cheek, as though on impulse and nodded. Then suddenly, as she noticed Monte coming into the doorway to the library, she was the dutiful servant once again. "Oh, miss, let me take a look at that gown."

Monte leaned against the doorjamb, his shirt open, his hair mussed, looking for all the world like an incredibly handsome buccaneer.

"Hey, Kimmee," he said.

"Hello, sir." She waved, then had second thoughts and curtsied. As she rose from her deep bow, Pellea was behind her and Kimmee risked an A-OK wink to show him plans were afoot and all was going swimmingly. "I hope things are going well with you," she added politely.

"Absolutely," he told her. "I've just had a nice little meal and I'm feeling pretty chipper."

She laughed and turned back to her work, completed it quickly, and turned to go.

"Well, miss, I just wanted to check on the gown and remind you I'll be here to help you get into it in about an hour. Will that suit?"

"That will suit. Magda should be through by then." She smiled at the young woman. "Thank you, Kimmee," she said, giving her a hug as she passed. "I hope you know how much I appreciate you."

"Of course, miss. My only wish is for your happiness. You should know that by now."

"I do. You're a treasure."

The maid waved at them both. "I'll be back in a bit. See you."

"Goodbye, Kimmee," Monte said, retreating into the library again.

But Pellea watched her go, deep in thought. In a few hours, she would be at the ball, dancing with Leonardo and preparing to have their engagement announced. People would applaud. Some might even cheer. A couple of serving girls would toss confetti in the air. A new phase of her life would open. She ought to be excited. Instead, she had a sick feeling in the pit of her stomach.

"Get over it," she told herself roughly. She had to do what she had to do. There was no choice in the matter. But instead of a bride going to join her fiancé, she felt like a traitor going to her doom.

Was she doing the right thing? How could she know for sure?

She pressed both hands to her belly and thought of the child inside. The "right thing" was whatever was best for her baby. That, at least, was clear. Now if she could just be sure what that was, maybe she could stop feeling like a tightrope walker halfway across the rope.

And in the meantime, there was someone who seemed to take great delight in jiggling that rope she was so anxiously trying to get across.

CHAPTER FIVE

TURNING, PELLEA MARCHED into the library and confronted Monte.

He looked up and nodded as she approached. "She's a good one," he commented on Kimmee. "I'm glad you've got such a strong supporter nearby."

"Why didn't you tell me you'd seen her, actually chatted with her?" Pellea said, in no mood to be mollified. "Don't you see how dangerous that is? What if she talks?"

He eyed her quizzically. "You know her better than I do. What do you think? Will she?"

Pellea shook her head. "I don't know," she said softly. "I don't think so, but…"

She threw up her hands. It occurred to her how awful it was to live like this, always suspicious, always on edge. She wanted to trust her best friend. Actually, she did trust her. But knowing the penalty one paid for being wrong in this society kept her on her toes.

"Who knows?" she said, staring at him, wondering how this all would end.

It was tempting, in her darkest moments, to blame it

all on him. He came, he saw, he sent her into a frenzy of excitement and—she had to face it—love, blinding her to what was really going on, making her crazy, allowing things to happen that should never have happened.

But he was just the temptor. She was the temptee. From the very first, she should have stopped him in his tracks, and she'd done nothing of the sort. In fact, she'd immediately gone into a deep swoon and hadn't come out of it until he was gone. She had no one to blame but herself.

Still, she wished it was clearer just what he'd been doing here two months ago, and why he'd picked her to cast a spell over.

"Why did you come here to my chambers that first time?" she asked him, getting serious. "That day you found me by the fountain. What were you doing here? What was your purpose? And why did you let me distract you from it?"

He looked at her coolly. He'd finished the chicken and eaten a good portion of the little loaf of bread. He was feeling full and happy. But her questions were a bit irksome.

"I came to get the lay of the land," he said, leaning back in his chair. "And to see my ancestral castle. To see my natural home." He looked a bit pained.

"The place I was created to rule," he added, giving it emphasis that only confirmed her fears.

"See, I knew it," she said, feeling dismal. "You were prepared to do something, weren't you?"

"Not then. Not yet." He met her gaze candidly. "But soon."

She shook her head, hands on her hips. "You want to send Leonardo and his entire family packing, don't you?" That was putting a pleasant face on something that might be very ugly, but she couldn't really face just how bad it could be.

He shrugged. "There's no denying it. It's been my obsession since I was a child." He gave her a riveting look. "Of course I'm going to take my country back. What else do I exist for?"

She felt faint. His obsession was her nightmare. She had to find a way to stop it.

"That is exactly where you go wrong," she told him, beginning to pace again. "Don't you see? You don't have to be royal. You don't have to restore your monarchy. Millions of people live perfectly happy lives without that."

He blinked at her as though he didn't quite get what she was talking about. "Yes, but do they make a difference? Do their lives have meaning in the larger scheme of things?"

She threw out her arms. "Of course they do. They fall in love and marry and have children and have careers and make friends and do things together and they're happy. They don't need to be king of anything." She appealed to him in all earnestness, wishing there was some way to convince him, knowing there was very little hope. "Why can't you be like that?"

He rose from the desk and she backed away quickly,

as though afraid he would try to take her in his arms again.

But he showed no intention of doing that. Instead, he began a slow survey of the books in her bookcases that lined the walls.

"You don't really understand me, Pellea," he said at last as he moved slowly through her collection. "I could live very happily without ever being king."

She sighed. "I wish I could believe that," she said softly.

He glanced back over his shoulder at her as she stood by the doorway, then turned to face her.

"I don't need to be king, Pellea. But there is something I do need." He went perfectly still and held her gaze with his own, his eyes burning.

"Revenge. I can never be fulfilled until I have my revenge."

She drew her breath in. Her heart beat hard, as though she was about to make a run for her life.

"That's just wicked," she said softly.

He held her gaze for a moment longer, then shrugged and turned away, shoving his hands down deep into his pockets and staring out into her miniature tropical forest.

"Then I'm wicked. I can't help it. Vengeance must be mine. I must make amends for what happened to my family."

She trembled. It was hopeless. His words felt like a dark and painful destiny to her. Like a forecast of doom.

There was no doubt in her mind that this would all end badly.

It was very true, what Monte had said. His character needed some kind of answer for what had happened to his family, some kind of retribution. Pellea knew that and on a certain level, she could hardly blame him. But didn't he see, and wasn't there any way she could make him see, that his satisfaction would only bring new misery for others? In order for him to feel relief, someone would have to pay very dearly.

"It's just selfish," she noted angrily.

He shrugged and looked at her coolly. "So I'm selfish. What else is new?"

She put her hand to her forehead and heaved a deep sigh. "There are those who live for themselves and their own gratification, and there are those who devote their lives to helping the downtrodden and the weak and oppressed. To make life better for the most miserable among us."

"You're absolutely right. You pay your money and you take your chances. I'd love to help the downtrodden and the poor and the oppressed in Ambria. Those are my people and I want to take care of them." He searched her eyes again. "But in order for me to do that, a few heads will have to roll."

The chimes on her elegant wall clock sounded and Pellea gasped.

"Oh, no! Look at the time. They're going to be here any minute. I wanted to get you out of here by now."

She looked around as though she didn't know where to hide him.

He stretched and yawned, comfortable as a cat, and then he rose and half sat on the corner of the desk. "It's all right. I'll just take a little nap while you're having your hair done."

"No, you will not!"

"As I remember it, your sleeping arrangements are quite comfortable. I think I'll spend a little quality time with your bedroom." He grinned, enjoying the outrage his words conjured up in her.

"I want you gone," she was saying fretfully, grabbing his arm for emphasis. "How do you get in here, anyway? Tell me how you do it. However you get in, that's the way you're going out. Tell me!"

He covered her hand with his own and caressed it. "I'll do better than that," he said, looking down at her with blunt affection. "I'll show you. But it will have to wait until we leave together."

She looked at his hand on hers. It felt hot and lovely. "I'm not going with you," she said in a voice that was almost a whimper.

"Yes, you are." He said it in a comforting tone.

Her eyes widened as she glanced up at him. He was doing it again—mesmerizing her. It was some sort of tantalizing magic and she had to resist it. "No, I'm not!" she insisted, but she couldn't gather the strength to pull her hand away.

He lifted her chin and kissed her softly on the lips.

"You are," he told her kindly. "You belong with me and you know it."

She felt helpless. Every time he touched her, she wanted to purr. She sighed in a sort of temporary surrender. "What are you going to do while I'm at the ball?" she asked.

"Don't worry. I'll find something to while away the time with." He raised an eyebrow. "Perfect opportunity, don't you think? To come and go at will."

She frowned. "There are guards everywhere. Surely you've seen that by now."

"Yes. But I do have your security setup to monitor things. That will help a lot."

"Oh." She groaned. She should never have let him see that.

She shook her head. "I should call the guards right now and take care of this once and for all."

"But you won't."

Suddenly, a surge of adrenaline gave her the spunk she needed to pull away from his touch, and once she was on her own, she felt emboldened again.

"Dare me!" she said, glaring at him with her hands on her hips.

He stared back at her for a long moment, then a slow grin spread over his handsome face. "I may be careless at times, my darling, but I'm not foolhardy. Even I know better than to challenge you like that."

The entry gong sounded. She sighed, all the fight ebbing out of her. "Just stay out of sight," she warned him. "I'll check in on you one last time before I go to the ball." She gave him a look of chagrin. "Unless, of course, you've left by then." She shrugged. "But I guess I won't hold my breath over that one."

He nodded. "Wise woman," he murmured as he watched her go. Then he slipped into her bedroom and closed the door before she'd let the hairdresser into the compound.

It was a beautiful room. The bedding was thick and luxurious, the headboard beautifully carved. Large oils of ancient landscapes, painted by masters of centuries past, covered the walls. He wondered what they had done with all the old portraits of his ancestors. Burned them, probably. Just another reason he needed his revenge.

But that was a matter to come. Right now he needed sleep.

He sat on the edge of her bed and looked at her bedside table, wondering what she was reading these days. What he saw gave him a bit of a jolt.

Beginning Pregnancy 101.

Interesting. It would seem Pellea was already thinking about having children. With Leonardo? That gave him a shudder. Surely she wasn't hoping to have a baby in order to reassure her father. That would be a step too far. And if she just had a yen for children, why choose Leonardo to have them with?

Making a face, he pushed the subject away. It was too depressing to give it any more attention.

He lay down on her sumptuous bed and groaned softly as he thought of the times he'd spent here. Two months ago everything had seemed so clean and simple.

A hungry man. A soft and willing woman. Great love-making. Good food. Luxurious surroundings. What could be better? He'd come back thinking it would all be easy to recreate. But he'd been dead wrong.

The wall clock struck the quarter hour again and tweaked a memory. There had been a huge, ancient grandfather clock in his mother's room when he was a child. There was a carved wooden tiger draped around the face of the timepiece and it had fascinated him. But even as he thought of that, he remembered that his mother had kept copies of her jewelry in a secret compartment in that clock.

What a strange and interesting castle this was. There were secret compartments and passageways and hiding places of all kinds just about everywhere. A few hundred years of the need to hide things had spurred his ancestors into developing ingenious and creative places to hide their most precious objects from the prying eyes and itching fingers of the servants and even of the courtiers. Life in the castle was a constant battle, it seemed, and it probably wasn't much different now.

Looking around Pellea's room, he wondered how many secret places had been found, and how many were still waiting, unused and unopened, after all these years. He knew of one, for sure, and that was the passageway that had brought him here twice now. He was pretty sure no one else had used it in twenty-five years. What else would he find if he tapped on a few walls and pressed on a few pieces of wood trim? It might be interesting to find out.

Later. Right now he needed a bit of sleep. Closing his eyes, he dreamed of Pellea and their nights together. He slept.

Pellea stood looking down at Monte, her heart so full of love, she had to choke back the tears that threatened. Tears would ruin her makeup and that was the last thing she would have been able to handle right now. She was on the edge of an emotional storm as it was.

Everyone had gone. She'd even sent the two men who were supposed to guard the tiara out into the hall to wait for her. And now she was ready to go and make the announcement that would set in stone her future life and that of her baby. But she needed just one more moment to look at the man she loved, the man she wished she were planning to marry.

If only they had met in another time, another place. If only circumstances were different. They could have been so happy together, the two of them. If there was no royalty for him to fight for, if her father was still as hale and hearty as he'd been most of her life, if her place weren't so precarious that she needed it bolstered by marrying Leonardo...

There were just too many things that would have to be different in order for things to work out the way they should, and for them to have a happy life. Unfortunately that didn't seem to be in the cards for her.

As for him—oh, he would get over it. He would never know that the baby she would have in a few months was really his. He was the only man she'd ever loved, but she had been very careful not to tell him that. She was pretty sure he'd had romances of one kind or another for years. It wouldn't be that hard for him. There would always be beautiful and talented women ready to throw themselves at him in a heartbeat.

Of course, if he did do as he threatened and try to take his country back by force, the entire question would be moot and they might all have to pay the ultimate price. Who knew?

In the meantime, she wanted just a moment more to watch him and dream….

When he woke an hour or so later, she was standing at the side of the bed. His first impression was benignness, but by the time he'd cleared his eyes, her expression had changed and she was glaring down at him.

"I don't know why you're still here," she said a bit mournfully. "Please don't get yourself killed while I'm at the ball."

He stretched and looked up at her sleepily. She was dressed to the hilt and the most beautiful thing he'd ever seen. His mother's tiara had been worked into a gorgeous coiffure that made her look as regal as any queen. Her creamy breasts swelled just above the neckline of her gown in old-fashioned allure. The bodice was tight, making her waist look tiny, as though he could reach out and pick her up with his two hands and pull her down…

His mouth went dry with desire and he reached for her. Deftly, she sidestepped his move and held him at bay.

"Don't touch," she warned. "I'm a staged work of art right now and I'm off to the photographer for pictures."

A piece of art was exactly what she was, looking just as she appeared before him. She could have walked right out of a huge portrait by John Singer Sargent, burnished lighting and rich velvet trimmings and all.

He sighed, truly pained. She looked good enough to ravish. But then she always did, didn't she?

"Forget the ball," he coaxed, though he knew it was all for naught. "Stay here with me. We'll lock the gate and recreate old times together."

"Right," she said, dismissing that out of hand, not even bothering to roll her eyes. She had other things on her mind right now. "The pictures will take at least an hour, I'm sure. Leonardo will meet me there and we'll go directly to the ball."

He frowned, feeling grumpy and overlooked for the moment. "Unless he has an unfortunate accident before he gets there," he suggested.

She looked at him sharply. "None of that, Monte. Promise me."

He stretched again and pouted. "When do you plan to make the big announcement?" he asked instead of making promises he might not be able to keep.

She frowned. "What does that matter?" she asked.

He grinned. "You are so suspicious of my every mood and plan."

Her eyes flashed. "With good reason, it seems."

He shrugged. "So I won't see you again until later?"

"No. Unless you decide to go away. As you should." She hesitated. She needed to make a few thing clear to him. He had to follow rules or she was going to have to get the guard to come help her keep him in line.

Right. That was a great idea. She made a face at herself. She was truly caught in a trap. She needed to keep him in line, but in order to do that, she would be signing his death warrant. There was no way that was going to happen.

At the same time, he showed no appreciation for the bind she was in. If he didn't feel it necessary to respect the rules she made, she couldn't have him here. He would have to understand that.

Taking a deep breath, she gave him the facts as she needed them to be.

"Once the announcement is made, our engagement will be official and there will be no more of anything like this," she warned him, a sweep of her hand indicating their entire relationship. "You understand that, don't you?"

His eyes were hooded as he looked up at her. "I understand what you're saying,"

"Monte, please don't do anything. You can't. I can't let you. Please have some respect."

His slow, insolent smile was his answer. "I would never do anything to hurt you."

She stared at him, then finally did roll her eyes. "Of

course not. Everything you do would be for my own good, wouldn't it?"

There was no escaping the tone of sarcasm in her voice. She sighed with exasperation and then the expression in her eyes changed. She hesitated. "Will you be gone?" she asked.

He met her gaze and held it. "Is that really what you hope?"

She started to say, "Of course," but then she stopped, bit her lip and sighed. "How can I analyze what I'm hoping right now?" she said instead, her voice trembling. "How can I even think clearly when you're looking at me like that?"

One last glare and she whirled, leaving the room as elegantly as any queen might do.

He rose and followed, going to the doorway so that he could watch her leave her chambers, a uniformed guard on either side. She could have been royalty from another century. She could have been Anne Boleyn on her way to the tower. He thought she was pretty special. He wanted her to be his, but just how that would work was not really clear.

Right now he had a purpose in mind—exploring the other side of the castle where his family's living quarters had been. That was the section that had burned and he knew it had been recently renovated. He only hoped enough would be left of what had been so that he could find something he remembered.

It would seem the perfect time to do it. With the ball beginning, no one would be manning their usual places.

Everyone would be gravitating toward the ballroom for a look at the festivities. A quick trip to Pellea's surveillance room was in order, and then he would take his chances in the halls.

The long, tedious picture-taking session was wrapping up and Pellea waited with Kimmee for Leonardo to come out. The photographers were taking a few last individual portraits of him.

"Shall I go check on the preparations for your entrance to the ballroom?" Kimmee asked, and Pellea nodded her assent.

It had been her experience that double-checking never hurt and taking things for granted usually led to disaster. Besides, she needed a moment to be alone and settle her feelings.

Turning slowly, she appraised herself in the long, full-length mirror. Was that the face of a happy woman? Was that the demeanor of a bride?

Not quite. But it was the face of a rather regal-looking woman, if she did say so herself. But why was she even thinking such a thing? She would never be queen, no matter what. Monte might be king someday, but he would never pick her to be his wife. He couldn't pick someone from a traitor's family to help him rule Ambria, now could he?

The closest she would get to that was to marry Leonardo. Did that really matter to her? She searched her soul, looking for even the tiniest hint of ambition and couldn't find it. That sort of thing was important to her father, but not to her. If her father weren't involved, she would leave with Monte and never look back. But that was impossible under the circumstances.

Still, it was nice to dream about. What if she and Monte were free? They might get on a yacht and sail to the South Seas and live on an island. Not an island like Ambria with its factions always in contention and undermining each other. A pretty island with coconut trees and waterfalls, a place that was quiet and warm and peaceful with turquoise waters and silver-blue fish and white-sand beaches.

But there was no time to live in dreams. She had to live in the here and now. And that meant she had to deal with Leonardo.

She smiled at him as he came out of the sitting room.

"All done?" she asked.

"So it seems," he replied, then leaned close. "Ah, so beautiful," he murmured as he tried to nuzzle her neck.

"Don't touch," she warned him, pulling back.

"Yes, yes, I know. You're all painted up and ready to go." He took her hand and kissed her fingers. "But I want to warn you, my beauty, I plan to touch you a lot on our wedding night."

That sent a chill down her spine. She looked at him in surprise. He'd never shown any sexual interest in her before. This put an ominous pall on her future, didn't it? She'd heard lurid tales about his many mistresses and she'd assumed that he knew their marriage would be for advantage and convenience only, and not for love or for anything physical. Now he seemed to be having second thoughts. What was going on here?

She glanced at Kimmee who'd just returned and had heard him as well, and they exchanged a startled glance.

Leonardo took a call on his mobile, then snapped it shut and frowned. "I'm sorry, my love," he told her. "I'm afraid I'm going to have to let the guards escort you to the ballroom. I'll be along later. I have a matter that must be taken care of immediately."

Something in his words sent warning signals through her.

"What is it, Leonardo?" she asked, carefully putting on a careless attitude. "Do we need to man the barricades?"

"Nothing that should trouble you, my sweet," he said, giving her a shallow smile that didn't reach his eyes. "It seems we may have an interloper in the castle."

"Oh?" Her blood ran cold and she clenched her fists behind the folds of her skirt. "What sort of interloper?"

He waved a hand in the air. "It may be nothing, but a few of the guards seem to think they saw a stranger on one of the monitors this afternoon." He shook his head. "We don't allow intruders in the castle, especially on a night like this."

He sighed. "I just have to go and check out what they caught on the recorder. I'll be back in no time."

"Hurry back, my dear," she said absentmindedly,

thinking hard about how she was going to warn Monte.

"I will, my love." He bowed in her direction and smiled at her. "Don't do any dancing without me," he warned. Turning, he disappeared out the door.

Pellea reached out to steady herself to keep from keeling over. She met Kimmee's gaze and they both stared at each other with worried eyes.

"I told him to go," she fretted to her lifelong friend and servant. "Now he's probably out running around the castle and about to get caught. Oh, Kimmee!"

Kimmee leaned close. "Don't worry, Pel," she whispered, scanning the area to make sure no one could overhear them. "I'll find him and I'll warn him. You can count on me."

Pellea grabbed her arm. "Tell him there is no more room for error. He has to get out of the castle right now!"

"I will. Don't you worry. He'll get the message."

And she dashed off into the hallway.

Pellea took a deep breath and tried to quiet her nerves. She had to forget all about Monte and the trouble he might be in. She had to act as though everything were normal. In other words, she would have to pretend. And it occurred to her that this might be a lesson for the way things would be for the rest of her life.

CHAPTER SIX

MONTE WAS BACK FROM EXPLORING and he was waiting impatiently for Kimmee to make good on her promises and show up with a costume he could wear to the ball.

He'd been to the other side of the castle and he'd seen things that would take him time to assimilate and deal with emotionally. It could have been overwhelming if he'd let it be. He'd barely skimmed through the area and not much remained of the home he'd lived in with his loving family. Most of what was rebuilt had a new, more modern cast.

But he had found something important. He'd found a storeroom where some of the rescued items and furniture from his family's reign had been shoved aside and forgotten for years. A treasure trove that he would have to explore when he got the chance. But in the short run, he'd found his mother's prized grandfather clock. More important, he'd found her secret compartment, untouched after all these years. That alone had given him a sense of satisfaction.

And one of the items he had found in that secret

hiding place was likely to come in very handy this very night.

But right now, he just wanted to see Kimmee appear in the gateway. He knew she'd been helping with the photo shoot, but surely that was over by now. If she didn't come soon, he would have to find a way to go without a special costume—and that would be dangerous enough to make him think at least twice.

"Don't give up on me!"

Kimmee's voice rang out before the gong sounded and she came rushing in bearing bulky gifts and a wide smile.

"I've got everything you need right here," she claimed, spreading out her bounty before him. "Though I'm afraid it's all for naught."

"Once more, you save the day," he told her as he looked through the items, thoroughly impressed. "I'm going to have to recommend you for a medal."

"A reward for costume procurement?" she asked with a laugh. "But there's more. I'm afraid you won't be able to use this after all."

"No?" He stopped and looked at her. "Why not?"

"The castle is on stranger alert." She sighed. "You must have gone exploring because some of the guards claim they saw you—or somebody—on one of the hall monitors."

"Oh. Bad luck."

She shrugged. "Leonardo is looking into it and he seems pretty serious about it. So Pellea sent me to tell you to get out while the getting's good, because there's no time left." She shook her head, looking at him earnestly. "I went ahead and brought you the costume, because I promised I would, and I knew you'd want to see this. But I don't think it would be wise to use it. You're going to have to go, and go quickly."

"Am I?" He held up the coat to the uniform and gazed at it.

"Oh, I think you'd better," she said.

"And I will." He smiled at her. "All in good time. But first, I want to dance with Pellea."

Her face was filled with doubt but her eyes were shining. "But if you get caught...?"

"Then I'll just have to get away again," he told her. "But I don't plan to get caught. I've got a mask, don't I? No one will be sure who I really am, and I'll keep a sharp eye out." He grinned. "Don't worry about me. I'm going to go try this on."

"Well, what do you know?" She sighed, wary but rather happy he wasn't going to give up so easily. "Go ahead and try it on. I'll wait and help with any last-minute adjustments."

He took the costume up as though it were precious—and in a way it was. He recognized what she'd found for him—the official dress uniform of Ambrian royalty from the nineteenth century—a uniform one of his great-great-grandfathers had probably worn. He slipped into it quickly. It all fitted like a glove. Looking in the mirror, he had to smile. He looked damn good in gold braid and a stiff collar. As though he was born to wear it.

When he walked out, Kimmee applauded, delighted with how it had worked out.

"Here's your mask," she said, handing it to him. "As you say, it will be very important in keeping your identity hidden. And it's a special one. Very tight. Very secure." She gave it a sharp test, pulling on the band at the back. "No one will be able to pull it off."

"Exactly what I need. Kimmee, you're a genius."

"I am, aren't I?" She grinned, pleased as punch. "Believe me, sir, I take pride in my work—underhanded as it may be."

He shook his head. "I don't consider this underhanded at all."

And actually, she agreed. "I'll just think of it this way—anything I can do to help you is for the good of the country."

He looked at her closely, wondering if she realized who he was. But her smile was open and bland. If she knew, she wasn't going to let it out. Still, it was interesting that she'd put it that way.

"I've got to hurry back," she said as she started toward the gate. "I'm helping in the ladies' powder room. You pick up all the best rumors in there."

"Ah, the ladies like to talk, do they?" he responded, adjusting his stand-up collar.

"They like to impress each other and they forget that we servants can hear, too." She gave him a happy wave. "I'll let you know if anything good turns up."

He nodded. "The juicier the better."

She laughed as she left, and he sobered. He'd been

lighthearted with Kimmee, but in truth, this was quite an emotional experience for him.

He took one last look in the mirror. For the first time in many years, he felt as if he'd found something he really belonged to, something that appealed to his heart as well as his head. It was almost a feeling of coming home.

And home was what he'd missed all these years. Without real parents, without a real family, he'd ached for something of his own.

He'd had an odd and rather disjointed life. For his first eight years, he'd been the much beloved, much cosseted Crown Prince of Ambria, living in the rarified air of royal pomp and celebrity. His mother and father had doted on him. He'd shown every evidence of being as talented and intelligent as his position in life warranted, and also as pleasant and handsome as a prince should be. Everyone in his milieu was in awe of him. The newspapers and magazines were full of pictures of him—his first steps, his first puppy, his new Easter clothes, his first bicycle. It was a charmed life.

And then came the coup. He still remembered the night the castle burned, could still smell the fire, feel the fear. He'd known right away that his parents were probably dead. For an eight-year-old boy, that was a heavy burden to bear.

That night, as he and his brother Darius were rushed away from the castle and hustled to the continent in a rickety boat, he'd looked back and seen the fire, and even at his young age, he'd known his way of life was crumbling into dust just as surely as the castle of his royal ancestors was.

He and Darius were quickly separated and wouldn't see each other again until they were well into adulthood. For the first few weeks after his escape, he was passed from place to place by agents of the Ambrian royalty, always seeing new contacts, never sure who these people were or why he was with them. People were afraid to be associated with him, yet determined to keep him safe.

As the regime's crown prince, he was in special danger. The Granvillis had taken over Ambria and it was known that they had sent agents out to find all the royal children and kill them. They didn't want any remnants of the royal family around to challenge their rule.

Monte finally found himself living in Paris with an older couple, the Stephols, who had ties to the monarchy but also a certain distance that protected them from scrutiny. At first, he had to hide day and night, but after a year or so, the Stephols got employment with the foreign service and from then on, they were constantly moving from one assignment to another, and Monte lived all over the world, openly claiming to be their child.

He grew up with the best of everything—elite private schools, vacations in Switzerland, university training in business. But he was always aware that he was in danger and had to keep his real identity a secret. The couple treated him with polite reserve and not a lot of affection—as though he were a museum piece they were protecting from vandals but would return to its proper shelf when the time came. They had no other children and were sometimes too cool for comfort. The couple was very closely knit and Monte often felt like an interloper—which he probably was. They were kind to him, but somewhat reserved, and it was a lonely life. They obviously knew he was special, though he wasn't sure if they knew exactly who he was.

He knew, though. He remembered a lot and never forgot his family, his country or that he was royal. That in itself made him careful. He remembered the danger, still had nightmares about it. As he got older, it was hard not being able to talk to anyone about his background, not having someone he could question, but he read everything he could about his homeland and began to understand why he had to maintain his anonymity. He knew that some saw him as cold and removed from normal emotions. That wasn't true. His emotions were simmering inside, ready to explode when the time was right.

Coming back to Ambria had done a lot to help put things in order in his mind. Finding Pellea had confused the issue a bit, but he thought he could handle that. Now, putting on the uniform that should have been his by rights cemented a feeling of belonging in him. He was the Crown Prince of Ambria, and he wanted his country back.

Monte DeAngelis, Crown Prince of Ambria, walked into the ballroom annex in a uniform that reflected his position, and he did it proudly. He knew the authorities were looking for him and it would only take one careless action, one moment of inattention, to make them realize he was the intruder they were searching for.

But he was willing to risk it. He had to. He needed to do this and he was counting on his natural abilities and intelligence to keep him from harm. After all, he'd had to count on exactly those for most of his life, and his talents had so far stood him in good stead. Now for the ultimate test. He definitely expected to pass it.

The announcer looked up at him in surprise and frowned, knowing that he'd never seen this man before in his life. He got up from his chair and came over busily, carrying papers and trying to look as though he were comfortably in charge.

"Welcome," he said shortly, with a bow. "May I have the name to be announced?"

Monte stood tall and smiled at him.

"Yes, you may. Please announce me as the Count of Revanche," he said with an appropriately incomprehensible Mediterranean accent, though he was blatantly using the French word for revenge.

The man blinked, appearing puzzled. "And Revanche is…?"

"My good man, you've never visited our wonderful region?" Monte looked shocked. "We're called the wine country of the southern coast. You must make a visit on your next holiday."

"Oh," the man responded dutifully, still baffled. "Of course." He bowed deeply and held out his arm with a flourish. "If you please, Your Highness."

He reached for the loudspeaker and made the announcement.

"Ladies and gentleman, may I present His Highness, the Count of Revanche?"

And Monte held his head high as he navigated the steep stairway into the ballroom.

Heads turned. And why not? Obviously, no one had ever heard of him before, and yet he was a commanding presence. He could see the wave of whispering his entrance had set off, but he ignored it, looking for Pellea.

He picked her out of the crowd quickly enough. For a moment the sight of all those masks blinded him, but he found her and once he'd done that, she was all he could see. She stood in the midst of a small group of women and it seemed to him as though a spotlight shone down on her. In contrast to the others around her, the mask she wore was simple, a smooth black accent that set off the exotic shape of her dark eyes and allowed the sparkling jewels of the tiara to take center stage. At the same time, the porcelain translucence of her skin, the delicate set of her jaw, the lushness if her lips, all added to the stunning picture she made in her gorgeous gown. She was so utterly beautiful, his heart stopped in his chest.

He began to head in her direction, but he didn't want to seem over-anxious, so he made a few bows and gave out a few smiles along the way.

Only a few stately couples were dancing as he entered the cavernous room, but he knew how this sort of ball operated, having been to enough of them on the continent. The older people did most of the dancing at first, and the music was calm and traditional. Then the younger ones would filter in. By a certain hour, rocking rhythms and Latin beats would be the order of the day, and the older people would have retreated to drink in the bar or queue for the midnight buffet table.

That was the structure, but it wasn't really relevant to his plans. He just wanted Pellea in his arms. Now all he had to do was to get there and claim her.

Many of the women had noticed him right away. In fact, a few were blatantly looking him over. One pretty little redhead had actually lowered her mask in order to wink at him in outright invitation.

Meanwhile, Pellea hadn't even noticed his arrival. She was deep in conversation with another woman, both of them very earnest. It was quite evident that the subject of their talk was more likely to be the state of world affairs than the latest tart recipe. But what did that matter? She was looking so beautiful, if one had to pick out a queen from the assemblage, she would take the night.

Why did that thought keep echoing in his mind? He turned away, reminding himself that the question was out of order. He wasn't going to think about anything beyond the dancing tonight. And in order to get things started, he decided to take the little redhead up on her offer.

She accepted his invitation like a shot and very soon they were on the dance floor. It was a Viennese waltz, but they managed to liven it up considerably. She chatted away but he hardly heard a word she said. His attention was all on Pellea.

As he watched, Leonardo asked her to dance, and she refused him, shaking her head. He looked a bit disgruntled as he walked away, but his friends crowded around him and in a moment, they all went straight for the hard liquor bar, where he quickly downed a stiff one.

Monte smiled. Fate seemed to be playing right into his hands. The music ended and Monte returned the redhead to her companions. He gave her a smile, but not many words to cherish after he was gone. Turning, he headed straight toward Pellea.

As he approached, she looked up and he saw her eyes widen with recognition behind her mask. She knew who he was right away, and that disappointed him. He'd hoped to get a bit of play out of the costume and mask before he had to defend himself for showing up here.

But then he realized the truth, and it warmed his heart. They would know each other in the dark, wouldn't they?

Not to say that she was pleased to see him.

"You!" she hissed at him, eyes blazing. "Are you crazy? What are you doing here?"

"Asking the most stunning woman in the room to dance with me." He gave her a deep bow. "May I have the honor?"

"No!" She glared at him and lifted her fan to her face. She was obviously finding it hard to show her anger to him and hide it from the rest of the people in the room at the same time. "Didn't Kimmee tell you that you'd been seen?" she whispered.

"Kimmee delivered your message and I acknowledge it. But I won't be cowed by it." He gave her a flourish and a flamboyant smile that his mask couldn't hide. "I have a life to live you know."

"And this stupid ball is that important to your life?" she demanded, trying to keep her voice down and astounded that he could be so careless.

Didn't he care? Or did he see himself as some kind of superhero, so over-confident in his own abilities that he scoffed at danger? In any case, it was brainless and dangerous and it made her crazy.

"Oh, yes, this ball is very important," he answered her question. His smile was slow and sensual. "It may be my last chance to dance with you. Believe me, Pellea, there is nothing more important than that."

She was speechless, then angry. How did he do it, again and again? Somehow he always touched her emotions, even when she knew very well that was exactly what he was aiming at. She felt like a fool, but she had to admit, a part of her that she wasn't very proud of loved it.

Monte knew he'd weakened her defenses with that one and he smiled. It might sound glib and superficial, but he meant every word of it.

She was beautiful, from head to toe, and as he gazed at the way the tiara worked perfectly with her elaborate ensemble, he thought about his memories of his own mother wearing it, and a mist seemed to cloud his eyes for a moment. In many ways, Pellea fitted into the continuity of culture here in Ambria the way no other woman he'd ever met could do. It was something to keep in mind, wasn't it?

Out of the corner of his eye, he saw Leonardo coming back into the room and looking their way, frowning fiercely. Monte smiled and glanced at Pellea. She'd seen him, too.

"We'd better get out on the dance floor or we'll be answering questions from Leonardo in no time," he noted. "He has that mad inquisitioner look to him tonight."

Quickly, she nodded and raised her arms. He took her into his embrace and they began to sway to the music.

"This is all so wrong," she murmured, leaning against his shoulder. "You know this is only going to anger him."

He glanced over at Leonardo, who was scowling, his friends gathered around him. Angering Leonardo was the least of his worries right now. He was gambling that the man wouldn't see him as the intruder he'd been studying on the castle monitoring system.

If he'd arrived in more normal attire, that might have been a problem. But because he'd appeared in such an elaborate costume, claimed to be royal and seemed to fit so well with the others who were here, he hoped Leonardo wouldn't connect him with the intruder until it was too late.

At first glance, he would have to say that he'd been right. Everything was influenced by context.

"I see that your handsome and valorous swain is celebrating his fool head off tonight," he noted as Leonardo threw back another shot of Scotch.

"Yes," she whispered. "He's already had too much. It's becoming a habit of his lately. I'm going to have to work on that."

He gazed down at her and barely contained the sneer he felt like using at her words. "Are you?"

"Yes." She lifted her chin and met his gaze defiantly. "After we're married."

She said the word loud and clear, emphasizing it to make sure he got her drift. And now he did sneer. He got it all right. He just didn't want to accept it.

He whirled her in a fancy turn, then dipped her in a way that took her breath away. But she was half laughing at the same time.

"Oh, that was lovely," she told him, clinging to him in a way that sent his pulse soaring.

"Your lover boy didn't like it," he told her blithely.

"Maybe not," she admitted, looking back at where Leonardo was standing a bit apart from his friends and watching her. "But you have to admit, until you arrived, all in all, he seems to be happy tonight."

"Why wouldn't he be?" He pulled her up against his chest and held her there for a beat too long, enjoying the soft, rounded feel of her body against his. "And you, my darling," he added softly. "Are you happy?"

Her dark eyed gaze flickered up at him, then away again. "You know the answer to that. But I'm prepared to do my duty."

That was an answer that infuriated him and he was silent for a moment, trying to control himself. But he couldn't stay angry with her in his arms. He looked down at her and his heart swelled. When was he going to admit it? This trip had been completely unnecessary. He'd already gathered all the reconnaissance data he needed on his last visit to Ambria. He'd only come for one thing. Trying to turn it into a Helen-of-Troy kidnapping of the enemy's most beautiful woman was just fanciful rationalizing. He'd come to find Pellea because he needed to see her. That was all there was to it. But now that he knew about this insane wedding to a Granvilli monster, he wanted to get her out of here with more urgency. She had to go. She couldn't marry Leonardo. What a crime against nature that would be!

And yet, there was the problem of her father. No matter what he might think of the man, if he ripped her away from him by force, without first convincing her to go, she would never forgive him. Knowing how important family was, and how traumatic it could be when it was torn apart, he might never forgive himself.

He had to find a way to make her come with him. Somehow.

He dipped her again, pulling her in close and bending over her in a rather provocative way. "I promise you, Pellea," he said, his voice rough and husky. "I swear it on my parents' graves. You will be happy."

Her heart was beating hard. She stared at him, not sure what he was up to. He was making promises he couldn't possibly keep. She didn't believe a word of it.

"You can't decide on my happiness," she told him bluntly. "It's not up to you."

"Of course not," he said, his bitterness showing. "I suppose it's up to your father, isn't it?"

She drew her breath in and let resentment flow through her for a moment. Then she pushed it back. It did no good to let emotions take over at a time like this.

"I know you hate my father," she said softly, "and you may have good reason to, from your point of view."

"You mean from a reasonable perspective?"

She ignored his taunt and went on.

"But I don't hate him. I love him very much. My mother died when I was very young and he and I have been our only family ever since. He's been everything to me. I love him dearly."

He pulled back, still holding her loosely in his arms. "You'd choose him over me?" he asked, his voice rough as sandpaper.

Her eyes widened. His words startled her. In fact, he took her breath away with the very concept. What was he asking of her? Whatever he was thinking, he had no right to put it to her that way.

And so she nodded. "Of course I would choose him. He and I have a real relationship. With you, I have…"

Her voice trailed off. Even now she was reluctant to analyze what exactly it was that they had together. "With you I had something that was never meant to last," she said finally.

He stared at her, wondering why her words stung so deeply. Wondering why there was an urge down in him that was clawing its way to the surface, an urge to do what he'd only bantered about, an urge to throw her over his shoulder as his own personal trophy, and fight his way out of the castle.

Kidnap her. That was the answer. He would carry her off and hide her away somewhere only he could find her. The need swelled inside him, almost choking him with its intensity. He was flying high on fantasy.

But he came back down to earth with a thump. What the hell was wrong with him? That whole scenario was just sick. He had no more right to force her into anything than he had to force anyone. If he really wanted her that badly, he would have to find a way to convince her to want him just as much. And so far, that wasn't working.

She preferred to stay with her father.

But that wasn't fair, to put it that way. Her father was her only living relative and he was very ill. Of course she was protective of him and wanted to stay with him. Her tenderness and compassion were part of what he loved about her.

"So I guess I come in third," he mentioned with deceptive calm. "Behind your father and Leonardo." He glanced back at her fiancé waiting for this long dance to end. "Maybe I ought to have a talk with your lover boy."

She drew her breath in sharply. "Stay away from him, Monte. The more he drinks the more dangerous he'll be."

She was passionate and worried, but also confused and torn and not at all sure how to handle this. Here she was in the same room with the man she loved and even in his arms, and just a stone's throw away from the man she was pledged to marry.

Let's face it, he was the man she *had* to marry, no way around it. She was pregnant. She needed a husband. Without one, she would be persona non grata in this community. And if those in charge ever figured out who the baby's father was, her child would be an outcast as well.

She really didn't have much choice in the matter. In a country like this, living in this rarefied sliver of the society as she did, and caring for her father as she did, there was no option to play the free spirit and defy the culture's norms. She needed protection. It was all very well to love Monte, but he would never marry her. She had to provide for her child—and herself. No one else was prepared to do it for her.

No one but Leonardo, and for that—though Monte might never understand it—she would be forever grateful to the man.

Leonardo knew she was pregnant, though he didn't know who the father was. He didn't really care. It wasn't love he was looking for in their relationship. It was the factions she represented, the power she could help him assemble, and the prestige of her name. Though her father had been mistrusted for a time because he had worked with the old DeAngelis regime, years had passed now, and his reputation was clear. Now, the magic of the old days and the old regime was what mattered. People were said to hold him in such high esteem, his reputation rivaled that of the Granvillis. And that was one reason Leonardo wanted her on his side.

It was well understood between the two of them. She was getting something she needed from him and he was getting something he needed from her. If Monte had just stayed away, everything would be going along as planned.

But Monte had appeared out of nowhere once again and upset the apple cart. She loved him. She couldn't deny it. And he was the father of her child, although he didn't know it. And here he was, inserting himself into the equation in a way that was sure to bring misery to them all. Did she have the strength to stop him? So far, it didn't seem possible.

The music finally came to an end. She knew Leonardo was waiting for her to return to her spot and she was resigned to it. Reluctantly, she began to slip out of Monte's arms.

But he didn't want to let her go.

"Do you find it oppressively hot in here?" he murmured close to her ear, his warm breath tickling her skin.

"Oh, I don't know, I guess…"

He didn't wait for a full answer. In the confusion of couples coming and going every which way to get on and off the dance floor, he maneuvered her right out the open French doors onto the dimly lit and almost empty terrace. As the small orchestra struck up a new tune, they continued their dance.

"Monte," she remonstrated with him. "You can't do

this. You're not the only one who wants to dance with me, you know."

"I know that very well," he said. "Why do you think I felt I had to resort to these guerilla tactics to have my way with you?"

She laughed low in her throat and he pulled her into the shadows and kissed her. His kiss was music by Mozart, sculpture by Michelangelo, the dancing of Fred Astaire. He was the best.

Of course, she wasn't exactly an expert on such things. Her experience wasn't extensive. But she'd had make-out sessions with incredibly attractive men in her time, and she knew this was top-tier kissing.

He started slowly, just barely nipping at her lips, and, as she felt herself enjoying the sensation and reaching for more of it, he found his way into the honey-sweet heat of her mouth, using his tongue to explore the terrain and sample the most tender and sensitive places.

She knew she was being hypnotized again and for the moment, she didn't care. His slow, provocative touch was narcotic, and she fell for the magic gladly. If he had picked her up and carried her off at that moment, she wouldn't have protested at all.

But he'd kept the clearer head and he pulled back.

"Oh, Monte, no," she sighed, the sweetness of his lips still branding hers. She felt so wonderful in his arms, like a rose petal floating downstream. The music, the cool night air, his strong arms around her—what could be better?

"Please," she whispered, reaching for him again.

"Not now, my darling," he whispered back, nuzzling behind her ear. "There are people nearby. And there are things that must be done."

"Like what?" she murmured rather sulkily, but she was beginning to come back to her senses as well and she sighed, realizing that he was perfectly right to deflect her. "Oh, bother," she muttered, annoyed with herself as her head cleared. "There you go, flying me to the moon again."

He laughed softly, dropping one last kiss on her lips. "There will be plenty of time for that later," he promised.

"No there won't," she said sensibly. "I'll be married. And if you think you're going to be hanging around once that has happened, you'd better think again."

She couldn't help but wince as she let herself imagine just how bereft her world was going to be.

But she managed to keep a fiercely independent demeanor. "There are certain lines I swear I will never cross."

He gazed at her, his blue eyes clouded and unreadable. "What time is the announcement planned for?" he asked her.

She looked up at him in surprise. "Just before the midnight buffet," she answered, then frowned, alarmed. "Wait. Monte! What are you planning to do?"

"Who, me? Why would you think I was planning anything at all?"

"Because I know you." She planted her hands on his

shoulders and shook him. "Don't do it! Whatever you're planning, don't!"

He pretended to be wounded by her suspicion, though his eyes were sparkling with laughter. "I can't believe you have so little faith in me," he said.

She started to respond, but then her gaze caught sight of something that sent her pulse racing. "Leonardo," she whispered to Monte. "He's found us."

"Oh, good," he said. "I've been wanting to talk to him."

CHAPTER SEVEN

PELLEA DREW IN A SHARP BREATH, filled with dread as she watched Leonardo approach.

"I'll hold him off if you want to make a run for it," she told Monte urgently, one hand gripping his shoulder. "But go quickly!"

"Why would I run?" he said, turning to meet the man, still holding her other hand. "I've been looking forward to this."

"Oh, Monte," she whimpered softly, wishing she could cast a spell and take them anywhere else.

Leonardo's face was filled with a cold fury that his silver mask couldn't hide.

"Unhand my fiancée, sir," he ordered, his lip curling and one hand on the hilt of the sword at his side. "And identify yourself, if you please."

Monte's smile was all pure, easy confidence. "You don't allow hand holding with old friends?" he asked, holding Pellea's hand up where Leonardo could see his fingers wrapped around hers. "Pellea and I have a special connection, but it's nothing that should concern you."

"A special connection?" Leonardo repeated, seeming momentarily uncertain. "In what way?"

"Family connections," Monte explained vaguely. "We go way back." But he dropped her hand and clicked his heels before giving Leonardo a stiff little bow. "Allow me to introduce myself. I'm the Count of Revanche. Perhaps you've heard of me?"

Leonardo looked a bit puzzled, but much of his fury had evaporated and a new look of interest appeared on his long face. "Revanche, is it?"

"Yes." Monte stuck out his hand and gave the man a broad smile. It was fascinating how the hint of royalty always worked magic, especially with dictator types. They always seemed a little starstruck by a title, at least at first. He only hoped the sense of awe would last long enough to save him from ending up in a jail cell.

"It is a pleasure to meet you at last, Leonardo," he said heartily. "I've heard so much about you. I'm hoping the reality can compete with the legend."

Leonardo hesitated only a moment, then stuck out his own hand and Monte shook it warmly.

"Have I heard of you before?" he asked.

Monte gave a grand shrug. "That's as may be. But I've heard of you." He laughed as though that was quite a joke. "Your father and I go way back."

"My father?" Leonardo brightened. "How so?"

Monte nodded wisely. "He's meant a great deal to me in my life. In fact, I wouldn't be the man I am today without his strong hand in my early training."

"Ah, I see." Leonardo began to look downright welcoming. "So he has mentored you in some way."

Monte smiled. "One might say that. We were once thick as thieves."

Leonardo actually smiled. "Then you will be happy to know he is going to make an appearance here tonight."

Monte's confidence slipped just a bit, but he didn't let it show. "Is he? What a treat it will be to see him again. I'll be happy to have a drink with him."

"Well, why not have a drink with me while we await his arrival?" Leonardo suggested. He was obviously warming to this visiting count and had forgotten all about the manhandling of his future bride. "Come along, Pellea," he said, sweeping them back into the ballroom with him. "We must make sure our guest is well supplied with refreshment."

Her gaze met Monte's and she bit her lip. She could see what he was doing, but she didn't like it at all. The moment an opportunity arose, she would help him make a run for it. That was the only thing she could see that would save him. This manly bonding thing couldn't last once the truth began to seep out.

But Monte gave her a wink and his eyes crackled with amusement. He was obviously having the time of his life fooling someone who didn't even realize he was dealing with his worst enemy.

They made their way to the bar, and by the time they got there, a crowd of Leonardo's friends and hangers-on had joined them.

"Come," Leonardo said expansively. "We must drink together."

"Of course," Monte agreed cordially. "What are we drinking?"

The bartender slapped a bottle of something dark and powerful-looking on the bar and everyone cheered.

"We must share a toast," Monte said, holding his glass high. "Let us drink to destiny."

"To destiny!"

Each man downed his drink and looked up happily for more. The bartender obliged.

"And to fathers everywhere," Monte said, holding his glass up again. "And to General Georges Granvilli in particular."

"Well. Why not?" Leonardo had just about decided Monte was the best friend he'd ever had by now. He pounded him on the back at every opportunity and merrily downed every drink Monte put before him.

Pellea watched this spectacle in amazement. But when Monte offered her a glass, she shook her head.

"Pellea, come share a toast with us," he coaxed, trying to tempt her. "I'll get you something fruity if you like."

She shook her head firmly. "No. I don't drink."

He blinked at her, remembering otherwise and sidling a bit closer. "You drank happily enough two months ago," he said to her quietly. "We practically bathed in champagne, as I remember. What's changed?"

She flashed him a warning look. "That was then. This is now."

He frowned, ready to take that up and pursue an answer, but Leonardo wrapped an arm around his neck and proclaimed, "I love you, man."

"Of course," Monte said with a sly smile. "You and I are like blood brothers."

Pellea blanched. Was she the only one who got a chill at hearing his words?

"Blood brothers." Leonardo had imbibed too much to be able to make head nor tails of that, but it sounded good to him.

Monte watched him with pity. "You don't understand that," he allowed. "I'm going to have to explain it to you. But for now, trust me." He raised his glass into the light, glad no one seemed to notice that he had never actually drunk what was in it. "Blood brothers under the skin."

"Are we, by God?" Leonardo was almost in tears at the thought.

"Yes," Monte said with an appropriate sense of irony. "We are."

Pellea shook her head. She could see where this was inevitably going and knew there would probably be no announcement of their engagement tonight. Unless Monte volunteered to prop the man up for it, and that wasn't likely.

All in all, this appeared to be a part of his plan. Didn't he understand that it would do no good? The announcement would be made, one way or another, before the wedding, and that was only two days away. He couldn't stop it. She couldn't let him.

He caught her eye, gesturing for her to come closer.

"Do you think Georges will really make an appearance?" he whispered to her.

She shook her head. "I have no idea. I haven't seen him in months. They always say he is in France, taking the waters for his health. For all I know, he's been right here this whole time, watching television in his room."

Monte glanced at Leonardo, who was laughing uproariously with a couple of his mates. One more toast and it was pretty obvious he wouldn't be capable of making an engagement announcement.

"Wait here, my love," he said softly. "I have to finish what I've started."

"Monte, no!" She grabbed his arm to keep him with her, but he pulled away and joined the men at the bar.

"A final toast," he offered to Leonardo. "To our new and everlasting friendship."

"Our friendship!" cried Leonardo, turning up his glass and taking in the contents in one gulp. Then, slowly, he put the glass down. Staring straight ahead, his eyes glassy, he began to crumble. His knees went first, and then his legs. Monte and a couple of the others grabbed him before he hit the ground. A sigh went through the crowd. And, at the same time, bugles sounded in the hallway.

"The General is coming!" someone cried out. "It's General Georges."

"Prepare for the arrival of the General."

Shock went through the crowd in waves, as though no one knew exactly what to do, but all realized something had to be done. Their leader was coming. He had to be welcomed in style.

One of Leonardo's friends sidled up to Monte. "We've got to get him out of here before his father comes," he whispered urgently. "There'll be hell to pay. Believe me, the old man will kill him."

Monte looked at the limp young gentleman who thought he was going to marry Pellea and had a moment of indecision. What did he care if Georges saw his son like this? It wasn't his problem.

And yet, in a way, it *was* his fault. Leonardo was not his enemy. His rival, yes. But it was Leonardo's father who was his mortal enemy. And perhaps it would be just as well if Georges wasn't distracted by focusing his rage on his hapless son.

Because he did plan to face him. How could he avoid the confrontation he'd spent his life preparing for?

"Let's go," he said to the man who'd approached him. "Let's get him to his chambers before his father gets here."

He looked back at Pellea, signaling her to his intentions. But she wasn't paying attention any longer. A servant had come to find her.

"My lady, your father is ill and asking for you," he said nervously.

Pellea reacted immediately. "My father! Oh, I must go."

Monte stopped her for only a moment. "I'll meet you at your father's room as soon as I can make it," he told her.

She nodded, her eyes wide and anxious. "I must go," she muttered distractedly, and she hurried away.

Monte looked back at the task at hand and gritted his teeth. It wasn't going to be a pretty chore, but it had to be done.

"Let's get him out of here," he said, hoisting Leonardo up with the assistance of two other men. And, just as they heard Georges arrive at the main ballroom entrance, they slipped out the side door.

"I'll be back, Georges," Monte whispered under his breath. "Get ready. We've got business between us to settle. Old business."

Monte slipped into Pellea's father's room and folded his form between the drapes to keep from being seen. Pellea was talking to the doctor and her father seemed to be sleeping.

The doctor began to pack his black bag and Pellea went to her father's bedside. Monte watched and saw the anguished love in her face as she leaned over the man. There was no denying this simple truth—she adored her father and she wouldn't leave him.

Monte closed his eyes for a moment, letting that sink in. There was no way he would be able to take her with him. All his kidnapping plans—in the dust. In order to get her to leave he would have to render her unconscious and drag her off, and that wasn't going to happen.

When the idea had first formed, he'd assumed she would come at least semi-willingly. Now he knew that was a fantasy. Her love for her father was palpable. She would never leave while he was still alive. And yet, how could he leave her behind? How could he leave her to the tender mercies of the Granvillis? The more he saw of her, the more he got to know her, the more he felt a special connection, something he'd never felt with a woman before. He wanted her with him.

But more than that, he wanted her safe. Leaving her here with Leonardo would be torture. But what could he do?

Invade, a voice deep in his soul said urgently. *The sooner the better.*

Yes. There really was no other option left.

So he would return to the continent empty-handed. Not quite what he'd promised his supporters waiting for him in Italy.

But all was not lost on that score. He had another plan—something new. Instead of kidnapping their most desirable woman, he would take their most valuable possession.

He was going to steal the tiara.

"Please tell me how he really is," she said anxiously to the doctor. "Don't sugarcoat anything. I need to know the truth." She took a deep breath and asked, "Is he in danger?"

"In other words, is he going to die tonight?" Dr. Dracken translated. "Not likely. Don't worry. But he is very weak. His heart is not keeping up as it should." He hesitated, then added, "If you really want me to be blunt, I'd have to say I wouldn't give him much more than six months. But this sort of thing is hugely unpredictable. Next year at this time, you might be chiding me for being so pessimistic."

"Oh, I hope so," she said fervently as she accompanied him to the door. "Please, do anything for him that you can think of."

"Of course. That's my job, Pellea, and I do the best I can."

The doctor left and Monte reached out and touched her as she came back into the room.

"Oh!" She jumped back, then put her hand over her heart when she realized it was him. "Monte! You scared me."

"Sorry, but once I was in, I was going to startle you no matter how I approached it."

She looked at him with tragic eyes. "My father…" Her face crumpled and she went straight into his arms and clung to him.

"Yes," he said, holding her tenderly, stroking her hair. "I heard what the doctor said. I'm so sorry, Pellea. I truly am."

She nodded. She believed him.

"He's sleeping now. The doctor gave him something. But a little while ago he was just ranting, not himself at all." She looked up into his face. "They are bringing in a nurse to stay with him tonight and tomorrow I'm going to sit with him all day."

He nodded, and then he frowned, realizing his fingers were tangling in her loosened hair. She was wearing it down. All the fancy work Magda had put into her coiffure was gone with the wind.

"Pellea, what happened to the tiara?" he asked.

She drew back and reached up as though she'd forgotten it was gone. "The guards took it back to its museum case," she said. She shook her head sadly. "I wonder if I'll ever get to wear it again."

He scowled, regretting that he'd let her get away before doing what he'd planned to do. Unfortunately, this threw a spanner into the works. Oh, he was still going to steal the thing. But now he was afraid he would have to do some actual breaking and entering in order to achieve his objective.

But when he looked at her again, he found her studying him critically, looking him up and down, admiring the uniform, and the man wearing it. He'd lost the mask somewhere, but for the rest, he looked as fresh as he had at the beginning of the evening.

"You know what?" she said at last, her head to the side, her eyes sparkling. "You would make one incredibly attractive Ambrian king."

He laughed and pulled her back into his arms, kissing her soundly. Her arms came up and circled his neck, and she kissed him back. Their bodies seemed to meet and fit together perfectly. He had a quick, fleeting thought that this might be what heaven was made of, but it was over all too soon.

She checked that her father was sleeping peacefully, then turned to Monte again. "Come sit down and wait with me," she said, pulling him by the hand. "And tell me what happened in the ballroom after I left. Did the General actually appear?"

He shook his head. "I didn't stay any longer than you did. With all the chaos that ensued upon Leonardo's… shall we call it a fall from grace…?"

He flashed her a quick grin, but she frowned in response and he sobered quickly, looking abashed.

"There you were, rushing off to see to your father. People were shouting. No one knew exactly what was going on for quite some time. And I and all my new mates picked up your fiancé and carried him to his rooms."

"I'm glad you did that," she said. "I would hate to think of what would have happened if his father had seen him like that."

"Yes," he said a bit doubtfully. "Well, we tucked him into his bed and I nosed around a little."

"Oh?"

"And I find I need to warn you of something."

She smiled. "You warning me? That's a twist on an old theme, isn't it?"

"I'm quite serious, Pellea." He hesitated until he had her complete attention. "Did it ever occur to you that you might not be the only one with a video monitoring system in this castle?"

She shrugged. "Of course. There's the main security center. Everyone knows that."

"Indeed." He gave her a significant look. "And then there's the smaller panel of screens I found in a small room off Leonardo's bedroom suite. The one that includes a crystal-clear view of your entryway."

Her eyes widened in shock. "What?"

He nodded. "I thought that might surprise you. He can see everyone who is coming in to see you, as well as when you leave."

She blanched, thinking back over what she'd done and who she'd been with in the recent past. "But not…" She looked at him sideways and swallowed hard.

"Your bedroom?" He couldn't help but smile at her reaction. "No. I didn't see any evidence of that."

"Thank God." But her relief was short-lived as she began to realize fully the implications of this news.

She frowned. "But how is it monitored? I mean…did he see you when you arrived? Or any of the other times you've come and gone?"

"I'm sure he doesn't spend most of his time sitting in front of the monitor, any more than you do."

"It would only take once."

"True."

"And how about when you arrived this time?"

Monte hesitated, then shrugged and shook his head. "I didn't come in through your entryway."

She stared at him, reminded that his mode of entering the castle was still a mystery. But for him to say flat-out that he didn't use the door—that was something of a revelation. "Then how…?"

He waved it away. "Never mind."

"But, Monte, I do mind. I want to know. How do

you get into my courtyard if you don't come in the way everyone else does?"

"I'm sorry, Pellea. I'm not going to tell you."

She frowned, not liking that at all. "You do realize that this leaves me in jeopardy of having you arrive at any inopportune moment and me not able to do anything about it."

He'd said it before and now he said it again. "I would never do anything to hurt you."

"No." She shook her head, her eyes deeply troubled. "No, Monte. That's not good enough."

He shrugged. He understood how she felt and sympathized. But what could he do? It was something he couldn't tell anyone about.

"It will have to do. I'm sorry, Pellea. I can't give away my advantage on this score. It has nothing to do with you. It has everything to do with my ability to take this country back when the time comes."

She searched his eyes, and finally gave up on the point. But she didn't like it at all. Still, the fact that Leonardo was secretly watching who came to her door was a more immediate outrage.

"Oh, I just can't believe he's watching my entry-way!"

Monte grinned. "Why are you so upset? After all, you're watching pretty much everyone in the castle yourself."

"Yes, but I'm just watching general walkways, not private entrances."

"Ah, yes," he teased. "That makes all the difference."

"It does. I wouldn't dream of setting up a monitor on Leonardo's gate."

He raised one eyebrow wisely. "Yes, but you're not interested in him. And he is very interested in you."

She thought about that for a few seconds and made a face. "I'm going to find his camera and tape it up," she vowed.

He looked pained. "Don't do that. Then he'll know you're on to him and he'll just find another way to watch you, and you might like that even less. The fact that you know about the camera gives you the advantage now. You can avoid it when you need to."

She sighed. "You're probably right," she said regretfully. It would have felt good taping over his window into her world.

There was a strange gurgling sound and they both turned to see Pellea's father rising up against his pillows.

"Father!" she cried, running to his side. "Don't try to sit up. Let me help you."

But he wasn't looking at his daughter. It was Monte he had in his sights.

"Your Majesty," he groaned painfully. "Your Royal Highness, King of Ambria."

Monte rose and faced him, hoping he would realize the man standing in his bedroom was not the king he'd served all those years ago, but that king's son. This was the first time anyone had mistaken him for his father. He felt a strange mix of honor and repulsion over it.

"My liege," Pellea's father cried, slurring his words. His thin, aged face was still handsome and his silver hair still as carefully groomed and distinguished as ever. "Wait, don't go. I need to tell you. I need to explain. It wasn't supposed to happen that way. I...I didn't mean for it to be like that."

"Father," Pellea said, trying to calm him. "Please, lie back down. Don't try to talk. Just rest."

"Don't you see?" he went on passionately, ignoring her and talking directly to the man he thought was King Grandor. "They had promised, they'd sworn you would be treated with respect. And your queen, the beautiful Elineas. No one should have touched her. It was a travesty and I swear it cursed our enterprise from the beginning."

Monte stood frozen to the spot. He heard the old man's words and they pierced his heart. It was obvious he had a message he'd been waiting a long time to deliver to Monte's father. Well, he was about twenty-five years too late.

He slid down into his covers again, now babbling almost incoherently. Pellea looked up with tears in her eyes.

"He doesn't know what he's saying," she said. "Please go, Monte. You're only upsetting him. I'll stay until the nurse comes."

Monte turned and did as she asked. His emotions were churning. He knew Pellea's father was trying to make

amends of sorts, but it was a little too late. Still, it was
good that he recognized that wrong had been done.

Wrong that still had to be avenged.

CHAPTER EIGHT

KNOWING PELLEA WOULD BE BUSY with her father for some time, Monte made a decision. He planned to make a visit to General Georges. Why not do it now?

A deadly calm came over him as he prepared to go. This meeting with the most evil man in his country's history was something he'd gone over a thousand times in his mind and each time there had been a different scenario, a different outcome. Which one would he choose? It didn't matter, really. They all ended up with the General mortally wounded or already dead.

The fact that his own survival might be in doubt in such an encounter he barely acknowledged and didn't worry about at all. His destiny was already set and included a confrontation with the General. That was just the way it had to be.

He strode down the hallways with confidence. He knew where the cameras were and he avoided them with ease. One of Leonardo's compadres had pointed out the General's suite to him as they'd carried Leonardo past it, and he went there now.

Breaking into the room was a simple matter. There

were no guards and the lock was a basic one. He'd learned this sort of thing as a teenager and it had stood him in good stead many times over the years.

Quietly, he slipped into the darkened room. He could hear the General snoring, and he went directly into his bedroom and yanked back the covers on his bed, ready to counter any move the older man made, whether he pulled out a gun or a cell phone.

But the man didn't move. He slept on. He seemed to have none of the effete elegance his son wore so proudly. Instead, he was large and heavy-set, but strangely amorphous, like a sculpture that had begun to melt back into a lump of clay.

"Wake up," Monte ordered. "I want to talk to you."

No response. Monte moved closer and touched the dictator. Nothing changed.

He glanced at the things on the bedside table. Bottles of fluid and a box of hypodermic needles sat waiting. His heart sank and he turned on the light and looked at the General again.

His eyes were open. He was awake.

The man was drugged. He lay, staring into space, a mere burnt-out shell of the human being he had once been. There wasn't much left. Monte realized that he could easily pick up a pillow and put it over the General's face…and that would be that. It would be a cinch. No problem at all. There wasn't an ounce of fight left in his enemy.

He stood staring down at the General for a long, long time and finally had to admit that he couldn't do it. He'd always thought he would kill Georges Granvilli if he found him. But now that he'd come face to face with him, he knew there was nothing left to kill. The man who had murdered his parents and destroyed his family was gone. This thing that was left was hardly even human.

Killing Georges Granvilli wouldn't make anything any better. He would just be a killer himself if he did it. He wasn't worth killing. The entire situation wasn't worth pursuing.

Slowly, Monte walked away in disgust.

He got back to the courtyard just moments before Pellea arrived. He thought about telling her where he'd been and what he'd seen, but he decided against it. There was no point in putting more ugliness in her thoughts right now. He could at least spare her that.

He was sitting by the fountain in the twilight atmosphere created by all the tiny fairy lights in her shrubbery when she came hurrying in through the gate.

"Monte?" she asked softly, then came straight for him like a swooping bird. As she reached him, she seized his face in her hands and kissed him on the lips, hard.

"You've got to go," she said urgently, tears in her eyes. "Go now, quickly, before they come for you."

"What have you heard?" he asked her, reaching to pull her down into his lap so that he could kiss her sweet lips once more.

"It's not what I've heard," she told him, snuggling in closely. "It's what I know. It's only logic. When all this chaos dies down and they begin to put two and two together, they'll come straight here looking for you. And you know what they'll find."

He searched her dark eyes, loving the way her long lashes made soft shadows on her cheeks. "Then we'd better get the heck out of here," he said calmly.

"No." She shook her head and looked away. "You're going. I'm staying."

He grimaced, afraid she still didn't understand the consequences of staying. "How can I leave you behind to pick up the pieces?"

"You have to go," she told him earnestly. She turned back to look at him, then reached up to run her fingers across the roughness of his barely visible beard, as though she just couldn't help herself. "When Leonardo wakes up, he's going to start asking around and trying to find out just who that man at the ball was. He'll want to know all about you and where you've been staying. And this time, they won't leave my chambers alone. They'll search with a fine-tooth comb and any evidence that you've been here will be…"

Her voice trailed off as she began to face the unavoidable fact that she was in as much danger as he was. She looked at him, eyes wide.

He was just thinking the same thing. It was torture to imagine leaving her behind. He'd turned and twisted every angle in his mind, trying to think of some way out, but the more he agonized, the more he knew there was no good answer. Unless she just gave up this obsession with staying with her father, what could he do to make sure she was protected while he was gone?

Nothing. Nothing at all.

He did have one idea, but he rejected it right away. And yet, it kept nagging at him. What if he showed her the tunnel to the outside? Then, if she was threatened, she could use it to escape.

They were bound to come after her, and even if they couldn't find any solid evidence of her ties to him, they would have their suspicions. Luckily her position and the fact that her father was so highly placed in the hierarchy would mean the most they would do at first was place her under house surveillance—meaning she would be confined to her chambers. But if her father died, or Leonardo became insanely jealous, or something else happened, all that might fall apart. In that case, it would be important for her to have a way to escape that others didn't know about. That was what made it so tempting to give her the information she needed.

Still, it was crazy even to contemplate doing that. Deep down, he didn't believe she would betray him on purpose. But what if she was discovered? What if someone saw her? His ace in the hole, his secret opening back into the castle which he and his invading force would need when he returned to claim his country back would be useless. He just couldn't risk that. Could he?

"And Monte," she was saying, getting back to the subject of her thoughts. "Leonardo's father is not a nice man."

"No?" Monte thought of the burned-out hulk he'd just been visiting. "What a surprise."

"I'm serious. Leonardo has at least some redeeming qualities. His father? None."

He looked at her seriously. "And do those redeeming qualities make him into a man you can stomach marrying?"

She avoided his eyes. "Monte..."

His arms tightened around her. "You can't kiss me the way you just did and then talk about marrying Leonardo. It doesn't work, Pellea. I've told you that before and nothing's changed." He kissed her again on her mouth, once, twice, three times, with quick hunger that grew more urgent with each kiss. He pulled her up hard against his strong body, her softness molding against him in a way that could quickly drive him crazy. Burying his face in her hair, he wanted to breathe her in, wanted to merge every part of her with every part of him.

She turned in his arms, reaching up to circle his neck, arching her body into his as though she felt the same compulsion. He dropped kisses down the length of her neck and heard her make a soft moaning sound deep in her throat. That alone almost sent him over the top, and the way her small hands felt gliding under his shirt and sliding over the muscles of his back pretty much completed the effort.

He wanted her as he'd never wanted a woman before, relentlessly, fiercely, with an insatiable need that raged through him like a hurricane. He'd felt this way about her before, but he hadn't let her know. Now, for just a few moments, he let her feel it, let her have a hint of what rode just on the other side of his patience.

She could have been shocked. She could have considered his ardor a step too far and drawn back in complete rejection. But as she felt his passion overtaking him and his desire for her so manifest, she accepted it with a willingness of her own. She wanted him, too. His marriage of the emotional need for her with the physical hunger was totally in tune with her own reactions.

But this wasn't the time. Resolutely, she pushed him back before things went too far.

He accepted her lead on it, but he had to add one thing as she slipped out of his arms.

"You belong to me," he said fiercely, his hand holding the back of her head like a globe. "Leonardo can't have you."

She tried to shake her head. "I'm going to marry him," she insisted, and though her voice was mournful, she sounded determined. "I've told you that from the moment you came today. I don't know why you won't listen."

This would be so much easier if she could tell him the truth, but that was impossible. How could he understand that she needed Leonardo even more than he needed her? She was caught in a web. If she didn't marry Leonardo, she would be considered an outcast in Ambrian traditional society.

Out-of-wedlock births were not uncommon, but they were considered beyond the pale. Once you had a baby out of wedlock, you could never be prominent in society. You would always have the taint of bad behavior about you. No one would trust your judgment and everyone would slightly despise you.

It wasn't fair, but it was the way things were.

He held her in a curiously stiff manner that left her feeling distinctly uncomfortable.

"You don't love Leonardo," he said. He'd said it before, but she didn't seem to want to accept it and act upon the fact. Maybe he should say it again and keep saying it until she realized that some things were hard, basic truths that couldn't be denied or swept under the rug.

She pulled away from him and folded her arms across her chest as though she were feeling a frost.

"I hate to repeat a cliché," she said tartly, "but here goes. What's love got to do with it?"

He nodded, his face twisted cynically. "So you admit this is a royal contract sort of wedding. A business deal."

"A power deal is more like it. Our union will cement the power arrangements necessary to run this country successfully."

"And you still think he'll want you, even if he begins to suspect…"

"I told you, love isn't involved. It's a power trade, and he wants it as much as I need it."

"Need it?" He stared at her. "Why do you 'need' it?"

She closed her eyes and shook her head. "Maybe I put it a little too strongly," she said. "I just meant… Well, you know. For my father and all."

He wasn't sure he bought that. There was something else here, something she wasn't telling him. He frowned, looking at her narrowly. He found it hard to believe that she would prefer that sort of thing to a love match. But then, he hadn't offered her a love match, had he? He hadn't even offered her a permanent friendship. So who was he to complain? And yet, he had to. He had to stop this somehow.

"Okay, I see the power from Leonardo's side," he said, mulling it over. "But where do you get yours?"

She rose and swayed in front of him, anger sparking from her eyes. She didn't like being grilled this way, mostly because she didn't have any good answers.

"For someone who wants to be ruler of Ambria, you don't know much about local politics, do you?"

He turned his hands palms-up. "If you weren't such a closed society, maybe I could be a bit more in the know," he pointed out.

She considered that and nodded reluctantly. "That's a fair point. Okay, here's the deal. Over the years, there have been many factions who have—shall we say—strained under the Granvilli rule for various reasons. A large group of dissenters, called the Practicals, have been arguing that our system is archaic and needs updating. For some reason they seem to have gravitated toward my father as their symbolic leader."

Monte grunted. "That must make life a bit dodgy for your father," he noted.

"A bit. But he has been invaluable to the rulers and

they don't dare do anything to him. And anyway, the Practicals would come unglued if they did."

"Interesting."

"The Practicals look to me as well. In fact, it may just be a couple of speeches I gave last year that set them in our direction, made them think we were kindred souls. So in allying himself with me, Leonardo hopes to blunt some of that unrest."

He gazed at her in admiration and surprise. "Who knew you were a mover and a shaker?" he said.

She actually looked a bit embarrassed. "I'm not. Not really. But I do sympathize with many of their criticisms of the way things are run. Once I marry Leonardo, I hope to make some changes."

Was that it? Did she crave the power as much as her father did? Was it really all a bid for control with her? He found that hard to believe, but when she said these things, what was he to think?

He studied her for another moment, then shrugged. "That's what they all say," he muttered, mostly to himself.

She was tempted to say something biting back, but she held her tongue. There was no point in going on with this. They didn't have much more time together and there were so many other things they could be talking about.

"Have you noticed that so far, no one seems to know who you really are?" she pointed out. As long as they didn't know who he was, his freedom might be imperiled, but his life wouldn't be. And if they should somehow realize who it was they had in their clutches… She hated to think what they might do.

"No, they don't, do they?" He frowned, not totally pleased with that. "How did *you* know, anyway? From the other time, I mean."

"You told me." She smiled at him, remembering.

"Oh. Did I?" That didn't seem logical or even realistic. He never told anyone.

"Yes, right from the first." She gave him a flirtatious look. "Right after I saved you from the guards, you kissed me and then you said, 'You can tell everyone you've been kissed by the future king of Ambria. Consider yourself blessed.'"

"I said that?" He winced a bit and laughed softly. "I guess you might be right about me having something of an ego problem."

"No kidding." She made a face. "Maybe it goes with being royal or something."

"Oh, I don't know about that." After all, he hadn't blown his cover all these years—except, it seemed, with her. "I think I do pretty well. Don't you think I blend in nicely with the average Joes?"

She shook her head, though there was a hint of laughter in her eyes. "Are you crazy? No, you do not blend in, as you so colorfully put it. Look at the way you carry yourself. The arrogance. There's no humility about you."

"No humility?" He was offended. "What are you talking about? I'm probably the most humble guy you would ever meet."

She made a sound of deprecation. "A little self-awareness would go a long way here," she noted as she looked him over critically. "But I could see that from the start. It was written all over you. And yet, I didn't kick you out as I should have."

"No, you didn't." Their gazes met and held. "But we did have an awfully good weekend, didn't we?"

"Yes." She said it softly, loving him, thinking of the child they had made together. If only she could tell him about that. Would he be happy? Probably not. That was just the way things were going to be. She loved him and he felt something pretty deep for her. But that was all they were destined to have of each other. How she would love to spend the next fifty years in his arms.

If only he weren't royal and she weren't tied to this place. If only he didn't care so much about Ambria. They could have done so well together, the two of them. She could imagine them walking on a sandy beach, chasing waves, or having a picnic by a babbling brook, skipping stones in the water, or driving around France, looking at vineyards and trying to identify the grapes.

Instead, he was planning to invade her country. And that would, of necessity, kill people she cared about. How could she stand it? Why hadn't she turned him in?

"Why does it matter so much to you, Monte?" she asked at last. "Why can't you just leave things alone?"

He looked up, his eyes dark and haunted. "Because a very large wrong was done to my family. And to this country. I need to make things right again. That's all I live for."

His words stabbed into her soul like sharp knives. If this was all he lived for, what could she ever be to him?

"Isn't there someone else who could do it?" she asked softly. "Does it have to be you?"

Reaching out, he put his hand under the water raining down from the fountain. Drops bounced out and scattered across his face, but he seemed to welcome them. "I'm the crown prince. I can't let others fight my battles for me."

"But you have brothers, don't you?"

He nodded. "There were five of us that night. Or rather, seven. Five boys and twin girls." He was quiet for a moment, remembering. "I hunted for them all for years. I started once I enrolled in university in England. I studied hard, but I spent a lot of time poring over record books in obscure villages, hoping to find some clue. There was nothing."

He sighed, in his own milieu now. "Once I entered the business world and then did some work for the Foreign Office, I developed contacts all over the world. And those have just begun to pan out. As I think I told you, I've made contact with two of my brothers, the two closest to me in age. But the others are still a mystery."

"Are you still looking?"

"Of course. I'll be looking until I find them all. For the rest of my life if need be." He shrugged. "I don't know if they are alive or not. But I'll keep looking." He turned and looked at her, his eyes burning. "Once we're all together, there will be no stopping us."

She shook her head, unable to imagine how growing up without any contact with his family would have affected this young Ambrian prince.

"What was it like?" she asked him. "What happened to you as a child? It must have been terrible to grow up alone."

He nodded. "It wasn't great. I had a wonderful family until I was eight years old. After that, it was hit or miss. I stayed with people who didn't necessarily know who I was, but who knew I had to be hidden. I ended up with a couple who were kind to me but hardly loving." He shrugged. "Not that it mattered. I wasn't looking for a replacement for my mother, nor for my father. No one could replace either one of them and I didn't expect it."

"Why were they hiding you?"

"They were trying to keep the Granvillis from having me killed."

"Oh." She colored as though that were somehow her fault. "I see."

"We were all hidden. From each other, even. You understand that any surviving royals were a threat to the Granvilli rule, and I, being the crown prince, am the biggest threat of all."

"Of course. I get it."

"We traveled a lot. I went to great schools. I had the sort of upbringing you would expect of a royal child, minus the love. But I survived and in fact, I think I did pretty well."

"It wasn't until I found my brother Darius that I could reignite that family feeling and I began to come alive again. Family is everything and I had lost mine."

"And your other brother?"

"A young woman who worked for an Ambrian news agency in the U.S. found Cassius. He was only four during the coup and he didn't remember that he was royal. He'd grown up as a California surfer and spent time in the military. Finding out his place in life has been quite a culture shock to him. He's trying to learn how to be royal, but it isn't easy for a surfer boy. I only hope he can hold it all together until we retake our country."

The old wall clock struck the time and it was very late, well after midnight. She looked at him and sighed. "You must go," she told him.

He looked back at her and wondered how he could leave her here. "Come with me, Pellea," he said, his voice crackling with intensity. "Come with me tonight. By late morning, we'll be in France."

She closed her eyes. She was so tired. "You know I can't," she whispered.

He rose and came over to kiss her softly on her full, red lips. "Then come and get some sleep," he told her. "I'll go just before dawn."

"Will you wake me up when you go?" she asked groggily.

"Yes. I'll wake you."

And would he show her his escape secrets? That was

probably a step too far. He couldn't risk it. He had to think of more lives than just their two. So he promised he would wake her, but he didn't promise he would let her see him go.

She lay down in her big, fluffy bed and he lay down on her long couch, which was almost as comfortable. He didn't understand why she wouldn't let him sleep beside her. She seemed to have some strange sense of a moral duty to Leonardo. Well, if it was important to her, he wasn't going to mess with it. She had to do what she had to do, just like he did. Lying still and listening to her breathe on the bed so near and yet so far, he almost slept.

CHAPTER NINE

THE MOMENT PELLEA WOKE, she knew Monte was gone.
It was still dark and nowhere near dawn, but he was
gone. Just as she'd thought.

She curled into a ball of misery and wept. Someday
she would have his child to console her, but right now
there was nothing good and beautiful and strong and
true in her life but Monte. And he was gone.

But wait. She lifted her head and thought for a
moment. He'd promised to say goodbye. He wouldn't
break his promise. If he didn't tell her in person, he
would at least have left a note, and there was nothing.
That meant…he was still somewhere in the castle.

Her heart stopped in her throat. What now? Where
could he be? Dread filled her since, surely, he would
get caught. He would be killed. He would have to leave
without saying goodbye! She couldn't stand it. None of
the above was tolerable. She had to act fast.

Rising quickly, she went to the surveillance room
with the security monitors and began to study them. All
looked quiet. It was about three in the morning, and she
detected no movement.

Maybe she was wrong. Maybe he had gone without saying goodbye. Darn it all!

That's when she saw something moving in the museum. A form. A tall, graceful masculine form. Monte! What was he doing in the museum room?

The tiara!

She groaned. "No, Monte!" she cried, but of course he couldn't hear her.

And then, on another panel, she saw the guards. There were three of them and they were moving slowly down the hallway toward the museum, looking like men gearing up for action. There was no doubt in her mind. They'd been alerted to his presence and would nab him.

Her heart was pounding out of her chest. She had to act fast. She couldn't let them catch him like this. They would throw him in jail and Leonardo would hear of it and Monte's identity would be revealed and he would be a dead man. She groaned.

She couldn't let that happen. There was only one thing she could do. She had to go there and stop it.

In another moment she was racing through the hallways, her white nightgown billowing behind her, her hair a cloud of golden blond, and her bare feet making a soft padding sound on the carpeted floors.

She ran, heedless of camera positions, heedless of anyone who might step out and see her. Who would be watching at this time of night anyway? Only the very men she'd seen going after Monte. She had one goal and that was to save his singularly annoying life. If only she could get there in time.

The museum door was ajar. She burst in and came face to face with Monte, but he was standing before her in handcuffs, with a guard on either side. Behind them, she could see the tiara, glistening on its mount inside the glass case. At least he didn't have it in his hands.

She stared into Monte's eyes for only a second or two, long enough to note the look of chagrin he wore at being caught, and then she swung her attention onto the guards.

"What is going on here?" she demanded, her stern gaze brooking no attitude from any of them. She knew how to pour on the superior pose when she had to and she was playing it to the hilt right now. Even standing there barefoot and in her nightgown she radiated control.

The guards were wide-eyed. They knew who she was but they'd never seen her like this. After a moment of surprised reaction, the captain stepped forward.

"Miss, we have captured the intruder." He nodded toward Monte and looked quite pleased with himself.

She blinked, then gestured toward Monte with a sweep of her hand. "You call this an intruder?" she said sternly, her lip curling a bit in disdain.

"Uh." The captain looked at her and then looked away again. "We caught him red-handed, Miss. He was trying to steal the tiara. Look, you can see that the lock was forced open."

"Uh." The second in command tugged on the captain's shirt and whispered in his ear.

The captain frowned and turned back to Pellea, looking most disapproving.

"I'm told you might have been dancing with this gentleman at the ball, Miss," he said. "Perhaps you can identify him for us."

"Certainly," she said in a sprightly manner. "He's a good friend of Leonardo's."

"Oh." All three appeared shocked and Monte actually gave her a triumphant wink which she ignored as best she could. "Well, there may be something there. Mr. Leonardo, is it?"

Just his name threw them for a loop. Everyone was terrified of Leonardo. They shuffled their feet but the captain wasn't cowed.

"Still, we found him breaking into the museum case," he noted. "You can't do that."

"Is anything missing?" she asked, looking bored with it all.

"No. We caught him in time."

"Well then." She gave a grand shrug. "All's well that ends well, isn't it?"

The captain frowned. "Not exactly. I'm afraid I have to make a report of this to the General. He'll want to know the particulars and might even want to interview the intruder himself."

Not a good outcome. Monte gave her a look that reminded her that this would be a bad ending to this case. But she already knew as much.

"Oh, I doubt that," she said airily. "If you have some time to question him yourself, I think you will find the problem that is at the root of all this."

The captain frowned. He obviously wasn't sure he

liked the interference being run by this know-it-all from the regime hierarchy. "And that is?"

She sighed as though it was just so tedious to have to go over the particulars.

"My good man, it was a ball. You know how men get. This one and Leonardo were challenging each other to a drinking contest." She shrugged elaborately. "Leonardo is now out cold in his room. I'm sure you'll find this fellow…" She gestured his way. "…who you may know as the Count of Revanche, isn't in much better shape. He may not show it but he has no clue what he's doing."

The guards looked at Monte. He gave them a particularly mindless grin. They frowned as Monte added a mock fierce look for good measure. The guards glanced away and shuffled their feet again.

"Well, miss," said the captain, "What you say may be true and all. But he was still found in the museum room, and the lock was tampered with and that just isn't right."

Pellea bit her lip, biding for time. They were going to be sticklers, weren't they? She felt the need of some reinforcement. For that, she turned to Monte.

"Please, Your Highness, tell us what you were doing in the museum room."

He gave her a fish-eyed look before he turned to the guards and gave it a try.

"I was…" He managed to look a little woozy. "I was attempting to steal the tiara." He said it as though it were a grand announcement.

"What on earth!" she cried, feeling all was lost and wondering what he was up to.

"Don't you understand?" he said wistfully. "It's so beautiful. I wanted to give it back to you so that you could wear it again."

She stared at him, dumbfounded at how he could think this was a good excuse.

"To me?" she repeated softly.

"Yes. You looked enchanting in it, like a fairy-tale princess, and I thought you should have it, always." His huge, puppy-dog eyes were doing him a service, but some might call it over the top for this job.

"But, it's not mine," she reminded him sadly.

"No?" He looked a bit puzzled by that. "Well, it should be."

She turned to the guards. "You see?" she said, throwing out her hands. "He's not in his right mind. I think you should let me take him off your hands. You don't really want to bother the General with this trifle, especially at this time of night. Do you?"

The captain tried to look stern. "Well, now that you mention it, miss…"

She breathed a sigh of relief. "Good, I'll just take him along then."

They were shuffling their feet again. That seemed to be a sign that they weren't really sure what they should be doing.

"Would you like one of us to come along and help you handle him?" the captain asked, groping for his place in all this.

"No, I think he'll be all right." She took hold of his hands, bound by the handcuffs, and the captain handed her the key. "He usually does just what I tell him," she lied happily. She'd saved him. She could hardly contain her excitement.

"I see, miss. Good night, then."

"Good night, Captain. Men." She waved at them merrily and began to lead Monte away. "Come along now, Count," she murmured to him teasingly. "I've got you under house arrest. You'd better do what I tell you to from now on."

"That'll be the day," he said under his breath, but his eyes were smiling.

Once back in her courtyard, they sat side by side on the garden bench and leaned back, sighing with relief.

"You're crazy," she told him matter-of-factly. "To risk everything for a tiara."

"It's a very special tiara," he reminded her. "And by all rights, it belongs to my family."

"Maybe so, but there are others who would fight you for it," she said, half closing her eyes and thinking about getting more sleep. "You almost pulled it off," she added.

"Yes."

She turned to look at him. "And you actually seemed to know what you were doing. Why was that? Have you been moonlighting as a jewel thief or something?"

He settled back and smiled at her. "In fact, I do know what I'm doing around jewelry heists," he stated calmly.

"I apprenticed myself to a master jewel thief one summer. He taught me everything he knew."

She frowned at him for a long moment. It was late. Perhaps she hadn't heard him correctly. But did he say...?

"What in the name of common sense are you talking about?" she said, shaking her head in bewilderment. "Why would you do such a thing?"

He shrugged. "I wanted to learn all I could about breaking into reinforced and security-protected buildings. I thought it would be a handy talent to have when it came time to reassert my monarchy on this island nation."

She stared at him in wonder, not sure if she was impressed or appalled. But it did show another piece of evidence of the strength of his determination to get his country back. This was pretty obviously an ambition she wasn't going to be able to fight.

Sighing, she shook her head and turned away. "Well, maybe you should go back for a refresher course," she noted.

He raised an eyebrow. "What are you talking about?"

She looked back at him. "Well, you didn't get the tiara, did you?"

"What makes you say that?" He smiled and reached back and pulled something out of the back of his shirt and held it up to the light, where it glittered spectacularly.

"You mean this tiara?" he asked her.

She stared at it as it flashed color and fire all around the room. "But I saw it in the case in the museum."

"You saw a copy in the case." He held it even higher and looked at it, admiring its beauty. "This is the real thing."

She was once again bewildered by him. "I don't understand."

"What you saw was a replica. My grandmother had it made years ago. I remembered that my mother had it in a secret hiding place. I went over to that side of the castle and, lo and behold, I found it."

"That's amazing. After all this time? I can hardly believe it."

"Yes. It seems that most of my family's private belongings were shoved into a big empty room and have been forgotten. Luckily for me."

She shook her head. "But now that you have the tiara, what are you going to do with it?"

"Take it back with me." He tucked it away and leaned over to take her hand in his. "If I can't take their most beautiful woman from them, at least I can take their prized royal artifact." He smiled. "And when you think about it, the tiara actually belongs to me. Surely you see that."

She laced her fingers with his and yearned toward him. "You're just trying to humiliate them, aren't you? You would have preferred to do it by stealing me away, but since that's not possible, you take the tiara instead."

"Yes," he said simply. "The answer is yes."

"But…"

"Don't you understand, Pellea? I want them thrown off-center. I want them to wonder what my next move might be. I want them to doubt themselves." The spirit of the royal warrior was back in his eyes. "Because when I come back, I'm going to take this country away from them."

He sounded sure of himself, but in truth, here in the middle of the night, he was filled with misgivings and doubts. Would he really be able to restore the monarchy? Would he get his family back into the position they'd lost twenty-five years before? Night whispers attacked his confidence and he had to fight them back.

Because he had to succeed. And he would, damn it, or die trying. No doubts could be allowed. His family belonged here and they would be back. This was what his whole life had been aimed at.

It was time to go. Actually, it was way past time to go, but he had run up against the wall by now. He had to follow the rules of logic and get out of here before someone showed up at Pellea's gate. It was just a matter of time.

But there was something else. He had made a decision. He was going to show Pellea the tunnel. There was no other option. If he couldn't take her with him, he had to give her some way to escape if things got too bad.

He was well aware of what he was doing—acting like a fool under the spell of a woman. If he were watching a friend in the same circumstances, he would be yelling, "Stop!" right now. Every bit of common sense argued against it. You just didn't risk your most important advantages like that.

After all, there were so many imponderables. Could he trust her? He was sure he could, and yet, how many men had said that and come out the loser in the end? Could he really take a woman who claimed she was going to marry into the family of the enemy and expect her to keep his confidences? Was he crazy to do this? He knew he was risking everything by placing a bet on her integrity and her fidelity—a bet that could be lost so easily. How many men had been destroyed putting too much trust in love?

For some reason the lyrics to "Blues in the Night" came drifting into his head. But who took their advice from old songs, anyway?

He had to trust her, because he had to protect her. There was nothing else he could do.

"Pellea," he said, taking her into his arms. "I'm going."

"Oh, thank God!" She held his face in her hands and looked at him with all the love she possessed. "I won't rest easy until you get to Italy."

He kissed her softly. "But I need you to do me a favor."

"Anything."

He was looking very serious. "I want you to keep a secret."

She smiled. "Another one?"

He touched her face and winced, as though she was

almost too beautiful to bear. "I'm going to show you how I get into the castle."

Her face lost its humor and went totally still. She understood right away how drastic this was for him. He'd refused even to hint at this to her all along. Now he was going to show her the one ace in the hole he had—the chink in the castle's armor. Her heart began to beat a bit faster. She knew very well that this was a heavy responsibility.

"All right," she said quietly. "And Monte, please don't worry. I will never, ever show this to anyone."

He looked at her and loved her, loved her noble face, loved her noble intentions. He knew she meant that with all her heart and soul, but he also knew that circumstances could change. Stranger things had happened. Still, he had to do it. He couldn't live with himself if he didn't leave behind some sort of escape route for her.

He frowned, thinking of what he was doing. It wouldn't be enough to show her where it was. The tunnel was old and dark and scary. He remembered when he'd first tried to negotiate it a few weeks before. He'd always known about it—it was the way he and his brothers had escaped on that terrible night all those years ago. And it had been immediately obvious no one had used it since. That was the benefit of having strangers take over your castle. If they made themselves hateful enough, no one would tell them the castle secrets.

When he'd come through, in order to pass he'd had to cut aside huge roots which had grown in through cracks. For someone like Pellea, it might be almost impassable.

It would be better if she came partway with him so that she would see what it was like and wouldn't be intimidated by the unknown.

"Bring a flashlight," he told her. "You're going to need it."

She followed him. He took her behind the fountain, behind the clump of ancient shrubs that seemed to grow right out of the rocks. He moved some smaller stones, then pushed aside a boulder that was actually made of pumice and was much lighter than it looked. And there, just underfoot, was a set of crumbling steps and a dank, dark tunnel that spiraled down.

"Here it is," he told her. "Think you can manage it?"

She looked down. It would be full of spiders and insects and slimy moss and things that would make her scream if she saw them. But she swallowed hard and nodded.

"Of course," she said, trying hard to sound nonchalant. "Let's go."

He showed her how to fill in the opening behind her, and then they started off. And it was just as unpleasant a journey as she'd suspected it would be. In twenty-five years, lots of steps had crumbled and roots had torn apart some walls. The natural breakdown of age was continuing apace and wouldn't be reversed until someone began maintaining the passageway. Even with a flashlight, the trip was dark and foreboding and she was glad she had Monte with her.

"Just ahead there is a small window," he told her. "We'll stop there and you can go back."

"All right," she said, shuddering to think what it was going to be like when she was alone.

"How are you feeling?" he said.

"Nauseated," she said before she thought. "But I'm always sick in the morning lately."

As soon as the words were past her lips she regretted them. How was it that she could feel so free and open to saying anything that came into her head when she was with him? And then she ended up saying too much. She glanced at him, wondering if he'd noticed.

He gave no sign of it. He helped her down the last set of stairs and there was the thin slit of a window, just beginning to show the dawn coming out over the ocean. They stopped and sat to rest. He pulled her close, tightening his arm around her and kissing her cheek.

She turned her face to accept his lips and he gave her more. Startled, she found in the heat of his mouth a quick arousal, calling up a passionate response from her that would have shocked her if she hadn't already admitted to herself that this man was all she ever wanted, body and soul. She drew back, breathless, heart racing and he groaned as she turned away.

"Pellea, you can't marry Leonardo. I don't care how much your father wants you to. It won't end up the way he hopes anyway. Nothing like that ever does. You can't sell your soul for security. It doesn't work."

"Monte, you don't really know everything. And you can't orchestrate things from afar. I've got to deal with the hand I've been dealt. You won't be here and you won't figure in. That's just the way it has to be."

"You don't understand. This is different. I'm making you a promise." He hesitated, steeling himself for what he had to do. "I'm going to move up operations. We'll invade by midsummer. I'll come and get you." He brushed the loose curls back from her face and looked at her with loving intensity. Here in the gloom, she was like a shining beacon in the dark.

"Leonardo's brand of protection won't do you any good by then. I'll be the one your father will have to look to."

His words struck fear into her heart. She turned, imploring him.

"No, Monte. You can't do that. You'll put yourself and all your men in danger if you try to come before your forces are ready. You can't risk everything just for me." She reached up and grabbed the front of his shirt in both hands. "I can't let you do that."

He gazed back steadily. "We'll have right and emotion on our side. We'll win anyway."

"Monte, don't be crazy. You know life doesn't work like that. Just being right, or good, or the nicest, doesn't win you a war. You need training and equipment and the manpower and…"

He was laughing at her and she stopped, nonplussed. "What is it?"

"You sound as though you've taken an army into the field yourself," he told her. "If I didn't know better, I would think you were a natural-born queen."

She flushed, not sure whether he was making fun of her. "I only know I want you safe," she said, her voice trembling a bit.

He took her into his arms. "I'll be safe. You're the one who needs protecting. You're the one ready to put your trust in the Granvillis."

She shook her head. "It's not like that," she said, but he wasn't listening.

He gazed at her, his blue eyes troubled. "I'll do anything I have to do to keep you from harm."

"You can't do it. You can't invade until you're ready."

"We'll get ready." He lifted her chin with his finger. "Just don't ruin everything by marrying Leonardo."

She turned away. Another wave of nausea was turning her breathless.

"What is it?" he said.

She shook her head. "I'm…I'm just a little sick."

He sat back a moment, watching her. "Have you been having that a lot lately?"

She couldn't deny it. She looked up and tried to make a joke out of it. "Yes. I imagine the situation in the world brings on nausea in most sane people at least once a day."

He frowned. "Possibly." A few bits of scattered elements came together and formed a thought. He remembered the way she seemed to want to protect her belly. The book at her bedside. The sudden aversion to alcohol. "Or maybe you're pregnant."

She went very still.

"Are you, Pellea? Are you pregnant?"

She paled, then tried to answer, but no words came out of her mouth.

"You are."

Suddenly the entire picture cleared for him. Of course. That explained everything—the reluctance to recreate the love they'd shared, the hurry to get him out of her hair, the rush to marry Leonardo. But something else was also clear. If she was pregnant, he had no doubt at all that the baby was his.

What the hell!

"You're pregnant with my baby and you weren't going to tell me about it?"

Outrage filled his voice and generated from his body. He shook his head, unable to understand how she could have done this. "And you plan to marry Leonardo?" he added in disbelief.

That rocked him back on his heels. He couldn't accept these things. They made no sense.

"Pellea…" He shook his head, unable to find the words to express how devastated he was…and angry.

She turned on him defensively. "I have to marry *some-one*," she said crisply. "And you aren't going to marry me, are you?"

She held her breath, waiting for his response to that one, hoping beyond all logic.

He stared at her, rage mixing with confusion. He couldn't marry her. Could he? But if she was carry-ing his child… This was something new, something he hadn't even considered. Did it change everything? Or was everything already set in stone and unchangeable?

He turned away, staring out at the ocean through the tiny window in the wall. She waited and watched the emotions crossing in his face and knew he wrestled with his feelings for her, his brand-new feelings for his child, and his role as the crown prince and a warrior king. He was torn, unprepared for such big questions all at once. She had to give him a bit of space. But she'd hoped for more. It wasn't like him to be so indecisive.

And, as he didn't seem to be able to find words that would heal things between them, her heart began to sink. What was the use of him telling her that they had to be together if he wasn't prepared to take the steps that might lead to something real? If he would never even consider making her his wife?

He had a lot of pride as the royal heir to Ambria. Well, she had a bit of pride herself. And she wasn't going anywhere without a promise of official status. If she wasn't good enough to marry, she would find another way to raise her child.

He turned back, eyes hard and cold as ice. "You have to come with me," he said flatly.

She was already shaking her head. "You know I can't go with you while my father lives."

Frustration filled his face and he turned away again, swearing softly. "I know," he said at last, his hands balled into fists. "And I can't ask you to abandon him."

"Never."

"But, Pellea, you have to listen…"

Whatever he was about to say was lost to history. An alarm went off like a bomb, echoing against the walls of the castle, shaking it to its foundations. They turned, reaching for each other, and then clinging together as the walls seemed to shake.

He looked questioningly at her. "What is it?" he asked her roughly.

"The castle alarm," she said. "Something must have happened. I haven't heard an alarm like this since...since Leonardo's mother died."

He stepped back, listening. "I thought for a moment it was an earthquake," he muttered, frowning. "Do you think...?"

"I don't know," she said, answering his unspoken question.

The alarm continued to sound. Pellea put her hands over her ears.

And just as suddenly as it had begun, it stopped. They stared at each other for a long moment.

"I'm going back," she said.

He nodded. He'd known she would. He had never wanted anything more strongly than he wanted her to come with him and yet he knew she couldn't do it. He was sunk in misery such as he'd never known before—misery in his own inability to control things. Misery in leaving behind all that he loved. And even the concept of a new baby that he would take some time to deal with.

"One more thing," he noted quickly. "Come here to the window." He waited while she positioned herself to look out. "Listen to me carefully. When you escape, wait until you get out into the sunlight, then look out across that wide, mowed field and you will see a small cottage that looks like something left over from a fairy tale. Go directly to it, ask for Jacob. I'll warn him that you may be coming. He will take you to the boat that will transfer you to the continent."

"If I escape," she amended softly, feeling hopeless.

He grasped her by the shoulders. "You will. One way or another, you will. And when you do, you'll come to me. Do you swear it?"

She nodded, eyes filling with tears.

"Say the words," he ordered.

"I swear I'll come to you," she said, looking up through her tears.

He stared into her eyes for a long moment, then kissed her.

"Goodbye," she said, pulling away and starting up the steps. "Good luck." She looked back and gave him a watery smile. "Until Ambria is free," she said, throwing him a kiss.

"Until Ambria is free," he saluted back. "I love you, Pellea," he called after her as she disappeared up the stairs. "And I love our baby," he whispered, but only to himself.

He would be back. He would come to claim what was his, in every way, or die trying. Cursing, he began to race down the stairs.

CHAPTER TEN

PELLEA GOT BACK without anyone knowing that she'd been gone and she covered up the escape tunnel exactly as Monte had in the past. She didn't find out what the alarm had been about until Kimmee came by with her breakfast.

"I guess the old General is really sick," she said, slightly in awe. "Can you believe it? I thought that man would be immortal. Anyway, someone went in to give him his morning coffee and thought he was dead. So they set off the alarm. Leonardo is furious."

"But he's not really dead."

"Not yet. But they say he's not far from it."

Despite everything, Pellea was upset. "How sad to come all this way home after all this time without really having a chance to see anyone he cares for," she said.

"Maybe," Kimmee said. "Or maybe," she whispered, leaning close, "the meanness finally caught up with him."

"Don't speak that way of the sick," Pellea said automatically, but inside, she agreed.

Still, she had a hard time dwelling on the sad condition

of the man who had been Ambria's leader for all her life. Mostly, she was thinking about Monte and his pledge to invade very soon, and she was sick at heart. She knew what danger he would be putting himself and his men in if he invaded now. If he did this just because of her and he was hurt—if anyone was hurt—she would never forgive herself.

Leonardo came by before noon. She went to meet him at the gate with her heart in her throat, wondering what he knew and what he was going to suspect. He looked like a man seriously hung-over and rather distracted by his current situation, but other than that, he seemed calm enough.

"Hello, my dear," he said. "I'm sure you've heard about my father."

"Yes. Leonardo, I'm so sorry."

"Of course, but it's not unexpected. He's been quite ill, you know. A lot worse than we'd told the people. It's a natural decline, I suppose. But for that moron to start the alarm as though he were dead!" He shook his head. "I've dealt with him." He slapped his gloves against his pant leg and looked at her sideways. "That was quite a night we had, wasn't it? I'm afraid we never did get around to announcing our engagement, did we?"

She realized he was asking her, as though he wasn't quite sure what had happened the night before. What on earth would she tell him? Nothing. That was by far the wisest course.

"No, we didn't," she said simply.

He studied her face. "Does that mean that the wedding is off?" he asked musingly.

She hesitated, not really sure what he wanted from her. "What do you think?" she asked him.

He made a face. "I think there was someone at the ball who you would rather marry," he said bluntly.

"Oh, Leonardo," she began.

But he cut her off. "Never mind, darling. We'll have to deal with this later. Right now I've got my hands full. I've got my father's ill health to come to terms with. And then there are the plans for succession."

"Why? What's going on?"

"You haven't heard?"

"No. Tell me."

"You know that my father arrived last night. They brought him in from France. I hadn't seen him for weeks. I didn't realize…" He stopped and rubbed his eyes. "My father is a vegetable, Pellea. I'm going to have to file for full custodial rights. And every little faction in the castle is sharpening its little teeth getting ready to try to grab its own piece of power." He shook his head. "It's a nightmare."

"Oh, Leonardo, I'm so sorry."

"Yes. It's all on me now, my sweet. I don't know if I have time for a marriage. Sorry."

Leonardo shrugged and turned to leave, his mind on other things. Pellea watched him go and sighed with relief. That was one hurdle she wasn't going to have to challenge at any rate.

Not that it left her in the clear. She was still pregnant.

She was still without a husband. What would become of her and her baby? She closed her eyes, took a deep breath and forced herself to focus. She had to think. It was time to find some new answers.

Pellea went to sit with her father later that day. He was much better. She wasn't sure what the doctor had given him, but she could see that his mind was clear once again and she was grateful.

She chatted with him for a few minutes and then he surprised her with a pointed question.

"Who was that man who was here yesterday?" he asked.

"The doctor?" she tried evasively.

"No. The other man. The one I momentarily mistook for King Grandor."

She took in a deep breath. "It was his son, the crown prince. It was Monte DeAngelis."

"Monte?" He almost smiled. "Oh, yes, of course it was Monte. I remember him well. A fine, strapping lad he was, too." He shook his head. "I'm so glad to see that he survived."

She paused, then decided to let honesty rule the day. "He makes a pretty good grown man as well," she said quietly.

"Yes." His gaze flickered up to smile at her. "I saw him kissing you."

"Oh." It seemed her father hadn't been as out of it as she had supposed. Well, good. He might as well know the truth. Did she have the nerve to go on with the honesty? Why not? What did she have to lose at this point?

"I'm in love with him, Father. And I'm carrying his child."

There. What more was there to say? She waited, holding her breath.

He closed his eyes and for a moment she was afraid what she'd said was too much for him.

"I'm so sorry, Father," she said, leaning over him. "Please forgive me."

"There's nothing to forgive," he said, opening his eyes and smiling at her. "Not for you at any rate. I would assume this is going to put an end to my plans for you to marry Leonardo."

She shook her head, sorry to disappoint him. "I'm afraid so."

He frowned. "The powers that be won't like it."

"No."

For the next few minutes he was lost in thought. She tidied things in the room and got him a fresh bottle of water. And finally, he took her hand and told her what he wanted to do next.

"I'd like to see the doctor," he said, his voice weak but steady. "I think we'd better make some plans. I'm about to leave this life, but I want to do something for you before I go."

"No, Father, you don't have to do anything more for me. You've done everything for me my whole life. It's enough. Just be well and stay alive for as long as you can. I need you."

He patted her hand. "That is why I need the doctor. Please see if you can get him right away."

She drew in her breath, worried. "I'll go right now."

The doctor came readily enough. He'd always been partial to Pellea and her father. After he talked to the older man, he nodded and said, "I'll see if I can pull some strings."

"Good," her father said once he was gone. "Leonardo will have his work cut out for him fighting off all the factions that will try to topple his new rule. He doesn't have time to think about me. I'm of no use to him now anyway and in no condition to help him." He took his daughter's hand in his and smiled at her. "The doctor will get me permission to go to the continent to see a specialist. And I'll need you to go along as one of my nurses."

"What?" She could hardly believe her ears. They were going to the continent. Just like that. Could it really be this easy?

"Are you willing?" he asked her.

"Oh, Father!" Pellea's eyes filled with tears and her voice was choked. "Father, you are saving my life."

Arriving in Italy two days later, Pellea was more nervous than ever. She wanted to see Monte again, but she was afraid of what she would find when she did. After all, how many times and in how many ways had he told her that he would never marry her? She knew there wasn't much hope along those lines.

And there was more. She knew very well that the

excitement of a clandestine affair was one thing. The reality of a pregnant woman knocking on the door was another. He might very well have decided she wasn't worth the effort by the time he got home. Was that possible? She didn't like to think so, but reality could be harsh and cold.

Still, one thing was certain. She had to go to him. She had to let him know that she was not in danger any longer, that she was not marrying Leonardo, and that her well-being was not a reason to launch an invasion. She was no longer in Ambria and no longer in need of any sort of rescue. The last thing in the world she wanted was to be the catalyst for a lot of needless killing.

She'd left her father in a clinic in Rome and she'd traveled a few hours into the mountains to the little town of Piasa where she knew Ambrian ex-patriots tended to gather. She found his hotel, and with heart beating wildly, she went to the desk and asked for him.

"He's not seeing visitors, miss," the concierge told her. "Perhaps if you left your name…"

How could she leave her name? She wasn't staying anywhere he would be able to find her. She turned away from the hotel desk in despair, losing hope, wondering where she could go.

And then, there he was, coming out of an elevator with two other men, laughing at something someone had said. Joy surged in her heart, but so did fear, and when he looked up and saw her, her heart fell. He didn't look happy to see her. He seemed almost annoyed.

He excused himself from the other men and came

toward her. He didn't smile. Instead, he pressed a room key into her hand.

"Go to room twenty-five and wait for me," he told her softly. Then he turned on his heel and went back to the men, immediately cracking a joke that made them laugh uproariously, one even glancing back at where she stood. Had he told them why she was here? Was he making fun of her? Her cheeks flamed crimson and, for just a moment, she was tempted to throw the key in his face and storm out.

Luckily, she calmed down quickly. There was no way she could know what he'd said to the other men, or even what he was thinking. He might have needed some sort of ruse to maintain his situation. She had no way of knowing and it would be stupid of her to make assumptions. Taking a deep breath, she headed for the elevator.

She found her way to the room, and despite her sensible actions, she was still numb with shock at the way he'd acted. Just as she'd feared, he was another person entirely when he wasn't in the castle of Ambria. What was next? Was he going to hand her money to get lost? And if he did that, how would she respond? She was sick at heart. This wasn't what she'd hoped for.

She paced the room for a few minutes, but she was so tired. After a few longing looks at his bed, she gave in to temptation and lay down for a rest. Very quickly, she fell asleep.

But not for long. The next thing she knew, someone was lying next to her on the bed and kissing her ear.

"Oh!" she said, trying to get up.

But it was no use. Monte was raining down kisses all over her and she began to laugh.

"What are you doing?"

"Some people welcome with flowers," he told her with a sweet, slow grin. "I do it with kisses. Now lie still and take it like a woman."

She giggled as he dropped even more kisses on her. "Monte! Cut it out. I'm going to get hysterical."

"Do you promise?"

"No! I mean… Oh, you know what I mean."

He did, and he finally stopped, but his hand was covering her belly. "Boy or girl?" he asked her softly.

She smiled up at him, happiness tingling from every inch of her. "I don't know yet."

"It's hard to believe."

She nodded. "Just another miracle," she said. "Are you happy about it?"

He stared into her eyes for a long moment before answering, and she was starting to worry about just what his answer was going to be, when he spoke.

"*Happy* isn't a strong enough word," he told her simply. "I feel something so strong and new, I don't know what the word is. But there's a balloon of wonderfulness in my chest and it keeps getting bigger and bigger. It's as though a new world has opened at my feet." He shrugged. "And now that you're here, everything is good."

She sighed. "I was worried. The way you looked when you saw me…"

"In public you'll find I am one person, Pellea. In

private, quite another. It's a necessary evil that some- one in my position has to be so careful all the time." He traced her lips with his finger. "But with you, I promise always to be genuine. You'll always know the real me, good or bad."

She was listening, and it was all very nice, but she still hadn't heard certain words she was waiting for. She told him about what had happened at the castle, and how she had accompanied her father for his visit to the specialist.

"I hope they can do something for him," she said.

"Does he plan to go back?"

"Oh, I'm sure he does. His life is in Ambria."

He nodded thoughtfully. "You're not going back," he said, as though he had the last word in the decision.

"Really?" She raised an eyebrow. "And just what is going to keep me here?"

"I am."

She waited. There should be more to that statement. But he frowned as though he was thinking about some- thing else. She was losing her patience.

"I've got to get back to my father," she said, rising from the bed and straightening her clothing.

Monte rose as well. "I'm going with you," he said firmly.

She looked up at him in surprise. "But…you hate him."

"No." He shook his head. "I hate the man he used to be. I don't hate the man he is today."

"You think he's changed?"

"I think we all have." He pulled her close. "And anyway, there are no good jewelers here in Piasa. I need to go to Rome. I need a larger city to find a real artist."

"Why would you want a jeweler?"

"I need a good copy made."

"Of the tiara?" She scrunched up her face, trying to figure out what he would want that for.

"In a way. I'd like to find someone who could reproduce the main part of the tiara as…" He smiled at her. "…as an engagement ring."

Her eyes widened. "Oh."

He kissed her on the mouth. "Would you wear a ring like that?"

And suddenly she felt as though she were floating on a cloud of happiness. "I don't know. It would depend on who gave it to me."

"Good answer." And he kissed her again, then took her two hands in his and smiled down at her. "I love you, Pellea," he said, his feelings shining in his eyes. "My love for you is bigger than revenge, bigger than retribution, bigger than the wounds of the past. I'm going to take care of all those things in good time. I'm going to get my country back. And when I take over, I want you with me, as my queen. Will you be my wife?"

She drew in a full breath of air and laughed aloud. There they were. Those were the words she'd been waiting for.

"Yes, Monte," she said, reaching for the man she loved, joy surging in her. "With all my heart and soul."

VALENTINE BRIDE

BY
CHRISTINE RIMMER

First published in Great Britain 2011
Harlequin Mills & Boon Limited,
Eton House, 18-24 Paradise Road, Richmond, Surrey TW9 1SR

ISBN: 978 0 263 88860 7

23-0211

Harlequin Mills & Boon policy is to use papers that are natural, renewable
and recyclable products and made from wood grown in sustainable forests.
The logging and manufacturing processes conform to the legal environmental
regulations of the country of origin.

Printed and bound in Spain
by Litografía Rosés S.A., Barcelona

Dear Reader,

Caleb Bravo is a player. He's got a big heart, but he loves fast cars, pretty women and, most of all, his freedom. He's about to get a lesson in love — and from the most surprising of women.

Irina Lukovic, Caleb's housekeeper, is quiet and hardworking, a recent immigrant from a war-torn Balkan country, a woman who keeps her head down and only wants to stay in America — and out of trouble.

They're about as unlikely a pair as anyone could imagine. But Caleb does have a gallant side. And when it looks like Irina could lose the one thing she wants most of all, well, what can he do but come to her rescue?

It's a marriage of convenience, one with strict parameters and a clear expiration date. Neither of them expects passion. Or love. Or the stunning revelation that Irina is not who she thinks she is.

These two are in for quite a ride!

Happy reading, everyone.

Yours always,

Christine Rimmer

Christine Rimmer came to her profession the long way around. Before settling down to write about the magic of romance, she'd been everything from an actress to a salesclerk to a waitress. Now that she's finally found work that suits her perfectly, she insists she never had a problem keeping a job — she was merely gaining "life experience" for her future as a novelist. Christine is grateful not only for the joy she finds in writing, but for what waits when the day's work is through: a man she loves, who loves her right back, and the privilege of watching their children grow and change day to day. She lives with her family in Oklahoma. Visit Christine at www.christinerimmer.com.

For my mom, Auralee Smith,
who just happens to be the best mom ever!
I love you so much, mom
and I'm so glad I'm your daughter.

Chapter One

Caleb Bravo stood in the doorway to his housekeeper's bedroom. He was holding the note she'd left propped on the kitchen counter. "What the hell, Irina?" He shook the note at her.

"Oh. Hello, Caleb. You are home early." She spoke without giving him so much as a glance, her head tipped down as she tucked a gray sweater into one of the two tattered suitcases spread open on her bed.

He entered the room. "I asked you what you're doing."

She straightened at last and faced him. "I am leaving," she said in her throaty, deadpan, Argovian-accented English.

"Just like that? Out of nowhere?"

"Is no other choice."

"Of course there's a choice." He held up the note again.

"Three sentences," he accused. "'Caleb, I must leave. I will not come back. Thank you for everything you do for me.'" He wadded it up and fired it at the wastebasket in the corner. "Couldn't you at least have told me why?"

She turned and took an envelope from the night-stand. "One hour ago, from the mail, this comes for me." She gave it to him.

There was a single sheet of paper inside—a letter, a very official-looking one, topped by the seal of U.S. Citizenship and Immigration Services. He scanned it swiftly. They were revoking her asylum. She was to report to her San Antonio service center immediately.

"What the hell?" he said again. "Don't you have a green card? Aren't those good for several years at least?"

"I have permit to work. I apply for green card. But there are…delays. Many delays."

"They can't do that, just…send you back to Argovia."

"But they do." She took the letter from him, refolded it, slipped it into the envelope, put the envelope on the nightstand—and returned to her packing. He watched her as she moved on silent feet from the bureau to the bed and back to the bureau again.

This was not happening. It *couldn't* be happening.

No way was he getting along without Irina. She was the best. She picked up after him, saw to his laundry, cooked tasty meals when he asked for them—and never batted an eye when she saw him or a girlfriend walking around the house naked.

She was the perfect live-in housekeeper. Quiet and competent and always calm. She anticipated his every need and also somehow managed to be next to invisible. He would never find another like her.

And what about Victor?

Her cousin, Victor Lukovic, was his best friend in the whole damn world. He owed Victor his life. He couldn't stand it if Victor thought he'd somehow chased his little cousin away.

"Irina."

"Yes?" She smoothed the folds of a brown wool scarf.

"Where exactly are you going?"

She frowned and shook her head. And then returned to the bureau for a stack of depressingly plain white cotton underwear.

He tried again. "So…back to Argovia then?"

She put the underwear in the larger of the two suitcases. "I never go back there." She flipped the suitcase closed and zipped it shut.

"But if not there, then…?"

"You have no need to know." She grabbed the laptop she'd bought a few months after she started working for him and stuck it in the side pocket of the smaller suitcase. Then she zipped that suitcase shut and dragged it to the floor. The larger one followed, landing with a heavy thump.

"Do *you* even know where you're going?"

No answer. She arranged the suitcases side by side, with a small space between. And finally she stepped into that space and faced him again.

"Thank you for everything you do for me, Caleb. You are good boss. The best." As usual, she was dressed from head to toe in nondescript gray. He'd never seen her in anything bright-colored, nor in short sleeves. And she wore high-neck shirts and sweaters year-round, in complete defiance of San Antonio's killer-hot summers. Her straight, dark brown bangs half-covered her enormous brown eyes. She looked…so pitiful. Lost. And alone.

He asked, "Have you called Victor about this?"

"No. My cousin does too much for me already. He does not need this trouble."

"Irina, come on…" Without thinking, he reached for her.

She flinched and ducked away from his outstretched hand. "Please. I must go now."

Damn. Bad move. He knew she didn't like to be touched. "I'm sorry. I didn't mean to—"

"You have done nothing wrong." She spoke gently as she hefted the suitcases, one in either hand. "Please. Move from in my way."

Like hell. "Come on. You can give me a little time, okay, before you…vanish into thin air? No one's coming to get you in the next ten minutes."

She shifted the suitcases and muttered something low in Argovian, her dark head tipped down. And then, glancing up, she said his name with a hopeless little sigh. "Oh, Caleb…"

He gave her a coaxing smile. "What can it hurt? Just a minute or two, to talk this over…."

"For what? Is no use."

"Irina. Please." He tried really hard to look pitiful and needy.

It must have worked. With a second sigh, she set down her bags. "Okay. You go ahead. You talk."

"I can't believe you were just going to walk out like this, just leave me worrying and wondering what the hell happened to you. If I hadn't come home early…" He shook his head in disbelief. "You *were* going to just go, weren't you? Just…disappear?"

"Yes. Are we finished with the talking now?"

The brilliant idea struck him right then, as he stared at her standing there, so lost and sad, between her two beat-up suitcases. He knew what he had to do. "We'll get married," he said. "It's the perfect solution."

She gave no response, only gazed at him steadily from behind those too-long bangs of hers.

He needed to get her away from the suitcases. "Come on." He gestured over his shoulder. "Into the living room. Let's sit down. We'll have a drink. We'll talk it over. We'll work it out, together."

She continued to stand there—silent, between her suitcases, watching him with an expression that gave nothing away.

"The living room?" he said again, almost afraid to turn his back on her for fear she might toss her suitcases through the window behind her and jump out after them.

There was another too-long moment while she continued to stare at him. And then, just as he was giving up hope, she spoke. "Yes. All right. We talk."

"Great," he said. "Fantastic." And he turned, ears attuned to the soft whisper of her flat black shoes on the hardwood floor. In the living room, she perched carefully on a leather club chair.

"Drink?" he asked, thinking he could use a nice stiff one about now.

But she pressed her lips together and shook her head. "No, thank you."

So he sat in the chair a few feet from hers and put on his most sincere expression. "Irina, I can't afford to lose you. That's all there is to it. You're too damn good at what you do. I could never replace you. It's just impossible."

Strange. She'd worked for him for two years. The whole hands-off thing had never been an issue before. But right now, it was a pain in the ass. If he could only touch her, he knew he could convince her. But he sat in his chair and she sat in hers, and since physical contact was off the table, he decided he'd have to settle for pitching his heart out. Luckily, he was a master at pitching. He did it for a living, after all.

He said, "You have to admit it. We get along great together. I have no complaints. Do you?"

She swallowed and shook her head, long bangs flying out and then settling like a dark veil over those big, haunted eyes.

"Plus, there's Victor. Irina, what would I say to Victor if we don't work this out? I can't believe you weren't even going to tell him."

She hung her head and softly admitted, "I…cannot tell him. He has *family* here. And he does too much for me already. It is better he is not involved."

"I owe him my life," Caleb said, with just the right touch of drama.

Or so he thought, until he realized she was trying not to smile. "You should not drive so fast."

Yeah, okay. He liked to drive fast, always had. While

they were still at UT, Victor had pulled him from a burning car after Caleb lost control of the wheel and crashed into a brick wall. He still regretted wrecking that car. A classic Mustang, a '68 fastback he'd restored himself in high school, with a little help from his brother, Jericho. They didn't make them like that Mustang any more.

"This isn't about my driving," he reminded her, in a tone both severe and reproachful. "This is about you and me and poor Victor, who's going to be beyond freaked if you just walk out of my house and disappear. This is about the fact that you need to let me do this one thing for you, for us, really—*and* for the man who saved my life."

Irina was watching him, her expression unreadable. Finally, she said gently, "You marry me so you will not have to marry that Emily person."

Bust-ed.

Yeah, all right. Getting Emily Gray off his back would be a nice bonus. What was he thinking, to sleep with a colleague, anyway? He never should have done that. But it was a problem he had when it came to women. How could a man resist? They smelled so good and they had such soft skin....

He cleared his throat. "Irina, you know I wasn't ever going to marry Emily."

"Too bad Emily does not know that."

True. Too true. Just the other night, Emily had followed him around the house chanting "Tick-tick-tick-tick!" For Emily, lately, it was all about her biological clock. She wanted a ring and a baby before she hit thirty-five. Caleb just wanted her off his back. But Emily was a driven woman. She refused to accept that he was not the man for her.

Enter Irina and her immigration issues.

He granted her his most charming smile. "Well, once you and I are married, Emily will get the picture crystal clear." There was a silence. A nerve-racking one, Caleb thought. Irina continued to study him from beneath the fringe of her bangs, her slim hands neatly folded in her lap. He kept his mouth shut, too, hoping she would agree with him that their getting married would be useful to both of them. But she just sat there. When he couldn't stand the silence any longer, he suggested, "Look, can we forget about Emily? Please?"

She nodded, a single regal dip of her head.

"So then it's settled," he said with easy confidence, assuming the sale as he had known how to do since before he could talk. "We'll fly to Vegas tomorrow and be married on Valentine's Day. Next week, you can visit the San Antonio service center with a marriage license in your hand."

"You do not understand."

"Understand, what?"

"A green card marriage is not so easy as the movies and the TV make you think. Your government is very—" she frowned, seeking the word "—very strict that the marriage must be a real one. There will be meetings, you understand? Meetings with Immigration officials. And the caseworkers could come to the door at any time, giving no notice, to try and prove us to be liars."

"Oh, come on. It's a government agency. I'll bet my Audi R8 that they don't have the personnel to have them wandering around dropping in on people randomly."

"It is not random. And you are right, home visits do not happen often. But they do happen, Caleb. If they are not believing the marriage is true and if they can prove we lie, that would be very bad."

"They would deport you, you mean?"

"Much worse than that. It is a crime to make a false marriage to get a green card. If Immigration discovers the marriage is not real, we both pay big fines and go to jail. And when I am released, *then* they deport me. *And* I am afterwards barred from ever in my life trying again to get a green card."

This began to look like something of a challenge. Caleb had always enjoyed a challenge. "We can do that. We can convince them. I'm real convincing when I put my mind to it."

"There is more."

"What do you mean, more?"

"The marriage must last for two full years."

Those words shut him up. For a half a second, anyway. "You're not serious."

"I am. Two years. Is it your wish to be married to your housekeeper for two years?"

It was not his wish, as a matter of fact. "Two years. That can't be. You're absolutely certain?"

"Yes. I am."

"It seems a little…extreme."

"Think. A true marriage is meant to last until there is death. Two years." She snapped her fingers. "Is nothing next to a lifetime. But is enough for Immigration to believe that the marriage is one that is made in good faith."

"Enough? It seems like too damn much to me."

She jumped to her feet so fast it startled him.

"Whoa. Irina. What?"

"I go and get the book for you."

"What book?"

"*U.S. Immigration Made Easy.* It has much about green card marriage. I show you the right page, about how it must be a marriage of two full years for a permanent green card, about what happens to you and to me if we make a false marriage." She drew herself up. "You think I am a fool? You think I do not consider all possible ways to stay in this country? I am many things, Caleb Bravo. But not a fool."

He put up both hands. "All right. Fine. I believe you. I don't need to see the book."

"You are sure?"

"I'm sure. Sit back down."

She perched on the edge of the chair cushion again and glared at him narrow-eyed from under her bangs.

He looked at her sideways. "Are you mad?" He tried to remember if he'd ever seen her mad before.

"You must know I never lie to you. I swear it. Without you to give me this job I will still be in Argovia."

"Irina. I believe you. Okay?"

Her expression softened and she said in a near-whisper, "Yeah. Okay."

Two years. Scary. He'd been thinking more along the lines of a few months, that she would get her precious green card quickly and then they could quietly divorce and go back to business as usual.

But really, now that he thought about it a little more, she might very well decide to quit working for him once she had permanent resident status.

But he would cross that bridge when he came to it. Whatever happened in the end, he did want to help. Plus there was the extra bonus of getting rid of Emily. *And* he would be doing right by Victor, who had trusted him to look after his precious cousin.

"It's going to be fine," he said. "We'll get married. For two damn years, if that's how it's got to be."

She folded her arms around her middle, a gesture that spoke to him of self-protection. And she dipped her head to the side. "There is another problem."

"What other problem?"

"You, Caleb. You are the problem."

He didn't get it. "Actually, I'm trying to be the solution."

"It is only…how you are."

"And how's that?"

She lifted one hand just long enough to give a dismissive little wave. "Always with the women."

What could he say? He did like women. "Yeah. So?"

"So, if we are married, *while* we are married, it has to be like a real marriage."

"Got that."

"It is not only as Immigration demands, it is as I demand."

He blinked. "As you…*demand?*"

Another regal nod. "It must be…how do you say it? The real thing. We must make the honest try. It is the only way I can see to rightness on this, the only way of making like real for Immigration. Even if it would not be truly real, it must be honest. For a man such as you, I know this is not easy to do."

He had no idea what she was saying. But it didn't sound all that flattering. "What does that mean, a man such as me?"

She shrugged. "You know…" She pantomimed with both hands out flat, a small space between her palms.

"Shallow. You're saying I'm shallow?"

She pressed a hand to her chest. "But good in heart."

"Gee, thanks—and why am I beginning to get the feeling you've already thought this through?"

Another shrug. "Because I do. I think about…the ways that it can be. I always know, if I have trouble, that you maybe start thinking to marry me for my green card. I am working for you for two years. I know how your mind is going." She tapped the side if her head with an index finger. "So I think about it, about if it happens. I think what I would need from you to say yes to marry you. I think about my…how do you say it? My conditions."

He tried not to gape. "I offer to save your butt and you've got conditions?"

"Um-hmm. I do, yes. While you are married to me, you give up the women."

Give up the women….

Two years without sex? It was impossible. "Come on. I'm a man, you know? A man with…needs."

"Yes," she calmly agreed. "I know."

So she was planning to sleep with him then?

Okay, that was hard to imagine. Caleb liked women.

All women. But never once in the whole time Irina had lived in his house, had the thought of sleeping with her so much as crossed his mind. Until just now. And now he *was* thinking about it, he wasn't really sure *what* he thought of it. It seemed…wrong, somehow.

But hey. She was a woman and he was a man. And they would be legally married. Why not, if she was the only woman available?

He asked, "You're saying you want it to be a real marriage then, while it lasts, a real marriage in every way?"

"No, I am saying that you can…make your own satisfying."

We're not really having this conversation. But they were. "Satisfy myself, you mean?"

"Yes. Please."

No way. If she had conditions, so did he. "Look. I hate to put you out. But that's not going to cut it. I do get your point. If we're going to convince Immigration that we're the real deal, I can't be seeing anyone else without risking everything. So I will agree to give up the women."

For a moment, he thought she might burst into tears. "Caleb. Thank you."

"Don't thank me yet. Because you've got to help me out here. I'm not gonna go two years without a woman in my bed."

The dewy-eyed gratitude vanished. Now her expression was not the least flattering. In fact, she looked kind of white around the mouth, her eyes even more haunted than usual. But she spoke in a reasonable tone. "I will not jump to the covers."

"You mean you won't hop into bed with me?"

"Yes. We cannot. I must have…time."

"Time."

"To…know you better in the way that a woman knows the man she marries. A month. Please. Can you hold your needs for a month?"

Hold his needs? He might have laughed. Or told her to forget it, that it was impossible. She clearly didn't want to have anything to do with him in bed— and he felt zero excitement at the idea of trying to change her mind.

She never dated, not that he knew of. And wouldn't he have known about it, if she did? Yeah, he could be oblivious sometimes. He'd grown accustomed to paying very little attention to her. He gave her a yearly raise and bonuses at Christmas. And at least every few months he made a point to tell her how much he appreciated the great job she was doing for him.

Most of the time, though, he forgot she existed and she seemed fine with that—but *come on.* He wasn't that damn oblivious. They lived in the same house, after all. He would have noticed if there had been a boyfriend.

Was she a virgin? He didn't know if he was up for dealing with a virgin. He'd had one virgin girlfriend, when he was a freshman in college. One had been more than enough. The first time he made love with her, there had been blood and she'd cried for hours. After that unpleasantness, he'd sworn off the innocent type. He didn't need the hassle.

But he wasn't about to let Irina go out the door lugging her battered suitcases and get lost in America, never to be seen again, either.

And really, maybe they were worrying about too much all at once. "How about if we just play it by ear then?"

She lifted a hand and brushed at her ear, a tentative, questioning touch. "Ear?"

"Figure of speech. What I meant was, we don't have to put any time limit on anything other than the two years we'll be married. Eventually, we'll, uh, have sex. But not until you feel you're ready."

"Maybe I never feel I am ready."

"Irina?"

"Yes, Caleb?"

"Forget about sex."

"But you said that you—"

"Stop. Listen. We'll just…fly to Vegas tomorrow and tie the knot and take it from there, just see how it goes."

"I know what that means." She looked pleased with herself. "To tie the knot is to marry."

"That's right. We'll get married. I'll give up the other women. And as far as the sex thing goes, I won't push you or anything. You don't have to worry about it, okay? We'll wait and see."

Chapter Two

"Repeat after me," the man called Father Ted instructed in a deep, booming voice that made her think of God Himself. "I, Irina, take you, Caleb."

She made herself stare up into Caleb's eyes. "I, Irina, take you, Caleb."

"For my husband...."

"For my husband."

"Before these witnesses I vow…"

"Before these witnesses I vow…" She repeated the rest, her higher voice echoing the deeper one. "…to love you and care for you as long as we both shall live. I take you, Caleb, with all of your faults and strengths… as I offer myself to you with my faults and strengths. I will help you when you need help, and I will turn to you when I need help. This I do promise until death do us part."

Father Ted turned to Caleb. "Repeat after me...."

And Caleb repeated. He said the same things to her that she had said to him. It was all very grave and solemn. She tried not to feel guilty, that it wasn't real.

Silently, she prayed that God might forgive her these lies. And then she reminded herself that it really wasn't a lie, that most of it was true. Only the parts about love and forever were lies. For the next two years, they would be every bit as married as any two people who planned to be together for all of their lives. Just without the love. And, for as long as she could avoid the inevitable, without the sex.

No love, no sex and not forever. Maybe they wouldn't be so very married after all.

But then she smiled to herself. Had she just prayed to God? She never prayed anymore. Not in years. Not since the terrible day she realized that if there was a God He had forsaken her.

"The ring," said Father Ted.

Her cousin Victor, huge and handsome in a black tuxedo, his broad face flushed and his dark hair slicked back, held the ring. He passed it to Caleb, who reached for her hand. She was prepared for that, for the necessity that there would be touching, including this—his taking her hand to put on the ring. As his fingers closed over hers and the panic tried to claim her, she reminded herself that he was Caleb, who had never done her harm, who had only been good to her.

The panic eased. She slowly let out her breath as he

slid the ring onto her finger. The diamond, large and bright, glittered at her. It all seemed so unreal—the long, high-necked white dress she wore, the ring, the Las Vegas chapel, with its walls painted to look like stone and its gold-veined pillars flanking the altar where they stood. Even the man who was marrying them, who had said to call him Father Ted. He looked suspiciously like an actor from Hollywood, with his thick head of silver hair and his too-blue eyes and deep tan.

She gazed up into her new husband's face. He smiled and she felt an answering smile tremble across her lips.

"You may kiss the bride."

She was ready for that, too. Caleb's hands brushed her arms and his eyes had a questioning look. She could almost hear him asking her if she was ready for a kiss. She gave him a tiny nod and he bent to press his lips to hers. It wasn't too bad. She closed her eyes and breathed evenly, in and out, steady and slow, reminding herself again that this was Caleb, who had always treated her with respect, with generosity and kindness.

A second later he lifted his head. His hands still pressed her arms—lightly, gently. She was aware of his warmth, of his scent that was not sour and dirty, but fresh and clean. And then he let go.

"May I present Mr. and Mrs. Caleb Bravo."

They turned together to the family sitting in the pews. On Caleb's side, there were his mother and father and his half sister, Elena. No one else in his immediate family had been able to get away on such short notice.

It had surprised Irina, to be truthful, that his family seemed to so readily accept the idea that she and Caleb were to marry—especially Davis, Caleb's father. More than once, she had heard Caleb speak in a tired voice of his dad. Davis wanted his children to marry women who came from families with money and power. In the past, when his sons chose women he considered unsuitable, Davis had made his displeasure known.

But not this time. This time, he had put up no resistance when Caleb announced he was marrying his housekeeper—or at least, none that Irina had heard about.

Besides Caleb's parents and half sister, there were also his Las Vegas cousins, Aaron and Fletcher, and their wives, Celia and Cleo, and their older children. The babies—Cleo's five-month-old boy and Celia's daughter of six months—were at home, watched over by their nannies.

On the bride's side, Victor's wife Maddy Liz sat with their two little ones, Miranda and Steven. Miranda, who was six, shouted gleefully, "Yay, Aunt Irina!" and she and her four-year-old brother started clapping. The other children joined in and then everyone else clapped, too.

Caleb put his arm around her. She hadn't been ready for that touch, but she accepted it. His hand felt warm and steady, there at the cove of her waist. She smiled up at him and he grinned down at her and everyone clapped even louder than before.

The recorded music played and Caleb offered her his arm. She took it without fear or hesitation. They went back up the aisle and out into the weak sunshine of the cool February afternoon.

The woman who helped Father Ted was waiting. She led them to a garden area, with a pond and a gazebo.

They took many wedding pictures there, she and Caleb smiling for the camera, the family around them.

After the pictures, as the sky grew dark with coming night, they got in the limousines lined up at the curb and returned to the twin casino hotels, High Sierra and Impresario, where they had all spent the night before. The Las Vegas men of Caleb's family were in the gaming business, Caleb had explained to her. Aaron was the boss at High Sierra and Fletcher the CEO of Impresario. Both men lived with their families within the lavish resorts, in top-floor penthouse apartments.

The ride wasn't far. Irina sat next to her groom, just the two of them, in their own private limousine. For a while they were silent. She watched the rows of tall palm trees file past beyond the tinted windows and stared at the darkening Nevada sky. Beside her, Caleb shifted slightly on the leather seat. She turned and found him watching her, a slow smile curving his mouth as she met his eyes.

"That went well." He seemed very pleased with himself.

"Yes," she replied, a strange heat rising in her cheeks as she stared into his eyes. "I am meaning to tell you that it surprises me, how everyone seems happy for us. And especially your father coming to the wedding, too."

"Why wouldn't they be happy?"

"Oh, maybe because until yesterday, I am your housekeeper only and you are a man with many girlfriends."

"Maybe they're relieved that I finally chose a good woman."

"Ah. Yes." She sent him a smile meant to tease him. "That must be it."

He made a low sound. "And you're surprised about my dad because he's always been such an ass before this?"

"Well, from what you say of him, he never likes his sons to marry a woman who has little money."

"I think he's changed. And I mean in a good way. You knew that my mother left him last year?"

"Yes. I remember. You speak of it many times with Elena." Irina liked Elena. After discovering that they were brother and sister the summer before, Caleb and Elena had become fast friends. Elena was often at Caleb's house. And she always treated Irina with courtesy, asking after Victor and Maddy Liz, teasing Caleb about how he was completely spoiled, to have someone so smart and capable to look after him.

"My dad's been a lot easier to deal with since my mom took him back," Caleb said. "And he's stopped trying to make us all over into his idea of who we should be." It was a big family. Caleb had six brothers and two sisters—three sisters now, including Elena. "It's kind of nice to have a father who's not always trying to work the angles with us. I hope it lasts," he added, as the limousine rolled under the deep porte cochere at the front entrance to High Sierra.

In the private dining room reserved for the wedding party, the tables were set with shining, gold-rimmed china and the walls were papered in stamped gold foil. The decorations were mostly red—including a lot of hearts tucked in among centerpieces of red and pink roses, in honor of Valentine's Day. A pile of beautifully wrapped gifts waited on a second table off to the side. Irina blinked at the sight.

The women all laughed at her surprise, and Elena said, "We went shopping this morning—me, Maddy Liz, Cleo and Aleta, while you and Celia were out looking for that gorgeous dress and getting pampered at the spa." Elena and Aleta shared a careful smile. Slowly, they were coming to accept each other: Davis's daughter by another woman, and his wife of more than thirty years.

"We bought out Macy's and Nordstrom and Williams Sonoma," Maddy Liz declared, in her Texas drawl. She had once been a debutante and also a cheerleader. Victor had met her in college when she was head of the cheerleading squad and he played football for the Longhorns.

"It was great fun," said Aleta of the shopping trip. Caleb's mom was a pretty woman, with sleek brown hair and eyes as blue as the Adriatic Sea. "Sit down, you two." She pulled out one of the two beribboned chairs at the gift table. "And open your presents."

Irina, laughing in pleasure, smoothed her long skirt and sat in the chair. Caleb took the chair at her side.

Maddy Liz handed her a big package wrapped in shiny silver foil, with a giant white silk bow. "Get to work."

Irina thanked her and tugged on the tail of the bow.

There were crystal goblets and wineglasses, fancy linens and silver candlesticks and many expensive kitchen gadgets.

Caleb leaned close to her. "Everyone knows how my bride likes to cook." She turned her face to him, and he brushed a kiss across her lips. It seemed very natural for him to do that. So swiftly, she was becoming accustomed to his gentle kisses, his light touch.

They shared a happy smile. He was enjoying himself. She knew that by his relaxed expression. She was having a fine time, too, which surprised her.

But why shouldn't she enjoy herself? Yes, it was a green-card wedding. But that didn't mean it couldn't be a happy one.

After the gifts came the dinner, with much toasting. And later a cake, which she and Caleb cut together like any American bride and groom might do. He put his hand on hers to guide the knife and she smiled back at him. In a traditional Argovian wedding, the cake had much significance. Its beauty and sweetness signified prosperity and fertility in a marriage. This cake was a fantasy of snow-white frosting decorated with swirls and cupids, with red hearts and soft red flowers. She licked a dab of icing off her finger. It was very sweet.

After the cake, the children grew wild. They ran around the table, laughing too loud, playing tag.

"Bedtime," said Fletcher's wife, Cleo. She and Celia and Maddy Liz took the young ones off to bed.

Their private dining room had a small dance floor and what Aaron called a combo of three musicians. The combo played background music during dinner, but once the children were taken off to bed, the musicians played a little louder. Caleb took her hand and led her onto the floor.

She whispered to him, feeling suddenly shy, "I do not dance."

And he answered low, "You do tonight."

He took her in his arms. He was careful and slow, each movement deliberate as he gathered her close. He didn't understand her fears of touching, but he knew of them, was considerate of them.

And it was like the kiss in the chapel after the vows. She danced, as he had said she would. Stiffly, yes. Feeling somewhat uncomfortable, with his body so close to hers. But it was somehow a right thing, a good thing, as it should be, the bride and groom dancing on their wedding night.

She closed her eyes and moved her body in time with his. He was careful not to pull her too close, to allow her the space she needed to feel safe. The song ended and another began. She and Caleb kept on dancing.

He whispered, "What did I tell you? You're an amazing dancer."

"Not so amazing," she whispered back. "But at least I don't trip on your feet. And what is this thing about you Americans?"

"What thing?"

"You are so enthusiastic. Everything is amazing or incredible or beautiful with you."

His broad shoulder lifted beneath her hand. "That's right. Amazing, incredible and beautiful. It's what you are."

She knew it was only Caleb's way, to flatter and lavish praise on a woman. Still, she enjoyed it, to have him say such lovely things to her. She kept her eyes closed and danced on.

Eventually, when she looked again, the little dance floor was full. The wives had returned from putting the children to sleep. They danced with their husbands, as she danced with hers.

Later, as Caleb went to dance with Elena, Davis

Bravo came to speak to her. She looked up at Caleb's tall, distinguished-looking father and wondered if there was about to be trouble from him after all.

But he only leaned close and said, "I had begun to wonder if Caleb would ever settle down. I'm so pleased to see it's finally happening—and I know that you and he will be very happy together."

She saw in his eyes that he was sincere. The awareness caused guilt to rise. Caleb's sometimes ruthless father was being so gracious and thoughtful to welcome her to his family. He had no idea that in two years there would be a divorce, that Caleb had only married her to save her from deportation.

Irina reminded herself that guilt was a luxury she could not afford. She intended to be a fine wife to Caleb, if only for a limited time.

"Thank you, Davis," she told him, meaning it. "Your kind words mean much. I do all I can to make your son a happy man."

"I know you will," he answered, the lines at the sides of his jade-green eyes crinkling more deeply.

Then Aleta came and slipped her hand into her husband's and told Irina how beautiful she was. "It's a joy to welcome you to our family," she said. "Caleb's a lucky man."

Irina said what was expected of her, that she was glad to *be* in the Bravo family, that she greatly appreciated their coming for the wedding and making the event a most special day for her.

The party continued until after eleven. There was champagne and laughter and the small band kept playing.

At the end, Irina threw her bouquet over her shoulder as American brides are known to do. Elena caught it, which surprised no one. She was the only single woman there.

Then, laughing and saying what a great time they'd had, they all left for their rooms, either there in High Sierra or at Impresario across the street. There was waving and fond see-you-tomorrows, and then she and Caleb and Victor and Maddy Liz were sharing an elevator up to their suites.

The elevator had mirrored walls—mirrors shot with gold. It was so strange, to see herself in her long white dress that Celia Bravo had helped her to choose, standing next to Caleb in his tuxedo—Caleb, who was no longer her boss, but her bridegroom.

Victor spoke to her in Argovian. She nodded, blushing, and thanked him formally.

Caleb and Maddy Liz demanded together, "What?"

"Come on you, two," Maddy Liz insisted.

So Victor translated. "May you know joy of your marriage bed and may your children be many."

"Well, all right," said Caleb, playing along with the fiction that they had made a forever union—a union they intended to consummate that very night.

And Maddy Liz, who was blond and beautiful and adored her big, Balkan-born football-star husband, made a growling sound and then giggled, "You know I love it when you speak Argovian." She stretched back a hand and curled her fingers around his powerful neck, craning her golden head back for a quick, hard kiss.

Irina envied them their love, their open passion for

each other. They seemed so young to her right then. She was only twenty-four, but sometimes she felt like a very old lady, an ancient *baba* with a cane and a wizened face, who had seen way too much of the world and its cruelty.

Caleb nudged her shoulder gently. "This is our floor. Good night, you two…."

"Congratulations," said Maddy Liz as the elevator doors slid shut on her and Victor.

Caleb led the way out of the elevator car and down the long hallway to their suite. He had his key card out and ready. He slipped it in the slot and then pushed the door open, holding it so that she could go in first.

So luxurious, their honeymoon suite. The walls were covered in a gold-leaf pattern and crystal chandeliers hung in the high-ceilinged sitting room and in the bedroom.

"Tired?" Caleb asked.

She shook her head. "I am too excited to be tired."

"It went pretty well, I thought."

She wanted, strangely, to throw her arms around him. But she didn't. It was one thing to feel the urge for such a gesture, another to actually go through with it.

"You're a beautiful bride," he said.

His words sent warmth coursing through her. She found it rather exhilarating, to have him looking at her and speaking to her in such an admiring way. Even if, to Americans, all brides were beautiful.

She complimented him in return. "Thank you, Caleb. And you are a very handsome groom."

He nodded, a gracious dipping of his head. "One more glass of champagne?" A bottle in a silver bucket waited over on the wet bar, and a pair of flutes as well, their stems tied with satin ribbons.

She rarely drank alcohol and she had been careful that evening to have no more than a few sips of the champagne that had flowed so freely. However, it seemed only right to share a glass with her groom.

"Yes, please," she told him.

He popped the cork and filled the twin flutes. Then he came and sat beside her on the sofa. He handed her a glass and held his high. "To two years of wedded bliss."

She laughed and touched her glass to his and then indulged in a long, fizzy sip. "Delicious," she said.

"It is, isn't it?"

She had a toast of her own. "To you, Caleb, my husband at least for a little while. Thank you for saving me from the need to choose between deportation and life…how do you say it? Life on the running?"

"On the run."

"Yes." Again, she tapped her glass with his. "That's it. On the run."

His green eyes, dark as rare emeralds, were shining. "And as for saving you? Anytime." They drank.

She asked, "Did you gamble today while I spend too much of your money getting ready for our wedding?"

"I played a little blackjack."

"Did you win?"

"I did all right. But I didn't play for long. I had an idea, so I spoke with my dad. He decided we should go for it. So he and I had a little meeting with Aaron and Fletcher."

She knew—or at least she had a general idea—of

what the meeting must have been about. "You think of something to sell to them."

"I did." He refilled his glass and topped hers off. "Last year, BravoCorp decided to get into wine importing as a sideline."

"Yes. I remember you speak of that. Wine from Spain."

"That's right. We import several varieties now. Good quality and good values, too. Recently, we've started bringing in some Italian wines. Chiantis, and some nice whites as well."

"So now High Sierra and Impresario, they will buy the wines from you?"

He raised his glass again. "Yes, they will." He looked so pleased with himself. "The wines we're importing are perfect for a tough economy. Good quality at a low price. That's what people want now."

Caleb loved to sell. He was always thinking of a way to put a deal together, which had made him the star salesman for his family's company. His father was forever trying to convince him to become a manager of the sales staff. Caleb refused. He liked the challenge of making the sale. Managing others was of no interest to him.

Too soon, her glass was empty.

"More?" He held up the bottle.

With a shake of her head, she set the flute on the low table in front of the sofa. Practical matters required discussing.

He seemed to sense her change of mood and put his glass down beside hers. "Go ahead and use the bathroom first. And I'll get myself a blanket and a pillow." He patted the sofa cushion. "I've slept on worse couches."

She had been dreading this moment. "Caleb?"

"Yeah?"

"Is…something we must discuss." Suddenly her poor heart was racing, beating at the walls of her chest like the frantic wings of a frightened bird.

"What? Who uses the bathroom first? It's okay, really. You go ahead."

"Uh, no. It is not about the bathroom. It is about… where you sleep. You must not sleep out here tonight."

"Don't be silly. I don't mind. Take the bed. I slept here last night. It was fine."

"Caleb." Embarrassment had her cheeks flaming. "I am so sorry…"

"About what?"

"Now we are married, we must share the bed."

Chapter Three

Irina added, "It is the best way. The safe way."

Caleb didn't get it. It made no sense at all. "The 'safe' way?"

"Yes."

"Okay," he said patiently. "Not following here. Didn't we have a long and really uncomfortable discussion a couple of days ago about how you weren't going to jump into bed with me?"

"I mean for the sex, not for the sleeping."

He wished she would begin to get a grip on the concept of the past tense. Carefully, he suggested, "You're talking about then?"

"Then?"

"When we discussed this before. You mean, you

meant you weren't going to have *sex* with me, not that you weren't going to sleep in the same bed with me?"

"Yes. Is correct. I *meant* not to have sex."

"So you want me to sleep with you, but not to have sex with you?"

She put her hands to her cheeks. "Is so much embarrassing. I am so sorry. I do not know how to tell you then."

"Fine. All right. But I think you'd better tell me now."

"Yes. Is time. You must know now."

"So. Why do you want us to sleep in the bed together?"

"Oh, Caleb. Is for Immigration."

He just didn't get it. "This is paranoia speaking. I don't know what it was like for you, in your own country. I don't know…what you suffered. But seriously, Irina. Immigration has no way of knowing whether or not we share a bed."

"But Caleb. They do have ways. They cannot know what we do in the bed. Is no way for them to be sure about that. But they can know if we are sleeping in the *same* bed."

"How the hell will they know that?"

"Is so simple. They come to visit when they want to visit. No appointment. They knock on the door maybe in the early morning. When they come in, they check if my clothing is in the room with your clothing, if only one bed is unmade. They keep…how do you say it? They keep a file about me. They add up the suspicious things that seem to say we are not truly married. Is better if we give them nothing to make them doubt."

"Oh, come on. This is America. It can't be that bad."

"Maybe you are right. But I hear stories. And I do not wish to take the chances."

"Look. They don't even know we're married yet. How are they going to knock on the door in the morning to check whether I'm sleeping on the couch or not?"

She made a small sound, a whimper of frustration. "Is just better, you know? We do it the right way from the first night. That way no one ever knows we are not truly together as a man and his bride."

He thought she was making a big deal out of nothing. But he could see by her tortured expression, by the way she twisted her hands in her lap, that she really believed what she was saying. And he ached for her, for whatever she'd been through in her young life that had made her so fearful, so certain that someone would come knocking on the door at all hours of the day or night, set on proving their marriage a fake and sending her back to the country to which she had sworn she would never return.

Really, it wasn't that big of an issue to him. A little bizarre, yes, to sleep next to a woman and *only* sleep. But he could get past it, if it would make her quit twisting her hands and looking so miserable.

"All right," he said. "If it's that important to you, we'll share the bed."

She drew in a deep breath as her face seemed to light up from within. "Oh, Caleb. Thank you. Thank you so much!" She grabbed for his hand, caught it— and then realized she'd actually touched him on purpose. She let go as if his skin had burned her. "Oops. Sorry." She covered her face with her hands. "Oh, I am such a fool."

"No. You're not." He wanted to clasp her shoulder,

at least, to reassure her with a touch. But he kept his hands to himself. "Irina. Come on, look at me."

Slowly, she lowered her hands. "Yes. I am a fool. I know I should tell you about the sleeping together when we agree to marry. I feel so bad that I do...that I *did* not."

"Irina."

"Yes?" She stared at him desperately through those huge, dark eyes.

"We worked it out. It's okay."

"Yes. All right." She forced a brave smile. "I am glad."

"You want some more champagne?"

"No. No more. More and I will get the headache."

"Then go ahead and get ready for bed, why don't you?"

"Yes. Of course. I make ready for the bed." She rose in a rustle of silk. He gazed up at her. Her dress had long sleeves drawing to points on the backs of her hands. The beaded neckline was practically a turtleneck. It covered just about everything. Still, she was beautiful in it. The gown showed off her narrow waist, her high, firm breasts. She looked like a princess in an old fairy tale, her dark hair pulled up and piled on her head, her bangs trimmed so they flattered rather than covered her enormous eyes.

He reached for the half-empty champagne bottle. "I'll be in soon."

She turned and left him. He filled his glass and sipped, feeling grateful to Aaron, who had provided the champagne. Cristal Brut 2002. Best of the best for the newlyweds.

He gave her ten minutes. And then he turned off the light in the sitting room and went through the darkened bedroom and the dressing area into the bath. He took off his tux and shoes and socks. As a rule, he slept naked. But for Irina's sake, he left on his boxer briefs. He brushed his teeth.

And then he switched off the bathroom light and moved through the shadows to the bed. As his eyes adjusted to the dimness, he could make out her slender form, curled up on the far side, clinging to the edge of the mattress, her back turned toward him.

With care and a nervousness that surprised him, he lifted the covers and slid under the sheet. He folded his hands behind his head and stared up toward the shadowed ceiling and the crystal chandelier that hung over the bed. A few of the glass prisms caught faint rays of light from outside and glittered dimly through the dark.

He realized that he was trying so hard to be quiet, he was barely breathing. How ridiculous was that?

"Irina, you asleep?" He whispered the question, just in case she was—or wanted to pretend that she was.

"No." Her voice was so small, from way over there on the other side of the bed.

He laughed. "Is this crazy, or what?"

She laughed too, a delicate, semi-smothered little sound. "Yes. Is pretty crazy, no doubt on that."

He wanted to ask her about her fear of being touched. But he didn't know how to even begin on that one. So he tried a less sensitive subject. "Victor told me once that you and your mother went to live with his family before you were born…."

"Is true. My mother gives birth to me when we are living with Victor's family." She sighed and shifted. A glance her way showed him her small, shadowed face. She seemed to be staring at the ceiling. "My father is brother to my uncle Vasili."

"Vasili was Victor's dad, right?"

"Yes. Uncle Vasili and Aunt Tòrja take my mother to live with them when my father dies." Her shadowed fingers were clutching something.

A charm? He remembered: she wore a necklace. Now and then he would see a bit of the gold chain above her collar. And occasionally he could make out the shape of whatever hung from it, outlined faintly beneath her clothing.

She said, "Then I am born. And then, when I am five, my mother dies from lung infection. Victor and me, we are like brother and sister, you know?"

"That's what he always said. That when he got that football scholarship to UT and left for Texas, he promised you he would find a way to bring you to America, too."

"Is true. But it is much later, before he can finally send for me. Much…terrible things happen first."

"Like what?"

"Well, the fighting. In my country, is always the fighting. Between the communists and the monarchists. Between the people and the soldiers. Between the Orthodox Christians and the ones of Muslim faith. When I am ten, the soldiers come to our house. They kill my Uncle Vasili and my Aunt Tòrja for lies the neighbors tell."

"What lies?"

"They say my aunt and uncle are loyalists to the

crown, that Uncle Vasili had once been working for the long-ago deposed king. That is lie. Uncle Vasili is not even born when the communists come, forcing the king and the royal family into hiding where they are eventually found and executed. But it is no matter to killers. My aunt and uncle are dead. Victor and I escape together."

Caleb knew the story. "But then you were found living in an empty building…."

"Is true. We are sent to the state home for orphaned children. At least for a few years we are together there." She let go of the charm at her neck and slipped her hand back under the blankets. "Always, Victor is watching out for me. And he is good at the sports. Is miracle that he gets the scholarship to go to America. And then finally, after college, when he is picked to play for the Cowboys and becomes permanent resident of the USA, he is ready to send for me at last. It takes five years of trying, but then it happens. I am getting the asylum. And here I am, working for you."

He wanted to reach for her hand under the covers. Would she pull away if he tried that? He was just unsure enough that he didn't.

And then he almost laughed. This had to be one of the weirdest moments of his life so far. In bed with his new bride, wondering if he dared to touch her hand.

"Argovia." He said the name of her country softly. He knew where it was on the map. Between Albania and Montenegro on the Adriatic Sea. It was about the size of Massachusetts. "Victor says it's a pretty country, a little like Greece."

She made a low sound, almost a growl. "Once.

Maybe. Before the Second World War. Before the communists come. In old days, I am told, Argovia is a quiet place where things never change too much. But the communists come and take over. We are part of Yugoslavia, under Tito, until the USSR becomes Russia once more. After that, after Tito, is one war and then another. And our peaceful, quiet country becomes a dangerous and brutal land."

"…where you will never go again."

"Is truth."

There was a silence. He glanced her way again and saw she still stared up at the shadowed ceiling above. He wondered if she could see the glints of light that somehow found the crystals on the chandelier, even through the darkness.

And then he felt her hand brush his. A tender, careful touch. A smile tugging the corners of his mouth, he turned his hand palm up, and waited.

Haltingly, with great care, she slid her palm over his and laced their fingers together. "Caleb?"

"Yeah?"

"Thank you. You save me. Thank you so very much."

He heard the tears that tightened each word. And he was proud to have been able to help her. "Anytime you need saving, Irina, you come to me."

"I will." A small sniffle. "I do."

Another silence. A long one. He lay there, her cool hand warming in his, and felt himself drifting contentedly toward sleep.

"Caleb?"

"Um?"

"If you want the sex tonight, is okay. We can do it."

Strangely, the idea of making love with her didn't seem nearly as wrong as it had two days before. But he knew she wasn't ready, though he could see them getting there. In time.

Not tonight, however.

"Caleb?" Her voice was so tiny, so scared and shy. "Do you hear what I am saying?"

"I heard you. Do *you* want sex tonight?"

Silence. And then he heard her draw in a shaky breath. "I am...willing. I will do it. With you."

"Thank you," he said gently. "But I think we should wait awhile, as we agreed."

"You do?" Hopeful. Relieved.

"I do."

"You are certain?"

"I am."

She said nothing for a time. He faded toward sleep again.

"Caleb?"

"Yeah?"

"Sleep well."

And he did sleep well.

When he woke, it was after nine in the morning. Her side of the bed was empty. And he smelled coffee. The low drone of the TV could be heard from the sitting room.

He dragged himself up against the headboard and called her name. "Irina?"

She appeared in the doorway to the sitting room, fully dressed in a loose brown sweater, the sleeves falling all the way to the tops of her hands, and trousers to match. She smiled at him, a shy, pleased little smile. "I have them bring breakfast. Are you hungry?"

"Starving."

"I bring it to you." She started to turn.

"Hold on."

She stopped, lifted a sleek dark eyebrow. "Yes?"

"I'll get up. Give me a minute."

She left him. He used the bathroom and pulled on some sweats, after which he found her at the table by the glass door to the suite's small balcony.

She sipped her coffee and then gestured at the place across from her where the covered dishes waited. "I get you Western omelet, home fries, bacon and English muffin." She set down her coffee, reached for the coffee carafe, and poured him a cup.

He sat in the chair, put the napkin across his knees and removed the covers from the food. It smelled great. There were clear advantages to marrying a woman who knew what you wanted for breakfast. "Just the way I like it."

She nodded and nibbled a piece of toast. "I am happy you get up before it turns cold."

He tucked into the omelet. Still hot and light as air. "Perfect." They had one more day and night in Vegas before they returned to San Antonio. "What are your plans for the day, Mrs. Bravo?"

"I take one hundred dollars from my savings to bring with me. Today, I gamble."

"You sound very determined."

"I feel the duty to experience new things. So I play

on the slot machines and maybe I try to play blackjack, too."

"You sure a hundred will be enough?"

"I study how to gamble on the Internet. Best is to take a certain amount of money to gamble with and not use more. Have a limit and stick by it."

"I'm just saying a hundred won't go far."

"Is far enough for me."

She lost her hundred dollars in the first twenty minutes of play. He offered more, but she wouldn't take it.

"I have my limit," she said. "And I am sticking on it."

She watched him play poker for a while. And then she and Maddy Liz took Steven and Miranda to Circus Circus.

That night, they saw a show at High Sierra's Excelsior Room. And later he ordered a limo. They drank champagne as they toured the strip.

Back at High Sierra, they went to bed at 2:00 a.m. He fell asleep with her hand in his.

The next day, Victor, Maddy Liz and the kids flew commercial back to Dallas. The Bravos, including the newlyweds and Davis, Aleta and Elena, returned to San Antonio on one the BravoCorp jets. Caleb and Irina were back at home by noon. Irina made lunch.

After they ate, they visited the San Antonio service center together.

She was nervous, he knew it. When Irina was nervous, she became very quiet. She didn't say a word the whole drive over there. And when they sat in hard plastic chairs and waited for their turn with a case-worker, she clutched a folder containing their marriage license and the necessary forms and other documents, and stared straight ahead.

He wanted to reach over, pat her hand, maybe lean close and whisper that it was all going to be fine. But she was strung so tight, he feared she might leap to her feet and run out the door if he spoke to her.

They were called in separately first, about ten minutes each, Irina and then him. The caseworker asked him questions about how he and Irina had met and what had made them decide to marry. Caleb told the story they had agreed on, that she had worked for him for two years and slowly he had come to realize that he loved her and wanted to spend his life with her.

The meeting went well, he thought. Then the woman who spoke with him called Irina back in. They were served up a short lecture about the trouble they would be in if their marriage was discovered to be a fraud.

Without missing a beat, Irina reached for Caleb's hand, twined her fingers with his the way she did when they were in bed together. "I love Caleb. I always love him, since he gives me job when I come to this country. When he tells me he loves me and asks me to marry him, I cry out with happiness."

Caleb lifted her hand and kissed the back of it, after which he gave a big smile to the woman across the desk from them. "I'm one lucky man," he said.

The woman didn't even blink. She took the forms and looked them over briefly, to make sure they were all in order. Excusing herself, she left them to make a copy of their marriage license, and also to copy his tax return, his birth certificate and the bills they had brought that proved they both lived at the same address. The tax return was to prove he had income, the birth certificate to testify that he was a U.S. citizen.

A few minutes later, they were in the car on their way back to the house. Once more, Irina sat staring out the windshield, looking frozen with fear.

He tried to ease the tension a little. "I think she was convinced we're sincere."

She turned and looked at him, her eyes full of shadows. He wanted to stop the car, grab her and hold her until the shadows filled with light.

"There will be home visits," she said.

"She didn't say anything about a visit."

"I tell you, they don't give warning. They simply come and knock on the door. We must be ready."

"We will be. Hey. We sleep in the same bed. We had a real wedding with the family and a damn fine party after. As far as they know, we're as married as it gets— we *are* as married as it gets for the next two years." He thought about the sex they weren't having. "Well, I mean, almost...."

She smiled then—or close to it—the corners of her mouth lifting the smallest fraction. "You are right. I try not to worry, okay?"

He gave her a nod and left it at that, though he really did think she was all tied in knots over nothing.

"Do you want to go on to the office?" she asked, when he pulled into the driveway.

"I can stay home for the rest of the day, if you'd like me to."

"No. You go on. I know you must have calls you are

needing to make." She jumped out of the car and went in through the garage by herself, pausing at the door to give him a wave.

As he drove to the BravoCorp building downtown, he thought how he could do a lot worse in a wife. Irina took great care of him. Now they were doing the married couple thing, he was actually finding her enjoyable to be around.

And she wasn't the needy type. She didn't cling. She had fears, clearly—serious ones—but she didn't expect anyone else to have to deal with them. He really liked that about her. It made him want to do all he could for her.

He parked in the BravoCorp lot and took the elevator up to his floor, where he had a small corner office and shared a secretary with the company's four other sales reps. His office was down the length of the floor from the elevators, so he walked past the cubicles of several coworkers on his way there.

They all congratulated him on his marriage as he went by, leaving him marveling at the efficiency of the office grapevine. Married for two days, and everybody had heard about it.

Which wasn't such a great thing, he realized maybe ten minutes later as he sat at his desk returning his calls. He hung up from touching base with a client and glanced toward his office door. He'd left it wide-open and instantly wished he hadn't.

Emily Gray, the woman he'd been sleeping with until last week, was standing there.

Chapter Four

Emily was looking sharp as a knife, in a fitted white shirt, pearls, a tight skirt and sexy high heels. She had her blond hair pulled back in a sleek twist.

And she was not smiling. "Caleb. Got a minute?"

What could he say? Might as well get it over with. "Sure. Come on in."

She swung the door shut and took the three steps needed to be standing in front of his desk.

"So what's up?" he asked, which was pretty damn lame, considering the expression on her face. She'd already heard what *he'd* been up to in the past couple of days. It didn't matter what he said. This conversation was not destined to end well.

"I heard you had a busy weekend." Every word had an icicle hanging from it.

He went for simple and direct. "I did. I went to Vegas. And got married."

"To that strange foreign housekeeper of yours." She spoke through gritted teeth.

"Her name is Irina. And now she's my wife."

"Why?"

"Because I'm in love with her." The lie came out a lot easier than he would have expected it might.

Emily didn't buy it, though. "The hell you are." She spoke quietly at least. Maybe because she didn't want to lose her job over this. "You're a son of a bitch, Caleb."

He really should have handled this differently. He could see that now. "Emily, look—"

"Look? Look at what? Less than a week ago I was in your bed. I admit I got a little overboard on the subject of my biological clock. I made something of an idiot of myself. I'm embarrassed about that. But you could have shown some class, you know? You could have dumped me to my face. If not that, you could have at least sent me an e-mail or shot me a text. *Something.* Instead, I got to hear about it at the water cooler. Just imagine how that made me feel."

"Okay. You're right. I was out of line not to tell you myself. If you want an apology, you've got it."

She made a low sound, like a growl. "I want a lot more than an apology."

"What is that supposed to mean?"

"Just wait. You'll see." She turned on her heel and marched the three steps back to the door. "My best to your bride."

"Damn it, Emily…."

But she wasn't listening. She yanked the door wide and stalked off down the hall.

He got up after a moment and shut the door again. Then he sat down at his desk and thought about what a complete jerk he'd been. And about what she might have meant when she said she wanted more than an apology.

He tried to think of ways she might sabotage him. There couldn't be a hell of a lot of them really, given that he was not only a Bravo in a company owned and run by the Bravos, but he was also about the best there was at what he did. If she wanted to keep her job, she wouldn't be messing with him, professionally or otherwise.

Uh-uh. The more he thought it over, the more certain he was that she'd just been blowing off steam. He'd treated her badly and she wanted him to know how she felt about it. Now they could both move on.

His phone rang. He answered it.

And a little later, his brother Gabe, second oldest in the family, who worked as a lawyer for BravoCorp, stopped by Caleb's office to congratulate him on his newlywed status. "Sorry Mary and I couldn't make it to Vegas for the wedding." Gabe had met Mary Hofstetter the previous spring. By late July they were married. They lived on a small ranch she'd inherited from her first husband. Mary loved that ranch. And Gabe had finally agreed to live there, too.

"No problem," Caleb told his brother. "It was short notice, I know."

"It wasn't that. Ginny had an ear infection." Ginny,

Mary's daughter by her first husband, was almost a year old now.

"Poor kid. I hope she's feeling better."

"Antibiotics. They work wonders. So how about you and Irina coming out to the Lazy H Thursday night? Give Mary and me a chance to break out the champagne and celebrate the family player getting married at last."

"Excuse me. *Who's* the player?"

"Not me. Not anymore. I'm a lucky man. Before Mary, I didn't know what I was missing."

Caleb laughed. "Two a.m. feedings and a rundown ranch?"

"I love that kid."

"I know you do."

"And the Lazy H isn't so rundown anymore. But you'll see. Thursday?"

"Sounds good to me."

"Check with Irina, then?"

"I'll let you know tomorrow."

By the time Caleb headed for home a couple of hours later, he'd pushed the unpleasant encounter with Emily to the back of his mind.

Irina had dinner waiting. They ate and watched a little television. Both of them laughed when Victor appeared in a commercial, advertising cough drops, wearing a bear suit—a little visual play on his football nickname, the Balkan Bear. Victor was one hell of a linebacker *and* a steady family man. That meant he got the primo endorsements.

"He is cute, my cousin," Irina said.

"Oh, yeah," Caleb agreed drily. "Six foot five and two hundred ninety pounds of cute."

He told her about Gabe's invitation and she said she'd love to go to dinner at the Lazy H. Somehow, he never got around to mentioning the encounter with Emily.

And really, what was the point of talking about that? It would only make her feel bad, and she didn't need that. Emily's depressingly justified anger at him was not in any way Irina's problem.

When it was time for bed, she shyly took his hand. "I make changes. I hope is all right?" She looked so nervous.

He found her way too charming. More so every hour that passed. "Like what?" He pretended to be doubtful, though really, however she wanted things was fine with him.

She pulled him into his bathroom and showed him how she'd taken over the cabinet under the second sink and arranged her stuff on the nearby section of granite counter.

"Look good to me," he said.

"I take half of your walk-in closet, as well. Is plenty of room in there."

"That was the plan."

She pulled him into the bedroom, where she let go of his hand and sank to the side of the bed. "I feel I am taking over your life."

He chuckled. "Isn't that what a wife does?"

"You are not feeling…like I am too much all over you? Too much…how do you say it? In your spaces?"

In his spaces. His Balkan bride did have a way with words. "No. It's all working out fine for me. What's not to like? You're easy to get along with and you know how to cook."

"Good." She rose. "I get ready for bed then." She disappeared into the bathroom and emerged about two minutes later wearing pajamas that covered as much as her daytime clothing did.

At least he could see her feet. They were slender, fine boned and pale. He tried not to stare at them, not to start thinking about the rest of her body, not to wonder what she would look like naked in the moonlight.

"Your turn," she said.

He brushed his teeth, got out of most of his clothes and joined her in the bed. When he turned out the light, he felt her hand brush his. It was getting to be a thing with them, holding hands in bed. If someone had told him a week ago that he would be lying beside his housekeeper tonight, longing for the simple touch of her hand on his, he would have walked away laughing, shaking his head.

He wove his fingers with hers and stared up into the darkness and thought about how he'd promised not to push her, how he had to remember that it had only been two days since their wedding.

"Caleb?"

"Um?"

"I feel I want to kiss you. Is that okay for you?"

Pleased all out of proportion, he whispered, "Absolutely." And then he waited. The kiss had been her idea, so it was only right that she should take the lead in it.

The bedcovers shifted as she slid toward him. He

felt her body heat. Her soft cotton pajamas touched his arm. Slowly, so as not to spook her, he turned his head toward her.

She was a darker shadow rising within the shadows of the room as she lifted above him. And then he felt her lips brushing his. Once. And then twice. He smelled her clean skin, and her breath—warmth and toothpaste— as she exhaled.

And then, with a second soft sigh, she retreated to her side of the bed. "Is okay," she whispered, more to herself than to him.

"I'm glad," he whispered back. He wondered what awful thing had happened to her to make it so hard for her touch him, to make it a really big thing just to ask for—and then claim—a kiss.

He wondered, but he didn't ask her about it. It seemed like an intrusion somehow. Plus, he wasn't really sure he wanted to know.

Thursday evening they drove up to the Lazy H. Caleb had been there once before, right after Gabe and Mary got married. The first thing he noticed when they drove into the yard in front of the house was the new barn, built to replace the one that had burned to the ground the summer before.

The house had been renovated, as well. When the barn burned, the fire had gotten away from Mary's ranch hands before the fire trucks showed up. The house had started to burn. They'd lost the master bedroom and the kitchen. The destruction had been fine by Gabe. It gave him the excuse he needed to convince Mary that they should hire a contractor and build what amounted to a new house. Now Mary had a big, modern, country-style kitchen with all-new appliances, handmade cabinets and granite-and-wood countertops.

There was also a new dining room. They ate dinner in there. Mary's daughter, Ginny, was eleven months old now and just starting to walk—which meant she was into everything. She staggered from one piece of furniture to the next, giggling in excitement at her newfound mobility. In the kitchen, Mary had special hooks on all the lower cabinets, to keep the curious toddler from pulling them open.

The little girl took an instant liking to Irina. She held up her baby arms and Irina scooped her up and gathered her close. For most of the evening, she had Ginny on her lap. Mary said what a nice change it was, to know that her daughter wasn't getting into anything she shouldn't be into.

Caleb had been kind of surprised when Gabe got together with Mary. Gabe used to go for the gorgeous, showy types. Mary was softly pretty and serious-minded.

And Gabe was completely gone over her. Unless he had to travel on business, he came home to Mary and Ginny every night. He'd never looked happier. Who knew that married life would agree with a guy like Gabe?

After dinner, Irina helped Mary put Ginny to bed. Gabe and Caleb put on their jackets and went out on the back patio, which had been fixed up just great, with drought-resistant landscaping and a covered slate patio. Gabe turned on the gas fire pit and they sat in the all-weather teak chairs and stared out at the sliver of moon hanging over the new barn.

"It's nice here," Caleb said.

"Yeah. Who knew I'd end up living on a ranch? Life is strange sometimes."

"But interesting."

"Oh, yeah." Gabe's white teeth flashed with his smile. "I always knew you would end up with Irina. We all kind of thought you would."

Okay, that was news. "You're kidding."

"Dead serious."

"All who?"

"The family."

"And all of you knew this, how?"

"Well, you always talked about her a lot."

"I did?"

"Yeah. And why not? She's taken damn good care of you. And she's…a sweet, good woman. For the long haul, a man needs a good woman in his life." Gabe's gaze shifted toward the house and Caleb knew he was thinking of Mary. Then his eyes were on Caleb again. "So how did Emily take the news that you and Irina had run off to Vegas together?"

"Not well. But I'm sure she'll get over it."

"A mistake, dating a coworker."

"Tell me about it."

"You thinking about having her let go?"

The idea had definite appeal. But no. "That wouldn't be right. All she did was make the mistake of going out with me."

* * *

It was after ten when Caleb and Irina headed home. Gabe and Mary stood on the wide front porch to wave goodbye to them.

"I like Mary very much," Irina said as they drove away. "She is smart and kind and...what is that expression? Ah. She has both of the feet on the ground."

"That she does."

"She is a writer. She writes articles for magazines. But I am guessing you knew that."

"Was that past tense I just heard you use?"

"Yes." She dimpled at him. "I am good with the English. I have a large vocabulary. But there is always room for improvements. I am working on those."

"Well, all right. Not that I don't love the way you talk right now."

"I can learn to be not so confusing, though, I think. That would be good. And about Mary..."

"Hmm?"

"She is writing a cookbook. A family cookbook. Will be many recipes. From Ida, to start. Ida is—was—Mary's mother-in-law before. Ida is born from German people."

"Yes, I know."

"And will be Latin cooking, too."

"Mexican, you mean?"

"Is correct." When he glanced her way, she was frowning. "Tex-Mex they call it, I think? From Elena and Mercy." Mercy, who had married Caleb's brother, Luke, was Elena's adoptive sister. "And cooking by your mother."

"My mom's a great cook."

"That is—was—what Mary says. I mean *said*. And some cooking by Mary, too. She makes the great home cooking, like her pot roast that we had tonight. And there are to be recipes also by Tessa." Tessa Jones Bravo was his oldest brother, Ash's, wife. "Tessa makes a mean chicken and rice casserole, Mary says to me."

He knew where this was heading. "And will there be a few favorite Argovian recipes included in this family cookbook of Mary's?"

She slanted him a glance. "How do you guess?"

"I am a very smart man."

"And you are so modest, too," she added playfully. "It is handsome in a man, to be modest."

"Attractive, you mean. It's attractive in a man, to be modest."

"That is what I am meaning." She sent him a shrewd glance. It was another thing he really liked about her. She might struggle with how to say things in English, but she was damn quick. A smart woman. And a perceptive one. "And yes," she added. "I am cooking the Argovian specialties for Mary's family cookbook. We do the cooking either in her kitchen, or at your house."

"Our house," he corrected.

She looked down at her lap, and then out the wind-shield again. "You are right. I should say 'our house.' Is important we are like real married people in all ways, even in how we speak of things."

"We *are* real married people. For the next two years. At least." He wasn't sure what had made him add "at least." And really, what the hell did it matter? They were going to be married for two years. Really, truly married.

Whether they ever got naked together or not.

"Yes, you are right," she said in a tone so obedient it made his teeth hurt. "We *are* married, for two full years."

He knew he should keep his mouth shut at that point. But then he thought about what Gabe had said, that the whole family just knew he and Irina would get together. And that really did kind of bug him, everyone assuming he would fall for Irina. And now they thought he *had* fallen for her, when in reality, it was something else altogether. A lie. A lie for a good cause—but a lie nonetheless.

"Look," he said gruffly. "Stop treating me like I'm your boss or something, okay?"

"But you *are* my—"

"I'm not your boss!" He was practically shouting. It was way out of line. He sucked in a slow breath, let it out with care. When he spoke again, he kept his voice even and low. "Not anymore. Not for two years, anyway."

"Yes, I know. You are right."

"Damn it. Come on, I told you to cut that out." He shot her a frustrated look—and instantly felt like an evil wife abuser. She was staring down at her folded hands, her shoulders tucked in and her soft mouth too tight. "Damn it," he said again, but softly that time. "Irina…"

She looked at him then. Her big eyes were shining with unshed tears.

Chapter Five

Caleb realized he'd never seen her cry.

True, she'd come close a couple of times, since that day a week ago when he'd offered to marry her. But before then not once. Now that he thought about it, before then she'd never shown much emotion at all.

And the few times she'd teared up since they agreed to elope, well, those had been tears of gratitude.

Not this time, though. This time he'd hurt her.

She asked softly, "Please. Can you drive more slowly?"

A glance at the speedometer proved he was getting near ninety. Another of his failings. Besides speaking harshly to his innocent wife, he drove too freaking fast. And his Audi R8 had been built for speed. He'd be up to a hundred before he knew it, with a state trooper on his tail.

He took his foot off the gas and slowed them down to the speed limit.

"Thank you." Her voice was small and way too forlorn.

At the next exit he turned off the highway. He drove about a mile and then eased the car to the side of the road in the middle of nowhere, with rolling, open pasture on either side. He turned off the engine, but left the lights on.

"Where is this place?" She sounded worried.

Was she afraid of him now?

The thought that she might fear him made him feel about two inches tall.

He gripped the steering wheel, then let his hands drop to his thighs. "It's nowhere. We'll get back on the road in a minute. I just…I wanted to tell you I'm sorry, that's all. If I upset you, if I…scared you."

She looked at him steadily. And then, out of nowhere, she laughed, a short, ragged sound.

It wasn't exactly the response he had expected. He frowned at her. "What'd I do?"

"Is only…oh, Caleb. Is not you, I think. Is me. You know?"

"Uh. Not really."

"I learn, in my life before, how to survive. I learn is better not to cry. Not to laugh. To be watching always. To be ready for trouble. For change. To live with even emotion—not up, not down. Always the same. Is making sense?"

"Yeah. I get it."

"But now…"

"What?"

"Everything is changing. I think I could not understand how much change is coming, when we agree to make our green-card marriage. Your family is so good to me. So…welcoming. All at once, I am like a different woman. Someone new. All at once, I find I am feeling so many things. Happy. Sad. I feel…too much, I think. Too many different ways. I am so thankful to you, I want to cry. When you speak in a mean voice, I want to cry. And then, for no reason, I want to laugh."

The urge was powerful to reach for her, to pull her close and wrap his arms tight around her. To soothe her. To make her feel safe. But grabbing her was the last way to make her feel safe.

He settled for a careful, steadying hand on her shoulder. She allowed that, without cringing or ducking away. And he knew that was progress, a big step, that already, in only a week, she could accept his touch without shrinking from him.

"It's okay," he said. "It's…good. Feelings are good."

She met his eyes. Hers were huge and full of shadows. And then she laughed again, a husky laugh that time. "You Americans and your feelings."

"Yeah, well, that's how we are." He sat back in his seat and stared out at the dark road ahead, at the lonely, rolling land to either side. "You're safe, Irina. No one is going to hurt you ever again."

He heard her sigh. And then she asked, "Caleb? Can we go home now?"

"You bet." He started up the car again, waited to make sure the road was clear going both ways. And then he crossed to the other side and headed back to the highway.

They rode in silence for several minutes.

Finally he asked, "So, will there be pictures in this cookbook of Mary's?"

"Yes, there will." She answered brightly, apparently as eager as he was to get back to a happier mood. "Zoe takes the pictures." Zoe was the baby of his family, a free spirit *and* an excellent amateur photographer.

"Good idea," he said. "Zoe's won awards with her pictures, even sold a few to magazines."

"Yes. That is what Mary says." Irina chattered on. "There will be pictures of all of us cooking the recipes, of the kitchens, which are the heart of family life, Mary says. Mary wants us to help each other with our recipes, so in Zoe's pictures family women are helping other family women. We go to each other's kitchens. It is more family-like that way."

"And Abilene and Corrine? Are they going to be included in the project, too?" Abilene was his other sister, a year older than Zoe. And Corrine was his brother Matt's wife.

"Mary says everyone. All the women of the family, as long as they are willing. And the men, too, if they wish to be contributing."

"Being total manly men, we're all pretty handy around a barbecue."

"Barbecue." She breathed the word in wonder. "Caleb. Is genius. I will tell Mary we must have whole section of Bravo men cooking the barbecue to be included with 'the man, the plan and the can' section."

"I'm not sure I want clarification, but...'the man, the plan and the can'?"

She laughed. The pleasured sound seemed to reach down inside him, bringing warmth and brightness. "Yes. Is about how a man can open a can and—"

"Wait. I get it. With a plan and a can, a man can make his own dinner."

"Yes!" She clapped her hands. "Is exactly right. Is already a cookbook with that name, *A Man, a Can and a Plan,* so Mary must find another title for that section. She gets this idea for the man section when she asks Gabe to be in the cookbook and he says he can open a can of salmon and add crushed crackers and corn to it and make patties."

He remembered. "Right. Gabe's famous salmon burgers. They're pretty good, too."

"That is what Mary says. She has Gabe make them for her and says that they will be in the book."

He suggested, "I know this is totally your deal, but I really think you should cook the Argovian recipes at our house."

"I should?"

"Yeah. We have a nice kitchen."

"We have a very nice kitchen." She sounded proud. He liked that. Plus, she'd said the all-important *we.*

He got to the main point. "And if you're at our house, when the food is done, I'll be the one eating it."

"Caleb. You are such a helpful man."

"I'm a man with a plan. In more ways than one."

In the weeks that followed, Irina remembered that conversation she'd had with Caleb by the side of the road on the way home from Mary and Gabe's house.

She remembered his gentle voice telling her it was okay to have feelings. She had laughed at him when he said that.

But as February became March, she often thought that he'd been right.

Sometimes, she would find herself thinking that this was the best time of her life. Like a surprise gift that was so much more greatly treasured for being unexpected. She kept house for Caleb, as always, cooking and cleaning and running his errands in the compact car he had bought for her use when she first came to work for him.

She slept in his bed at night, holding his hand until they both fell asleep. Sometimes she kissed him. Carefully. And slowly. Each kiss was a little easier than the one before. She would concentrate on the softness of his lips, on his clean, manly scent. She wanted so much to please him. And she knew that to give him sex would be a good way to do that.

He was so patient with her, and that did surprise her. Caleb had many good qualities, but never in the time she had worked for him had she considered him a patient man. He liked his pleasures—good food, good liquor and soft, willing women in his bed—and he liked them often. But to help her, he had agreed to give up other women *and* not to push her to make love with him.

And he was keeping his agreement.

She was taking advantage of his kindness, she knew that. It wasn't fair to ask so much of him and not willingly offer her body, such as it was, for his enjoyment. Yet still, she put off the time when she would be naked in his arms. She wasn't ready yet. She feared the demons of the past, that in the act of loving, her terror would rise up and overwhelm her with panic. And pain.

She feared her own ugliness under her clothes.

Sometimes, in the night she would lie awake beside him and imagine reaching for him, melting into his strong arms. But she never quite made that move.

And then there were nightmares, the reliving of that terrible time, of the rough hand on her mouth, the smell of sour breath, the whispered threats, and the promise of the pain....

She would wake from the terror, whimpering. Twice, her furtive moans woke Caleb, too.

"Irina?" His voice, through the dark, cutting a big hole of light and hope through her fear.

She reached for him, found him, gripped his strong hand tight. "Shh. Go back to sleep. Is nothing. Only a nightmare...."

He would squeeze her hand then. Just that, nothing more. His voice and the touch of his fingers pressing hers brought her back to the clean sheets, the safety, the goodness of her life in America.

And apart from her doubts and worries in the darkness, and the occasional nightmare, the world she knew now was all goodness. And light.

She went to gatherings with his family: a baby shower for Mercy, who lived at the Bravo family ranch, Bravo Ridge, with her husband, Luke, and was expecting their first baby in May. And a party at Corrine and Matt's house, where she met their five-year-old daughter, Kira, and learned they were expecting a second child in late summer.

And she spent much time with Mary, who quickly became a good friend to her.

Irina had never had a real girlfriend before. She loved the simple joys of this new friendship: to sit in Mary's kitchen, holding Mary's little girl, making plans for which recipe section of the cookbook they would tackle next. Or to have Mary and Gabe over to the house she shared with Caleb.

It was Mary who had encouraged her when Irina said she would like to have a family dinner party. Caleb's house—her house, too, now, at least for a time, she kept reminding herself—was big enough to hold them all. The date was set for the second Saturday in March.

Irina cooked all the food herself, the good, filling food her Aunt Tòrja had taught her to prepare when she was a child: mushrooms stuffed with feta cheese and herbs, walnut rice salad and braised lamb with spinach. And chicken wings marinated in yogurt and thyme, for those who didn't care for lamb. She offered two desserts—*tikvenic*, which was her country's version of pumpkin pie, and also a special Argovian egg custard served with brown-sugar syrup on top and vanilla ice cream on the side.

It was a wonderful party, full of laughter and happy voices and smiles around the big dining room table. Zoe came with her cameras and took many pictures. Mary planned that the party—Irina's recipes and Zoe's photos—would be in the cookbook, a shining example of a special family gathering.

Caleb's family had always treated Irina well. They had known her and had been kind to her, as Victor's little refugee cousin who had needed a job to get her asylum in the U.S. and who took such good care of Caleb. But now she felt their acceptance and approval so totally. It made her heart feel full. And it also brought the bitter aftertaste of guilt, that she was lying to these fine people, pretending to be someone she wasn't—or wouldn't be, after a specified length of time.

Always, when the guilt tried to rise, she would push it down again. She would remind herself that it had been her choice to walk this path, and Caleb's choice, as well.

Maybe, when their time as husband and wife was over, she would be able to keep the relationships with his family that she was forging now. Not the same, of course. But close enough. Oh, she did hope so. The Bravos were good people. She hoped they would forgive her deception. That they would understand.

And beyond her guilt over deceiving the Bravo family, on top of her feeling that she cheated her husband by not providing sex, she began to worry about money.

She hadn't considered the money question at first. They had so quickly agreed to marry and then followed through with it, they'd hardly had time to discuss all the details of their agreement. He had paid for her wedding gown, for the expensive wedding party and their beautiful wedding suite. It had all been so exciting and new, she hadn't considered at the time how much money it must have cost him.

On the first of March, when her usual automatic deposit had appeared in her bank account, transferred from his, she had experienced a slight twinge, a feeling that this wasn't right, that a man did not pay his own wife for things like cooking dinner and doing laundry. At that time, though, she'd avoided giving the problem serious thought. She had pushed it from her mind and gone on with her new life as Caleb's bride.

But then, when she was planning the dinner they gave for the family, he had written her a check for five hundred dollars to pay for everything. Yes, lamb was expensive. But there was no wine or liquor to buy. Caleb had a well-stocked bar. And last year, Victor had sent two cases of good-quality Bulgarian wine, which she planned to serve with the meal.

When she tried to argue that five hundred was too much, he had waved her objections away. He said that a party like that was a lot of work and he didn't want her worrying about something so minor as money.

So minor as money...

She had lived in a bombed-out building with her cousin, lived on garbage and whatever they could steal. Later, in the state home for orphaned children, there was food. They didn't starve. But it was never enough.

To her, money mattered. It meant the difference between stealing in the streets and a full belly and warm clothes on her back, and the deep comfort of knowing she was safe and not a thief. Sometimes she dreamed of a day she might have enough money of her own to know that that she would never be hungry. Enough to help others, to feed and clothe the needy. To make it so that at least one other person would be as fortunate as she, to find a safe place to live and people to care for her.

She didn't know how, exactly, that she would accomplish her dream of giving aid to others. But she did know she had to get beyond relying on Caleb's generosity. That, at least, would be a start.

On the Sunday morning after the big party, she let Caleb sleep in and got up early to finish cleaning up the kitchen and the dining room. She put away the dishes and the serving pieces and then swept the floors in the dining room and kitchen.

At a little before eleven, Caleb found her in the laundry room loading the tablecloth and napkins from the night before into the washer.

"You work too hard," he said.

She shut the door to the washer and started the cycle and then went to him, putting her hands on his strong shoulders, lifting her mouth for a kiss. He gave her one, a light brush of his lips against hers.

"I do not mind working," she said. "How about breakfast?"

"Did you eat already?"

Her stomach growled. She put her hand on it and laughed. "I was busy. I waited for you."

"I'll do the bacon if you'll scramble the eggs."

"Sounds like a perfect deal to me." She had been making an effort to use her articles, her a's and the's. And to remember, as much as possible, to speak in the past tense when appropriate. She didn't always succeed, but she was proud of the progress she was making.

"I had a good time last night." He looked at her warmly, with real affection.

"I, too."

In the kitchen, she made coffee and prepared the eggs for the pan as he put the bacon on the griddle.

When it was ready, they sat at the table in the bow window that looked out on the pool. She admired the way the sun made reddish glints in his light brown hair, and she tried to think of how to bring up the money issue gracefully.

He asked, "Something bothering you? You keep doing that scrunchy thing." He pointed to the space between his eyebrows. "You'll get a corrugated forehead if you're not careful."

"Corrugated?"

"Wrinkled."

"Ah." She gave up trying to be graceful about it and pulled the two-hundred-dollar check she'd written that morning from the pocket of her jeans. "Here." She slid it across the table to his side.

He picked it up and made an angry face at it. "What the hell, Irina?"

She sipped her coffee and tried not to feel defensive. "You always say 'what the hell' to me when you don't like something I am doing. Well, this is not a bad thing. This is because I do not need all the money that you gave me for the party. So I return—am returning—the rest to you."

"It's not necessary." He slid the check her way again.

"Yes, Caleb. It is necessary." She pushed it back toward him.

He had picked up his coffee mug. But he set it down without drinking from it. "You worked all week on that party. You cooked and you cleaned. You made everything perfect. Then this morning, you left me to get my beauty sleep and got up and worked your ass off without any breakfast. The work you did was worth a damn sight more than three hundred bucks. Worth more than five. In fact, I probably owe *you* money." He picked up the check, tore it in half, and then wadded up the pieces.

She wanted to laugh. She wanted to cry. He made her feel all confused inside. It hurt. And it was so beautiful, both at the same time. She reminded herself to speak calmly, to use reason. "It is not right."

"What is not right?"

"A man does not pay his wife to cook his food and clean his house."

"*Our* house."

"Yes. Okay. *Our* house. What I am telling you is that you must stop paying me."

"Like hell."

They glared at each other.

She tried again. "If you will not consider the rightness—"

"I am considering the rightness, damn it."

"Will you please let me complete my sentence?"

"Yeah. Sure. Go for it." He pushed back his chair and folded his big arms across his broad chest.

She spoke with measured care. "If you will not consider the rightness, then you must remember Immigration."

"As if I could damn well forget."

"If you are paying me, it looks like I am working for you, not like we are two people who are truly married."

"That's crap."

"No. Is the truth."

"Irina, get real. When two people are married and one stays home and takes care of the house, the one who brings home the cash has to share it. Immigration is not going to think twice about me giving my wife the money she needs to run our house—and maybe have little extra for herself. Your argument is weak."

"Weak?"

"That's what I said."

"I have...pride, Caleb."

"I know you do. And that's fine. But so do I. This marriage is no hardship on me."

Her throat clutched up. "Is not?"

"No. It's great. It's working out just fine. And you're working as hard as you ever did. So you will damn well be paid for what you do."

She swallowed down the lump of emotion that had clogged up her throat. "I...all right."

He pulled his chair close to the table again and picked up his coffee cup. "Well. Good. I'm glad that's settled." He drank.

"There is something else...."

He peered at her over the rim of the big mug. "You're ruining my Sunday breakfast, you know that?"

"We should have made an agreement when we got married, so I cannot steal your money when we are divorced."

He set the cup down. "What are you talking about?"

"I see this in a movie. A prenup, they call it."

"Irina, we didn't have time for a prenup."

"But there is also a *postnup*. Did you know that?"

"Think about it this way," he said, without answering her question.

"What way?"

"Just the fact that you're talking to me about wanting

me to have a postnup is proof enough that I don't need one. You're not going to try and steal my money, Irina." He grabbed up the pieces of the torn check and held them out to her. "If you were, you wouldn't be writing me checks to pay me back when there's nothing to pay me back for."

She watched his face across the table, knowing he was right. About all of it. And yet, still feeling that she owed him so much, wishing there might be some way to repay him.

"Eat your breakfast," he said gruffly. "You'll waste away to nothing."

Sex, she thought, as she picked up her fork. She could at least do that for him. He had been so patient with her. It was only right that she give him pleasure, at least....

But that night she did nothing to show him she was willing to make love with him.

She took his hand as she always did, once they were in bed. But nothing more. There seemed to her so many difficult steps to take before they could share intimacy. Just taking off her clothes, letting him see her naked, was going to be a challenge, one she cringed at having to face.

And then there were the terrible things that had happened in Argovia, after she was grown up and on her own, after Victor had left for America. The things she had never imagined she would share with another soul.

She was beginning to think she needed to tell him those things. And that scared her more than being naked in front of him. It was...a whole other kind of nakedness. The most difficult kind.

The next day he left for Los Angeles on a business trip, he and his brother Matt, who was the BravoCorp financial expert. They were to meet with the bosses of a large agricultural firm about selling the firm wind energy.

Caleb would be gone until Friday.

Irina felt such relief to be able to put off the issue of lovemaking for a few more days. And on the heels of her relief came anger with herself. It was one little thing that she could do for him, when he did everything for her. Yet she constantly found ways to avoid making it happen.

And he seemed willing to leave it alone, not to push her—to simply wait until she gave him some kind of sign. At this rate, he would be waiting a very long time.

Tuesday afternoon Mary came over with Ginny. Irina held the sweet little one in her lap as they pored over the pictures Zoe had taken at the dinner party. Later, as Ginny napped, Irina and Mary worked on the Argovian recipes, editing them, making them simpler and clearer. Mary described what she called the layout—how the pictures and the recipes would appear on the page in the finished cookbook.

Before Mary left, she asked Irina if something was bothering her.

Irina's heart gave a small lurch in her chest. Had she been so obviously upset that Mary had noticed the turmoil within her? But then she put on a smile and shook her head. "No. There is nothing."

"You seem…I don't know. Preoccupied, maybe? And a little sad. You know I'm here, if you need me. If there's anything I can—"

"No. Is nothing. Truly," she baldly lied.

After Mary was gone, she almost wished she had confided in her. But there was far too much to say, and none of it appropriate. It wouldn't be right to burden her sister-in-law with her secrets and her fears. Let alone with the information that she and Caleb had never made love.

No. Better to leave it. If she started talking, she might end up confessing that Caleb had married her so she could get her green card. That would be wrong. No one but she and Caleb could know that. As completely as she trusted Mary, it was unwise to tell anyone that her marriage was not as it seemed.

Wednesday, Mercy Bravo called and invited her out to the family ranch, Bravo Ridge, for dinner. Irina accepted, feeling that warmth within, that the Bravo women were looking out for her, taking care of her while Caleb was gone. It was a lovely evening. Matt's wife, Corrine, came, too, and brought her little girl, Kira.

Thursday morning, Elena called. "Mercy said you were out at the ranch last night."

"Yes. We had very nice time."

"Good. So you're doing okay on your own?"

"I am fine, thank you," Irina assured her.

"Call me if you need anything. School's in session." Elena was a middle school teacher. "But after four, I can be right over."

"I will call if I have need of you, I promise. And thank you so much for thinking of me." She hung up feeling good, feeling a part of Caleb's family in the truest sense.

She ate her breakfast and then she spent a couple of hours reading. Irina tried to read daily, for an hour at least. She read American history and novels and the occasional self-help book. She also practiced writing in English. She kept a journal where she wrote about things she learned, about her life in America. Everything from recipes to her thoughts on things she saw on television. She enjoyed learning. And reading and writing in English helped her to become more fluent in the language. Now and then, in recent weeks, she had found herself actually thinking in English. That was a big step. It made her feel closer to her ultimate goal of becoming an American in every way.

Around eleven, she tackled the job of sealing and polishing the granite counters in the kitchen. And after she finished the counters, she decided to go ahead and take a mop to the floor. First, she got out the vacuum cleaner and ran that. Then she started in with the mop.

It was a big kitchen and mopping was sweaty work. She'd already grown hot from polishing the countertops.

"Oh, what the hell?" she said to the empty kitchen as she blew her damp bangs out of her eyes and braced the mop against the edge of the counter. And then she laughed in delight. *What the hell?* It was something that Caleb would say.

She was, after all, home alone until tomorrow. Who was going to see her, if for once, she wasn't all covered up?

Swiping the beads of sweat from her brow, she took the hem of her long-sleeve T-shirt and whipped it up over her head—and off. The necklace her mother had left to her lifted with the shirt, and then dropped into place again above her breasts.

She lifted her arms and drew in a deep breath. Oh, if

there was a heaven, surely this was it: the feel of her bare skin, cooling, without the usual layers of protective clothing to hold in the heat.

The mop waited. She grabbed it and danced in a circle, remembering the way she had felt in Caleb's arms, dancing on the night they were wed. And then she went to work in earnest, mopping the floor, singing an old Argovian work song at the top of her lungs as her locket swung in and out at the end of its chain in rhythm with each stroke.

It was the singing that betrayed her, the loud, rousing song that made it so she didn't hear the garage door going up and, a moment later, rumbling down again.

She went on singing and mopping until a movement at the corner of her eye made her stop. And turn.

Caleb.

Oh, dearest God. It was Caleb. He stood in the open doorway from the laundry room, his suitcase beside him and a big bouquet of bright flowers in his hand.

He stared at her.

She wanted to die. Die right then, holding that mop, sweating in her plain white bra, without anything to cover the ugly scars from his gaze.

Finally, he spoke. "I…got home early."

With a strangled cry, she dropped the mop and ran from the room.

Chapter Six

Fury. Pure rage.

It coursed through Caleb, hot and fast.

What had they done to her? The scars, so many of them, white and puckered, marring her pale skin. As if someone had shot her with a gun full of nails. It must have hurt so damn bad.

He wanted to kill with his bare hands. He wanted to beat the life out of whoever had done that to her.

He dropped the flowers on the counter and went after her. Halfway down the hall, he heard a door slam in the bedroom. He followed the sound to the shut door of their bathroom.

"Irina?" He rapped on the door lightly, forced his voice to be gentle, though his anger at whoever had hurt her still burned. "Irina, come on...."

"Go away. Please."

"No." He said it firmly. "Come on. Let me in."

A silence on the other side of the door. He waited for her to tell him again to get lost.

But then he heard the click as she disengaged the privacy lock. The doorknob turned and the door opened. She stood there, tall and proud in her plain bra and gold necklace, crying without sound, the tears pouring down her sad, beautiful face. Revealed to him in a way she had never allowed herself to be until then.

She asked, her voice husky and weighted with hopelessness, "What do you want?"

You.

But he didn't say that. It seemed too much of an invasion, to confess it right then. To make that kind of demand on her. In fact, he figured any answer he gave at that moment, any words he chose to speak, were bound to be wrong.

At a loss, he said nothing. He simply held out his arms, not really believing that she would let him hold her. She never had until then.

But she surprised him—as she so often did. With a sigh, she came to him. He gathered her in, whispering, "Shh. Hey. It's okay. It's all right.…"

She clung to him, wrapping her arms around him and holding on tight. "Oh, Caleb. I am so embarrassed. So much ashamed…"

"Uh-uh. No." He captured her tear-wet face between his hands and made her look at him. "There is absolutely no reason for you to be ashamed."

Her breath caught on a sob. "But I…make such big fool of myself."

"No. Never."

"Yes. I do. Always hiding myself, always covered. I make such a big important thing of that, you know? Since we marry, I am trying to think how to show you, how to…tell you. And now, today, you find me singing in the kitchen, wearing only my bra. Is…not how I planned for it to be."

"Irina." He held her dark gaze, thumbs brushing the wetness from her soft cheeks, willing her to hear him, to believe. "You are no fool. You're brave and strong. Sweet. And good…"

"I know it is stupid. I am too proud. I never want anyone to see my scars." She glanced down. "Not even you. It becomes—became, like a habit, to keep covered up. To hide. A habit I never knew how to break." A tear trembled at the corner of her eye.

He wiped it away. "Well. Now I've seen your scars. You're not covered up. And look. It's turning out great."

She made a small disbelieving sound. "Great? To be dancing around the kitchen without my shirt, singing a silly song?"

"Well, here you are. In my arms. If singing with your shirt off is what it took to get you here, it's all good to me."

A laugh that was also a sob escaped her. "Oh, Caleb. Always, you see on the brighter side."

"I'm a very cheerful man—though I don't feel the least cheerful toward the bastard who did that to you. I'd like to get my hands on him."

She reached up, touched the side of his mouth. He felt that touch all the way to the center of himself. "You are angry?"

"At the son of a bitch who hurt you? You bet I am."

"Forget about him."

"Like hell."

"He is dead. Is what often happens to suicide car bombers."

"Crap. I was hoping I might get a shot at him."

"You are too late. But I agree. If he wasn't dead, I would want to kill him, too. In addition to himself, he murdered ten innocent people whose only crime was to go shopping, or to enjoy an afternoon snack in the café where I was working then. It was…how do you say it? A terrorist act, an attempt to disrupt the current government. In my country, it is happening all the time. Of the victims, I am one of the lucky ones. I am still alive. Still whole. All my parts are still working. It is so…random, you know? Bits of metal and glass hit me, cut me so deeply. But only on my upper chest and a few places on my arms. My face, my breasts, my belly, the rest of me. All untouched. Others were not so fortunate."

He gathered her close again. She didn't resist, only rested her shining, dark head on his shoulder with a small, quivery sigh. He wondered at himself, that it meant so much, just to be able to hold her.

She lifted her head and gazed up at him. "There is…more." The ghosts were back in her eyes.

"Will you tell me?"

Her soft mouth trembled. "Is very…it is very difficult to talk about."

He took her hand, led her to the bed and dropped to the edge of it, pulling her down to sit beside him.

She tugged her fingers free of his grip and crossed her arms over her breasts. "I feel...so bare."

"You're beautiful."

She smiled then. "Always ready with a compliment."

"I mean it. You are."

"And you are so patient with me." She let her arms relax, let her hands drop to her lap. "You surprise me, in so many ways."

"In good ways, I hope."

She nodded. "Only good ways." And then she stood and gazed down at him. "It is wrong, I know, to ask you. But again, I need time—and not only to be with you as a woman is with her husband. I need time also to tell you the rest of my sad, ugly story."

He looked up at her flushed face, into her eyes, red-rimmed from crying. And he realized that he didn't want to be anywhere else but right there, with Irina. He realized he was glad that they had two years—at least—to be together.

To come to know each other.

Something was happening to him. He wasn't sure what. A shifting of priorities. A difference in the way he viewed the world. What had mattered a lot a month ago didn't seem all that important now. He didn't have to be in a big rush anymore to get what he wanted. To find pleasure and quick satisfaction. She was showing him a side of himself he'd never known existed.

He reached out, caught her hand. "I brought you some flowers."

A smile quirked the corners of her mouth. "I saw them...right before I screamed and ran and hid in the bathroom."

"You should put them in water."

She twined her fingers between his, the way she did when they were in bed. "Yes. All right. I will."

He released her. She turned and left him. He watched her go, admiring the fine, slim shape of her back, the way her hips flared gracefully out from the tight, inward curve of her waist.

The next day Irina went shopping. She bought some blouses, two lightweight knit shirts and two dresses. She was frugal in her purchases, as always. But nothing that she bought was brown, gray or black.

Before going home, she even dared to stop at Victoria's Secret. She bought underthings that weren't white. And a nightgown that was nothing like what she usually wore to bed. The new tops and dresses revealed a few of her scars. But the thought that people would see them didn't bother her as much as it once had.

She showed most of her purchases to Caleb when he got home from work that night—everything but the nightgown. That, she would show him when she was ready. She even modeled one of the dresses for him.

He said she looked amazing, which made her smile. Partly because it was one of those things Americans are always saying. And partly because she could see in his eyes that he meant it.

She thanked him. And then she went into his arms and kissed him. A longer, slower kiss than ever before.

The next morning, Victor and Maddy Liz brought the children down from Dallas for the weekend. Irina took her cousin aside soon after they arrived. She told him of the car bombing, removing the sweater she wore over her new blouse, showing him for the first time what had happened to her.

He was hurt that she hadn't confided in him before. And he told her so.

She apologized for keeping her injuries secret. "I didn't want to talk about it. And I didn't want you to feel bad. But now I am thinking that it was worse, keeping it all locked up inside myself."

He put his giant hands on her shoulders and stared into her eyes. "You keep too much inside, I think, little cousin. But things are better now, no? You are happy with Caleb?"

"Very happy."

"Well, then, I am happy, too."

They went to Six Flags in the afternoon. Caleb rode on all the rides.

Irina liked to watch him with Miranda and Steven. He was so good with children. He didn't talk down to them, and he seemed completely at ease with them.

Victor put his big arm across her shoulders as they watched Maddy Liz, the children and Caleb going around on the Ferris wheel. "Life is good, no?"

She tipped her head back to give him a grin. "Life is very good."

"Who knew we would get so lucky?"

She went on tiptoe to kiss his cheek.

After Six Flags they went out for pizza. The kids were

asleep in the car as they drove back to the house. Maddy Liz put them to bed. And then Caleb opened a bottle of the Bulgarian wine Victor had sent the year before.

They grabbed sweaters against the evening chill and went out to sit by the pool. Maddy Liz told them she was pregnant again, due in September. Irina saw the look that passed between Victor and his wife. She felt Caleb watching her and turned to him. They shared a glance, one that was both warm and intimate.

Oh, yes. Life was good.

Victor and his family went home after lunch the next day. And Caleb went to his office for a while. He was still catching up on his regular work after the week in California.

Irina tried to do her daily reading. But she kept finding herself just sitting there, the book open on her lap, staring at the far wall, remembering the special moments of the previous day—watching Caleb with the children, sharing that private glance with him after Maddy Liz told them about the new baby.

It was time. And she knew it.

Past time, to be truthful.

Eventually, she gave up on reading. She went out to the kitchen and started cooking.

When Caleb got home at six, she had him open the wine. They sat down to the meal she had so carefully prepared. He ate, praising the food, looking so happy— with the good food, the wine. And with her.

After the meal, he helped her clear off. They watched a little television.

At nine, she left him to get ready for bed.

In the dressing room off the bath, she took off all of her clothes and put on her new pink nightgown. Petal-pink, the saleswoman had told her. The nightgown fit her like a second skin, leaving very little to the imagination. It had pink lace straps and trim. It dipped low between her breasts and revealed all of her scars. She let her hair down and brushed it until it fell, smooth and shining, to just below her shoulders.

And finally, straightening her spine, ordering her heart to stop pounding so fast and so loud, she opened the door to the bedroom.

Caleb was on the other side of the door, waiting for her.

She gasped at the sight of him. "Caleb! You surprise me."

"It seemed like you were taking a long time in there." He looked at her slowly, his gaze traveling down to her bare feet and then following a leisurely path back up again. "Well," he said, when he finally met her eyes once more.

"Well, what?" She really did wish she didn't feel so nervous.

"You're beautiful. And anytime you want to wear that nightgown, you're welcome to take as long as you want getting ready for bed."

"You like it?"

"Very much." His voice was rough and soft at once. The sound of it touched her all over, caressing her.

She let out the breath she hadn't even realized she was holding. "I am so relieved."

"What? You were worried? One glance in the mirror should have eased all your fears."

"It is not about what I see when I look in the mirror."

He tipped up her chin and looked deep in her eyes. She thought he would speak then, but he didn't. He brushed the backs of curved fingers along the side of her neck, the light touch arousing and also a little bit frightening.

No man had touched her intimately in more than three years. And the last man to do so…she shuddered at the thought.

He felt that shudder. His expression changed—from tender to determined. He ran his fingers, so lightly, across her shoulder and down her bare arm to capture her hand.

"Come on," he said. He led her to the bed and pulled her down with him, so they sat together on the edge of it, the way they had done the other day, when he came home and found her in the kitchen, mopping and singing, without her shirt.

She lifted his hand and rubbed her cheek against the back of it. "I want…to be your wife, Caleb. In all ways. For the time that we are together, I want us to have everything a man and a woman can share. I want to make love with you. Tonight. I want to sleep in your arms."

"Irina…" He seemed not to know what to say.

She lowered their joined hands into her lap. "Yes, Caleb?"

"I have to ask…" Again, the words faded away.

She held his hand tighter. "Anything. It is okay. Just ask." She turned and met his waiting eyes.

He blew out a breath. "Is this your first time?"

She wished that it was. That she could come to him all fresh and clean, with no painful, ugly memories to mar what should be a beautiful thing. "No. It is not my first time."

He leaned closer, bending down slightly, until their foreheads touched. "Whew. Good news."

She chuckled. "Is it?"

"Oh, yeah. Making love with a virgin is…a big responsibility."

She reached up, touched the side of his face. Warm. Clean. Temptingly rough, with a hint of beard. "You underestimate your…capabilities, I think. Your girlfriends always seem very happy with you in that way."

"Irina."

"Hmm?"

"Let's not talk about other women. You're the only one who matters to me now." He kissed her, a tender nibble of a kiss, like the flutter of warm wings against her lips.

She spoke, her mouth brushing his, he was so close. "Zoe tells me that you can sell a surfboard to an Eskimo. Elena says that you can charm the birds down out of the trees. I think your sisters are right about you."

"Shh." His breath was warm against her lips. He lifted a hand, eased it under her hair and clasped the nape of her neck in a touch both intimate and possessive, a touch that caused a lovely, warm shiver to spread outward, along her arms, down her back, over her hips and thighs. Everywhere.

He kissed her again, his lips coaxing her to open. When, with a soft sigh, she did, he deepened the kiss, easing his tongue beyond her parted lips, tasting her fully.

She let her eyes droop shut. Down low in her belly,

she felt a faint fluttering. Like an ember, small and shy, one in need of gentle, steady fanning.

He lifted his mouth from hers. She opened her eyes again and saw that he was watching her. He touched her shoulder, clasping, and then he laid his hand flat on her upper chest, over her mother's necklace and the worst of her scars.

She stared into those green, green eyes and allowed him to trace the upper curves of her breasts, his gentle finger traveling along the pink lace at the edge of her nightgown, bringing shivers in its wake.

And then he caught her locket in his hand. "I always used to wonder about this."

"My locket?"

He nodded. "Sometimes I would see the outline of it under your clothes."

"It was my mother's. It is all I have from her."

He turned the locket so the battered gold case gleamed dully in the light, touching his thumb to the single, ornately engraved letter on the front. "*G.*"

"Yes."

"*G*, for…?"

"I have no idea. My mother's name was Dafina— same as Daphne in English. Her maiden name was Sekelez. And my father's first name was Teo." She took the locket from him and opened it to show him the two miniature portraits inside. "My mother." She pointed to the dark-haired woman. And then to the other image. "And this is my father, Teo Lukovic, my Uncle Vasili's younger brother." Her father had worn a moustache. And had dark hair, like her mother's and her own.

Caleb studied the pictures. "A handsome couple."

"I think so, too. And I am happy at least to have a picture of each of them. I hardly remember my mother."

"…and your father died before you were born."

"Yes."

"It's so damn sad."

"Yes."

"Have you ever tried to find out what the *G* stands for?"

She laughed. "Caleb. In my life, up until recently, I have been keeping very busy simply trying to survive." She took the locket from his hand and snapped it shut. Then, sweeping her hair over one shoulder, she showed him her back. "Unhook the chain, please."

He made no move to do as she asked. "Irina…" He said it so softly.

"Please." She sent him a glance over her shoulder.

He undid the clasp.

She held out her hand and he dropped the necklace into her palm. Rising, she went to set it on the nightstand, turning back to face him as she spoke. "I think, for now, for tonight, I would like to forget the past."

His gaze scanned her face. "All right."

She went to him, took his big shoulders in her hands and pushed him back on the bed. He didn't resist. She followed him down, her hair falling forward, the ends just brushing his face. "For now, there will be only you and me in this room. The sad mysteries of the past do not exist. All the old ghosts can stay away."

"Fair enough."

She held his gaze. "You have condoms?"

He tipped his head toward the nightstand. "In the

drawer…" His voice had gone husky, his eyes soft and intent.

"I have…another request."

"Anything. Always."

"Remove your clothing."

Chapter Seven

He didn't move for a moment. His eyes sought answers from hers.

She had no answers to give him.

"Whatever you want," he said at last, and started to sit up.

She gently pushed him back down. "There is more."

He threaded his fingers up through the fall of her hair to press his warm palm along the side of her face. "I'll say it again. Whatever you want, I'm up for it." And then he gave her a slow, playful smile. "And that I mean literally."

She glanced down the length of his body. The bulge at the front of his trousers said it all.

Her stomach tightened, irrational fear trying to own her.

She wouldn't let it. This was Caleb. *Caleb,* who would never do her harm.

He guided her chin up so she looked in his eyes again. "What's wrong?"

"Nothing. It is all right," she whispered. "It is... good." She bent close, scenting him. He smelled so fine—clean, with a faint hint of manly aftershave.

The fear settled, retreated.

She brushed her lips across his, back and forth, enjoying the feel of her mouth barely touching his, taking pleasure in that, savoring the promise in a simple caress. She whispered, "After you undress, you lie back down. You...let me touch you. You let me to do whatever I want to you. But you must not touch me. You must...let me be the boss of your body. Let me make the pace and do the touching."

He searched her face again, breathed her name, "Irina..."

"Is it...okay with you? Will you do that?"

"Of course I will. And it's more than okay with me. It's only, well, a minute ago, you looked so scared."

"I am not afraid." The denial burst from her too loud, sounding defensive. She made herself repeat it, softly. "Not afraid. Truly."

"You're sure this is what you want?"

She nodded. "I am very sure. Please. Will you do this for me?"

He gazed up at her steadily. "Yes."

She bent and kissed him again. "Thank you." And then she lifted away from him. Retreating to the lower corner of the bed, she gathered her knees up and smoothed her nightgown over them. "Undress."

He rose. He took off everything swiftly, each movement deft and purposeful. He sat to remove his shoes and socks. She stared at his powerful back as he bent to the task, admiring the play of muscles beneath his firm skin and the sweet, tender bumps of his spine.

Naked, he rose and turned to her. His eyes held hers for a moment. And then he glanced down. Waiting. Letting her look at him.

And oh, she did look. At his fine, broad shoulders, his deep, muscled chest, lightly furred with golden hair that grew in a T, over his small male nipples and down the center of his hard belly, pointing the way to his full arousal.

She admired more than his body right then. She admired his heart. Such a big heart he had. And a kind one. And what a fine man he was. Man enough that he had nothing to prove. Man enough that he could let her take the lead, give the orders, be the boss.

Rising, she pulled back the covers, revealing the clean, white sheets, smoothing the blankets, folding them neatly at the end of the bed. "Please." She touched his pillow, stroked a palm along the exposed lower sheet. "Lie down now."

He did as she asked, stretching out face up, arms at his side, legs together.

"Don't...reach for me, please. Let me touch *you*."

"All right."

"And say nothing."

He gave her a nod.

She came back onto the bed and crouched on her knees beside him. She still wore the lace-edged nightgown and had no intention of removing it.

Not this time.

His hardness taunted her. Something dangerous. She

wanted to touch it, to wrap her fingers around it, to prove that it was no harm to her, to find, in conquering his maleness, her complete confidence as a woman again.

And yet...

No. Later. He was willing to be patient. So could she.

She stretched across his body, her thigh pressing the hard muscles at the side of his waist, and pulled open the drawer in the nightstand. She knew he watched her, that he saw the way the nightgown stretched tight over her breasts, that he wanted to touch her, to take her breasts in his hands. She knew it by the sharpness of the breath he drew, by the way his arousal jumped higher even than before.

But he did not reach. He remained still, at her command, save for the slight ragged edge to his breathing, and that single sharp twitch of his desire.

She removed the box of condoms from the drawer, took one out, put the box back, slid the drawer shut. Retreating again to her side of the bed, she set the condom on the nearer nightstand. She had no idea if she would be using it—if she would have the courage to go that far.

But it was there. Waiting. Available, if she decided she was ready for that.

She turned to him again. He hadn't moved. But he was watching her. Waiting. And so clearly ready for whatever she was going to do to him.

Touching was her prerogative. So she indulged herself. She touched his face first. It seemed the safest part of him. She traced his thick, golden-brown eyebrows, his ears, which were just about perfect—not too large, and set close to his head.

She ran her fingers into his hair, which was thick and slightly spiky, warm with his heat. He shut his eyes then, and she bent close to press her lips to his eyelids, which fluttered beneath her kiss.

A low, controlled groan escaped him as she lifted her head. When he looked at her again, his eyes dark and knowing, she knew he wanted more.

He wanted everything.

And she thought of his great patience. A month and more, in this very bed with her, holding her hand every night, letting her kiss him, accepting the occasional light touch she gave him, but keeping his own desires in check. Such a man deserved so much. He deserved everything a woman had to give.

More, certainly, than her battered body and damaged spirit could provide.

But for now, hers was the body available to him. They would have to make the best of the situation. She would have to rise not only *to* the occasion, but beyond it. She would have to get past her own crippling fears.

And she did want that—to cast off the cruel chains of the past. She wanted it for him *and* for herself.

She pressed her cheek to his cheek, and she whispered, "You are amazing."

And she saw the smile twitch the edge of his mouth. *Amazing*: it was what he was always calling her.

"I love that you are silent now," she whispered in his ear, before catching his earlobe between her teeth and worrying it lightly, bringing another low groan up from deep in his chest. "It's a gift that you give me now," she said softly. "A gift among so many others…this little bit of time while I am touching you, having it all as I want it to be, having *you*, Caleb, under my hands…"

His groan was louder that time.

She smiled as she kissed him, opening her mouth over his, waiting for his lips to part, so she could dip her tongue inside and taste the slick wetness within, finding it to be sweet and clean. Caleb, only.

And no other.

She stretched out beside him and rested her head on his chest. She listened to his heartbeat, so hard and deep. And then she kissed him, there, over his heart. She kissed the hollow space just below where his ribs met.

And she moved lower.

Caleb. Only Caleb…

The knowledge of him filled her mind, opened her heart.

Boldly, she took him in her hand. He surged against her, the flared tip weeping slightly. But he kept his word. Not to touch. Not to reach. To say nothing.

He was warm. Strong. Hard. Silky.

She stroked him. He lifted his hips, moaning, his big hands fisting up handfuls of sheet to keep from reaching for her.

It was…all right. To be with this man in this so-intimate way. She could do this. She *was* doing this.

She lowered her mouth to him and slowly, with great care, she took him inside. Panic threatened, constricting her throat.

But all she needed was a slight retreat. And then she could take him in again.

Such progress made her bold. It seemed she might do it…might take this scary experiment all the way to its ultimate conclusion.

She released him.

That brought a heavy, hungry groan from him. He lifted an arm—but only to put it across his eyes.

She rose to her knees, sank back to sit on folded legs—and told herself that she was going to reach for the condom, going to take it out of the wrapper, slide it down over him.

But she didn't.

After a moment or two, he lowered his arm from across his face. He rolled his head toward her, his eyes watchful and so dark. Waiting.

She bit her lip, shook her head.

He held out his hand. She took it, kissed it, held on tight.

In time, he stretched out his free hand and switched off the lamp by the side of the bed. She reached for the blankets, pulling them up to cover them.

When he gathered her close to his naked body, she didn't resist, didn't even flinch. His warmth and his strength felt good. Felt right.

"Go to sleep," he whispered, his lips brushing her temple.

She listened to his breathing grow soft and shallow and knew that he slept. And then, in time, she closed her eyes and let sleep have her, too.

When she woke it was daylight, but still very early. Caleb lay on his side, his head resting on his folded arm, eyes open. Watching her.

With a finger, he guided her bangs out of her eyes. "You were having a bad dream, I think. Making those soft, scared noises."

"I don't remember…"

He gazed at her steadily. "Sometimes bad dreams are like that."

She glanced away.

And he touched her chin to make her look at him again. "What?"

If she couldn't give him sexual pleasure, at least he deserved the truth. "I lied." She let the confession out on a sigh. "I do remember what I was dreaming. It's the same dream I've been having for three years. It never changes. But at least, now, it's a bad dream I can wake up from."

He didn't say anything. But then, he didn't have to. She could see by his tender expression that he was waiting, giving her the time she needed to tell him the things she had so much trouble talking about.

Eventually, she said, "I had a boyfriend, after I left the state home. We lived together for two years in Terejevo." Terejevo—the *J* pronounced like the English *H*—was Argovia's capital city. "He was…a wonderful man. His name was Neven. Neven Mozi. We lived together in a small apartment a few blocks from the café where we both worked."

Caleb's eyes were the clearest green right then. She could see by the way his brow had furrowed that he knew what must have happened to Neven.

She went on, "I was happy with Neven. We talked of marriage. Always before, I had dreamed of coming to America. But while I was with Neven, I could see myself staying there, in my country, being his wife, having children." She sucked in a shaky breath. "I guess you know where this is going. Neven died. He was one of the ten who didn't survive the car bomber's attack."

He clasped her shoulder and then slowly stroked her hair. It felt good, his touch. "I'm sorry, Irina."

She moved close enough to kiss his mouth lightly, and then retreated. "I didn't know at first that he was dead. It was chaos after the bombing. I remember being carried on a stretcher, people yelling, giving orders, the terrible sounds of other victims screaming in pain. The smell of smoke filled my head, greasy and foul. I think I passed out from the horror of it, from the pain of my injuries. Next time I came to myself, it was much later. I woke in the hospital, tubes running everywhere. Bandaged. Still hurting so bad. I screamed until a nurse appeared and turned up my morphine drip. I kept asking about Neven. No one would tell me. I don't think they knew."

Caleb laid his hand on her cheek. The warm touch helped. It grounded her, brought her back to the safety of the present.

It made it so she could tell the hardest part of the story.

"There was a man. An orderly. He came in the night. More than once. He moved the blankets out of the way, lifted my flimsy hospital gown…"

Caleb was lying so still. Too still.

"Caleb. Are you…is this all right?"

He brushed her hair out of the way and clasped her nape, so gently. And then he moved a little closer, to kiss her. It was a slow kiss, but a chaste one. A kiss that lingered even after he retreated to his own pillow again, a kiss that spoke of tenderness and complete acceptance of whatever she might say next.

"It's okay," he whispered. "Tell me. All of it. Please."

So she told him. "He…raped me. More than once. And when he did it, he whispered to me, that I would tell no one. That if I did tell, he would kill me. Lying there beneath him, I thought of death, thought that it would be a mercy if he would just murder me. But there was still Neven. Still hope—until a woman with a kind face and a gentle voice came to tell me that Neven was dead. After that, the orderly appeared beside my bed one more time. He hurt me as he had the other times. By then, I hardly felt what he did to me. I was dead inside— except for thinking of how I would kill him."

"Did you?" Caleb spoke so calmly, but there was murder in his eyes.

She smiled at him, sadly. "No. He was caught while I was still in the hospital, caught in the act of abusing some other poor patient. He was sent to a work camp. They don't last very long in the work camp."

"Good."

"Oh, Caleb. It was so hard for me, when I heard that they caught him. Then I had nothing to live for, not even the expectation of my revenge."

"But you did live." He touched her again, tracing the line of her jaw, the shape of her ear. "Not only beautiful. But strong. And so brave."

"Not brave enough."

"More than brave enough."

She dared to move in closer to him, to tuck her head beneath his chin. He wrapped her close in his big arms. She nuzzled his neck, breathed in deeply through her nose, letting the scent of him fill her and banish the lingering, too-powerful memory of sour breath and stale sweat that thinking of her attacker always brought with it.

"Last night…" She pressed her lips to his neck, opening them, touching his beard-rough skin with her tongue. He tasted as good as he smelled. "I was trying to…how do you say it? Put the past behind me."

"I kind of figured as much." He was smiling. She could hear it in his voice. She tipped her head back to look at him and he touched her mouth with his thumb, rubbing the fleshy pad back and forth against her lips. "I enjoyed what you did last night."

A soft laugh escaped her. "Even if it was a little…incomplete?"

He didn't answer. Instead he kissed her, a kiss that lingered, that made her sigh.

When he lifted his warm mouth from hers, she whispered, "But now I am thinking…"

Now his thumb pressed the tip of her chin. "Thinking what?"

"Maybe if we work together on this task, things will turn out better for both of us."

He kissed the tip of her nose. "You consider it a task?" His tone was teasing.

"Activity then?" She clasped his shoulder. Touching him had become increasingly easier. And also more pleasurable. Sometimes it was difficult to remember the way she had felt only a month before—how afraid she'd been to touch and be touched.

"Activity…" He considered the word, and teased, "Maybe we should call it what it is."

"Yes. All right. Sex. Lovemaking."

He grew more serious. "You're sure?"

"You asked me that last night."

"And the question remains as valid now as it was then." He shifted, moving his legs beneath the covers.

And she felt him, a silky warmth against her hip. He was already hard. She waited for the panic. It didn't come. Was it possible that the sudden, gripping fear was gone forever?

If not, it was fading. In time, she might be free of it. What a miracle that would be.

He asked again, "Are you sure?"

"I'm sure," she said. "I…" Heat rose in her cheeks. "Maybe you could take the lead this time."

"I'd be happy to. But I want you to promise you'll speak up if I do anything that scares you…anything that even makes you nervous. Or anything you just plain don't like."

"Caleb. I trust you. It will be fine."

He chuckled then. "Listen to you—reassuring *me*."

"Should I just…lie back and close my eyes?"

"If that's what you want to do."

She thought about that—and then nodded. "Yes. I believe that is what I will do."

He braced up on an elbow and waited, looking lazy and patient, like a golden lion basking in the sun.

"Would it…be all right if I leave my nightgown on?"

"However you want it, that's how we'll do it."

"Well. Yes. Then, good." She turned over, pushed up on

an elbow, plumped her pillow, and then flopped back down on her back. "Should I close my eyes, do you think?"

"However you want it," he said again.

She closed her eyes, tugged at her nightgown under the covers. And finally, with a hard sigh, she made herself lie still. "Okay. I am ready."

He didn't move. And he didn't say anything, either.

She had to resist the powerful urge to peek.

And then, at last, she felt the air on her skin as he drew the covers back.

Now she *really* wanted to look. If she opened her eyes just a tiny bit, well, what would that matter? He had said she should do whatever she wanted to do.

But no. She made herself breathe slowly and evenly, and she kept her eyes closed.

What was he looking at? At least, she thought with some relief, she wasn't naked.

He touched her wrist. A good choice, she thought, not to do anything too scary right away....

His fingers drifted, stroking lightly, playing along the flesh of her arm, up to her elbow, then back down to where he had started. Her hand, palm up, fingers loosely curled, tightened reflexively as he brushed the sensitive inner flesh of her wrist.

It felt...nice. A little shivery, but in a good way. He caressed his way back up her arm in one long stroke. And then he clasped her shoulder, a companionable touch, a touch that said all would be well, that there was nothing to be nervous about.

He moved again, bending close. She felt his breath across her cheek. He kissed her temple, the bridge of her nose. And then he stopped moving, with one hand clasping her shoulder, his mouth a breath's distance from hers.

Oh, she could feel him so acutely, feel his body heat all along her side, feel his breath across her lips. An inch closer, and he would be kissing her.

But he didn't take that inch.

After several seconds of such tender torture, she couldn't bear it. With a small moan, she lifted her head off the pillow...until her lips met his.

Delicious.

She sighed in pleasure against his mouth, and opened to him instantly, reaching blindly to touch him, to feel the warm, hard shape of his arm, the bulge of his shoulder. She let her fingers drift inward to the fine musculature of his chest. She stroked his skin, there, below his throat.

Because she wanted to. Because she could.

And as she caressed him, he kissed her, an endless kiss, one that was thorough, deep and somehow lazy as well. She thought again of a lion in the sun, as she offered her mouth to be plundered by his.

He put his hand in the center of her belly, pressing down slightly. She gasped when he did that. It was the first time he had ever touched her there, and the thin fabric of her nightgown provided very little barrier between his hand and her vulnerable flesh.

At her gasp, he made a questioning sound in his throat, a sound that vibrated through her, since her lips were fused with his.

She realized he might take that hand away. And now that she'd had a moment to adjust to the feel of it on her stomach, she didn't want him to pull back. So she pressed her own hand over his, so he would know that she wanted him touching her there.

He smiled, a slow smile, against her lips.

And he deepened the touch, made it more of a caress. It felt…so good. And exciting, too.

Below, in the womanly center of herself, it happened— that delicate liquid flutter, the one she had felt just for a moment the night before, the one that, for three long, lonely years, she had never thought to feel again.

More. The word took form inside her mind. She wanted more. She wanted everything.

He seemed to know. Or maybe it was the way her body was moving beneath his hand, her hips rocking, her back arching, as she urged him on.

The kiss they shared was so lovely, deep and endless. And he seemed to know he had her full permission to explore her body.

He cupped her breast, over the nightgown. When she only moaned into his mouth and arched her back higher, he dared to ease the lace straps down her arms, freeing her for a more intimate touch. He kissed his way over her chin and along her throat with hot, soft, nipping little kisses.

And then he reached her breast. He took it into his mouth, sucking, teasing her nipple until she grabbed his head close and speared her fingers into his spiky hair and murmured, sighing, "Oh, Caleb. Oh, yes…"

By then, it was like a dream to her. The sweetest kind of dream, a dream of pleasure, a dream where she was truly free at last, to enjoy her own body and the touch of a man.

A good man. A very patient man…

He raised her nightgown and she needed no urging by then. She parted her legs for him, accepted his touch on her most private places. *More* than accepted.

She wanted his touch. She wanted *him,* wanted every caress, every whispered word, every sweet, wet press of his mouth to her yearning flesh.

When he eased himself between her thighs, she opened her eyes and pushed at his shoulders. "Wait…"

He misread her panicked look. "Too fast?"

"Oh, no." She stroked the side of his face. "It's perfect…"

"But?"

"The condom. We need to—"

"It's handled," he said gruffly, lifting away enough that she could see.

She looked down, saw he had already had it on and laughed, a breathy, excited sound, as she let her head drop back to the pillow. "I don't even remember when you put it on…."

"That's good, right?" He arched a brow at her.

"It is good, yes. Oh, Caleb, it is very, very good…." She lifted her arms, reaching for him.

He settled close. And she felt him, there, where she was wet and waiting. A low, rough sound escaped him. A questioning sound.

She closed her eyes. "Yes. Oh, please. Yes."

Her body was so ready, so eager for him, that she gave no resistance. Only wet and heat and welcome as he came into her.

He groaned when he filled her. And she pulled him down hard on top of her, lifting her hips at the same time, taking him even deeper. He rested on his elbows, his hands to either side of her face, palms warm against her cheeks.

And he kissed her. Slow and deep and so intimately. And below he moved within her, long, careful, strokes that drove her higher, that had her digging her nails into his back, had her pressing up to welcome him, had her body moving like one long, endless wave.

Her climax rose slowly. She felt it upon her, at first like a faint promise, a promise that became a surety, a surety that began with a slow glow and opened up like a flower of fire, blooming hot and wide into a shattering finish.

She cried out as it rolled through her, a pulsing so powerful it claimed every nerve, surging out, taking the whole of her, drawing tight—and then releasing. And then doing that again.

And again.

And again.

Her fulfillment called to his. No sooner did the high waves of pleasure within her begin to settle into satisfaction, than he was coming, too, pressing hard into her, throwing his head back, as his release shuddered through him.

When he went limp above her, she gathered him in. She whispered his name and stroked his damp skin and caught his face between her hands so she could press a series of small, happy kisses on his lips, his cheeks, his nose, his proud chin.

"You're crying…." He brushed at her cheek. His finger came away wet with her tears. He swore. "I hurt you."

"No. You didn't hurt me. You never hurt me." She wrapped him tight in her arms again and whispered to him, "You only bring me happiness. And a safe place. And joy. Oh, Caleb. So much joy…"

Right then, the doorbell chimed.

"What the hell?" He lifted away again and they frowned at each other. "You expecting company?"

"No."

"Me neither." He kissed her one more time. "You stay here. I'll get rid of whoever it is." He rolled away and rose from the bed.

She saw the red marks on his back where her nails had dug in. "Oh, Caleb. I scratched you."

"Am I bleeding?"

"No, but—"

"It's fine. It doesn't hurt."

"You're sure?"

"Absolutely."

She wanted to reach out and drag him back into bed with her. But she didn't. She settled against the pillows again, swiping the tears from her cheeks. At least she had the pleasure of watching his beautiful body as he yanked on a pair of sweats and turned for the door.

"I'll be back," he said over his shoulder.

A warm shiver went through her at the promise in his eyes—and the doorbell rang a second time. "I'll be here."

It took him several minutes to return. And when he did, his eyes were no longer soft with passion.

"It's all right," he said softly. "It's going to be fine."

"Caleb, what…?"

"Put on a robe and come out to the living room."

"Caleb?"

"A woman from Immigration Services is here."

Chapter Eight

Caleb watched her face turn sickly gray and feared she was going to chuck her cookies right there in the bed.

"I must dress," she said frantically, shoving back the covers, jumping to her feet.

He went to her, took her by her shoulders. "Wait."

"Caleb. Please. I must—"

"Stop. Listen."

"Caleb—"

"You want to convince her we're for real, right? What better way to do that than if I'm half-dressed and you're looking all soft and satisfied in your nightgown?"

Even freaked, she caught on quick. "I'll put on a robe and comb my hair." She started to turn.

He held her there. "Don't."

She blinked. "Excuse me."

"Your hair. Let her see it wild like that. Let her know that you just got out of bed. *Our* bed."

She blinked. And then she nodded. "Yes. All right. I'll get the robe...."

He let her go. She vanished into the dressing room, returning a moment later wearing a beige terry-cloth robe over the sexy pink nightgown. She belted the robe. It covered pretty much everything but a small V of her sweet, scarred chest.

Still, with her very kissed-looking mouth, the flush on her cheeks, and her hair loose and wild, anyone with half a brain would know exactly what she had been doing—with *him,* a fact that he was going to be more than pleased to make perfectly clear. She looked sexy as hell, and he couldn't wait to get rid of the lady from USCIS and take her back to bed.

"Is okay?" she asked, nervously.

"It's perfect." He took her hand. "Let's go."

The woman from USCIS—who had given him her card and introduced herself as Tracy Lee—was sitting on the couch where he'd left her. Her expression when she spotted Irina reminded him of those old MasterCard commercials: "Marriage license: fifty-five dollars. Wedding dress: four thousand dollars. The look on the Immigration lady's face when she realizes you really are married? Priceless."

"Hello." The woman rose and held out her hand. "Irina, I'm Tracy. Tracy Lee."

Irina took the woman's hand. "Nice to meet you, Tracy." She sounded like royalty, so proud and gracious—and not in the least intimidated. It was a damn good act, considering that a minute or two before, back in the bedroom, she'd been openly terrified. "You are up early."

"Yes. I thought I would drop by, and see…how you're doing."

"I am doing well, thank you. *Very* well—and happy to be safe here in America with my husband." Irina sent him a warm glance. "A good man is so hard to find."

They both turned and looked at him. Bare-chested in his oldest pair of sweats, he tried to look modest and unassuming—and good as well.

"Uh, yes," Tracy agreed. She seemed slightly at a loss. He got the feeling that she'd shown up at their door expecting something completely different than what she was getting.

"Please." Irina gestured at the couch. Tracy sat back down again. "Would you like coffee? It will only take a few minutes to prepare."

Tracy cleared her throat. "No. Really. That won't be necessary."

Irina sat down, too. "All right, then." She glanced at Caleb, hovering above her, and tipped her head toward the empty chair.

He got the message and dropped into it. "Tracy, what can my wife and I do for you?"

Tracy straightened the hem of her blazer. "Hm. Well. As you may have been told, on occasion—rare occasion—we visit the homes of immigrants who claim resident status through marriage to a U.S. citizen. It's—" she waved a hand "—only a formality."

He doubted that. And she hadn't answered his question. So he tried again. "And how exactly can we help you?"

Tracy shifted on the couch cushion and her lips tightened a fraction. "As a matter of fact, you already have." He took that to mean she'd gotten the message he'd been hoping she would get. She went on. "The main reason for my coming here is to see that you and Irina are sharing the same residence. Given that, I am here to gain assurance that you are living as a couple, rather than merely as co-occupants."

"Well, we are—on both counts."

"Yes. I can see that." Tracy stood again. Apparently, she was ending the interview before it had really begun. And she had started to seem a little ticked off, hadn't she? Why? She added, "It's more than apparent that there is no attempt to perpetrate a sham marriage here."

"Oh, no," said Irina. "We marry for love and we are very happy together." She reached across the distance between their two chairs. He met her in the middle, clasping her hand. They stood at the same time.

Tracy said, "Your paperwork is in order, and now that I'm here in your home and can see for myself, I'm more than satisfied that everything is aboveboard."

Caleb had to ask, "So…what made you think it wasn't?"

Irina sent him a quick, freaked-out glance, one that warned him to leave it alone. He squeezed her fingers to reassure her.

Fortunately, Tracy Lee just happened to glance down at her sensible pumps at the crucial moment, so she didn't see the flash of panic in Irina's eyes. Irina had a split second to compose her expression before the case-worker looked up again.

"Not to worry," Tracy said briskly. "I can see that your marriage is authentic, and I intend to make that very clear in my report." She settled her big purse over her shoulder. "There's no need to take up any more of your time. I'll be going now." She slid out from behind the coffee table and headed for the foyer. Caleb and Irina followed.

In the entry, Irina slipped ahead to open the door. "Have a nice day, Tracy."

Caleb tried again. "Did someone tell you that we weren't really married?"

"Caleb," Irina said softly, with a smoldering glance that made him want to grab her and haul her back to bed. "Who could possibly think that?"

Tracy looked more than a little relieved that Irina had answered his question for her. "Irina is right," she said. "You're obviously very happy together. Congratulations, to both of you." And she hustled on out to the porch and down the steps.

Before she made it all the way out to her midsize sedan that was the same dark blue color as her blazer, Irina shut the door and sagged against it. "Caleb." She didn't sound happy.

He tried to look innocent. "Yeah?"

"You scared me to death." She shook her head. "Asking her questions like that. Is not smart to ask questions. *They* are the ones who ask the questions."

"Irina, it's okay. This is America, remember? We have rights here—and one of them is the right to try and find out what the hell's going on when a situation stinks."

"I told you they sometimes do surprise home visits."

"And I told you they don't have the personnel or the funding to start dropping in on every immigrant who happens to marry a U.S. citizen. They only do that when they're suspicious. And we gave them nothing to be suspicious about. Which means somebody else did."

She wasn't listening. "I almost had a heart attack, you know that?" She pressed a hand to her chest. "My heart was beating so hard, I thought it would jump right out of my throat."

"Irina, hey." He could see that she really was upset, so he spoke more gently. "It's okay, I promise you. It worked out just great. That woman was not the least suspicious."

"I know she wasn't. But you scared me so bad, I nearly gave myself away."

"You were great. Seriously. You gave nothing away. And even if you had, so what?"

She made a small, frustrated noise. "So what? You know so what. She might suspect the truth."

"How? We live in the same house, sleep in the same bed. And we've told everyone we're in love. We're the only ones who know that we got married so you could stay in the country. And anybody who wasn't blind could guess what we were doing when Tracy Lee knocked on the door." He dared to take a step closer to her. "Come on. It's all right. It's all good. You have to realize that."

A ragged sigh escaped her. "It is only…I was so frightened that something would go wrong."

"But it's fine. You can see that, right? Tracy Lee is now absolutely convinced we're for real. And that's what she'll write in her report. The visit worked in our favor." He moved in closer. "I promise you." With a gentle hand, he smoothed her tangled hair. "You were terrific. Tracy absolutely believes that we're a couple."

"Oh, Caleb...." She swayed against him.

He gathered her close and kissed her hair, her cheek, her temple. And then he framed her face between his hands and took her mouth. She gave no resistance, only parted her lips for him with a small, hungry moan.

Damn, but it was something, to be able to touch her at last—to feel her arms around him. To know she not only accepted his touch; she wanted it, invited it.

He took her hand and led her back to the bedroom. Once there, he untied the robe and eased it off her shoulders. She gazed at him steadily, those big dark eyes trusting and soft with desire, as he guided her back onto the tangled sheets of their bed.

It was after ten when they got up and went to the kitchen for breakfast.

"You are very late for work." She faked a scolding tone as she sliced a banana onto her high-fiber granola.

"Yes, I am." He brought her the thick, dark espresso that she liked.

"You do not sound especially regretful." She tipped her head back to look at him.

He set the small cup down. "Well, after all, it's your fault."

"For shame. Blaming your innocent wife."

"It's true." His kissed her, a light, playful kiss, before

he returned to the counter to get some coffee for himself. "I have no remorse. None."

She finished slicing her banana.

He poured his own plain black coffee and sat down across from her. "I'd really like to know who's been talking to the Immigration people about us."

She sent him a sharp look. "You are like a cat."

"Oh, really?"

"Um-hmm. Curiosity is bound to kill you."

He sipped his coffee and regarded the bowl of cereal in front of him. She'd been making him eat high-fiber cereal at least four mornings a week for two damn years. He didn't like it any more now than he ever had. "At one time, I would have known it had to be my father. But he really has changed in the past few months." He shook his head. "Uh-uh. Not my dad."

"Caleb. Eat your cereal."

He set down his coffee mug. "I'm guessing it's Emily."

Now he had her attention. "Emily Gray? Why? Has she said something to you?"

He realized about then that he never had told Irina about the confrontation with Emily on the day they got back from Vegas.

Irina cleared her throat. "Caleb?"

"Uh, yeah?"

"What happened with Emily?"

He aligned his spoon so that it was precisely parallel to his cereal bowl. "We, um, well, Emily and I had a brief conversation right after you and I got married."

She sat back in her chair and looked at him sideways. "You never told me about any conversation with Emily."

He straightened his shoulders. "One conversation, Irina. It lasted maybe two minutes—is that even long enough to be considered a conversation? It was more like an exchange. One exchange. After that, she avoids me and I return the favor."

"What happened in this *exchange?*"

Crap. "You know, the usual…." He grabbed the spoon. Suddenly he was only too happy to shove some high-fiber cereal into his mouth.

She wouldn't let it go. "Tell me what she said, please."

He made a face and chewed dramatically.

She simply waited, watching him patiently, until he swallowed. "Okay. Now. Your mouth is empty and you can tell me what happened, what was said between you and Emily in that one, so-short *exchange.*"

He blew out a breath. "Fine. Sure. She was angry and embarrassed. She said that at least I could have dumped her to her face."

Irina shrugged. "Well. She was right."

"Thanks," he said drily. "I really appreciate your support."

"What else?"

"There was something about how I would be sorry, how she would get even."

"*'Something'?*"

"Okay, okay. For your information, I know I was a complete jerk in the way I handled ending it with her."

"Which was not to handle it at all."

"Thank you for the input. Mind if I continue?" At her regal nod, he went on, "I said if she wanted an apology, she had it. And she said she wanted a lot more than an apology. I asked her what she meant by that. And she said I should just wait, that I'd see. And then she said, 'Give my best to your bride' in a really bitchy tone, and she left."

Irina took her espresso by its tiny little handle and sipped. When she set it down, she said gently, "You should have told me."

He admitted, "Yeah. I know. I didn't want to upset you. And then, when nothing else happened with her, I just let it go. I haven't said a word to her since the day we came back from Vegas, I swear it."

She scooted closer to the table and sipped her espresso again. "It does sound as if she planned to take revenge."

"No kidding." He had to know. "You mad at me?"

She shook her head.

"Whew."

"So, will you talk to Emily?"

"I was thinking about it. But then, what good will that do? If she tipped off the Immigration people about us, she's certainly not going to admit it." He sipped his coffee. "Uh-uh. I think I'm just going to have to talk to Ash, which I should have done a month ago." Ash was CEO. Emily answered to him.

"Talk to Ash about what?" Like she didn't know.

Patiently, he laid it out there in plain English. "About how Emily has got to go."

A silence. Irina stared at him, her soft mouth slightly open. Then she pinched it shut. "You will have her fired?"

"Hell, yes."

"But Caleb. You do not even know for certain that she is the one who called Immigration about us."

"If she didn't, who did?"

"I don't know. How would I know?"

"That's right. And we'll never know for certain. But Emily is the only one I can think of who threatened me with payback because I married you, the only one who would even consider dropping a tip with Immigration."

"Because you hurt her. You humiliated her."

"Come on, Irina. Whose side are you on here?"

"The side of doing right. You plan to fire a woman, to take away her livelihood, when you have no proof of her wrongdoing. It is not right. It is…beneath you, Caleb."

He swore under his breath.

She looked at him levelly. "Saying bad words is not making you right."

"Well, what the hell do you want me to do, then?"

She considered the question. And then she set her napkin on the table, pushed her chair back and circled around to his side of the table. He watched her come, not sure what she was up to.

When she moved behind his chair, he craned his head back to keep an eye on her. "What are you up to?"

She put her hands on his shoulders. And rubbed. It felt good. Too good. And then she bent close. He got a whiff of her scent—soap, shampoo and woman. All woman. She pressed her cheek to his. "Caleb…"

"What?" He growled the word.

She caught his chin and turned his head again until she could reach his mouth. She kissed him, a soft, wet, long kiss, a kiss that had him seriously considering scooping her up and carrying her back to the bedroom. Again.

When she finished driving him nuts with that mouth of hers, she straightened and gave him her sweetest, most innocent smile. He pushed back his chair, enough that he could pull her down onto his lap. She wrapped her arms around his neck and kissed his cheek.

"Okay," he said huskily. "What was that about?"

Her smile was all innocence. Looking at her then, he would never have believed the terrible things she had endured in her short life. She looked pure and untouched as a princess in a fairy tale.

"You are a wonderful, kind, loving man." She fluttered those dark, thick eyelashes at him.

"Thanks. And go ahead. Whatever it is, hit me with it."

She fiddled with his shirt collar, smoothing it the way a wife would do. "We must consider that if Emily did call Immigration about us, she did us a favor."

"What the hell?"

"Think on it. If not for whoever called them about us, Tracy Lee would never have come to the house. She would never have seen us together, never have been made so certain that we are truly married."

"Maybe so. But Emily still set out to mess us over."

She put an index finger to his lips. "You do not know that. There is no way for you to know."

He caught her hand and pressed it, palm flat, to his chest. "True. I need to find out."

"Caleb, please. Do not call Immigration. Do not get them all—how do you say it?—stirred up. Do not get their attention. Attention from them is the last thing we need."

"You're severely limiting my options here, you realize that?"

"I am serious. Please honor my wishes in this. Do not call them. It is too dangerous."

"You worry too much. You really do. We're about as married as it gets—for the time being, anyway. And that's all they're ever going to know."

She said something low in Argovian.

"Say it English," he instructed.

"I will be happy to. 'If you poke at a nest of wasps, you are bound to get stung.'"

"I would hardly call USCIS a nest of wasps."

"Of course you say that. You are a citizen. To you, they are only doing their job. To me...well, I do not want to give them any reason to reconsider my status as the wife of an American. Caleb. Please. Do not contact them."

He couldn't stand to see the worry in her eyes. "Look. If it bothers you that much..."

"It does."

"All right then. I'll leave them alone."

"Thank you." She tucked herself tight against him. "Oh, thank you...." And then she pulled back to look at him. "And what about Emily?"

"I'll talk to her, okay? I'll try to find out for certain if she was the one, try to get a read on her."

"But you said that it would do you no good to talk to her."

"Well, you've just eliminated the option of trying to get anything out of Immigration. I can ask around the office, see if anyone heard her talking about doing a number on us. And then I'll confront her, see what she says."

"Maybe you only see what you want to see. That is not fair to poor Emily."

"Oh, now she's *poor* Emily, is she?"

"Do not fire her, Caleb. It is not right."

"Let's just take this one step at a time, okay? I'll ask around and I'll talk with her. Then I'll figure out what to do next."

Chapter Nine

On further consideration, Caleb decided to forget asking around the office.

He had to get real. No one was going to rat out Emily. She was generally well liked and respected. And if one of his brothers had heard something, they would have taken him aside and told him already.

Plus, if Emily had decided to screw him over by tipping off Immigration that his marriage was a fake, she would hardly have shot herself in the foot by flapping her mouth about it. Emily was a very capable, intelligent woman. She would get her revenge and keep quiet about it.

So that left having a little private talk with her.

He got to BravoCorp at five after eleven and went directly to her windowless office on the second floor.

She was there at her desk, busy at the computer, her slim fingers flying over the keys.

She glanced up when he loomed in the doorway. Her mouth tightened and her blue eyes grew wary. Was there guilt in her expression?

He couldn't tell. "I need a word with you."

She studied him for a long count of five. Then she shrugged. "Sure." He stepped into the cramped room and shut the door. She didn't offer him the single guest chair and he didn't take it. "What do you need?" She grabbed a pen, leaned back in her chair, and braced her elbows on the chair arms, ready for battle.

He stood right up against the desk, giving her its solid bulk between them, but nothing else. "Been talking to U.S. Citizenship and Immigration Services lately?"

She looked him square in the eye as, with an angry thumb, she clicked the pen three times in rapid succession. "What *are* you talking about?"

"Somebody sent the Immigration people to my house this morning to terrorize my wife."

She glanced away. But only for an instant. Then she was staring at him, unblinking, again. "Are you accusing me?"

"No, I'm asking you. Did you contact Immigration about my marriage to Irina?"

She licked her lips. It was mistake. A definite tell. He knew at that moment that she was the one. "Of course not," she said.

He felt better then, at least marginally. He pulled back the extra chair and dropped into it. "I should have you fired."

"If you do, I'll sue your ass off."

"Good luck with that."

He thought about Irina, about what she would say if he told her he'd had Emily fired because she'd licked her lips when he'd asked her the big question. Irina would be outraged. She'd start saying mean things in Argovian.

Emily tossed the pen on the desk blotter and pulled her chair in close again. "Listen. I don't want to make any trouble, okay? I just want to do my job—which you know damn well I am very good at."

"You mean you don't want to make any *more* trouble."

She leaned toward him, resting her arms on the blotter, folding her hands, but not looking at him, showing him the vulnerable crown of her head. "You treated me like crap, you know?"

He found he couldn't argue with that, since it was the truth. "That doesn't give you the right to carry lies to USCIS."

She slanted him a fierce glance. "Lies? Oh, please. You're still trying to convince me that you married your strange little immigrant housekeeper because you love her?"

"I'm not trying to convince you of anything. I'm trying to decide if I'm willing to call it even at this point, and accept your word that you've had your revenge, and now we can both just go on with our lives—or not."

She sat up straighter. "You're serious."

"Yeah."

"We can just…let it end here?"

"Yeah."

"I keep my job."

"That's what I said."

She pinned him with that cool blue gaze. "I'm not admitting to anything."

"It's not the confession that matters. It's that you quit with the payback scenarios. And also, well, you might think it over. Maybe you'd be happier working somewhere else."

Her lip curled in a sneer. "Now you're trying to chase me away."

"Emily. It was just a thought."

"I like my job."

"Fine. Keep it, then. And stop trying to screw up my life."

She jerked up a hand, palm out, like a witness taking an oath. "Okay. I swear. I'll never do anything against you or your wife—not that I ever did."

He rose. "Fair enough, then."

She nodded. He saw relief in her eyes. Maybe she'd been feeling a little ashamed of what she'd done. But ashamed or not, he believed that she was through planning reprisals against him. That was the main thing.

And Irina would be happy to learn that "poor Emily" still had her job.

After Caleb went to work, Irina drove up to the Lazy H to have lunch with Mary.

She wore one of her new blouses, one that showed her scars. And she was just a little nervous at having Mary see them for the first time—nervous and unsure how much to tell her friend.

But it was a funny thing about Mary. She was so easy

to talk to. And now that Irina had told everything once, to Caleb, it ended up being such a natural thing to tell Mary all of it—about Neven and the car bomb and even the man who had raped her in the hospital.

Mary cried. And Irina cried. They hugged each other so tight.

Later, Irina held Ginny as they discussed the next section of the Bravo Family Cookbook, which was to showcase Mercy and Elena and their mom, Luz. They would be cooking green chile burritos in the big kitchen at the family ranch, Bravo Ridge.

Mary said, "We're set for Saturday, at eleven a.m. Zoe's agreed to take the pictures. Gabe's coming. And Luke will be there. What about Caleb?"

"I think so. I'll ask him."

"Great. There's a reward, you know?"

Irina guessed, "When they are through with the cooking, we eat."

"That's right. And Mercy will have the beer on ice." She chuckled. "Be sure to tell Caleb there will be beer." They shared a grin.

Ginny, still in Irina's lap, poked at Irina's chest with a little finger. "Owie." She gazed up at Irina with such sweet affection. "Tiss, tiss." She puckered up her little mouth.

Mary said, softly, "She wants to kiss it all better."

And then Ginny kissed the tip of her tiny finger and pressed it to one of the white, puckered scars.

"Oh, thank you. I feel so much better!" Irina hugged her close as Ginny giggled in delight.

A little later, while Ginny napped, Mary said how terrific it was that Irina had started wearing brighter colors, that she no longer felt she had to cover herself from head to toe.

"It is a little strange," Irina confessed, "the way people stare when they first see the scars."

Mary suggested, "You could look into plastic surgery, if it really bothers you."

Irina shook her head. "I don't think so. Not for me. I find I am growing proud of my scars. They tell a story, *my* story. And when people first see them, well, there is maybe a moment of awkwardness. But it quickly passes. Is this making sense?"

"Absolute sense." Mary grabbed her and hugged her.

When Mary let go, Irina confessed, "For three years, after what happened in the hospital, I hate to be touched. But now I am finding I like it very much. Especially the hugging."

So Mary, laughing, hugged her again.

When Irina got home from the Lazy H, she went right to the kitchen to start dinner.

The doorbell rang just as she stuck the thermometer probe into the chicken. She put the chicken in the oven, washed her hands and hurried to answer as the doorbell rang again.

A woman she had never seen before was waiting on the front porch. A woman who might have been any age, from thirty-five to fifty. Petite, with short brown hair and a determined look in her dark eyes, the woman said, "Hello, I'm Daisy English. And you must be Irina."

Irina frowned. "Yes. I am Irina. Irina Bravo."

"Golacek," the woman corrected her. "You are Irina Maria Sekelez Golacek."

The woman's words shocked her. Irina knew the name Golacek. In Argovia, every last one of the Golaceks had been hunted down and killed. Was the woman from Immigration?

Irina didn't think so. People from Immigration made a point to identify themselves as such.

"No, I'm sorry," Irina said firmly. "You have the wrong person. I told you, my name is Irina Bravo."

The small, determined woman would not be swayed. "But you were born a Golacek."

"No. What you say is incorrect." Instinctively, Irina raised a hand and wrapped her fingers around the gold locket at her neck. She was more than aware that she should tell the woman to go away and then shut the door.

But she didn't. She stood rooted to the spot, mesmerized by the small woman's sharp, knowing gaze, by her very insistence that the impossible was true.

"Irina, please. Let me just show you—"

"No," Irina insisted. "Before I am married, my last name is Lukovic."

"I'm sure that's what you were told."

"What are you saying, what I am told? It is my *name*."

Was there pity now, in that sharp little face? "I'm sorry. But it's not your real name."

Irina felt driven, for no logical reason, to explain her own identity to this total stranger. "My father's name was Teo Lukovic and my mother was called Dafina. After my father died, my mother went to my father's brother, my uncle Vasili and his wife, my aunt Tòrja. I was born in their house and I lived with my uncle and his family until I am ten, when—"

"Wait." Daisy cut her off with an impatient wave of her small hand. From a side pocket of her laptop case, she removed a piece of paper. She held it up so that Irina could see the pair of images printed on it. They were enlarged copies of the two tiny portraits she held clasped tight in her sweating hand.

"Your parents," said Daisy. "Crown Prince Laslo Teodore Lekalovic Golacek and his bride, the Baroness Dafina Maria Sekelez, whom your father met in exile."

Chapter Ten

Caleb let himself in the front door at a little after six. He dropped his briefcase on the long table in the entry hall and followed his nose to the kitchen, where Irina was taking a nicely browned chicken out of the oven.

Funny how lately, just the sight of her pleased him. All that time she had worked for him, and he'd never realized how gorgeous she was. But now, in her fitted red blouse and snug jeans, with her shining, straight dark hair falling loose below her shoulders, she took his breath away.

She set the pan on the cooktop and used a pot holder to remove the long temperature probe. "Hello, Caleb." She sent him a smile over her shoulder, that tempting dimple appearing in her cheek and the diamond hoop earrings he'd bought her a couple of weeks ago sparkling as they moved against the smooth white skin of her neck. "The chicken must cool a bit. And the potatoes are almost done...."

He came up behind her, smoothed her hair to the side and kissed her neck. "You smell good—as good as that chicken."

"Are you hungry?"

"I am. And not only for dinner."

She laughed. "Move out of my way, or I will poke you with my probe."

"Whoa. Scary." He put up both hands and stepped aside.

She carried the probe to the sink to wash it. "Have an appetizer." A tray of them waited on the central island. "And will you open some wine?"

He grabbed an appetizer and went to the wine cabinet to choose a nice white. Once he had the wine opened, he poured them each a glass.

"Thank you." She took the glass he offered, sipped and then set it on the counter as she began putting together a salad—spinach and strawberries, a favorite of his. He sat at the island and watched her as she finished preparing the meal.

Strange that she hadn't asked him what happened with Emily. He'd expected her to be on him about that the minute he walked in the door.

In fact, she seemed a little preoccupied.

But about what? "Everything...okay?"

"Of course." She didn't look up. Maybe because she was slicing strawberries with a sharp little knife and needed to keep her eyes on the job. "Is fine."

He finished a second appetizer. "So what did you do this afternoon?"

She sent him a bright smile. Maybe she wasn't pre-occupied after all. Just willing to wait until he volunteered the information about his ex-girlfriend.

"I went to Mary's." She rinsed and dried her hands. "We worked on the cookbook—which is reminding me. Will you go with me to Bravo Ridge Saturday? Elena, Mercy and their mother are cooking green chile burritos. After the cooking, we eat. Gabe and Luke will be there, too. Mary says to tell you there will be beer."

"I'm there."

"Mary said that would convince you."

"Men are easy. A beer, a good woman. It's all we need."

"What about your fast cars and football?"

"Yeah, well. Those, too."

"Carve the chicken?"

He got his favorite knife and went to work. Five minutes later, they sat down to eat.

Really, it was kind of surprising that she still hadn't asked about Emily. It wasn't like her. She had a mind like a steel trap. Once she got something in there, it didn't get away.

But somehow, the issue of Emily had managed to escape.

He waited until they were clearing off the table before he said offhandedly, "I had that talk with Emily Gray today."

She gasped—and set down the platter she was carrying. "Emily. I do not believe it. I forgot all about poor Emily."

"Not so poor, believe me. Emily makes a very nice salary, and she can definitely take care of herself."

Irina was shaking her head. "I don't know how I could have forgotten about Emily. It's only that I…" She let the sentence trail away unfinished. "Never mind."

He took her hand and pulled her closer. "Something wrong?"

"No. Nothing."

He tipped up her chin. "Sure?"

She laid her palm along the side of his face. "I am sure." And then she kissed him—a long kiss, slow and deep.

When she finally pulled away, he said, "Okay. Now *I've* forgotten all about poor Emily."

Looking thoughtful, she studied his face. "I am thinking that since you are teasing me about her, you have not fired her. That you have…worked out your problem with her."

He guided a thick swatch of coffee-colored hair back over her shoulder and touched her earring so it swayed against her neck. "I have no problem with Emily. Not anymore."

"But what *happened?*"

"You're right. She's keeping her job."

Her smile bloomed wide. "I am so glad."

He pulled her closer. "You amaze me, you know that? The woman tries to mess you over royally, and you're just happy nothing bad is going to happen to her."

Irina's big eyes got bigger than ever. "She confessed that she went to Immigration about us?"

"She confessed nothing. But I know she did it."

"How?"

"Take my word, will you? I just know."

"But—"

"Shh." He brushed his thumb across her lips. "It doesn't matter anyway, because it all worked out."

She frowned, puzzled. "In what way did it all work out?"

"We reached an understanding. Emily's agreed to leave us alone from now on. And she wants her job. So, as long as she keeps her agreement she can keep working for BravoCorp, too. Everybody wins."

She beamed. "Well. So. Is all good."

"Looks that way. You sure you don't want to talk about whatever's bothering you?"

"How can anything bother me when you hold me in your arms?"

"Good answer." He lowered his mouth to claim her sweet lips again.

But something *was* bothering her. Caleb sensed it. He didn't push her about it, though. He figured that she would tell him when she was ready.

The week went by. A good week. A *great* week. They made love every night. And each time was better than the time before. Her fear and shyness fell away, and beneath them he found an eager and adventurous lover, one he couldn't wait to come home to when the workday was through.

Saturday, they went out to the ranch in the late morning and stayed until after ten that night. There was plenty of beer, as promised, and Luz Cabrera's amazing burritos. Caleb hung with his brothers and watched his green-card wife laughing and chattering with the other women.

She was smart and brave, and she had a great sense of humor. They had an excellent sex life. Who knew that was going to happen? And she could cook. And on top of all of that, she was beautiful.

Sometimes he almost forgot that they weren't really married—or, rather, that their marriage had an expiration date. Sometimes he found himself thinking that maybe they could just go on like this, stay married, even after the two years were up.

But then he would remind himself that she had her whole life ahead of her. With permanent residence and the freedom that brought with it, she might want to get out on her own for a while. She might want a college degree, so she could pursue a career. She might *not* want to be tied down to a husband, now that the world was opening up for her.

And, come on—he wasn't exactly the settling-down type. He'd always liked to keep his options wide-open. He hardly understood himself lately, to be so over-the-moon about his temporary wife.

After going in circles, deciding how it would end up with them, and then deciding it would work out completely different, he would shake himself and wonder what the hell was wrong with him. Two years was a long time. Why worry about the end, when they'd barely gotten started?

It was completely unlike him to get all tied up in knots over things that hadn't happened yet. He kept having to remind himself that he seriously needed to chill.

* * *

It had rained on and off all day, but the sky was clear and thick with stars when they got home from the ranch that night. At the door, he scooped her up in his arms and carried her into the bedroom.

He let her slide to the floor by the bed, kissing her as he lowered her down. They undressed and went into the bathroom, where they filled the big tub and got in together.

It was a long, relaxing bath. And satisfying on more than one level.

Later, in bed, they made love again. Slowly. He looked up at her face above him as she rode him. "Beautiful," he whispered, reaching up to take her breasts in his hands.

She let her head fall back and cried out as her climax shuddered through her. He followed her lead, surging up into her, spilling his release as her body milked the last drop from his.

They lay holding hands afterward, the way they used to do before they became lovers. It was a kind of a habit with them now. And a nice one, he thought.

She whispered, "It was good at the ranch. I laughed so much."

"Must have been the beer."

She clucked her tongue at his teasing. "It was not the beer. It was…the company. It is good to have family around you."

Under the covers, he rubbed his thumb over the back of her hand, to let her know he understood what she was telling him.

"Without my Aunt Tòrja and Uncle Vasili…I cannot imagine what my life would have been. Without them to take care of me, what would have happened to me when my mother died? And Victor. He was all I had, my blood, my family, for so long. No one, ever, can take them away from me. Victor and my aunt and uncle are…who I am. The foundation of my life, you know?"

Was she crying? How had that happened? A few seconds ago she had been talking about all the fun she'd had at the ranch.

"Hey…" With his free hand he reached for her. She turned her face away from his touch—but not before he felt the wetness of her tears. "Irina, what is it? What's wrong?"

She eased her fingers from his grip and turned on her side, facing the other way. "Is nothing." Muffled. Miserable. "Go to sleep."

He was getting a little fed up with this crap. It worried him, made him feel powerless. "You're lying."

She didn't deny it. "Please, Caleb. I cannot speak of it. Not now."

When, then? The question was right there, begging to be asked. But he didn't ask it. He held it in.

Since he had no clue what was bothering her, how could he figure out what to do about it? It hurt that she turned away from him. And that—the fact that it hurt—freaked him out.

Which made him wonder if things were getting a little out of hand between them. What kind of a wuss was he turning into? He'd always been a guy who took life as it came. He never let himself become tied up in knots because his current girlfriend got emotional over something she wouldn't even talk to him about. He'd always kind of figured that if a woman wanted him to help out, she at least had to admit to what the hell her problem was.

But with Irina, well, he did care if she was hurting, if she was upset. And he found that disturbing. He wasn't in this to become some guy he didn't even know anymore.

Yeah, a little change was good.

He could stand to become a little more…sensitive. To develop some patience. But he was starting to wonder if he was carrying this sensitivity thing too far, getting into this too damn deep.

Then again, she *was* his wife—for now, if not forever. And she didn't play games. So, if something was eating at her, it was probably something serious. Something serious that she wasn't letting him help her with.

He hated that.

But she'd asked him to back off. And he would. He wasn't like his dad or Gabe, both of whom had an inbred need to control outcomes, to fix anything that they considered broken. Part of being a killer salesman was knowing when to wait. There was an art to closing a sale—and timing was a major part of it.

He turned on his other side and closed his eyes. Eventually, sleep settled over him.

When he woke again, it was still dark. He turned over and saw that Irina's side of the bed was empty.

But she hadn't gone far. She'd pulled on her terry-cloth robe and gone to sit in the easy chair by the window.

He sat up. "Irina?"

"It is okay." Her voice was low, soothing. It didn't sound like she was crying. "I am here. I am…thinking."

He watched her rise from the chair. She came to him, a shadowed shape in the darkness. Dropping the robe from her shoulders at the side of the bed, she lifted an arm to toss it back across the chair. He held up the covers and she slipped beneath them, turning to tuck herself against him, drawing his arm across her waist, so that he held her close from behind.

"You were right," she whispered on a sigh. "I lied. There is much that is bothering me."

He smoothed her hair away from her face. "Tell me. All of it."

"Oh, Caleb…"

"Come on. You'll feel better once you get it out there."

A small, unhappy sound escaped her. And then, finally, she confessed, "Last Monday, while you were at work, a woman came to the door, a reporter. She said her name was Daisy English. And that my name was not as I had always believed it to be."

Chapter Eleven

"**W**hat the hell?" said Caleb.

Irina snuggled in closer. "You say it rightly. 'What the hell?'" She let a moment elapse before she continued. "At first I stood in the doorway and argued with her, telling her I was Irina Bravo, that I had been born Irina Lukovic, listing my mother's name and my father's, my aunt's and uncle's."

He wanted to tell her that she should have shut the door in the woman's face, that there was no sense in arguing with a nut job. But Irina already knew that. If she'd continued confronting this Daisy English, she must have had a reason.

Irina said, "And then Daisy took a picture from her laptop case. She held it up for me to see. It was an enlarged copy of the pictures in my locket, my mother and father."

"No."

"Yes. And she tells me they are not Dafina and Teo Lukovic, as I always believe. They are Crown Prince Laslo Golacek and his bride, Princess Dafina."

"Whoa."

"That is what I think: *whoa.* And I insist again that it is impossible, that I know who I am and I am not this Irina Golacek. I am no lost princess. I am an ordinary woman."

Caleb suggested, gently, "The *G* on the locket…"

"Yes. I know. Oh, Caleb. I know."

"And your mother's name is the same. But you said your father was Teo."

"For Teodore, Daisy says, which was Prince Laslo's middle name."

"So about then, you invited Daisy in?"

"I did. She told me she is writing a story, for *Vanity Fair.*"

"Did she give you a card?"

"Yes." She stirred. "I'll get it…."

"Later." He pulled her close to him again. "You think she was being straight with you?"

"I wondered at first. But so much of what she said fits with what I already know. She knew my mother's middle name, Maria. And her maiden name, Sekelez. And after she went away, I checked on the Internet."

"And?"

"Daisy English writes for a Canadian newspaper, *The Globe and Standard.* And she has also contributed to many magazines, including *Vanity Fair.* I read some of her articles. They are very…sensational. She likes to write about rich people and murder and royalty."

"But are you sure the Daisy English you found on Google is the same woman who came to the door?"

"I checked for images and found them. She is the one."

"Wow."

"Yes. What is it they say? OMG!"

He hugged her tighter, pressed his lips to her bare shoulder. "So—what next?"

"There is so much to think about."

"I hear you."

"There is money, Daisy says. In Swiss bank accounts. A lot of money, for the royal heir, the last surviving member of the Golacek line. All I must do is prove beyond doubt that I am the baby that Princess Dafina was carrying when she disappeared."

"How could you prove that?"

"A DNA test."

Now that made no sense at all. "But don't they need DNA from the parents to do that?"

She moved her head against the pillow in a nod. "And they have that."

"How? Your parents are dead—and the prince and princess are presumably dead, right?"

"Yes. But they know where Princess Dafina was buried, in a Terejevo graveyard not far from where my aunt and uncle…" Her voice trailed off and then she corrected herself. "Not far from the Lukovic home."

"Who knows that? And how?"

"The Argovian government. They knew that the Lukovics, loyalists to the crown, took the princess in when she came to them for help, and were able to provide her with a new identity as a member of the Lukovic family."

He was putting it all together. "So…when the soldiers came and killed Victor's parents…"

"Yes. Tòrja and Vasili *were* loyalists after all. Only later, years after Tòrja and Vasili were murdered, did someone look through the old records and learn that Vasili Lukovic was an only child."

"An only child who had his supposed sister-in-law living with him and his family for five years."

"Until she died, yes."

This was way more than enough proof, as far as Caleb was concerned. "So…your mother and the princess are one and the same."

"It would seem so. They have taken samples from her body. And from Prince Laslo's body, too."

"How did your father—I mean, the prince—how did he die?"

"He was detained and executed as they tried to re-enter the country."

"He and the princess returned to Argovia together, after living in exile?"

"Um-hmm. When he was young, Prince Laslo was sent to live in Spain, to keep him safe. He met the Baroness Sekelez, also in exile, there in Spain. They fell in love, married and, as the story has it, she became pregnant."

"And then he decided to take her back to Argovia?"

"That is right."

"Why would he do that, bring his wife and unborn baby to a place where they would be in danger?"

She turned over so she was facing him and he rolled to his back, easing an arm beneath her so he could gather her close again. "Because he believed he had to," she whispered, her breath warm against the hollow of his throat. "By the old laws, kings of Argovia must be born on Argovian soil."

"You're saying they returned to protect their child's birthright?"

"Yes. And the prince was caught and executed. They burned his body, but not...well. And there were witnesses who knew where the remains were buried. They took DNA samples from those remains."

"You're telling me that Daisy English managed to convince the Argovian authorities to let her dig up two bodies to get DNA from them?"

"No." She kissed his shoulder. "I am not telling you that."

"Well, then...?"

She sighed. "Since I was a small girl, there were always rumors that the murdered Prince Laslo's wife lived to deliver her child, and that the child was saved, somehow, and raised in hiding by loyalists to the crown. Others—young men and women—have come forward, claiming to be the missing Golacek heir. And in recent years, things have changed in my country, Daisy says. The new president insists he feels no threat from the long-deposed Golaceks. He claims he wants to let bygones be bygones and has allowed the samples to be taken from the bodies for the DNA tests to be performed. So far, the samples have been used to disprove wrongful claims."

He touched her chin, guiding her face up for a quick kiss. "What does Daisy want out of this?"

"A story. *My* story. She says it would be very 'big' for her—and for *Vanity Fair*—to get the exclusive story of the lost Golacek princess. She says with pride that she has been working on this story for two years, that she is the one who discovered the Lukovic 'connection.'"

He couldn't hold back a laugh. "The Lukovic connection. It sounds like a novel. A thriller, for sure."

"Daisy thinks so, too. She told me that after the *Vanity Fair* exclusive, she will write a book as well."

"And what, exactly, *is* this Lukovic connection?"

"The Lukovics were loyal servants of the Golaceks while they ruled Argovia. When the Golaceks were deposed, the Lukovics went with them to their hideout in the Argovian mountains, where Prince Laslo was born. According to Daisy, the man I knew as my uncle, Vasili, was also born in the mountains while the Lukovics were in hiding with the royal family. My 'uncle' Vasili was Prince Laslo's sworn supporter and loyal retainer."

"So Daisy is certain that you're the one she's looking for."

"Yes. She says she wants to help me claim what is mine. She also wants me to sign a contract, a promise that I will make myself available to her, and her exclusively, so that she can write my story, as I lived it, once the DNA results can prove my rightful claim to the Golacek name and fortune."

He put his hand to her cheek and brought her face close to his. In the darkness, he couldn't read her expression. "And what do *you* want?"

A shudder went through her slim body. "Oh, Caleb. I want to run and hide. I want...it is the one thing I ever had, you know? My cousin, Victor. My Aunt Tòrja, my Uncle Vasili. Now I am to find out they are not mine, after all? I can hardly bear it." He heard the tears rising in her voice.

"Shh." He pressed his lips to her forehead, smoothed her hair again. "You know your aunt and uncle loved you. And Victor would die for you. No matter what happens, they are as much yours as they ever were."

"Oh, Caleb...I feel like the world is not the same, you know? That all is changed. I am not who I used to be. I am someone...all new. Someone else. A princess. I want to run away from that. I just want to be as I have always been. And yet, at the same time I want to know the truth. It is very confusing. It tears me apart." She caught his hand and brought it to her breast. "Here. In my heart."

He tightened his arm around her. "No matter what, you're still the same person. And you don't have to do anything you don't want to do."

She watched his face. Even through the shadows, he could see her eyes, so dark and deep. "I know. Yes. I know you're right, but..." She didn't finish. Maybe she didn't know how to.

He wanted to protect her. It was another new side of him—one he wasn't sure he was ready for. "Has this Daisy woman bothered you again since Monday afternoon?"

"She called once, on Thursday. She asked if I was ready yet to...make my move. I told her to leave me alone, that I would call her after I decide what I want to do. She was not happy."

"Too damn bad for her. And good for you. Don't let her railroad you."

"Railroad?"

"It means run over you, push you into doing something you don't want to do. Don't let her do that."

"I won't."

"Good."

"Caleb?"

"Yeah?"

"I don't want to tell her about what happened in the hospital. It is not her business, that a bad man raped me, how I suffered from that. I don't want that in a magazine, or in a book, for the world to see." She drew in a shaky breath. "It is not that I am ashamed. I am not. It is only…it is such a personal thing. A *hard* thing. Not a thing I want strangers to read about."

"So don't tell her. You're right. It's none of her damn business. It's got nothing to do with the story she wants from you."

"The only ones I ever told were you and Mary."

"Well, *I'm* sure as hell never telling her. Or anyone, unless you want me to. And you can count on Mary, too."

"I know that. I…sometimes I think that someday I might tell Victor, too. But only those I trust. Those I…care for in a deep way. But Daisy said I must tell her everything, all of it, my whole life, so that she can write down the truth as I have lived it."

"That's crap. Don't buy into it. She'll get one hell of a story if you agree to talk to her. Even without what happened in the hospital. And you don't have to tell her anything you don't want her to know."

"You speak truth."

"Yeah, well. Daisy English had better watch herself. It's not like you're all alone with no one looking out for you."

"Caleb?" Her voice was soft. Inviting.

He dipped his head, so his lips just touched hers. "When you say my name like that, all I can think about is getting you naked."

"I'm already naked."

"Yes, you are."

"Kiss me. Please."

He settled his mouth on hers and she opened for him.

"Make love with me," she whispered, her breath warm against his lips. "Make it so there is only you and me, just for now. For a little while. Please."

He kissed her again, more deeply than before, sweeping a hand down between them, finding wetness. And heat. He dipped a finger into the soft, moist silk of her. And then two.

She pulled him closer, moaned into his mouth.

A few moments later, when he eased himself between her thighs, she took him into her with a soft, welcoming sigh. He put his mouth against her throat, and then scraped his teeth where his lips had been.

She groaned and pressed herself tighter against him. "Yes, Caleb. Oh, yes. Like that."

He braced up on his hands so he could look down at her. In a sliver of moonlight that found its way in through the closed blinds, he could see her sweet face, those dark eyes that watched him, melting. Hot.

"Beautiful," he whispered.

And she reached up, lifting her hips at the same time to hold him inside, bracketing her legs around him and rolling, taking the top position.

He settled back against the pillows, letting her take him, enjoying the ride. She was right. Things were changing. She had come a long way from the watchful, wary housekeeper with her slow, tortured English, her unwillingness to be touched.

Who knew what a miracle had been waiting under all those ugly clothes?

She bent close, her hair falling against his face, her gold locket, warm with her body heat, sliding along his throat. He caught her mouth, speared his tongue inside. She moaned and pushed her hips against him. He wrapped his arms around her and rolled them both a second time.

On top again, he surged hard into her. She tightened her legs around him and took him, all of him. So deep. So good. So perfectly right.

When he came, she followed right after him, her hair like a cloud of midnight across the white pillows, her soft lips crying his name.

Over Sunday breakfast, she said she would call Daisy the next day.

He could think of one or two things she should handle beforehand. "You should give Victor a heads-up, don't you think?"

Those wide brown eyes got even wider. "You are so right. I must call him first. He must know of this before I go any farther with it."

"I'm with you on that. And for more reasons than one."

She frowned. "What reasons?"

"I'm guessing Daisy English will be wanting an interview with Victor, too. Not only did you and he escape together and live on the streets when his parents were killed, he made it possible for you to come to America."

"And he's a famous football player, too."

"He adds a whole new dimension to her 'Lukovic connection.' You'll want to be in agreement with him ahead of time about what part he's willing to play in this."

"I will call him right now." She started to rise. And then she lowered herself back into her chair. "I can't. It is too much to tell about on the phone."

Caleb ate another bite of his eggs Benedict. He really liked Sundays. Saturdays, too. She never made him eat high-fiber cereal on the weekends. "So fly up there. Tell him in person."

"Yes. That's good. I'll go to him. I'll tell him everything. I'll do it today."

"Hold on."

Halfway to her feet, she sank back into her chair for the second time. "What now?"

"I was hoping we could maybe get together with my dad and Gabe today."

"But why?"

"I'm thinking you need Gabe for this." Gabe, after all, was the family lawyer. "This is too big to deal with on your own. You should have representation."

She put her hands to her cheeks. "Representation? Is a little extreme, don't you think?"

"It may turn out that all Gabe will do is some over-seeing, looking for any red flags."

"What red flags?"

"If I knew, we wouldn't be asking Gabe."

"But I have not taken the DNA test yet. Maybe it will all turn out to be nothing, a mistake. Then we will have your family involved for no purpose."

He looked at her levelly. "Do you really believe that it will turn out to be a mistake?"

She dropped her gaze and let her hands fall to her lap. "No. No, I fear I do not." She lifted her head, squared her shoulders. "All right then. Gabe will be my lawyer." She slanted him a doubtful look. "And I am needing to tell your father because…?"

"See, it's like this. Yes, my dad can be a pain in the ass. But lately he's been acting downright reasonable with everyone in the family. He's a good man to have on your side. He's brilliant and cagey. And connected. He knows everybody who's anybody in the great state of Texas. It can't hurt to have him in on this. Between him and Gabe, they'll make sure nobody is taking advantage of you."

"Caleb. No one is going to take advantage of me."

"I didn't say they would succeed, but they'll sure as hell try. If the DNA test proves that you're who we think you are, you're not only a princess, but you've also got a fortune waiting for you in Switzerland. You'll have them standing in line to offer you whatever they're selling."

"This is not encouraging."

"Sure it is. In the end, if you've got a choice in the matter, it's better to be rich. You just need the right people watching your back."

* * *

They met that afternoon at the Lazy H—Caleb and Irina, Gabe and Davis. Mary was there. After all, it was her house. And Caleb's mom, Aleta, came with Davis.

Irina was glad for Mary's steady presence. And for Ginny, who climbed into Irina's lap and instantly fell asleep. Her warm little body felt so good. Comforting. And *real,* in a world suddenly turned upside down.

Caleb told the story for her, as she had asked him to do on the drive to Mary's ranch. If she hadn't been so worried over how it was all going to turn out, she might have smiled at the expressions on the Bravos' faces as Caleb explained it all.

When he finished, no one said anything for several seconds. Irina shifted Ginny so she was resting on her other arm. She wasn't surprised at the silence. Listening to Caleb, she had found herself thinking it was fantastical, really. Not the kind of thing that happens to an everyday person like her.

Davis spoke first—which didn't surprise her, either. "This Daisy English, you sure she's who she says she is?"

Irina kissed the top of Ginny's head. "Yes. I am sure."

Caleb said, "Irina did some research on her. She's for real."

Mary spoke up then. "I've read some of her work. She's pretty well known. You have to be good, to write for *Vanity Fair.*"

Davis had more to say. "I'm only talking about options here, Irina. It looks to me like you have plenty of them. You don't have to tell a reporter anything if you don't want to. We have enough information to approach the

Argovian government on our own. With all the evidence you have pointing to the authenticity of your claim, they're not going to refuse you access to the DNA."

Caleb must have noticed that she was frowning. "What, Irina?"

"Without Daisy English, I would never know about any of this. Daisy told me she has worked on this story for two years, to follow what she calls her 'Lukovic connection,' until she found me. I would want someone looking out for my interests, yes." She glanced at Gabe, who gave her a reassuring smile in return. "I would want Daisy to understand what I will do and what I will not do for this story she wants so much. But I will not bypass her. If I go forward, she will have her story."

Davis shrugged. "Fair enough. And I imagine she can set up the test a lot more quickly than we could, since we would be starting from scratch. She's probably already established the contacts to get it done. So there's an upside to giving her what she wants."

"An upside beyond the fairness aspect," Aleta added, with an indulgent glance at her husband. "Which *does* matter."

Davis cleared his throat. "Absolutely."

Gabe asked, "When will you meet with this reporter again?"

"I have to go to Dallas and speak with Victor tomorrow. When I return I will call her."

Caleb said, "My guess is that Daisy will be jumping right on it. She's already called once after that first surprise visit, to try and hurry Irina into agreeing to go forward."

"Don't make any arrangements with her until I'm

present," Gabe advised. "When you call her, tell her you want to meet with her and set up a time. Agree to nothing on the phone. I'll be there, at that first meeting you have with her. Try to set it up for Tuesday, in the afternoon. Have her come to the BravoCorp building. We can talk in my office. Then, after she leaves, you and I can talk it over and decide what your ground rules will be."

"Will there be a contract?"

"I imagine she'll have something for you to sign. But you and I can go over it before you put your signature on it."

Irina thanked Gabe—and all of them—for their help. Mary had Sunday dinner ready. They shared a family meal. Irina thought how good it was to be with the Bravos, to laugh with them. To feel a part of their family, even though she knew it wasn't real, wasn't forever.

At home, she made a reservation for her flight to Dallas the next morning. She and Caleb went to bed early and made tender love.

In the middle of the night she woke. Her mind was racing—with memories, with visions of the past. Some good, some so terrible she had to stifle the whimper of pain and sorrow that tried to rise in her throat.

All that time, all her life, she had known herself as Irina Lukovic. Now it could turn out that she was someone altogether different. She felt like a stranger inside her own skin.

She clutched her locket for comfort and tried to lie still, to let poor Caleb sleep. But he must have sensed her troubled wakefulness.

"You okay?" he asked, sounding groggy, half-asleep.

"Yes," she lied.

He reached out and pulled her close. She rested her head against his big chest, listened to the steady rhythm of his good, strong heart. And took comfort in the warmth of his body, in the soothing feel of his flesh pressed to hers.

It would be all right, she promised herself. It would work out fine. Her life had never been an easy one. And yet, somehow, against all odds she had managed to survive.

She would survive this, as well. Survive being—or not being—a princess.

Survive telling Caleb goodbye when the time came, the time that was supposed to be almost two years away, and yet somehow, since the visit from Daisy English, seemed to loom ever closer, day by day.

Chapter Twelve

"If it's what you want, I'll meet with this reporter and tell her what I know," Victor said, the next day when they sat in a Dallas restaurant, just the two of them, over lunch.

Irina studied his broad face. "You don't seem all that surprised."

"Because I'm not—at least not too much. When I think it over, it makes perfect sense."

Irina laughed. "To you, maybe. To me, it is just…" And then, out of nowhere, tears were pushing at the back of her throat. She gulped them away and made herself finish what she had been trying to say. "Unbelievable. Impossible."

And then she stared down at her lunch and tried to blink the foolish moisture from her eyes. Truly, this ridiculous, constant crying had to stop. In the past month and a half, since Caleb had saved her from deportation by making her his bride, she so often found herself bursting into tears over the smallest things. She couldn't understand it. Not after all those years, the endless tragedies she'd lived through, all without shedding a single tear.

Victor set down his enormous club sandwich. "Cousin, are you crying?" He asked the question in Argovian. And he looked somewhat stunned—much more surprised, in fact, than he had been at the news that she could be a princess.

She swiped at her eyes, lifted her head and answered, "Of course not," also in their own language. Then she sipped her iced tea and switched back to English. "Why do you say that it makes sense? How can it make sense that I might be the last of the Golaceks?"

"There were things…" He ate more of his sandwich, his dark eyes thoughtful.

"What things?"

He swallowed, and then took another bite.

She reached across and poked at his big shoulder, the way she used to do when they were children and he was being obstinate. It was like poking a boulder. "Tell me."

He chewed and swallowed and then, finally, he said, "Aunt Dafina, for one. She never treated Mother and Father and me like her family. With her, there was always a certain…reserve. She was gracious and kind, but not familiar. And she never cooked or cleaned. Mother did everything around the house."

"I don't remember any of that."

"How could you? You were barely five years old when she died. I was ten, old enough to remember more than you. Father took me aside the day of her burial. He said I was always to watch out for you. That you are my sacred trust, precious beyond price."

Irina rolled her eyes. "Lucky you."

He drank some milk. "Even at ten, when a lot of what grownups talked about went straight over my head—even then, I took note of his words. I understood that there was more going on than I was being told. I could see no reason why he would think he had to tell me to watch over you. He knew I would always take care of you. Because you are my little cousin, not because of anything so huge and serious as my father made it seem...." His voice trailed away.

"What else?" In her eagerness, she leaned across the table toward him.

He stared into the middle distance, and she knew he was back there in Argovia, with Uncle Vasili, all those years ago. "Father also said there was...much I must know and understand—that when I was sixteen and ready to shoulder the burdens of a loyal retainer, he would tell me everything."

"*A loyal retainer.* You're serious? He said those words?"

Victor nodded. "I remember thinking that the whole conversation was really...weird."

"Weird how?"

"The intensity of his expression, the way he lowered his voice as if he was afraid an enemy might hear. The way he grabbed my shoulder, his big, work-hardened fingers digging in. I was so relieved when he was through talking and let me go back out to play."

"And then, just five years later, the soldiers came and killed him."

"And Mother, too."

"For being loyalists to the crown, remember?" She realized she was whispering, as though what she was saying was somehow a secret.

"Yeah. I remember."

"I was so angry, that they would kill two innocent people for being something I knew they weren't."

Victor's gaze was steady. True. "It begins to look like they were, though. Loyal to the royal family until death."

"And you saved me, Victor." Again, she had to swallow down the tears. "You dragged me away, out of the house we had both been born in, though I was so frightened and didn't want to go. I often think of that, you know? If not for you, the soldiers would have had me, too."

"You were my little cousin," Victor said softly. "And you still are. You always will be, no matter what."

At home that afternoon, she called Daisy English and left a message on her voicemail. Daisy called back ten minutes later. Irina agreed to meet with her the next day, at BravoCorp.

As promised, Gabe was at the meeting. Caleb came, too. They sat in the sitting area of Gabe's corner office. Daisy seemed a little wary at first, to have the two big, handsome Bravo men hovering close—one of whom was an attorney.

But she quickly became excited as she spoke of finally getting to hear the story of Irina's life. She said she could hardly believe that the project she'd been working on for so long was finally coming to fruition.

She did have a contract, but it was a simple one. She wanted only what she'd originally asked for: exclusive rights to Irina's life story. Gabe made her put a time limit on those rights. For the next two years, it was agreed, Irina would tell her story to no one else.

Daisy got an appointment at a certain lab and took Irina there on Friday. The technician swabbed the inside of Irina's cheek. Daisy explained that the swab would be sent to the Armed Forces DNA Identification Laboratory in Rockville, Maryland. Irina's DNA would be compared with that taken from the bones of Princess Dafina and Prince Laslo.

Along with the tests in the Maryland lab, other labs in Scotland and in Argovia would be enlisted to prove or disprove the validity of Irina's claim. It was all to be done in what Daisy called a "strict chain of evidence." And it was likely to take several weeks.

Daisy didn't want to wait for the results. "We're going to go ahead with the interviews," she said.

That surprised Irina. "But what if the results show I am not who you believe me to be?"

"They won't," said Daisy. "I've got a golden gut about this, after all the digging I've done on this project. And my gut tells me there's no need to hold up this project waiting for the lab results."

The following Monday, Tuesday and Wednesday, Daisy came to the house at nine in the morning and stayed until late afternoon. As Irina's story came out,

Daisy said she was only more certain she'd finally found the lost princess.

On Thursday Daisy met with Victor. Later that afternoon she called Irina.

"I'm pumped," Daisy announced as soon as Irina said hello. "This is it. Talking to your cousin—or I guess I mean the man you always *believed* to be your cousin—has only made me more certain that *you,* Your Royal Highness, are exactly who I always knew you were."

Irina smiled at her own reflection in the master bathroom's mirror. Over the past week, she'd actually become fond of Daisy and her excited way of talking. "Wait for the DNA," she said.

"I'm going to make some calls, see if we can't move things along a little faster on that. Stay available."

Irina set down the bottle of window cleaner she'd been using on the mirror. "Are we finished with the interviews?"

"For now. I have all those hours of tapes to go through. A rough draft to cobble together. Then I'll be in touch with a list of questions, stuff that comes up in the writing that I forgot to ask you, things you told me that weren't clear. Whatever. And as soon as we get the DNA findings, there will be the cover shoot. Probably in at least two stages. We'll do shots at your house, there in San Antonio. And at that ranch your husband's family owns. Nothing says 'the princess moved to Texas' like a ranch, don't you think?" She went on, as she often did, without waiting for an answer. "And I'm pushing the magazine for some studio pictures, too. With appropriate props, in Manhattan."

"I will be going to New York?"

"Yes, you will. And maybe to…" Daisy didn't finish. "Never mind. You have a point. We should wait for the DNA. We want to think positive, but there's no reason to get too far ahead of ourselves. I'll let you know later about any other locations."

Irina swallowed. Hard. "And…did you say that my picture is to be on the cover of *Vanity Fair?*"

"You bet it is, my darling."

"*If* it turns out I am who you are so certain I am."

"Stop being negative. It's happening, baby. I'll be in touch."

A click, and the line went quiet. Clutching her locket in plastic-gloved hands, Irina hung up and stared at herself in the mirror some more. Soon she would know if the face she saw belonged to a princess.

She shivered, picked up the bottle of window cleaner, and gave the mirror several hard squirts, until her own image was blurred and impossible to recognize. Then, with the clean rag, she started polishing.

After the bathroom, she put dinner in the oven and ran the duster on the hardwood floors. Next, she tackled the stainless steel in the kitchen. Caleb came in from the garage as she was polishing up the refrigerator.

"Is this my own private Cinderella I see, slaving away with her rag and her spray can?"

She set down the can and the cloth and turned to him. Slowly, she began peeling off her plastic gloves, making a show of it, tossing the first one over her shoulder and then the other after it. They made slapping sounds as they landed in the sink. He set down his briefcase as she went to him.

Bracing her arms on his shoulders and fluttering her eyelashes at him, she said, "You are home early. Not that I am complaining."

He sniffed. "Prime rib?"

"Only the best for my favorite husband."

"I do like your attitude." He kissed her—and frowned when he lifted his head. "We *are* alone, right?"

"Yes, we are."

"The interviews…?"

"Over, at least for now. Daisy is going back to New York, to write her rough draft, she says. And to wait for the DNA results—which she claims she is somehow going to try to speed up."

"The woman is relentless."

"Yes, she is."

"She seems pretty damn certain that you are the lost princess."

Irina was getting a little tired of talking about Daisy English. "Kiss me again. Talk later."

"Dinner?"

"It's in the oven for another half hour, at least."

"A half hour will do it." He put a hand at her back and bent to slide the other under her knees. Then he lifted her high in his arms. She laughed and kissed him again as he carried her to the bedroom.

He let her down by the bed and set about swiftly stripping off her clothing. "Stand right there," he commanded as soon as she was naked. She stood where he told her to, as he stripped off his own clothes, too.

Then he guided her down to the bed and began kissing his way slowly along the center of her body.

When he pressed his mouth over the womanly heart of her, she cried out.

Two months they had been married. She wished it might never end. And at times like this, she liked to pretend that they would go on together forever.

His clever tongue stroked her. She moaned and reached down to him, urging him to come to her, to fill her. But he only gently pushed her hands away and continued driving her crazy with that endless, so-intimate kiss.

Easter came. They spent the day at Bravo Ridge with the family. Everyone had questions. About the interviews with Daisy, about the DNA test, about when Irina's story would appear in *Vanity Fair.*

Irina told them that the interviews were over and they were waiting for the test results before they could go forward. She warned them that it was not a settled thing yet, that until the results came through they didn't know for certain that she was really the Golacek heir.

Caleb said, "My wife, the cautious princess."

She teased him. "You sound like Daisy." She put on Daisy's excited voice. "'It's happening, baby. Take my word.'"

"Well, it is," he insisted. "You wait. You'll see."

A week passed. And another. Daisy called twice. But only to ask questions, to clarify information that she had found on the interview tapes.

"Soon," Daisy promised. "We'll be moving forward soon...."

April became May. Mercy had her baby, a sweet boy they named Lucas, after his father—and Emilio, after

Mercy's adoptive grandfather, who had owned Bravo Ridge before Luke's grandfather won it from him on a bet. Back then, in the 1950s, the family ranch had been called La Joya. It had been in Mercy's family for hundreds of years.

Another month passed. By mid-June, two months after Daisy had interviewed Irina, everyone had stopped asking when the article in *Vanity Fair* would appear, and it had been over a month since Daisy had called.

All the furor back in April began to seem like a dream to Irina, a scary fantasy she had indulged in. As far from real as the movies she and Caleb watched in his media room on the big flat screen TV.

Did it matter? Irina came to the conclusion that it really didn't. She was happy—with her husband for two years, with the life they shared and with his family, each one of whom she was enjoying so much. She would get her green card as planned, and go on with her life in America. Back in January, she had received her high school equivalency diploma. And she'd already signed up to attend San Antonio College in the fall.

The only real benefit she could see to being proven a princess was the money waiting in those Swiss banks. With a lot of money, she could more easily live her dream of helping others.

But why make a lot of plans for how to spend a fortune she might never see? She decided she wasn't going to think about. Not until the DNA results came back—if they ever did.

July settled over San Antonio like a stifling blanket. For the Fourth, they held a big family barbecue out at

Bravo Ridge. The men manned the grills and barrel smokers, and Zoe brought her cameras, partly to get family pictures of the party, and partly because the Independence Day barbecue was to fill a whole section of Mary's cookbook.

Irina spent much of that day sitting in the shade playing UNO with Corrine and Matt's daughter, Kira, and holding Ginny in her lap. When Mercy needed a break from the new baby, Irina took little Lucas into the house where it was cool. She carried him upstairs to change his diaper and then sat with him in the white nursery room rocker, rocking and softly singing him an old Argovian lullaby.

When he drifted off to sleep, she put him in his crib and turned on the baby monitor. She took the receiver back out to the party and gave it to Mercy, who thanked her with a tired smile.

Kira found her a minute or two later. "Where have you been, Aunt Rina?" She had her little hands braced on her hips. "I was looking *everywhere!*"

Ginny called to her. "Rini, Rini!"

So she sat with the children for another hour, cuddling Ginny, listening to Kira chatter away and playing the answering voice to her endless chain of knock-knock jokes.

"Knock-knock."

"Who's there?"

"Lettuce."

"Lettuce who?"

"Stop asking questions and lettuce in!" Kira crowed and burst into a fit of helpless giggles.

"I think you have the magic touch with children," said a masculine voice behind Irina.

She glanced over her shoulder. It was Davis Bravo. "I...enjoy them," she replied, feeling vaguely foolish, and suddenly shy.

Kira wasn't shy at all. "Grandpa!" She jumped to her feet. "Make me tall." He went to her and scooped her up and set her on his broad shoulders. She stretched her hands to the cloudless summer sky. "I'm so tall! Walk me around, Grandpa."

Davis obeyed, striding off with her toward the picnic tables, where Mercy, Mary and Aleta were supervising the preparations for the meal. Irina watched them go, longing stirring within her—for this fine family she couldn't keep, for Caleb's baby, which she would never have.

She glanced around, seeking him. And found him over by one of the grills, flipping hamburgers. He seemed to sense her gaze and turned his head to meet her eyes, raising his big spatula in a salute. She smiled at him, her heart so full. She had loved him from the first—when he gave her a job so that she could come to America.

But she hadn't intended to fall *in* love with him. She had truly believed that her heart, like her body, was dead to that kind of loving.

But he had awakened her. Like a princess in a fairy story. He had awakened her to love with his goodness and generosity of heart, with his tender touch.

"Tiss, tiss," said Ginny, reaching up a little hand. Irina bent close and gave her a quick peck on her small, puckered mouth.

* * *

A few days after the barbecue, Irina drove out to the Lazy H to see the pictures Zoe had taken and to help Mary organize the barbecue section of the family cookbook, which included a number of recipes from Davis and the Bravo sons. Since the men didn't write their recipes down, Mary had carried around a small digital recorder during the barbecue and gotten each of them to explain to her the ingredients and preparation of dishes like Davis's Hot Turkey Wings and Luke's Killer Pork Ribs. Mary said she was almost ready to turn the book in to her publisher. She was hoping it would be in bookstores by next spring, but said she couldn't be sure. They might hold off publishing until the holidays next year.

At home, Irina decided on lasagna for dinner and began gathering her ingredients. She was setting a big pot of water on to boil when the phone rang.

It was Daisy. "Did you get the letter?"

She felt weak in the knees, so she pulled a chair close and lowered herself into it. "Letter?"

"From the Maryland lab?"

"No."

"You will. By FedEx. By tomorrow, for sure."

Irina put her hand over her mouth—and then took it away so she could talk. "What will the letter say?"

"That you are the lost Golacek princess."

Chapter Thirteen

In the weeks that followed, everything changed.

There were photo shoots—at the house and at the ranch. Caleb flew with her to New York for more pictures. They stayed in a fine hotel on Park Avenue, ate at wonderful restaurants and saw two Broadway shows.

Caleb also took her shopping. She bought more new, bright-colored clothes. And more sexy nightgowns to tempt him in bed.

The story spread that the lost Golacek heir had been found at last, that she was young and pretty—and scarred. They really seemed to like that she was scarred. Scars, Daisy explained to her, spoke of tragedy, of a whopping good story.

Reporters showed up at the house.

Irina learned to say, "No comment," and quickly close the door.

Closing the door on them didn't stop them. Her name turned up anyway—on the Internet, in weekly magazines and daily newspapers. Her picture, too. A simple trip to the grocery store became an obstacle course, with paparazzi popping up out of nowhere, cameras ready.

There were visits with bankers—*her* bankers. Her fortune was over two billion, she learned. It used to be near five, before the recent world-wide recession. Two billion sounded like plenty to her.

Enough to help many people—although she still didn't know exactly *how* she would help those in need. She was waiting for her life to settle down a little, waiting to become accustomed to being a princess. It wasn't easy, having her world turned over on its axis.

By the last week in July, the *Vanity Fair* issue that contained Daisy's story about her had gone to press. Irina received a stack of advance copies of the September issue with her picture on the cover, wearing nothing but a satin sheet, her gold locket and a diamond tiara.

She passed the copies around to the family. They were all very flattering about the article. They said she looked beautiful in the pictures, that her story touched them deeply. Elena said that it had made her cry.

Daisy had moved on to her book deal.

"Which is major," she told Irina proudly. "You are making me a very rich woman, you know that?" She gave Irina a wink. After which she broke the news that she wanted Irina to fly to Argovia. "The book will have a large photo section. Readers will want to see you in your homeland. And I'm thinking we'll get some shots in the palaces." She meant the former residences of her grandfather, King Ladislaus, one of which was now a museum and the other the home of the president. "And some in the mountains," Daisy went on, "where the royal family lived in hiding. And of you outside the house where you were born. And the state home. Mustn't forget the orphanage."

Irina knew that she was never going back, not even to visit. But she felt like a coward to confess that to Daisy. So she proposed other objections. "I don't even know if my aunt and uncle's house still stands."

"It's there. Trust me. It's my job to keep on top of these things."

Irina squared her shoulders. "I am not returning to Argovia."

"Oh, sure you are, baby. It's time you went back. It'll be a cathartic experience for you."

"Cathartic?"

"You know. Transformative. A healing thing."

"No."

"How can you say that? Of course you will go. And you're going to love it. It's going to be great."

"You don't understand. Even if I want to go—which I do not—I cannot leave the USA. If I do, I will not get back in."

"What *are* you babbling about, my darling?"

Irina patiently explained that she didn't dare leave the country, not until she at least had notice from USCIS that her green card had been approved.

"Start packing," commanded Daisy. "I don't want to hear any more excuses. I'll make some calls."

"Make some calls? Daisy, you must be realistic. Nobody tells Immigration what to do."

Daisy made a snorting sound. "The rules have changed for you, baby. You're no longer a sad little refugee who keeps house for a living. You're royalty."

"In name only. In case you didn't notice, my country has not been a monarchy for over fifty years."

"Royalty is royalty, deposed or not. And royalty with money…oh, baby. Don't you see? It's the money part that really matters. The State Department will be jumping through hoops to make you happy in the good old USA."

"You cannot be sure of that."

"Oh, yes I can. And I am. Next April fifteenth, you'll be reporting your billions to the IRS. No, they can't tax everything. Your excellent money managers will make sure of that. But you will pay taxes, serious taxes. You're an asset to this country now, not someone who is taking a job a citizen might fill—and think about this. You can live anywhere now. Anywhere in the whole wide world. You can spend your life on a beach in the tropics, or in a luxury hotel on the Champs Elysees."

"I want to live in America," she said. "I *will* live in America."

"Fine. No problem." Daisy waved a hand. "Call your banker. Tell him you need it in writing from Immigration that your green card is on the way."

"My banker? Why?"

"Bankers know lawyers. The right lawyers. Things will be settled before you know it."

"The right lawyers? I have a lawyer. Gabe will—"

"No, baby," Daisy said in that too-patient voice that set Irina's teeth on edge. "You need a lawyer who specializes in immigration. You need the best."

"Gabe *is* the best."

"Yes, I'm sure he is. But he's not an expert in immigration law."

"I still do not intend to go to Argovia."

"Just get the lawyer. Get your green card. We'll talk again once that's settled."

That night, over dinner, Irina told Caleb what Daisy had said.

"The woman is too damn pushy by half," Caleb grumbled. "But she's right. Maybe we should have gotten you a good lawyer from the first...."

"Why? I do not like to waste money when there is no need."

Caleb laughed. "I'd hardly call it a waste if it settles your immigration issues, would you?"

"No," she admitted with a sigh.

"Make the call. Get the lawyer."

The next day, she did. And the day after that she had a new lawyer. Her name was Rita Rodriguez. Irina went to see her. Rita was tall, with black hair and sharp black eyes. She wore beautiful designer suits and spike heels that showed off her excellent legs.

Rita went right to work. She had a good look at Irina's financial records and then determined that Irina had never broken the law. She had Irina bring in all of the papers she'd filed with USCIS so far.

"I think we can definitely speed things up here." She

told Irina when they met for the third time. "You sit tight. I'll be in touch."

Two days later, Rita's secretary called and asked her to come to the office.

"It's handled," the lawyer said. "You should get your notice—a letter from USCIS that says your conditional status as a resident is approved—within the week. The actual green card will take longer. Weeks or months. But the notice of action letter is as good as the card. When you get it, take it to your local USCIS office and have them stamp your passport. Keep the stamp current, by renewing as needed."

"I will."

"So you're all set," said the lawyer. "For now. If you don't get the notice within ten working days, call me. And when you've been married for two years and are ready to apply for permanent status, come and see me again. We'll prepare your petition. And in the meantime, I notice that you and your husband share no assets. You need to fix that. When you apply for permanent residence as the wife of a citizen, USCIS is going to be looking for assets in common."

"Assets in common…" Irina repeated, sounding as uncomfortable as she felt. She had known about them, had read about the necessity for them in the books on immigration that she studied so diligently.

But she'd been putting off thinking about taking that step, putting off bringing it up with Caleb. It seemed just one more way she was entangling herself in his life. One more way that this supposedly simple deception had become so very complicated.

Rita tapped her beautifully manicured nails on the desktop. "You should apply for credit cards jointly. Buy a house together—or have him put you on the deed to the house you live in now."

Buy a house together.

Well, they could do that, couldn't they? *She* could buy a house and put *him* on the deed.

She was a wealthy woman now, she had to remember that, learn to think of herself as someone with the means to accomplish just about anything. After years of struggling merely to get by, having more money than she could possibly use in her lifetime still didn't seem real to her.

Rita was watching her through those black eyes that always made her feel uncomfortable, as if the lawyer could see inside her head. Rita said, cautiously, "I'm sure your marriage is solid."

"It is." Irina stiffened it in the chair. "Very…solid."

Did Rita look at her pityingly? Or was that just her own guilt, for making a sham marriage—a sham marriage that, in recent months, felt so much like the real thing.

Even though it wasn't.

She had to remember that. It wasn't.

Rita said, "As your lawyer, I must make certain you are aware that to engage in a sham marriage to get a green card is against the law."

"Of course I know that."

"Well, all right then." Was that a smile trying to lift the corner of Rita's mouth? "That said, there are always other options. So, if your marital situation should change—"

"It will not." Irina said, with a finality she didn't feel.

"I'm sure it won't." Rita spoke mildly. "But if it does, come to me right away."

All the rest of that day, Irina thought of what Rita and Daisy had said.

There are always other options....

The rules have changed for you, baby....

She thought about Caleb. About how good he had been to her. How much she cared for him—*loved* him. Was *in* love with him.

And now she might be able to free him—from her.

He didn't exactly seem like he *wanted* to be free, though, did he? He seemed happy with her. She took excellent care of him, as a real, forever wife would. He seemed to like being in bed with her, too, now that she had moved beyond her fears and came to him with eagerness.

Yet, he did have the right to be free. It was...a gift she longed to offer him. He could be free, if he chose freedom. Free, before the required two years were up; free without having to worry that she would be sent away.

She thought about how Daisy had said that she could live anywhere in the world if she wanted to. If they denied her residency now, she could live elsewhere, and live well, dependent on no one. She wouldn't have to return to Argovia.

And she thought about how, for most of her life, she had tried to keep her head down, to simply get by. It had taken all of her energy and focus just to survive. She thought about how it *did* bother her, that her marriage to Caleb wasn't the real thing, the forever thing.

How, as much as she loved her life with him, it was a life and a love forged of bleak necessity. Of a lie.

Six months ago, when she and Caleb agreed to marry, the possibilities for her had been severely limited. But everything was changed now. The world was wide-open to her.

Maybe it was time for her to take a few chances. Time for her to move beyond merely surviving. Time for her to free the man she loved.

And herself, as well.

A week later, as Rita had promised, her notice that she had been approved for a conditional green card came in the mail. She went right out and got her passport stamped. The stamp was good for a year, and would serve as proof that she was in the country legally.

That night, when Caleb came home, she had his favorite dinner of lamb chops and new potatoes ready for him. She told him her news and he said how great it was. In honor of the occasion, he even opened an expensive bottle of champagne he'd been saving.

They ate and he told her again how happy he was for her. She tried to be happy, too.

They watched some television in the media room and went to the bedroom about ten. He caught her hand as they stood near the bed, and pulled her close to him. They shared a tender kiss. When he lifted his head and gave her a smile, she stared up at him and wished it might never end between them.

But it *was* going to end. And the longer it went on, the worse the pain was going to be when it did.

He looked at her sideways—teasing, but doubtful.

"Okay, what's going on? You look so strange. You've seemed a little edgy all night. Was it something I said?"

She stepped free of the circle of his arms. "I think we should buy a house together," she blurted out.

He frowned. "Why? Something wrong with this one?"

"Oh, no. I love this house."

"Well, then, why move?"

"My lawyer said we need assets in common—that USCIS will be checking for common property when I apply to make my conditional green card a permanent one."

"Well, all right. How about this? I'll put your name on the papers for this house—unless you want a vacation house? Is that what you mean? We could do that. A vacation house in the Hill Country maybe—but you know, the family already has a cabin up there. I keep meaning to take you, maybe for a weekend sometime soon. You'll like it, I'll bet. And now that I'm thinking it over, if we bought a place, we should choose somewhere more exotic. The Bahamas. Or Cancun, somewhere with beaches and sun and sand."

She put her hands over her face. He was so good to her. She should just go on as they had been, tell him a vacation house would be great and leave it at that.

But somehow she couldn't.

He moved close again, touched her shoulder, a tentative caress. One that spoke of his real concern for her. "Irina. Talk to me. Tell me what's the matter?"

She pressed her hands to her mouth. And then let them fall. "Oh, Caleb. You don't understand."

"Understand what?"

"I want us to buy a house together. Here in San Antonio."

"Why, if you like this house?"

"So that I can move in there. By myself."

Chapter Fourteen

Caleb wanted to break something. "You *what?*"

Irina flinched and jumped back away from him. "Please don't yell at me."

He instantly felt like a jerk. He shouldn't have shouted at her.

But he didn't get it. What was she talking about? Moving out? *Why?*

And, okay, he had to admit that it hurt to hear her say it. It hurt a lot. And that—how damn much it hurt—kind of freaked him out.

He made himself speak more calmly. "Look. Is it something I did?"

"No. No, it's not you. Never you. You have to believe that." She looked so desperate. So miserable.

He blew out a slow breath and tried to calm down.

"I'm seriously not following. We have a plan here. And suddenly you want to mess it up royally? I don't get it. You've always been so careful about this."

"I know." Her soft mouth was a bleak line.

"Think about it. We took a vow of silence. We agreed not to tell anyone, not even Victor, that we weren't strictly for real. You had us sharing a bed from the beginning, even though you hated to be touched, you were so afraid that Immigration might come knocking, checking to see that only one bed was slept in. My family thinks we're completely in love. And now you want to move out?"

"It is only that, now that I have the green card approved, we don't have to be quite so careful."

"Not *quite* so careful? Come on. Face it. If you move out, you're not being careful at all."

"But I want to…give you your freedom."

"My freedom." The word tasted sour in his mouth. "Did I ask for that? I don't remember asking for that."

"I just…I feel so bad."

"About what? I told you I was in this for the whole two years. Why, suddenly, are you wanting to screw around with the program?"

"I don't."

"Yeah. You do. If you move out, you're screwing with the program."

"But I'm not." She raked her bangs back with spread fingers. "Not exactly."

"What the hell? You are or you aren't."

"I only mean that I am not so frightened now, to take a small chance. I am…stronger now. I see things in a new light. I have options now that I did not have before."

Options. She had *options*....

He wanted to yell at her again, to demand to know who had been filling her head with crazy, dangerous ideas.

He stopped himself—barely. Yelling, after all, didn't solve anything. And besides, whoever had told her about her damn options was right. She was a princess, after all. And a hell of a lot richer than he would ever be.

She must have taken his silence to mean he was starting to see it her way, because she said, "You would have to be...discreet, until the two years are up and I have permanent residency. And I would hope that when the time comes, you would vouch for me, fill out the forms as my husband, the way we planned."

"*Lie* for you, you mean. The way I've *been* lying for you."

"Caleb." She looked sad. And determined, too. She had reached behind her to unzip her yellow sundress. But then she didn't. She let her hands drop to her sides. "Yes. I would ask you to lie for me, as you have been doing." She went over and sat on the edge of the bed. "As we have *both* been doing. And at the same time, I would be giving you a chance to have your life back— right away, rather than a year and a half from now."

His fury spiked all over again. "This is crap. Just plain crap."

"No. You do not understand what I am—"

He cut her off with a slicing motion of his hand. "I understand, all right. I understand that you're not thinking straight, for some reason I'm not getting at all. After all we've done to make sure that you can stay in America, you're suddenly deciding to move out on your

own, to take a chance on getting your ass put in jail—
and then kicked out of the country permanently. Have
you lost your mind?"

"No. My mind is right here." She touched her
temple with a finger. "Inside my head." And she
refused to back down. "I do not believe I will be kicked
out. We proved already that we are married. And we
will stay married for the full two years—at least
legally. It is enough."

"But it's not enough. You said it yourself. It has to
be a *real* marriage. If you're living on your own and I'm
spending time with other women—discreetly or otherwise—it's not a real marriage." He shook his head. "I
just don't get it."

She looked at him so strangely. "Don't you?"

"Hell, no."

She stared at him for several seconds more. Then she
bent to slip off her sandals. Rising with the sandals in
her hand, she disappeared into the dressing room.

He resisted the urge to follow her. If he did, he would
only start yelling again. Instead, he took off his shirt and
tossed it over a chair. He got out of his trousers and his
shoes and socks. In only his boxer briefs, he went and
sat on the side of the bed where she had been a few
minutes before.

Really, what was the matter with him? He wasn't the
type who yelled at women. He was a guy who took relationships—and life in general—as they came.

He was still wondering what his problem was when
she emerged from the dressing room wearing the short
summer robe that he'd bought her when they went to

New York for the *Vanity Fair* cover shoot. The thin, pink satin clung to every luscious curve. She looked good enough to eat. At least from the neck down.

The expression on her face kind ruined the effect. It wasn't nearly as inviting as the rest of her.

She perched on the edge of the easy chair by the window, several feet away from the bed—and him. "May I say the rest of what I wanted to tell you? Will you listen, please?"

"Go for it." He pushed the words out through clenched teeth—at the same time as he wondered why this made him so mad. What they had was bound to come to an end. He had always known that. He never would have entered into it otherwise.

She said, "Everything is changed for me, don't you see? At last, I have the chance to…be independent. And you, Caleb, you have a chance to have your life back, to be free again, the way you always wanted to be."

He had to ask, "Is that what you want, to be free of me?"

She looked at him for a long time. And finally she answered, "No. It's not. I love you, Caleb. I want to be with you—to stay with you. But sometimes a woman does not get everything she wants."

The knot of tension in his gut eased. At least a little. "You're serious. You want to be with me?"

"Oh, yes. I am. I do."

"Well then, what's the problem? I'm fine with going on as we have been. It's no hardship on me."

She stared at him. "No hardship."

"No. And it's safer. You know it is. Safer if we just go on, live together for the full two years."

She hung her head. "Caleb. No."

"Why the hell not?" He came very close to yelling the question. But he didn't. Not quite.

She answered with careful control. "I just told you why. I don't want to *have* to be married anymore. I have a choice now. And my choice is not that."

"What choice? You're making no sense. If you move out, you'll still be married, you just won't be living with me."

She glanced away. "You know what I mean."

"Do you realize what you're risking? If it all blows up in your face, you're in big trouble. We both are."

"I do not think so. We got married. Everyone believes it was a real marriage. I've never told a soul that it was otherwise. Have you?"

"Hell no. When *I* make an agreement, I keep it."

"Caleb." She spoke with careful patience. "Sometimes even a real marriage doesn't work out. People have problems. Even Immigration will understand that."

"So, all right, we don't end up in jail. They could still deport you. You always swore that you would stay here, in America, no matter what. Suddenly you've changed your mind?"

Her pretty chin was set. "If America doesn't want me, fine. I will go elsewhere. At least now, if I have to go, I have the means to choose *where* I go."

He wanted to jump up, go to her, grab her, shake her until her good sense returned. "This doesn't sound like you."

"But it *is* me." Her big eyes pleaded with him to understand. "Oh, Caleb. I am not the same sad little refugee you married. Can't you see? It is all…so different for me now. And not only because I am suddenly a wealthy woman, a lost princess, finally found. No. More than all that, the real change in me is due to you. And for that, I am so grateful. You cannot know how much.…"

He didn't want her damn gratitude. He wanted…

Okay—he wasn't sure what he wanted. Just what he didn't want. And that was to lose her.

Which was pretty damn twisted, if you thought about it. Of course he would lose her. That was the plan. She would get her green card. And after two years of pretending to be married, it would be adios.

It was only, well, they were supposed to have a year and a half left together. He'd gotten used to that idea, been happy with it.

Really happy.

Maybe too happy.

"Caleb?" She rose. He watched her come to him, loving the fluid motion of her body beneath the wisp of robe. When she stood above him, she put her hand on his bare shoulder. "Please don't be angry with me."

He gazed up into her dark eyes. She had a right to her own choices, a right to be free, to run her own life. To live on her own, if she wanted. He should be man enough to support her in that. "You surprised me, that's all."

She bent close, kissed him. A light, questioning kiss. "It will be all right. You will see."

He breathed in the scent of her—so sweet and womanly. "One way or another, you are getting that damn green card."

"Yes, Caleb."

"I like the way you say that."

"Yes, Caleb."

He slid a hand around her nape and pulled her close for another kiss.

They went to bed as always, and made passionate love.

But in the days that followed, Irina felt the difference in what they shared. There were...spaces now. Distances between them.

Somehow, they never made love again after that night she told him of her plans to move out. And he didn't come home early from work anymore. Sometimes he came home at six. Sometimes he stayed at the office even later.

They still went to family events together—Sunday dinner at Bravo Ridge, a barbecue at Gabe and Mary's.

Mary asked her if anything was wrong. Irina lied and said there was nothing. She couldn't tell her the truth, not without making Mary complicit in her sham marriage.

Irina knew Caleb remained true to her, that he respected their agreement, their two-year bond. But he was pulling away from her, making her a smaller part of his life than she had been before.

And she was pulling away, too.

She kept remembering that she had told him she loved him and wanted to stay with him. And he hadn't said a word about loving her, too. Yes, she did realize that she had done it badly, that the way she had told him was awkward. And not fully clear.

She should have said that she not only loved him, she

was *in* love with him. That if he would only love her back, she would never leave him.

But those words wouldn't come. Because he had said nothing about wanting her to stay with him. And, well, she did have a little pride after all.

She believed that he did care for her—not in the passionate, complete, forever way that she had come to love him. But he cared. He did. And now it was as if he was removing himself from her, little by little. So that when the final break came, it would be a simple thing, easily accomplished. In essence, already done.

She moved her belongings back to the room she had stayed in before they got married. She began sleeping in there, too. He didn't comment on that.

Somehow, so swiftly, they had become like roommates rather than husband and wife. They were courteous and distant with each other. What they had shared was over. Irina told herself she was learning to accept that.

She started college. Just a few hours a week. Still, it made her feel that she was keeping busy, keeping her mind off her marriage that had ended up meaning so much more to her than it should have.

As September blew in on hot, dry winds, he went to California on business for a week. Maddy Liz had her baby—another boy. They named him Andrew Vasili. Irina went up to Dallas for a couple of days to help out. She found some comfort in taking care of Steven and Miranda, in holding sweet little Andrew in her arms.

When she returned to San Antonio on Wednesday, Daisy came from New York for a two-day visit. As usual, Daisy had more questions, more details she needed in order to fill out her book that was going to be over six hundred pages and cover a sweeping timeline, from the fall of the Golaceks, to the life of her grandparents in hiding, to the escape of the crown prince to Spain and his romance with the Baroness Sekelez, to his untimely death when he tried to smuggle the pregnant Dafina back into the country.

And onward, all the way to the final discovery that Irina was the lost princess.

Irina wanted to know when the book would be published. Daisy gave her one of those so-patient looks. "I'm still on the first draft. It will be a while."

"A while?"

"This is publishing, darling. I need at least another six months to finish the writing—realistically, more like eight. Then it goes to production. A year and a half, at least. And then there's placement to consider. Maybe the summer after next. And by the way, what about the trip to Argovia?"

Irina told her again, "I am never going back there."

"Is this about the green-card situation? I thought you got that worked out."

"Daisy. It is not because I cannot. It is because I will not. Probably never. And definitely not for this. Not for a few photographs."

Daisy peered at her closely. "You're afraid to go."

Irina didn't flinch. "No. I do not *want* to go. I do not live there anymore, and there is nothing for me there but memories of death and suffering."

Daisy grunted. "You are becoming altogether too obstinate and independent-minded, my darling. Do you know that?"

Irina grinned. And then Daisy grinned. And then both of them burst out laughing.

Daisy went back to New York and Caleb returned from California even more polite and distant than before. Irina admitted to herself that she was dragging her feet about moving out. Elena's mom was a Realtor. Irina called Luz and described the kind of house she was looking for.

Luz took her to several different properties. Nothing seemed quite right. Gently, Luz asked her if she was sure she really wanted to move.

That night in bed, in the room she had slept in when she was Caleb's housekeeper, she longed for him so powerfully. It took all of her will not to go to him, to beg him to take her back into his bed and his life, to give her a chance to be his wife again, for as long as he would have her, to beg, shamelessly, for the rest of the time they had left in their green-card marriage.

She dreamed of him that night, of his touch on her body, his kisses on her mouth, her breasts. All of her. Everywhere. She woke up moaning, touching herself. Crying.

It had to stop.

The next day, after she got home from her two classes, Luz showed her a house only a few blocks from Caleb's house. It was two stories, with a fine modern kitchen, a spa tub in the master suite and a beautifully landscaped yard, complete with pool. A house a lot like Caleb's, the kind of house she had never dreamed she might own.

It was vacant. She told Luz she wanted it.

Luz laughed. "At last I believe you really want to move."

"I love it. And I want it."

"When do you want to bring Caleb to see it?"

Irina only smiled. "He doesn't need to see it. He… has complete trust in my judgment."

So they made the offer. Luz tried to get her to bargain for it, but Irina felt it was worth the asking price. She would have paid cash for it that very day. But Luz convinced her to hold off closing on it long enough to get the various routine inspections.

Irina kept Caleb informed about the house hunt. And she told him the day she had her offer accepted.

He solemnly congratulated her. And then he turned around and left the room. She stared after him, feeling as if he had ripped her heart out and taken it with him.

Finally, on the last Friday in September, Irina got her house. Luz was surprised when Caleb didn't come to the closing, but since Irina had him put on the deed as co-owner, it didn't look that much out of the ordinary. After all, everyone knew Irina had a fortune. People with lots of money did things differently.

That night she told Caleb that she had her house and would be moving into it as soon as she chose the furnishings.

"Good for you," he said.

"You are on the deed with me, as we discussed."

"Right. To look good for the Immigration people."

"Yes."

He held her gaze. A sudden, hot shiver went through her. She wondered what he might be thinking. And then he said, "We should have champagne."

She felt like a sad little beggar, offered a crumb at

last. She should have told him no, thank you. She had studying to do, a shopping list of furniture and housewares to make.

But instead she smiled at him. "Yes. That would be so nice."

He got a bottle from his fancy wine cooler, popped the cork, and poured them each a glass. He handed her the flute and then tapped his against it. "To my favorite princess. May all your dreams come true."

"And yours." She drank. All of it. In one long, fizzy gulp. When she set the glass down, he was watching her.

He set his glass down, too. And then he reached for her. "One more time." His voice was low, rough. His green eyes burned with dark fire.

Should she have refused him? Probably. But her body was as hungry for him as her heart and her spirit were.

She went into his arms with zero resistance, only a willing sigh. He kissed her hard, spearing his tongue into her mouth, claiming her. She moaned her eagerness to be his.

He scooped her up high in his arms and carried her into his bedroom—once, for far too short a time, *their* bedroom—and bent long enough to lower her feet to the floor. Still kissing her, he began taking her clothes away. He did that quickly, ruthlessly.

She wasn't shy either. She tugged at his belt, ripped his fly wide, shoved down his trousers and his boxer briefs with them, careful only of his manhood that stood up so stiff and proud. Dropping to her knees, she helped him off with his shoes and his socks, too.

She sighed at the sight of him, so hard. So ready for her. She took him, wrapping her hand around his silky hardness, stroking him. He pulled her upright and claimed her mouth again.

Taking her by the shoulders, he guided her down to the bed. She kicked off her sandals, the last scrap of covering she had left.

His kisses burned her, set her on fire. He took her breasts in his hands and claimed one with his mouth, biting her nipple a little and sucking, hard and rhythmically, so that she rocked her hips against him, pulling at him, digging her nails into his broad shoulders.

Wanting more. All of him.

But he didn't give in to her whimpered pleas.

Not yet.

He went on kissing her. Everywhere. It was like her dream, the one she'd had the night before she finally chose her new house, the dream where he claimed every inch of her, with his mouth, with his searing touch.

When at last he eased his lean hips between her thighs, she took his hard buttocks in her two hands, digging her nails in, pushing her body up to him, demanding all of him.

He gave her what she wanted, filling her with one strong, consuming thrust. And then he braced up on his fists and he watched her as he rode her.

She looked up at him, met his eyes that burned like green fire. So much she wanted to tell him. So much she longed to give him…everything. All that she had. All that she was. All she would ever be.

So much he had given her. Including this magic. This

wild, sexual beauty. Never, until Caleb, had she believed she could know this kind of joy again.

It was a gift and she was so grateful for it. A gift among so many. A gift she would cherish.

She would not become bitter. She would remember that he had never been hers to keep, that he had never promised her his heart or his love. That all he *had* given her was going to have to be enough.

When his climax took him, he pressed into her so hard. She rose up to meet him, her body answering his, going with him over the edge into fulfillment. She held on tight as the waves of pleasure claimed her, and lost herself in the searing magic of that perfect moment.

Their last time. She wished it might never end.

But it did end.

And in the morning, before dawn, she returned to her own bed. Two hours later she got up and ate her breakfast alone.

She straightened up the kitchen and then went to school. That afternoon she started shopping. Amazing, how many things a woman had to buy to fill an empty house.

One week later she moved to her new place. She had Mary over for lunch as soon as she was settled in. She explained that things weren't going so well with Caleb. She didn't give details. Mary hugged her hard and reminded her that she would always be there for her, and if she needed anything—*anything*—all she had to do was call.

The next day Victor appeared at her door. "I talked to Caleb," he said in Argovian. "He asked only that I speak with you before I smashed in his so-handsome face."

Irina grabbed him and hugged him and then dragged him inside to see her new house. She made him espresso and asked him, please, not to hurt Caleb.

"You love him, I think," said her cousin. "He does not deserve you."

"He's been so good to me, Victor. I can never explain how good."

"I think I know," her cousin said.

They left it at that.

In the days that followed, Irina had visits from Elena, from Aleta, from Mercy and from Ash's wife, Tessa, too. They all wanted to help any way that they could. They all said they loved her and were there for her anytime she needed them.

Corrine, Matt's wife, also came by. She brought Kira and Kira's new baby sister, Kathleen, with her. Irina listened to Kira's latest knock-knock jokes and held the month-old Kathleen in her arms.

Irina confided in each of the Bravo women that she was looking for good causes to support. They all had suggestions. She talked to her investment counselor and arranged to give large sums of money to a woman's center, an afterschool program for the disadvantaged, the YWCA and a state-wide English as a Second Language project.

Her life was so full. And so much of what she had was due to Caleb. If not for him, she would have run far and fast when she learned that her asylum was to be revoked. Instead, she had shared months of happiness with him. With his help, her deepest wounds had been healed. Now she had so many true friends, and money enough to live a prosperous life and also give generously to others.

What more could any woman ask, she would remind herself whenever she started missing him too much. She prayed that he was happy, that he enjoyed being free.

After Irina left him, Caleb tried to tell himself that it was for the best.

She had it all now. The horrors of her past were behind her. She had a right to a new life, a fresh start. She had married him out of simple necessity. Yeah, she had said she loved him. But he knew that would pass. People always loved the ones who rescued them. He didn't want to keep her with him because she was grateful. He wanted her to have her chance. To start over. To be free.

He tried to remember how much he used to like his own freedom. But that wasn't working out all that well. The house seemed so damn empty without her. Not to mention a mess.

The mess part he could fix easily, by hiring a housekeeper. But he didn't do it. If he came into his kitchen and saw another woman at the sink, well, he figured that would probably break him. And he wasn't in the mood for cleaning up after himself.

Might as well just live with the mess.

He tried to get out more. After all, he used to love to party. So he tried going to bars. But he didn't even want to drink—let alone to dance with strange women. So he would head for home, driving too fast.

He was a hazard on the highway and he knew it. Always had been. He tried to remember to keep it within a few miles of the speed limit, but didn't always succeed.

After Victor almost punched his lights out, his father came to talk to him, to ask him what his problem was, letting a wonderful woman like Irina get away from him. Caleb told him to butt out. His dad called him a damn fool before he finally left him alone.

Luke came next. He said, "This place looks like a pig lives here."

Caleb said, "Want a beer?"

Luke accepted a Corona and then asked Caleb if he had lost his mind. "Remember what you said when I was dating Mercy? That what we had was what mattered? That when you looked at us together, you thought, 'That's it. That's what it's all about.' Remember that?"

"And your point is?"

"Why are you letting Irina go? You're in love with her. You know it. We all know it."

"She send you here to talk to me?" He growled the question. But inside he felt a flicker of hope.

"Nobody sent me. I came because you're my brother."

Hope faded to an ember and died. "So mind your own damn business. Please."

After Luke, he got visits from Matt. And Gabe, too. He told them that what was going on between him and Irina was no concern of theirs.

Eventually they left him alone. He wasn't sure if that was better or worse than them dropping in unannounced to lecture him about his marriage breaking up. They didn't know crap. None of them had any idea why he and Irina had gotten together, or why they were separated now.

Not that it really mattered why. What mattered was he had lost her, that he wasn't going to get her back.

And that was for the best.

Elena started coming over two or three times a week. They would have a beer, maybe watch a movie. She told him what she thought about his breakup with Irina—and she wouldn't let him chase her away.

She said, "You're an idiot. She loves you. You love her."

He said, "It's not that simple. Stay out of it."

She said, "Take my advice. Go to her. Tell her you love her and you miss her so much, you won't even hire another housekeeper, that the laundry is piling up and your heart is broken and won't she please, please come back to you."

"And to think, a little over a year ago, I didn't even know you were my sister."

"Yeah, well. Now you have me, *mi hermano*. I'm the one who's willing to tell you what a fool you're being."

"No. Actually, everyone has told me."

"But then they went away and left you alone. I keep coming back."

"And this is *good* news?"

"Go to her. She lives three blocks away."

"I know where she lives."

"Take flowers. Knock on the door. When she opens it, tell her you love her and your house is a mess. Everything from there on will be good. Trust me on this."

"Shut up and pass the popcorn."

And Elena *would* shut up. At least until the next time she started in on him. "You're afraid, aren't you? I don't know why. It's not like you had a bad upbringing or anything. Yeah, your dad fooled around once. That almost cost him everything—and ended up creating me. But they have mostly been happy together, your mom and dad. And it's so obvious that they're still madly in love, even after all these years. You really need to get over yourself and go after your wife."

The most annoying thing was that, after a while, the things Elena said started to kind of make sense to him. He had never felt for any woman the way he felt about Irina. While he was helping her get her green card and get over the rough stuff that had happened to her, she had somehow managed to sneak into his heart. Until she filled it completely, took total possession.

Life was a hell of a lot easier when a man didn't care that much.

Shallow, Irina had called him, that day they agreed to get married. *Shallow, but good in heart.* Maybe he *was* shallow. Maybe he had liked it that way. And maybe he had sent his wife away and called it for her own good, when in reality it was because she had changed his life, changed *him* so completely.

And that scared him to death.

He gave up going to bars. It was just too depressing. And afterward, he only ended up driving home too fast.

In fact, since he knew he would end up wrapping his car around a tree if he didn't watch it, he took considerable care to drive at or below the speed limit every time he got behind the wheel.

Which only made what happened so damn ironic.

Thirty-five days after Irina left him, on a Thursday afternoon, two weeks before Thanksgiving, he was driving home from the office, going twenty-eight in a thirty-mile-an-hour zone.

He saw that the light ahead was red. So he slowed to stop. But then it went green, so he continued on through.

In the middle of the intersection, a flash of movement to his left had him turning instinctively to glance through his side window. A giant pickup was barreling down on him. He could see the guy behind the wheel— an old guy, eyes wide and terrified, clutching his chest.

He thought *This is it. I'm a dead man. And I wasn't even speeding.*

And then he thought *Irina.*

And then came the impact, metal crunching, the whole damn world spinning, a screaming sound that might have been human—or not.

When the screaming stopped and there was stillness except for the hissing sigh of a busted radiator somewhere, he looked through the blood in his eyes and what was left of the windshield and it seemed he saw her face, her beautiful face.

He whispered, "Irina." But he knew she wasn't really there.

Chapter Fifteen

The ambulance came fast. They pried him out of his once-beautiful car and put him on a stretcher, then loaded him into the ambulance.

"You're going to be all right," said the EMT guy bending over him, taping an IV lead to the back of his hand. Caleb was really relieved to hear that, since everything hurt, especially his chest, where the restraint had dug in hard, keeping him in his seat. And his damn head felt like someone had taken an axe to it.

He asked, "The old guy…in the pickup?"

"Cardiac arrest." The EMT tipped his head at the other cot in the ambulance. They were working the old guy over, too. "So far, he's hanging in there."

In the emergency room they stitched up the three-inch gash in his forehead where a piece of flying metal from the pickup had cut him. They told him he was lucky for the Audi's reinforced steel passenger compartment and side airbag.

He knew they were right. He just wished his chest would stop aching—and his head, too, for that matter.

They finished cleaning him up, wheeled him into a private room and a woman came in with a handheld device. She gave him a smile and poked at the device with a stylus.

He asked, "The guy who hit me, they say he was having a heart attack…?"

"He's still in surgery," she said, briskly. "But there's hope. Our cardiac center is one of the best in the state. I'd say that he's got better than a fighting chance. And *you* are going to be fine."

"Great. Can I go then?" With a groan, he started to rise.

She hustled over and gently eased him back down. "Stay in the bed, please. We want you to remain with us overnight, to keep an eye on that head wound. Is there anyone you would like us to call?"

"My wife," he said, without even stopping to think about it. He rattled off her phone number, which he'd been too chicken to use for the whole, endless five weeks since she left him.

Then he lay back and stared at the round institutional clock on the wall, and waited, chanting her name inside his aching head, praying she would come.

It took her twenty minutes.

The door slowly opened and she slipped inside. She wore her dark hair down on her shoulders, a white V-neck sweater, tight jeans, great-looking high-heeled boots. And the diamond hoop earrings he had bought her.

"Beautiful," he whispered.

"Oh, Caleb." Those big, dark eyes had tears in them. She came and took his hand. "What have you done to yourself?"

"Nothing. I swear it. I wasn't speeding. An old guy had a heart attack and ran into me."

"Oh, Caleb…"

"He's still in surgery, they told me. They say it's a good chance he'll pull through."

She pressed his hand to her chest. It felt really good there. "But you…?"

"I'll be fine. They're making me stay overnight for observation, that's all."

"Oh, I'm so glad." She said it with feeling, like she really meant it.

He remembered what Elena had told him to say. "I love you, and my house is a mess—and I'm sorry, I know there should be flowers."

"Oh, Caleb…"

"You keep saying, 'Oh, Caleb.'"

"I…don't know what else to say. Except you look terrible and I'm so glad you're alive."

"Everything hurts. Especially my heart. Come back to me."

"Oh, Caleb…" A smile tipped the corners of her soft lips. Was that a yes? But then she gently put his hand back down on the mattress.

He suggested, hopefully, "Start with this. Just a kiss."

"Your poor head." Her slender fingers hovered near the bandage on his forehead.

"I'll probably be scarred. That's okay. Scars are hot."

"Yeah?"

"Yeah. What about that kiss?"

"Oh, Caleb…" She bent close. He sucked in the scent of her. So sweet and clean, so well remembered. He would know her scent anywhere, could pick her out in a light-less room crowded with a hundred other people. She kissed him, a gentle kiss, one that ended much too soon.

"Do that again. Only longer. And deeper."

She hesitated.

And before he could figure out what to say to banish the doubts from her eyes, the door opened again.

It was his mom and dad.

His mom said breathlessly, "Caleb? Oh, honey…"

And his dad squeezed her shoulder. "Aleta, he's all right. Look at him. A little battered, maybe. But okay."

Irina murmured, "I called them. I knew they would want to know." And then she stepped out of the way, so they could get close.

They rushed over, surrounding him, one on either side of the bed.

He loved his parents. He shouldn't have resented the hell out of them for showing up right when he was working every angle to try and get his wife back. But he did resent them—at least for a second or two.

Then he couldn't help giving them a grateful smile. "Thanks for coming."

His mother kissed his cheek. "You do look like you'll survive." She wore a worried little frown.

His father patted his arm. "He's a tough one. All our boys are."

"That's right," Caleb agreed. "Hardheaded as they come. Just like my old man."

His father laughed. His mother sighed.

And Caleb reassured them. "Really. It's not that serious. They're keeping me overnight, but only as a precaution."

"But what *happened?*" asked his mother. She narrowed her eyes at him suspiciously. "Were you speeding?"

"No, I was not. I was driving *under* the speed limit, as a matter of fact." He told them about the old guy having a heart attack in his ginormous pickup.

A nurse came in.

She took his blood pressure, checked his pupils, asked him if he felt dizzy or nauseous. When he answered in the negative, she promised his mother and father that there was nothing to worry about.

The nurse left.

Caleb was beginning to worry that Irina might decide he didn't need his parents *and* her at his bedside. She might leave. That couldn't happen. He wouldn't let it.

He caught his father's eye. "So, see? You guys can stop worrying. Irina will watch out for me."

His dad got the message. "Ahem. Well then…" Davis glanced at his mom.

She nodded. "All right." She kissed Caleb's cheek again. "I'll tell the nurse to call us immediately, if there's some further complication."

"Okay, Mom. But there won't be."

She patted his shoulder. "I'm just happy you're all right."

At last, convinced that he wasn't going to die after all, they turned for the door, pausing there to say goodbye to Irina. He heard his mom whisper, "I'm so glad you're here."

His dad said gruffly, "You take care of him."

Irina made a low sound in her throat that might have meant yes. Or just as likely *What else can I do?*

And then, finally, it was the two of them, alone again. There was a moment—awkward. Strained. He wondered what to say next, how to convince her that he had truly seen the light.

While he tried to figure that out, she got the visitor's chair and dragged it over next to him. That was a good sign, he decided, that she had come closer, rather than just sitting down in it halfway across the room.

And then she took his hand.

He knew then, for certain, that he was getting some-where.

"Remember..." His throat kind of clutched up. He had to swallow, hard, before he could go on. "...the way we used to sleep?"

Her mouth trembled and she nodded. "You on your side of the bed, me on mine. With only our hands joined." A tear cleared her lower lid and slid down her cheek. "What you said, before Aleta and Davis came...."

"I meant it." His voice came out low, ragged with emotion. "Every word. Just come back to me. It's all I want. All that matters."

She stood up from the chair—but only to bend over

him. She kissed him again, lightly. And she whispered, "You were…perfectly content, I think, as a bachelor." She touched his cheek, a tender brush of her hand.

He dared to reach up, to stroke her shining hair. "I had no clue what I was missing. You showed me that there could be so much more. I thought…I told myself that letting you go was the *right* thing. Because I was scared out of my mind, of how much I love you, of how much you mean to me."

"You must be sure. You must be absolutely certain." More tears spilled over. She swiped them away. "My poor heart. It is so weary of being broken. I have lost too much in this life already."

"I know. It's a lot to ask of you. Two whole years was bad enough."

A trill of laughter escaped her, but then she grew serious again. "Caleb, I am not joking."

He met her eyes without wavering. "Neither am I. I know what I want now. I want you. I love you, Irina. And I want you to give me the rest of our lives. I want to make our marriage the real thing, in every way. I want us to be together, for Thanksgiving and Christmas. For New Years and our first anniversary, on Valentine's Day. I want every Valentine's Day after that. I want us to have kids. I want us to be lying in our bed, side by side, holding hands, when we're both old and gray."

"Oh, Caleb…"

He pressed his palm to her cheek, cherishing the feel of her tear-wet skin beneath his touch. "If you only knew how much I've missed you. How empty every-thing seems without you beside me. I don't think I can ever get it clear to you, how rotten and crappy it's been since I let you walk out my door."

She closed her eyes. "Caleb…"

He waited, hardly daring to breathe, as her dark eyelashes lifted. And at last she gave him the answer he longed for.

"Yes," she whispered. And then, more firmly, "Yes."

"Forever," he vowed.

"Forever," she answered. "I love you, Caleb."

"And I love you, Irina." He said it with feeling. With passion. With awareness of his absolute commitment to her and the life they would share. Together. Always.

She was so much more than he had bargained for— his refugee princess, beautiful, scarred and proud. And still standing, still strong, no matter what they'd tried to do to her.

He'd agreed to two years at her side and ended up with forever. It was the deal of a lifetime. No doubt about it.

* * * * *

Turn the page for a sneak peek at
The Nanny and the CEO, *the heartwarming new novel from favourite author Rebecca Winters, available this month from all-new Mills & Boon® Cherish™.*

CHAPTER ONE

"Ms. CHAMBERLAIN? You're next. Second door on the left."

"Thank you."

Reese got up from the chair and walked past the woman at the front desk to reach the hall. At ten o'clock in the morning, the East 59th Street Employment Agency in New York's east side was already packed with people needing a job. She'd asked around and had learned it was one of the most reputable agencies in the city. The place reminded her of her dentist's office filled with patients back home in Nebraska.

She had no idea what one wore for an interview to be a nanny. After changing outfits several times she'd opted for a yellow tailored, short-sleeved blouse and skirt, the kind she'd worn to the initial interview on Wednesday. This was her only callback in three days. If she didn't get hired today, she would have to fly home tomorrow, the last thing she wanted to do.

Her father owned a lumberyard and could always give her a job if she couldn't find anything that suited her, but it wouldn't pay her the kind of money she needed. Worse, she didn't relish the idea of seeing Jeremy again, but it would be inevitable because her ex-fiancé happened to work as a loan officer at the bank where her dad did business. Word would get around she was back.

"Come in, Ms. Chamberlain."

"Hello, again, Mr. Lloyd." He was the man who'd taken her initial application.

"Let me introduce you to Mrs. Tribe. She's the private secretary to a Mr. Nicholas Wainwright here in New York and has been looking for the right nanny for her employer. I'll leave you two alone for a few minutes."

The smart-looking brunette woman wearing a professional business suit was probably in her early fifties. "Please sit down. Reese, is it?"

"Yes."

The other woman cocked her head. "You have excellent references. From your application it's apparent you're a student and a scholar. Since you're single and have no experience taking care of other people's children, why did you apply to be a nanny?"

Reese could lie, but she had a feeling this woman would see right through her. "I need to earn as much money as possible this summer so I can stay in school until graduation. My academic scholarship doesn't cover housing and food. Even those of us born in fly-over-country have heard a nanny's job in New York can pay very well, so I thought I'd try for a position." Hopefully that explanation was frank enough for her.

"Taking care of children is exceptionally hard work. I know because I raised two of my own."

Reese smiled. "I've never been married, but I'm the oldest in the family of six children and did a lot of babysitting over the years. I was fourteen when my youngest sister was born. My mother had to stay in bed, so I helped with the baby. It was like playing house. My sister was adorable and I loved it. But," she said as she sighed, "that was twelve years ago. Still, taking care of children is like learning to tie your shoes, don't you think? Once you've figured it out, you never forget."

The other woman eyed her shrewdly while she nodded. "I agree."

"How many children do they have?" *Please don't let the number be more than three.* Although Reese wouldn't turn it down if the money was good enough.

"Mr. Wainwright is a widower with a ten-week-old baby boy named Jamie."

The news concerning the circumstances came as a sobering revelation to Reese. She'd assumed she might end up working for a couple with several children, that is if she were ever offered a job. "Then he's still grieving for his wife." She shook her head. "How sad for him and his little boy, who'll never know his mother."

Reese got a swelling in her throat just thinking of her own wonderful mom still remarkably young and vital, probably the same age as Mrs. Tribe.

"It's a tragic loss for both of them. Mr. Wainwright has arranged for a nanny who's been with another family to start working for him, but she can't come until September. Because you only wanted summer work, that's one of the reasons I was interested in your application."

One of the reasons? She'd aroused Reese's curiosity. "What were the others?"

"You didn't name an unrealistic salary. Finally, one of your professors at Wharton told me you've been on full academic scholarship there. Good for you. An opportunity like that only comes to a very elite group of graduate students. It means you're going to have a brilliant career in business one day."

To run her own brokerage firm was Reese's goal for the future. "That's my dream."

The dream that had torn her and Jeremy apart.

Jeremy had been fine about her finishing up her undergraduate work at the University of Nebraska, but the scholarship to Wharton had meant a big move to Pennsylvania. The insinuation that she was too ambitious led to the core of the problem eating at him. Jeremy hadn't wanted a future-executive for a wife. In return Reese realized she'd had a lucky escape from a future-controlling-husband. Their breakup had been painful at the time, but the hurt was going away. She didn't want him back. Therein lay the proof.

Mrs. Tribe sat back in her chair and studied Reese. "It was my dream, too, but I didn't get the kind of grades I saw on your transcripts. Another of your professors told me he sees a touch of genius in you. I liked hearing that about you."

Reese couldn't imagine which professor that was. "You've made my day."

"Likewise," she murmured, sounding surprised by her own thoughts. "Provided you feel good about the situation after seeing the baby and discussing Mr. Wainwright's expectations of you in that regard, I think you'll do fine for the position. Of course the final decision will be up to him."

Reese could hardly believe she'd gotten this far in the interview. "I don't know how to thank you, Mrs. Tribe. I promise I won't let him, or you, down. Do you have a picture of the baby?"

A frown marred her brow. "I don't, but you'll be

meeting him and his father this afternoon. Where have you been staying since you left Philadelphia?"

"At the Chelsea Star Hotel on West 30th."

"You did say you were available immediately?"

"Yes!" The dormitory bed cost her fifty dollars a night. She couldn't afford to stay in New York after today.

"That's good. If he decides to go with my recommendation and names a fee that's satisfactory to you, then he'll want you to start today."

"What should I wear to the interview? Do I need some kind of uniform? This is completely new to me."

"To both of us," came her honest response. "Wear what you have on. If he has other suggestions, he'll tell you."

"Does he have a pet?"

"As far as I know he's never mentioned one. Are you allergic?"

"No. I just thought if he did, I could pick up some cat or doggie treats at the store. You know. To make friends right off?"

The woman smiled. "I like the way you think, Ms. Chamberlain."

"Of course the baby's going to be another story," Reese murmured. "After having his daddy's exclusive attention, it will take time to win him around."

Mrs. Tribe paused before speaking. "Actually, since his birth, he's been looked after by his maternal grandparents."

"Are they still living with Mr. Wainwright?"

"No. The Hirsts live in White Plains. An hour away in heavy traffic."

So did that mean he hadn't been with his son for the

last couple of months? No…that couldn't be right. Now that he was getting a nanny, they'd probably just left to go back home.

"I see. Does Jamie have paternal grandparents, too?"

"Yes. At the moment they're away on a trip," came the vague response.

Reese came from a large family. Both sets of grandparents were still alive and always around. She had seven aunts and uncles. Last count there were twenty-eight cousins. With her siblings, including the next oldest, Carrie, who was married and had two children under three, that brought the number to thirty-four. She wondered if her employer had any brothers and sisters or other family.

"You've been with Mr. Wainwright a long time. Is there anything of importance I should know ahead of time?"

"He's punctual."

"I'll remember that." Reese got to her feet. "I won't take any more of your time. Thank you for this opportunity, Mrs. Tribe."

"It's been my pleasure. A limo will be sent for you at one o'clock."

"I'll be waiting outside in front. Oh—one more question. What does Mr. Wainwright do for a living?"

The other woman's eyebrows lifted. "Since you're at Wharton, I thought you might have already made the connection or I would have told you. He's the CEO at Sherborne-Wainwright & Co. on Broadway. Good luck."

"Thank you," Reese murmured in shock.

He was *that* Wainwright?

It was one of the most prestigious brokerage firms in

New York, if not *the* top one with roots that went back a couple of hundred years. The revelation stunned her on many levels. Somehow she'd imagined the man who ran the whole thing to be in his late forties or early fifties. It usually took that long to rise to those heights.

Of course it wasn't impossible for him to have a new baby, but she was still surprised. Maybe it had been his second wife he'd lost and she'd been a young mother. No one was exempt from pain in this life.

EXPECTING ROYAL TWINS! *by Melissa McClone*

Mechanic Izzy was shocked when a tall handsome prince strode into her
workshop and declared he was her husband! Now she's about to face an
even bigger surprise...

TO DANCE WITH A PRINCE *by Cara Colter*

Royal playboy Kiernan's been nicknamed Prince Heartbreaker. Meredith
knows, in her head, that he's the last man she needs, yet her heart
thinks otherwise!

HONEYMOON WITH THE RANCHER *by Donna Alward*

After Tomas' fiancée's death, he sought peace on his Argentine ranch.
Until socialite Sophia arrived for her honeymoon...*alone*. Can they heal
each other's hearts?

NANNY NEXT DOOR *by Michelle Celmer*

Sydney's ex left her with nothing, but she needs to provide for her
daughter. Sheriff Daniel's her new neighbour who could give Sydney the
perfect opportunity.

A BRIDE FOR JERICHO BRAVO *by Christine Rimmer*

After being jilted by her long-time boyfriend, Marnie's given up on love.
Until meeting sexy rebel Jericho has her believing in second chances...

Cherish™

0211/023a

THE DOCTOR'S PREGNANT BRIDE?
by Susan Crosby

From the moment Ted asked Sara to be his date for a Valentine's Day dinner, the head-in-the-clouds scientist was hooked; even if she seemed to be hiding something.

BABY BY SURPRISE
by Karen Rose Smith

Francesca relied on no one but herself. Until an accident meant the mother-to-be was forced to turn to fiercely protective rancher Grady, her baby's secret father.

THE BABY SWAP MIRACLE
by Caroline Anderson

Sam only intended to help his brother fulfil his dream of having children, but now, through an IVF mix-up, enchanting stranger Emelia's pregnant with his child!

Nora Roberts' *The O'Hurleys*

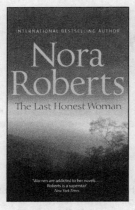

4th March 2011

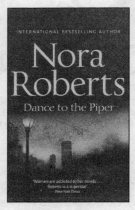

1st April 2011

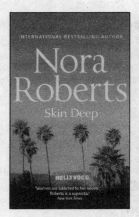

6th May 2011

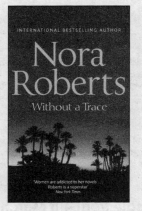

3rd June 2011

2 FREE BOOKS
AND A SURPRISE GIFT

We would like to take this opportunity to thank you for reading this Mills & Boon® book by offering you the chance to take TWO more specially selected books from the Cherish™ series absolutely FREE! We're also making this offer to introduce you to the benefits of the Mills & Boon® Book Club™—

- **FREE home delivery**
- **FREE gifts and competitions**
- **FREE monthly Newsletter**
- **Exclusive Mills & Boon Book Club offers**
- **Books available before they're in the shops**

Accepting these FREE books and gift places you under no obligation to buy, you may cancel at any time, even after receiving your free books. Simply complete your details below and return the entire page to the address below. You don't even need a stamp!

YES Please send me 2 free Cherish books and a surprise gift. I understand that unless you hear from me, I will receive 5 superb new stories every month, including two 2-in-1 books priced at £5.30 each, and a single book priced at £3.30, postage and packing free. I am under no obligation to purchase any books and may cancel my subscription at any time. The free books and gift will be mine to keep in any case.

Ms/Mrs/Miss/Mr _____ Initials _____

_____

Surname _____

Address _____

_____

_____ Postcode _____

E-mail _____

Send this whole page to: Mills & Boon Book Club, Free Book Offer, FREEPOST NAT 10298, Richmond, TW9 1BR